Saving Grace

Deception. Obsession. Redemption

H D Coulter

Ropewalk Publishing

For my own Saving Grace.
My editor, my friend.
Thank you.

Contents

Chapter 1

April 1832, Beacon Hill, Boston.

"You are my child; you are not his – you are innocent – you are loved – you are mine."

Bea rubbed the protruding foot stretching outward from under the swollen skin of her belly. Tipping her head from side to side, she hoped restlessly that the tormenting dream would trickle out of her ears and leave her in peace. The polished wooden arm felt cold and smooth as she gripped tight on to it with her free hand, planting herself back in reality. Without realising it, her hand gradually crept up to her neck, following the pale mauve line that stretched from ear to ear. The mark left by the rope had faded but it had left a scar, an irremovable brand on her skin that would never allow her to truly forget. Her mind still enjoyed torturing her regularly, and now and then she would relive a moment from the harrowing night of the attack to the last second, the moment she had thought she was dead. Minor aspects would change in her memory until she wasn't sure what was real, or what was now a fantasy. She felt a sudden kick from the tiny foot, and this time the jolt brought her firmly back to the present. She repeated the same mantra again, reminding herself this child, formed in an act of hate, was going to be born into love. Tiredness engraved in the lines across her face and a dull ache in her bones. She breathed deeply, in and out, rubbing her distended belly in a repetitive motion. Pulling tighter the shawl around her shoulders, her Da had given her at home however many Christmases past.

How much she missed him. She stared out of the large window and down to the street below. The gas street-lamps filled Boston with a warm golden glow all night long, seeping into the house and creating shadows in the corners. She missed the stars, a simplicity she had taken for granted back in Ulverston, and instead of the soothing noise of the swelling waves and the night-time birds, the city was brimming with voices, with bodies, with the hustle and bustle. It didn't stop for the night; it never stopped.

Joshua stirred in the bed, peacefully ignorant of her wakefulness. She was envious of his ability to sleep. Each night, he would cradle her in his arms as they both drifted off, allowing her to feel safe. But in her dreams, it would all come flooding back, haunting her with vivid images of Hanley's face; that night; the jury laughing at her; and eventually, the sensation of the noose tightening around her neck. She had tried to stop herself. She remembered that keenly. She had tried to walk away from them both, but she knew in the end, despite all her efforts, it was all her fault; she had made the choices which lead her down this path. Guilt ate her up. A clammy, twitching sensation ran through her body. Her heart pounded, fearful of the shadows in their room. Then she felt it again, the baby shifting in position, kicking her bladder or a rib. Her forever-reminder of him.

At first, the pregnancy hadn't felt real. For the first month, she had still expected to see her monthly blood staining the sheets every morning. Convincing herself it was a lie, she willed herself to believe that she and Joshua would have the life they had dreamt of, and they would leave everything dark and violent behind them. Watching him contemplate bringing up Hanley's baby as his own made her morning sickness worse. But as the bump grew out of her slim frame, the idea became too real to ignore. They could no longer hide it and instead acted to the best of their ability like the joyous soon-to-be parents of a wedding-night baby. No one could know the actual truth. Each time she had thought about having the child, the questions brought forth images of the recent past, and her entire body shook with fear. She couldn't love this child, not *his* child... Joshua would sooth her, tell her all the right words, every assurance she needed to hear, but he couldn't look at the growing reminder, or touch her around that area. Every day he told her he loved her, that he didn't blame her. And yet she saw a darkness grow inside him, and a quickening temper when there used to be patience.

During the first few months in Boston they had secured rooms in a Boarding House; one bedroom and a small sitting room, where the lady of the house, a Ms Huddersfield, would bring their breakfast and dinner every day. During the worse of her morning sickness, it had been a blessing, spending her time in a fractured sleep; numb to life passing her by. Joshua, unable to watch his new wife disappear, would spend his days out, from early morning until late evening, telling her not to worry and that he was working everything out; that he would find a job soon and they would finally find additional security.

But she didn't worry, she didn't care. The only thing that consumed her was the growing reminder and the thin line between nightmare and reality. It wasn't until the first time she felt it kick that the movement in her belly became a baby, and her mind shifted away from its relentless anguish.

Sitting in the darkness, Bea felt the baby wiggle, followed by a spattering of tiny hiccups, and she watched her bump gently jump with each one. It was one of the few times she smiled. The first time it had happened the sensation had felt strange, like tiny bubbles popping in her belly, but once the realisation had kicked in, so did the memories of her sisters. An image of little Rowan or Holly when they had had the hiccups, giggling at the silly noises coming from their mouths as they tried and failed to talk through them. In that moment she had known that this child, her baby, would be an innocent boy or girl, untainted by her wounds or its father's crimes, deserving only to be loved. She embraced each movement as a sign of the child's character, instead of a painful reminder of all they had lost. Coming up with her line, she had repeated it to herself, to banish away the fear and hatred: "You are my child; you are not his – you are innocent – you are loved – you are mine."

"Come back to bed, my love". Joshua's half-asleep voice filtered through the dark room.

Bea slipped back under the covers, whispering gently: "She has the hiccups again – feel her." She guided his hand over the bump. He let out a sleepy chuckle.

"Why are you convinced it's a girl?"

"Just a feeling I have."

Bea lay on her side with Joshua's arms wrapped around her. She heard his breathing getting deeper once more, but she couldn't rest; the baby was awake, and it scared her to close her eyes, fearful of the endless that might occur if she did. Her mind wandered over the simple tasks which lay ahead, making brief lists until she fell asleep.

Chapter 2

Ulverston 1832.

"That is quite a debt you are racking up, dear Max." Hanley stacked the gold coins into a pile as he held the owing slips of paper in his left hand.

"I can pay you; I just need a couple of days to free up the money." Max licked out the last dregs of whiskey from his glass. There were three other tables surrounding them in one of the smaller rooms in the club where high stakes were thrown away more often than anyone involved cared to note.

Hanley grinned and gestured to the serving staff to bring two more. "On me." They placed the tumblers down in front of them within seconds. With a simple nod, Max lifted his and swallowed the contents in one gulp. "We both know you are running out of capital. That's the dreadful business with ships, you never quite know when you're going to lose them like that."

Max relaxed back in his chair and allowed the haze of alcohol to blur his thoughts. "Storms happen... we have insurance."

"Yes... and yet I had heard they are refusing to pay - and that would suggest you owe me a great deal of money that you simply do not have." Hanley laid the pieces of paper in front of him like tarot cards, then gathered five more from his pocket and added them to the spread. "Your friends were more than happy to allow me to buy your debt."

Max jumped forward in his chair and stared at the extra pieces of paper on the cards table. "You will get your money – I just need time." He could no longer hide the panic in his voice.

"But Max - I can make sure the wheel of fortune turns again and makes all your troubles disappear." Hanley drew an invisible wheel in the air in front of them, turning it around with his hand. Max watched the motion as if Hanley were casting a spell over him.

"What... what would you want in return?"

"Information... tell me where they are."

"Who?"

The Captain's face twitched in anger and his tone became darker. "The boy and his whore."

"I don't know. I cut ties with him after that dreadful... situation." Max paused, remembering who he was speaking to and the lengths that person would go to to achieve their aims.

"A little birdie has told me he has been sending you letters." Hanley held the younger man's gaze, warning him to weigh his next words.

Max leaned in a little closer and lowered his voice from the other gentlemen in the room. "If I told you, then – then it would all disappear – the debt?"

Hanley mirrored his actions playfully. "You have my word."

"They... they are in America. Boston, to be exact."

"Excellent, what else?"

"He wants help to find work. Once word spread of their situation, none of the usual employers would send him a reference after they heard his own father had washed his hands of him. Without a reference, he can't get a decent situation, not one that would... suit." Max stared down at his empty glass, longing for it to fill once more with whiskey. Hanley paused, his hand in the air, and waited. "Joshua seems to think I can help him, that I know of people in Boston. I told him... I couldn't -

I can't... I won't, I won't help him now, not anymore - but the letters keep coming." Hanley moved two fingers, a sign for a refill.

"I want you to send him a letter back, informing him of the contrary – a convenient position in Boston has manifested itself, and you can furnish him with the relevant names and addresses."

"Why? What's in it for you, Hanley? Why would you want to help him get a job?" Max paused, the glass touching his lips, the smell of the single malt intoxicating.

"That is none of your business now, is it, Max? But, if you do this, I will sweeten the deal by having a word with your insurance company."

Even through his hazy thoughts, Max realised the power that this man held, and knew it would not be wise to cross him, especially on the behalf of a disgraced and former friend. "If you tell me what to write, I... I will send it." He masked the taste of guilt and betrayal in his mouth as he gulped down the whiskey. "I must say, it will make him pleased, especially with the news... *Oh* -"

"What news?" Hanley tilted his head, and a curious grin fell across his mouth.

"That he... well... he is to be a father, you see. A wedding night blessing, he said, but if that's the case why ask for me to keep it quiet...?"

"Now... that is excellent news!" Hanley looked elated as he ordered two more drinks. "We must toast to their newfound fortune."

Confused as to what he might have said, Max kept his thoughts to himself on the transaction. "You will... keep to your part of the deal, won't you, Victor?"

"You doubt me?"

"No, no, of course not." Max lowered his eyes from Hanley's stare; the world was moving around him, a sign he needed to call it a night.

Hanley played with the pieces of paper in his hands, shuffling them like a deck of cards. "A man will deliver a letter to you tomorrow. You must copy it, word for word, and hand it back to him. In return you will get your little pieces of paper, and the good news you've been waiting for." Max nodded in agreement, finished the last of his drink, and made his move to leave. Hanley rose to his feet and remarked loudly, "A pleasure doing business with you, Sir Max Elliot."

Max held his head high and staggered out of the club, doffing his hat to familiar faces and disapproving looks.

Hanley sat back in his chair and gestured for another drink. Joyous news. His plan was taking effect and now, on top of everything, he was going to be a father. He knew there was no way the baby was a wedding-night blessing. He relived the event in his head for the hundredth time, knowing he had left his seed in her. There was no doubt in his mind that the baby was his, but what was he going to do about it? He smiled at the imminent chaos, wishing he had been there when she had realised, when she had told the Mason boy of the news.

An image of Bea popped into his head, smiling at her sisters in their old cottage kitchen. How much they had looked like her; how sweet she had seemed... how innocent. The scene shifted to her standing in front of him, holding out their child. His child. And in that moment, he knew the game had shifted.

Chapter 3

April 1832, Beacon Hill, Boston.

T he landlady entered the small living-room with a pot of coffee in one hand and a letter in the other. "Morning sir - a letter came for you in the early hours." She placed both on the table, side by side.

"Good morning, Ms Huddersfield." Joshua noticed the writing straight away to be that of Max Elliot. "Thank you." He nodded to her gratefully as he held up the letter, impatient to know its contents.

"Would you like any breakfast today? Do you think Mrs Mason could manage anything?" She stared at the mound, still lying motionless in the bed through the adjoining door.

"She was up again through the night."

"A bit of fresh air will do her good, that's what she needs." Ms Huddersfield nodded to herself. She reminded Joshua of one of his mother's former housemaids, plain-speaking and clear in their opinions, a definitively northern trait.

"Thank you, Ms Huddersfield. I will pass that on." She replied with a low huff and made her way back through to the stairway. Joshua waited until the door clicked shut and tore at the envelope.

"Dear Mr Joshua Mason.

I received your letters and sent out inquires on your behalf. Recently, I received word that a position has opened in Boston Harbour with the Wentworth Shipping Company, and therefore took the liberty to arrange a meeting for you with the proprietor, a Mr Goldstein, on the 8th of April at midday. I have enclosed the address below.

I hope this news is agreeable to you and concludes our business for the foreseeable.

Yours sincerely,

Sir Max Elliot."

Joshua read through the note several times. Felt the loss of his friend in the lack of emotion with each word more keenly, though undoubtedly grateful for the effort. He had heard about Wentworth Shipping during his initial investigations and knew they were the large firm with multiple ventures and opportunities; exactly what he was looking for. He checked the date on the letter and then back at the blank calendar which hung next to the door, holding no invites or events. They had been in Boston for about six months now, but the friendly connections he thought he'd made in Liverpool and London that he'd banked on setting him up in Boston had turned their back once they had heard of the circumstances. The only favour they would agree to was not spreading the rumours further, so not to spread the disgrace into Boston society and allow a fresh start for him. Therefore, each day, the only choice open to him was to sit by this small fire, and watch his new wife being consumed by guilt, grief and her own piercing fear of bringing Hanley's child into the world. That, or drift from one firm to another in the bleak winter, without a reference or connections, receiving rejection after rejection, each less civil than the last. Existence was a lot harder than he thought it would be. And the money he had saved wouldn't last them much longer. He glanced back at the letter. Today was the 8th. He had a few hours to make himself presentable and race down to the docks. *Thank you, Max.*

He changed into his wedding suit, the best one he had, and studied himself in the small, tarnished mirror hanging in the bedroom. Looking back at him was a man he barely recognised. A man with forlorn eyes set in a complexion as pale as milk and a face framed with unruly hair. He slicked it back as much as the tousled blonde waves would allow and smoothed down his suit.

"You look nice, is that-

"I have a meeting for a potential job."

"What time is it?" Bea sat up in bed and searched for a clock, half of her mind still in a dream world. Her growing bump, which stuck out from under the bedcovers, seemed visibly larger this morning.

"Just after ten – I'd better be off." He shifted his gaze to her eyes, that were staring back at him. For the first time in a while, they were smiling. He leaned in and gave her a slow kiss on her forehead as she placed her hand on top of his, giving it a light squeeze. He pulled back and made his way back to the small seating area. "I'll get Ms Huddersfield to bring up some ham and eggs, and a nice pot of tea." Having a Yorkshire landlady meant it really would be a good cup of tea and a consistently decent breakfast.

"Thank you. Good luck, my love. I'm sure you will impress them." She smiled at her husband for a brief second before the shifting bump stole her attention once more.

"I will be back soon - rest and eat." She bobbed her head in agreement, then chuckled as her hand got kicked. He picked up his thin satchel off one of the dining chairs and couldn't help but grin at the sight of love on his wife's face and soon to be a mother.

"Someone is awake today." She said tenderly and looked back at Joshua. "Good luck – I love you." Today would be the day he'd changed their luck around, for her sake, for his and soon to be family.

"Love you too." He waved before closing the door behind him.

T he sun held a little heat today, and the sign of spring in the trees and flowers lifted his spirits. *Today was going to be a good day.* He ambled up the hill to the nearby stables and borrowed his usual horse. If he got this job, he could own a horse again, and pay for the lodgings, knowing he could indulge occasionally in the long rides he used to. In that aspect Joshua missed the countryside and the familiar fields around his former family home. Each time he looked out towards the distant trees and landscape stretching outward from the city fringes, an image surfaced of their house, and his mother standing outside as if waiting to welcome him home, and with it a winding punch to his stomach, removing all air out of his lungs. He pushed the thoughts back to the corners of his mind, where they belonged, and focused once more on the task at hand. He paid the usual fee and greeted the dark brown mare gently. He trotted through the new streets and watched how the houses changed character as he got closer to the docks. The boarding house wasn't grand and was in one of the less desirable parts of Beacon Hill, but it was better than these terraces. He studied the grubby children playing in the streets, throwing rocks at a wall in some form of game. Their back-broken mothers were cleaning clothes nearby, with yet another child in their bellies they could not feed. Had he brought Bea from one hopeless situation to another?

If he could not secure this job, would this be their fate in a year's time, once all the money was gone? Instead of owning ships, he would become just another labourer, wringing out an impossible living at the docks, and leaving Bea to raise her baby in a room shared by three other families? Bob Lightfoot flashed into his mind, as did their many late-night conversations about the reform and the fight for equality and the vote. At least Bob was on the brink of achieving something; a lasting legacy, not only for his own family, but for the families of countless others. What had Joshua achieved, apart from turning his world upside down? But today he would change it. He felt luck for the first time in a while.

The narrow streets opened at last to the vast expanse of the harbour. It was larger than both Liverpool and Southampton combined. The horse, nervous at the harsh sounds and constant bustle of the harbour, danced on the spot, flaring at any sudden noise. He spotted the Wentworth Shipping docks almost immediately, the largest wharf by far on the west side, and encouraged his horse over, ignoring a burst of laughter that erupted behind his back as he made his way through the clusters of working men along the walk.

"Mr Mason, here to see Mr Goldstein. I have an appointment." Joshua left the horse in the stables around the back of the office and warehouse and now greeted the freckled young man in front of him more curtly than he had intended.

"Of course, sir. I am George Carter, a senior clerk here for Mr Goldstein." George held his hand out and gave Joshua a broad smile. George reminded him of himself in younger years, with an eager smile and ink-stained fingers. "He is expecting you, if you follow me." He gestured his hand up the stairs and then down the corridor to some larger offices.

"Yes – come in!" a robust voice boomed back from the other side of the plain door.

George slid his head around the opening and held out a hand

for Joshua to wait. "Mr Mason is here to see you, sir."

"Very good, send him in." George gave a bow in response and then stepped back to allow Joshua to pass, whispering: "Good luck, sir."

"Mr Mason, come in and take a seat. Coffee?" Joshua nodded. "Get me two cups of coffee, George." Mr Goldstein seated behind a large wooden desk, sparsely furnished with ink and an impressively thick ledger. He was a broad man, dressed in the finest tailoring, but it was his presence that filled the room.

"A pleasure to meet you, Mr Goldstein. May I say how grateful I-"

"I hear good things about you, Mr Mason." Mr Goldstein gestured for him to sit, and ignored the younger man's outstretched hand. "Cambridge, then working at various firms in London and Liverpool before taking your place in the family business, under your father. So, what has brought you here? Why leave your family for Boston?" He leant back in the leather desk chair and waited, his hands resting in an arch over his chest, fingertips lightly poised.

Joshua had heard this question almost a hundred times now. He certainly couldn't reply with the entire truth. But enough to please most preoccupied business owners with only a hint of a lie. "I believe the future of shipping belongs to the Americans. What you have achieved here, by becoming one of the central trading ports, it has changed the industry for good. All other major ports now want to go through America, and Boston in particular. Where better a place to raise my child, to continue my journey in a progressive environment where innovation and ambition are welcome?"

"A silver tongue indeed," Mr Goldstein muttered to himself. "Very good, Mr Mason," he remarked in a louder tone. "I need a manager that will oversee the logistics of all our trading routes - make doubly sure there are no unnecessary complications or setbacks. The hours are long, but the pay is fair, and if you impress me, there is plenty of room in the company for advancement. Does that sound reasonable enough to you?"

George bounded in with two cups of coffee that he'd poured a little too generously. He placed one on the desk, and the other he passed to Joshua with a broad smile, who took the dripping vessel gingerly.

"So, you have a family, a wife? Where are you staying now?" Mr Goldstein asked while George made his way back out of the doorway.

Joshua almost choked on his coffee as he tried to swallow and speak simultaneously. "In a boarding house on Garden Street. Yes, I have a wife and a baby on the way. But that won't..."

"Good, I like a family man. I prefer a family man. More settled, more reliable; shows me he is ready to commit."

"Yes sir, I am ready..."

"But you can't stay at a boarding house, that won't do for my manager. You must find a house; George will help you."

"I- er... Thank you, sir!" Mr Goldstein was already perusing his ledger and making notes in a small book he had produced from a concealed pocket. Joshua sat awkwardly for a moment, unsure whether the interview was really over so soon.

"Excellent. You can start on Monday. Good day, Mr Mason – I shall expect great things from you." He lifted his head briefly and gestured towards the door.

"Thank you, sir. I won't let you down. Good day." Joshua stood up and bowed, still holding onto his coffee. He left his new superior to his lists, a little stunned that something had actually gone his way. This evening, he would tell Bea everything was going to be alright, that their new life can begin.

Chapter 4

May 1832, Beacon Hill, Boston

Bea stood in the kitchen, picking herbs from the small clay pots dotted along the windowsill. How she wished they had a small garden, enough space to grow a few vegetables and flowers. The back of the house had a little yard, with two clotheslines for their servant Sarah to use next to the washhouse, but the walls were too high for any sun to last more than an hour, and the plants she had tried to grow lay dead in the larger clay tubs dotted around the hard ground.

You could have fitted the ground floor of her family home into this kitchen as it stretched half the length of the house. There was a backdoor which lead to the yard, and cupboards filled with pans, tins and umpteen dinner sets to host endless dinner parties. In the centre was a large, beaten-up wooden table with four chairs pushed neatly underneath. Bea loved the table, and cooking dinner off it reminded her of her Granda's one in her family home in England. She chopped up some carrots and onions, and laid them roughly on the bottom of the roasting pan, then stuffed the mixture of fat, breadcrumbs, nutmeg, sage, thyme and a few sprigs of rosemary into the small chicken and placed it jauntily on top. Finally, she rubbed a small nob of butter across the skin and finished with a sprinkle of salt and pepper. The spices and seasonings were such a luxury to her. She never became tired of lifting the lids of each small but precious pot and daintily spooning out a pinch of the magic substances for every meal.

Across the table, Sarah leaned against a wooden stool in her simple tailored dress of golden yellow, the same colour of the almond scented flowers on the gorge bush, with an apron wrapped around her waist. Sown together from the remains of an old dress and a bunch of white Dogwood embroiled in the corner as she peeled the potatoes over a small tin bucket. Her head was wrapped in an astonishing colourful scarf, to the likes Bea had never seen before, tied with a knot on top. Sarah's foot tapped the stone slabs in time to the humming tune as she got lost in her tasks. Bea listened to the beat and the soft melody as she worked; one she hadn't heard before. She would sometimes ask what the song was about, but: "Jus' an old work song, Mistress," would be all she received, and then silence. The baby that afternoon was full of excitement, shifting around in her belly, annoyed with the lack of space it now had to endure. It was less than two months until the birth, and Bea still wasn't ready to welcome it into the world. She had been putting off preparing the nursery, falling in love with the tiny wriggling person inside her, but painfully afraid to look into its face and see Hanley staring back.

Across the kitchen, Sarah knocked over the tin pail as she turned to fetch more potatoes, and a loud crash bounced off the walls. Bea instinctively grabbed the chopping knife again and crouched low to the floor behind the nearest leg of the table, turning pale, her breathing rapid.

"Mistress – mistress – 'was only me; I knocked the pale to the ground. Mistress?" Sarah crouched down next to her and teased the knife out of her shaking hand, placing it on the table. "Mistress, let's get you to a seat, hmm?" Sarah helped Bea to rise and guided her to a chair by the warm stove. She picked up a small glass tumbler and poured some water out of the jug, and handing it to her carefully. Bea sat in silence as the colour slowly returned to her cheeks. She rubbed the wiggling bump, repeating the usual soothing series of words in her head.

"Thank you, Sarah, I'll be alright now. It just took me by surprise, that's all." She put the glass down on the table and twisted and spun the piece of lace wrapped around her left

17

wrist. Red and white lines embedded into her skin came through the delicate tiny flowers and leaves, the silk threads fraying at the edges.

"Yes, Mistress." Sarah stood to walk back to the spilt potatoes and picked up the handful of skins darted across the floor. She paused. "Mistress, may I speak freely?"

"Of course, you can."

"Since workin' for you and Mr Mason, there has been a shadow hangin' over you. I have watched you take many a wicked spell, turnin' white as a ghost, wid' your body shakin'. There is what we call a demon-tormentin' you. I do not ask to know whad' that demon is, it is not my place. But I do fear for you mistress – I fear that if you do not find yo' peace and expel this demon from yo' mind – learn to live wid' what has happened to you, then I fear one day it might consume you - and the baby."

"I thank you for your words, Sarah, but... we-well, we all have demons from our past we do not wish to talk about, do we not?" Bea twisted the lace wrapped around her left wrist until it became a rope coursing against her pearly white line. Her heart slowed to a steady beat, the thread between her fingers.

Bea gazed at Sarah's dark honey-toned skin, knowing that her own journey in life would most likely have been less than simple, and wondered, just for a moment, how she came to Boston. It was possible she had been born a free woman, but equally likely that she hailed from somewhere else, and had faced hardship to find her place at this table. She guessed the woman in front of her would have her own demons to face, and yet they didn't seem to bring her down to her knees. She, on the other hand, crumbled in seconds over a fallen tin pail. She felt like a coward, brimming with guilt, unable to control herself.

Sarah nodded. "We do, mistress." Then she carried on with the potatoes calmly, as though nothing had happened, tapping her foot to a rhythm.

Bea felt the heat off the flames and sipped at her water, repeating the familiar lines in her head and stroked the protruding shape of the baby's bottom.

"Sarah, would you mind finishing the rest of the dinner? I want to lie down before Joshua comes home. This little one had me up again at all hours last night."

"Of course, mistress."

"Thank you, Sarah."

Bea slowly raised herself from the chair and waddled out of the kitchen, up the stairs and into the tall hallway. The owner had painted the walls in an elegant off-white colour that stretched up to the high ceiling, covered in strangers, and places she has never been to, rented images which had come with the house. She made her way to the stairs and climbed slowly. The simple task of walking upstairs became more difficult with each passing day as the baby grew. The scant breath became harder as the baby pressed up against her lungs. She felt as though she were back home, climbing the fells, instead of a couple flights of stairs up to her own bedroom. Relieved to get to the top, she made her way through the door and towards a small wooden chest. She lifted the lid and was greeted by a ruby red cushion and long pearly white threads with bobbins at the ends. After a month of unfamiliarity in Boston, Joshua had sourced out a little haberdashery shop and brought her enough supplies to start her lace-making again. He had meant it as a helpful distraction, but it only reminded her of what she had lost through the naivety and wilfulness of her own actions. She hid it out of sight and out of mind. But then, as she slowly bonded with her unborn baby, she had developed a notion to create some tiny pieces of lace that she could attach to the baby's clothing. A simple gift from mother to baby; at least some small token of love. Her fingers started moving in and out as though they had never stopped, and in a few days, she needed more supplies.

Bea had lost all track of time as the baby daisies flourished in her hands. She hadn't heard the front door open or Joshua climbing the stairs.

"I am glad to see you creating your beautiful lace once more. Can I ask what it is?"

"Evening my love." Bea smiled up at him.

"Sorry, forgive me - good evening, my darling." Joshua walked around the side of the bed and leaned in for a kiss on the top of her head. He still hadn't kissed her, not properly, not since their stilted wedding night. On board the ship, during their crossing, the nightmare haunted her by day, and he knew she saw Hanley's face everywhere she went. But after the news and the baby bump grew, it was he who had created the actual distance in their intimacy. An arm at night and a kiss on the head was the best she could ask for now.

"It's a lace ribbon to go round a plain summer dress I bought her weeks ago. Can you see the daisies running along it?" Her fingers continued as he took a step backwards.

"I love watching your hands moving back and forth, weaving in and out. And out of nowhere, a stunning picture reveals itself. I am still touched by that gift you gave my mother, when we were sitting at the harbour that day ..."

Bea could see the pain in his eyes and across his face at the memory, the loss she knew he felt for his family, and his honour. She wanted to reach out to him, pull him closer and comfort him as he had once done for her. And yet, he wasn't ready for it. Neither was she, and they both knew it. Would their relationship ever return to how it used to be, when they had first felt love, and known the excitement of a free future, with new prospects? He took a step away, out of her reach, and walked through the small side door into his dressing room.

"Sarah said dinner will be ready in twenty minutes. Do you... would you like to join me this evening?" he shouted through the door.

"Yes, I would love to."

"Only if you think you're up to it. I don't want you to tire yourself out on my account."

The words jolted in her ears, and her heart sank, suspecting he wanted to give her a way out, that he couldn't even last a meal with her, let alone a whole day.

"I have rested, and I would love your company this evening."

"Really?" Joshua popped his head around the door frame, half-dressed. Something stirred inside of Bea at the sight of him. She didn't know if it was the pregnancy, or simply missing her husband's closeness, and how they used to be. Either way, seeing him standing in front of her now, with his naked chest, she suddenly craved the touch of his skin.

"We prepared a roast chicken tonight, Sarah and I. A reminder of home, with fresh herbs. Joshua... I was thinking - I know we have talked about this before, but it doesn't seem right – I mean, that Sarah helps us to prepare dinner and then doesn't eat with us."

"She has a home to go to. You have asked her before, and she said no. We have to respect her wishes." He came out of the doorway and stood a foot away from her; she could smell his sweat and the grime from the harbour. She almost reached out to stroke his muscles, but stopped herself at the last second. "You haven't had servants – help - around the house before. I suppose it doesn't seem normal, but trust me, that's simply... how it is."

"Just because that's *how it is*, doesn't mean that's how it *ought* to be." She gave him one of her stern-but-playful looks that always made him smile.

"Maybe one day, my love." He hovered for a moment, an awkward temptation hanging between them. His eyes held a spark of lust as they gazed downwards from her face to her breasts before resting on the undeniable bump. There they froze for a second, then drifted back upward as he placed another kiss on top of her head. He strode back into the dressing room abruptly. The high-pitched dinner bell called out below. Bea tried to heave herself up off the bed, one hand on the bed post and the other on the mattress.

"Would you like a hand?" Joshua called as Bea rocked herself back and forth to gain some momentum.

"No, no, I can..." Joshua scrambled back into the bedroom just as Bea had swung herself to a standing position. Their two bodies collided; their lips pressed tightly together as Joshua bent forward trying to catch her. Joshua felt Bea about to fall back onto the bed as he wrapped his arms around her. Without thinking, she kissed him. Her hand stroked the side of his cheek and felt the evening stumble breaking through. How much she had missed him. The hunger stirred inside of him in return as he kissed her back with force, sending a shiver trickling through her body.

He stroked one hand firmly down her back as his tongue played with hers. Then the baby kicked, softly at first, then harder. As if startled awake, Joshua jumped back, looking at Bea with a stunned expression. Slowly, a stiffness crept over his face as the past seven months flooded back.

"I... had better finish getting ready – it's not fair on Sarah if the food goes cold." His head lower, he strode back into the dressing room.

Bea collapsed onto the bed. She forced herself not to cry at the sudden rejection from her only love. She closed her eyes and stroked the now active bump. She repeated the same lines, "You are loved – you are mine," muttering away to herself as usual. It was not their fault her husband couldn't touch her anymore. None of what was happening was their fault. Her fault; she was sure it was a girl.

"Bea... would you mind if I ate my dinner in my study this evening? I have just realised I have some paperwork to look over before tomorrow - and I wouldn't want to bring work to the dining table."

"Of course, I understand." She adopted on a falsely bright voice, almost happy to the point of being uncomfortable. "I'm a little tired. I might have Sarah bring a tray up to the room."

"That's a good idea. You rest, and I will tell Sarah. I'll see you at bedtime, love." He hovered in the doorway, unsure if he should give her another customary kiss on the head; perhaps they had had enough kissing for one day. Without another word, he left by the other dressing room door so as not to walk past her.

Chapter 5

Each Tuesday and Thursday Bea took her morning walks around Beacon Hill. At first Sarah insisted on accompanying her, telling her that some streets weren't as friendly as she would like to believe them. But Bea dismissed the notion, uncomfortable with the concept of a servant walking two steps behind, as was the custom in the area, especially a person of colour.

Sarah handed her the simple teal cloak Bea had bought when they first arrived off the ship, now too small with her bump sticking out in front.

"I'll be gone an hour."

"Yes, Mistress," came the gentle reply as Sarah opened the door.

Bea nodded her head. Over the past couple of weeks, she had asked Sarah many times not to address her as 'Mistress'. But Sarah had refused, saying that it wasn't the done thing, and giving her a suspicious look as if the suggestion was some sort of trick, a way to make a fool of her. After that, Bea had stopped trying. It only made their relationship uncomfortable. One day, she hoped Sarah would trust her, and then she would approach the subject again. One day.

The streets were alive, carriages travelling up and down the main road, gentlemen on horseback docking their hats at the image of an elegant woman with child. Bea bowed at each gesture, as per Joshua's painstaking instructions of how a lady of her standing must behave. The actions felt strange, mimicking other gentile ladies strolling down the street, their heads held high and on constant display. She had been born a coastal cottage girl and now she was a lady. But it was all a lie. It wasn't how she had thought it would be. She carried so many secret labels that she had given up wondering which one was her true calling; a lace-maker, a cottage girl, a wife, a mother, a murderer; a fugitive?

Bea headed right and walked up the hill towards Boston Common. It would have been easier to turn left, to walk downhill, past Louisburg Square and their own private garden, and on to Mount Vernon Street, to walk past the more elite homes. When they had moved to their new home, Joshua had encouraged her to become more involved with society, to accept an invitation from the wife of a new business acquaintance for afternoon tea. She had agreed tentatively, but when the onslaught of questions came about her background and her family back in England, Bea had all but crumbled. Her former life had been all over the newspapers, as had the trial, and her escape from the hanging. She couldn't tell a living soul the truth for fear of their judgement, and the prospect of Joshua losing the precious job he had barely begun. So, she lied. She could no longer be Beatrice Lightfoot, and Beatrice Mason was full of lies. Upon her return home, full of anger and shame, she had told her husband that she never wanted to attend another social event without him at her side leading the way. After responding thereafter to similar events with a handful of rejections, blaming it on the pregnancy, the invites had stopped, and Bea Mason had made a point of avoiding that area of town.

S pring had arrived in Boston Common. The extensive area of greenery was a welcome relief. It wasn't the wilds of nature she was used to, but the chance to sit under the trees and listen to the birdsong, helped her to rediscover a part of her former self. The large space was elegant in design, with old, solid-looking trees lining the edges, two simple paths crossing from one side to the other, and a few iron benches dotted here and there along the way. She made her way to the base of the common, the delicate sweet scent of almonds and floral blend drifted towards her. Her back ached with the pressure and the bench looked inviting for a brief rest. After taking a quick glance left and right, she leant her head right back luxuriously onto the cool curved iron, and gazed straight upward, eyes narrowed. The sky was clear blue, almost the shade of cornflower. The sun soaked into her aching bones and warmed her face. She placed her hands over the bump and felt it roll from one side to another, distorting the shape of her stomach as the baby turned over in its sleep. For a moment she could believe she was back at the harbour wall, in that pocket of time which was filled with happiness, before the night that changed everything. It was strange; she had earned for adventure across the water, wanted away from Ulverston, and create a new beginning. But now that it had happened, she had escaped with the man she loved; reality didn't match that of her daydreams. Part of her yearned for home. She smiled as a woman walked past, pushing a grand pram with ornate, golden markings on the sides. Reminding Bea of some of the more spectacular carriages she had seen around Boston. The woman glanced at her, then put her head down once more and kept walking. Hauling herself up reluctantly, Bea cut through the trees lining the East side of the common, and watched the men landscaping the Back Bay, the once-great rope yard of Boston, into a new bespoke park everyone was talking about. She watched the workers dig out holes for the trees and new plants, in places where there had once been large wooden wheels and spokes hammered into the ground for the rope to run through. How practicality gave way to grandeur, she thought sadly, much like herself. She made her way back onto the path, and then out on to Charles Street. The road was full of shops, from Ladies fashion, grocers, butchers and ironmongers, to bookshops, jewellers, and a tiny haberdashery. The quiet stillness of the common gave way almost instantly to the bustle of gentlemen, soldiers, entrepreneurs, servants, and ladies. People of all shapes and colours, people from distant countries she had never even seen in pictures before strolling past. Bea kept her head down, bracing herself for each noise and smell, praying she didn't get one of her episodes. The rules of society were hard to get used to; where she had once been useful, needed and wanted, she was now forbidde. Sarah had to be the one who ordered the weekly supplies of food, coal, and wood for the house, and the one who was responsible for all the cleaning and washing. Bea could only enter the more lady-like shops and occasionally help prepare the meals. Still getting used to the fact she had a disposable income, she struggled to enjoy spending it. To Joshua it was a very little, to Bea it was a fortune. Twice a week she would get a popular novel from the bookshop, and then on the way home drop by Mrs Potter's Emporium for more thread and wool for her bonnets. Mrs Potter was a friendly, older woman, who loved to chat to her customers and took a genuine interest in Bea. She was saddened, and not a little confused when, each time she tried to make conversation about the projects she was working on or enquired about the baby, Bea would merely nod her head, and give the briefest, stumbling replies. She suspected Mrs Potter was lonely, and once upon a time she would have enjoyed the odd meaningless conversation with an older woman who knew something of the city. But these days she was in no mind to filter the words and expand on her false story more than was necessary. So she would her bid good-day and leave as quickly as possible with her purchasers, and an empty smile.

Bea, uneasy at the concept of knocking on her own front door to have it opened for her, let herself in. Relieved to be in the sanctuary of her home and away from the hordes of unknown people, she closed her eyes and smiled when she heard Sarah in the kitchen, singing. Her joyous songs were the opposite of any hymn Bea had heard in Ulverston - one of her 'workin' songs' she called them. Bea held back for a moment, listening to the words and the power of her voice behind them. She filled it with love, loss, soul, and heartbreak. Sarah never sang in Bea's presence, and she only hummed when sufficiently distracted by her task to forget where she was. Twice, Bea had asked if Sarah could sing to her, or teach her the songs, but straight away the quiet, dark-eyed woman would softly refuse, and remain guarded for the rest of the day. Bea understood somehow and didn't press the matter further. There was a loneliness to her home that wore Bea down, but Sarah relieved that a little, and Bea relied on her in ways she didn't fully understand.

She was about to head up the stairs when she remembered Sarah had asked her to make herself known upon her return, so she knew her mistress had arrived back home safely. Bea took her foot off the first step and followed the singing towards the kitchen. She knocked on the kitchen door so as not to startle her companion and waited.

The singing stopped. "I'm back," remarked Bea with a small smile, standing in the doorway.

"Would you like a cup of tea?"

"Oh - yes please." Bea waddled into the kitchen to take a seat at the table.

"I will bring it up in a minute - I've made some lemon cake." Being able to buy lemons was one benefit of having money that was entirely acceptable to Bea.

"Thank you, Sarah, that's lovely - I would prefer to take it down here; if you're not too busy?"

"Yes mistress – take a seat."

"Thank you, this little one is really pressing on my hips today."

Sarah was nodding, as if she knew exactly what Bea meant. "It will get into position – you only have a month to go."

Bea picked at the cake in front of her, ignoring the cake fork at its side. "Nothing is ready – I'm not ready."

"I know a talented carpenter who can make you a cot." Bea glanced up at the unexpected remark and smiled again. "Really? Back in- I mean, back home, Da would know the men to ask, or there'd be handed down one, from my Mam – but here, I don't know who to ask, and Joshua…" There was a note of doubt in her voice.

Sarah poured out the tea and placed a cup out for Bea and one for herself. She sat down at the table opposite. "Tell me what you think you'll need, and I'll see if I can help – there are lots o' men I know who would welcome the work – it might help you prepare yourself too, Mistress." She cut Bea another slice of cake.

"Thank you, Sarah, you're very kind." Bea tasted the sharp tang of the lemon, followed by the sweet crunchy sugar dissolving on her tongue, and felt a slight loosening around her shoulders, and in her chest. "I'll work on the list this afternoon – if you will help me – I would be grateful for your guidance." There was almost a plea to Bea's voice that she hadn't intended to show.

"I shall do me cleanin' first – but yes, I can help – I will make a start on the dinner and then come up to you."

"What if… what if I help you prepare the dinner, and then… you can help me?" Bea smiled hopefully.

She was surprised and more than relieved to see Sarah smile back. "You have yourself a deal, Mistress."

Chapter 6

Joshua had been aware of Bea's restlessness during the night, blaming it on the baby, as she apologised for waking him again. All too often he had watched her wriggle in her sleep, fighting against the nightmare, reliving the same events in her mind, and covered in a cold sweat. These past months he had felt helpless, as a part of Bea disappeared and became lost. He longed for the young lady he had met at the old harbour wall or at the ball, and the spark of hope and confidence she had carried inside. So much had happened in a year. It shook him daily how much a person could change.

He gazed at her, lying there asleep, like a fell protruding out in its humble surroundings. He watched as the baby inside wriggled, the shape of the bump shifting ever so slightly. He wanted to reach out, stroke and sooth the child; bond with his future son or daughter. But then, it wasn't really his, however much he told Bea the contrary. He knew he could never love it in the same way as if it had been his own child in there. There were moments he would forget, as Bea grabbed for his hand and placed it on the kicking child; to please her, he would smile and make an encouraging comment. He saw all too keenly how her sanity hung delicately on a cliff's edge, clinging on to the possibility of normality finding its way back into their lives once again.

He left her sleeping and made his way to his dressing room. Downstairs, Sarah had already arrived. She was a good worker and a kind woman; she had been recommended by a neighbour, and her experience, and her living on the North Slope, a few streets away, had made her the ideal candidate. He had known immediately after meeting with her she would be a steady, friendly source of company for Bea. Bea herself had resisted the idea of a servant at first, insisting she could look after the house alone, uncomfortable at the idea of another person coming into their home and taking care of the work. Joshua had tried to see it from her point of view, realising the contrast of his own comfortable upbringing against her own. But the truth of the matter was, she wasn't able to look after the house. She could barely look after herself. The arrangement gave her the space and freedom to focus on the baby, and after a shaky start, they had settled into a routine.

"Mornin', Mr Mason," Sarah said, handing him his morning cup of coffee. "Breakfast?"

"Morning Sarah, yes, thank you." Sarah nodded, then made her way out of the room and downstairs to the kitchen.

Joshua sipped his first cup of the day. The coffee in Boston was stronger than he was used to, with a rich nutty taste. Next to his place setting lay the daily paper, 'The Boston Morning Post'. He scanned over the morning headlines and articles. It was an unusual layout compared to what he was used to, with narrow articles running down, side by side, unlike the more leisurely paragraphs of the Lancaster Gazette. His eyes scanned over the morning poetry, 'Summer Fete' by Thomas Moore, Esq, knowing Bea would read it later. He skimmed the rest of the front page before turning to the shipping news on the second page.

Sarah returned with a pot of coffee in one hand and a plate of gammon and eggs in the other.

"Thank you, Sarah."

"Anyt'in' else I can do for you, Sir?"

"No, that will be all... Mrs Mason is sleeping in late this morning."

"Very good, Sir." She nodded and left the room.

A stillness descended on the breakfast table. Joshua broke the perfectly made egg yolk and watched the golden liquid trickle towards his slice of gammon. He finished his breakfast absent minded and downed his last cup of coffee. Sarah stood at the front door, in time, holding his leather shoulder-bag and coat. He peeked in the hallway mirror, straightened his white cravat, and tugged down his grey waistcoat and jacket. Satisfied with his appearance, he placed his arms into the held-out overcoat and took the bag from Sarah's hand.

"Thank you, Sarah." He gave her a sincere smile, knowing Bea would be well looked-after in his absence, sighing heavily as the door closed behind him.

Along Pinckney Street, there was a hive of activity. The coal merchant was dropping off his goods with the help of skinny soot-covered lackeys, dragging large sacks to each front door; children shouting and racing a small dog down the street, whilst more familiar men of Joshua's class strolled to work. There was no need of carriages and horses if you lived and worked on Beacon Hill, unless you belonged to the Gentry or the Brahmins of the area. Instead, there were common stables, where you could stable your horse, hire one, or rent a carriage if you had occasion to attend a business meeting in the centre of Boston, or, like Joshua, worked at the harbour, on the Back Bay. He had bought the mare from an acquaintance of their landlord, and she was a beauty, her chestnut coat stamped with a creamy marking below her ears, and possessing a pleasant temperament. Joshua had wanted a horse which was used to the loud noises at the harbour, not a gentile animal used to the quiet streets of Beacon Hill. He felt himself awaken fully as he trotted on to the Exchange and Merchant Row. There was current, a charge flowing through him; this was where he knew he could breathe freely, forge a path, build his name up to a new respectability. For miles, the piers stretched out along Boston harbour, from the slim, shorter lengths owned by small, independent family companies, to the large, overbearing ones belonging to entire countries, asserting their own share of Boston Harbour for all to see. The largest piers were owned by the big shipping companies who had claimed harbours across the world, from the Far East, Africa, Europe, England, to South America and the West Indies. The Wentworth Shipping Company was one of the largest in Boston; owned by a Brahmin, the central figure of power both in Beacon Hill and Boston itself. Joshua guided his mare to the back stables attached to the large company building, running along its grand pier. Already the harbour was full of ships, sailors and business-owners as far as the eye could see. The beating heart of Boston was up and ready for business.

He made his way upstairs, where George Carter, now his clerk, hurried towards him with another cup of coffee and read out the morning tasks with unfeigned enthusiasm. On his first day, the clerk had sketched out his full personal history for Goldstein's new manager, hardly pausing for breath, or to drink his own brew. George was a young, sharp-eyed lad of twenty-four, born in Boston into an elite trading family, and eager to make his own mark on the world. He was undeniably keen, and furthermore had a thick, nasal accent, which Joshua had struggled to understand at first.

"Slow down, George, allow me to drink my coffee, and leave the list on my desk – I'll call you in for your thoughts when I've had time to digest both."

George blushed with embarrassment, handed Joshua his steaming cup, and dodged past him quickly to place the list on his desk. "Thank you, George." With a nod and an apologetic grin, George strode back into the adjoining office and continued with his tasks.

Joshua mopped the drips from the bottom of his cup along the rim of the saucer and stared out of the window down to the harbour below. He had arranged a surprise for Bea, which should arrive today, if weather permitted, and he hoped that when he arrived home that evening, his reception might hold a little more life than usual. He had kept in contact with Bob Lightfoot, exchanging updates on the effects of the upheaval they had left behind them, and letting him know how his daughter was doing. In one particular letter, Mr Lightfoot had confided in Joshua just how much Bea's misfortune had cost the family. Business had become slow, and Beth had eventually lost her job when the family for whom she had worked for no longer wanted to be connected with the scandal. He had remarked hopelessly that if Beth was to have any chance of a loving suitor or a suitable position in life, she would need to leave Ulverston. In response, Joshua came up with a plan to help both Lightfoot women. In previous letters, he had informed Mr Lightfoot of Bea's condition, and the sad difficulties she was experiencing after her ordeal. He had suggested that if Beth came to Boston, she could help support Bea, and they could both give her a fresh start in a society that knew nothing of her past. The second Lightfoot sister would arrive today by three, God willing, and perhaps be all the difference they needed.

Joshua congratulated himself for a moment. He felt constantly responsible for what had happened to the Lightfoot's after he and Bea had fled. Perhaps worst of all, in an act of revenge, his father had blacklisted Bob's rope business, convincing four other companies to pull their contracts nigh on simultaneously. Gritting his teeth in shame, he turned back from the window. He should have known his father was more than capable of such bitterness and pride.

Joshua stared at the immediate list of jobs burning a hole in his desk and finished his coffee, keeping one eye conscientiously on the clock.

T he docks were suffocating. The air was thick with sweat, waste, spices, and sugar. On one side stood the grand ships, with the smaller vessels cast in their shadow. Opposite the piers there were warehouses lining the bank, with everything else crammed in between. One man, with sweat running down his grubby face, leaving behind shining lines from hairline to chin, glared at the Englishman as he jumped out of the way from an oncoming crate. Joshua made his way to the pier where the passenger ships were coming in and whiled away the spare minutes, pacing on the spot as he watched people disembark. He had met Beth twice, and on neither of those occasions had he spoken to her, his attentions guided only towards Bea. What if, in fact, she hated him for what he had put her family through? What if this was all a mistake? He watched as each man and woman paused at the top of the ramp in wonder and fear as they contemplated the scene and the skyline in front of them.

Then, for a moment, he thought he saw Bea standing on deck. The sun was shining down on her, and she had a wide-eyed, youthful appearance, the way she used to look when they had first met. Taken back, he found himself catch his breath at the memory. He waited for her to descend and stepped forward.

"Miss Beth Lightfoot?" Joshua tapped her on the shoulder.

"Yes?" She jumped.

"Hello, may I introduce myself – properly, for once - I am Joshua Mason." He held out his hand for her to shake.

Her expression relaxed as a smile spread across her face and a little chuckle ebbed out at her initial surprise as she took hold of his hand. "Hello, Mr Mason, it is a pleasure to see you again."

"The pleasure is all mine. Is Miss Crookshank with you? How was your journey?"

"Yes, thank you, it was strange; oddly, given my Da's profession, I have never been on a ship before, and there were moments it was very choppy – Rose, Miss Crookshank, is somewhere just behind me." Joshua spotted another lost soul a few feet away, scanning the people around her for a sight of her friend. "Rose, over here!" Beth waved her hand in the air.

"There you are -"

"Rose, Miss Crookshank: Mr Joshua Mason, my brother-in-law."

"Hello Sir." Rose did a strange little curtsy as Joshua doffed his hat towards her, trying not to smile.

"A pleasure to meet you. I have a carriage waiting to take us straight to the house. Bea will be happy to see you again, Miss Lightfoot."

"Call me Beth, please, it feels too strange now for you to call me Miss Lightfoot."

"Then you must call me Joshua."

"Agreed." smiled Beth.

Joshua gestured to the two men standing behind, holding their luggage towards the carriage, and they turned as one away from the ship.

Joshua shut the door, blocking out the sounds of passage and toil, and thumped the roof to signal they wished to set off.

"I have not told Bea you are arriving, I wanted it to be a surprise for her."

"How is she?" Beth lowered her voice.

"She..." He looked at Miss Crookshank for a moment and filtered his words carefully. "She is... resting, preparing for the baby." He forced a weak smile, and Beth understood.

Chapter 7

S arah came racing down the stairs with a distressed expression toward the three people standing in the doorway. Joshua sprang forward immediately. "Sarah, what has happened? Where is Bea?"

"Sir, I sent a boy to your work, but you'd gone – it is Mistress..." Joshua dropped the bags and ran towards the stairs taking two at a time, with Sarah explaining breathlessly from behind: "she been funny all day Sir, never really waking, not eating, and then she started a-shoutin' and a wailin', and nothin' I could do would-".

"*They are going to kill my baby.*" Bea's scream through the bedroom door was so high-pitched that it pierced their ear drums.

"Bea?" Joshua barged into the room. He saw his ghostly-white wife stumbling back and forth, muttering to herself with protective arms wrapped round her bump. "Bea, what's wrong?"

"*They are trying to kill my baby.*"

"Who are?"

"*The rope, it is tightening around her neck.*"

Joshua spun round and stared at Sarah. "What has happened? Why is she talking like this?"

"She just woke this way – about two hours ago, I heard a scream from downstairs, so I came up, and saw Mistress covered in sweat, shoutin' nonsense. I did not want to leave her, so I got the runner-boy to fetch you – but you'd gone."

"Bea, its Joshua, I need you to sit down and talk to me."

"Who?" She stared at him blankly, broke out of his hold and

kept moving. "They need to be stopped – they can't have her – they had me once – they can't have her." Joshua froze in shock, his outstretched arms vacant.

Beth moved past Joshua and placed an arm around Bea's shoulder as she walked beside her. "Bea, its Beth, love."

"Beth? Beth! Beth, fetch Da, please, quickly."

"That's a good idea. I'll fetch him. You just sit here now, alright, on the bed? That's it, good girl."

"He'll know what to do." Bea muttered to herself, rocking back and forth on the edge of the bed.

"What are you talking about, your Da isn't here, I'm here -" Joshua looked from one sister to the other, with wide, hopeless eyes. He tried to reach out to Bea once more, but Beth grabbed his arm.

"Joshua, may I have a word – out in the hallway?" Beth funnelled Joshua out the open door and closed it quietly behind them. "Joshua, you need to fetch a doctor. I will stay with Bea."

"Why does she not know me?" Pain and exhaustion were all too clear in his face, and Beth could finally see the toll the last six months had taken on the man in front of her.

"It's the pregnancy. I have seen other women go through this. She needs a doctor - now."

"What, is she - ... will she be...?"

"We must not think that way. If you hurry, you can save them both."

He placed a hand on her shoulder and looked directly into her eyes. "I can't lose her."

She rested her hand on top of his and gave him a look of determination, a look he knew well. "Who is her doctor? Fetch him or a midwife, Sarah might know of one in the community. Either way, she needs someone now." She gave him a light pat on the hand before letting go and headed back to her sister.

"Sarah?" Sarah stood two feet away from him, still clutching onto the damp cloth in her hand. "Do you know anything about birthing children? Or of any women who have helped others through labour, a midwife perhaps?"

Sarah thought of the wise woman who visited her when it was time for her child to come into the world. The fear gripped her heart, knowing her child would become a slave the minute it was born. She hadn't wanted to let go of it, to bring an innocent life into that hateful world. She saw the same look now on her Mistress's face. "I know only a little sir, but there is another, someone who all our women use."

"Can you get your boy to fetch her? I'll pay for her time – please?"

"I can, but... sir..."

"What?"

"She is black, Sir... a Negro."

Joshua let out a small laugh of relief. "It makes no difference to me; all I care is that she can help my wife." There was no judgement in his voice, only concern as he headed towards the stairs.

"Yes Sir – I'll send for her."

"Thank you, watch over her." He gave her the same look of trust and thankfulness he had given her every morning as he left the house. "I'm going to fetch the doctor, but I hold little store by him." Another scream from Bea followed as he bounded down the stairs, jumping the last three, and sprinted out the door.

Sarah quickly shuffled after him and made her way to the kitchen where the little boy sat by the fire eating a chunk of fruitcake.

"I need y'to head over to Miss Fishers, now, as fast as you can."

"For her, who's screaming?"

"Tell her it's my Mistress and her unborn babe."

He nodded his head, placed the rest of the cake in his mouth, grabbed another slice for his pocket, and made his way out the back door toward the alleyway.

Sarah gathered a small bowl of cold water and replaced the fabric in her hand with new ones before making her way back up to the bedroom.

∞∞∞

"Beth, I saw it, I can feel it: the rope is around my baby's neck, she can't breathe..."

"Bea, I need you to sit down. Your baby is fine, she is still in your belly, you are protecting her." Beth stood in front of her, wanting to grab her, to hold her tight, but fearful all the while, sensing her sister could feel something wrong with the pregnancy and having no clue herself as to the best course of action.

"You don't understand, none of you do."

Balancing the bowl in one hand with the fabric draped over her shoulder, Sarah opened the door. She placed the items on top of the dresser, rolled one piece of fabric into a wad, and dipped it into the cool water.

"Mistress - Bea, I need you to sit." Sarah gently rested her hands on the trembling outstretched arms and guided the clammy woman towards her small velvet chair, a few feet away. She rung out the water from the cloth and placed it on Bea's feverish forehead. Bea calmed, as the soothing relief of the wet cloth penetrated her chaotic mind.

"None of them know... to think you're going to die... to feel the rope around your neck, snapping tight..." For the first time, Sarah wondered exactly what had happened to her Mistress all that way across the sea. She saw a woman who had been on a torturous journey, much like herself, to escape her past and find some kind of freedom.

"Thank you - Sarah, is it? I'm Beth, Bea's second sister. I've seen this... this thing, before - have you? Back home, another woman close with child. As the due date neared, she became feverish, and seeing things that weren't there. The baby came into the world *already dead*," she whispered the last words. "And the mother, she... she died giving birth. The amount of blood was too much. I was her maid, but also her friend."

40

Her voice was distant. "She wanted me there, I held her hand and then I - cleaned up the room afterwards. I never thought that..."

"That thing won't happen today." Sarah's voice was firm and controlled.

Beth nodded, and squeezed one of Sarah's hands, damp from the cloth, both keeping an ear out for the door, praying the boy found Miss Fisher before it was too late.

Bea drifted in and out of consciousness, moaning in pain and spouting randomly chosen words. Sarah kept cooling down the rags and placed them back on her head and over her collarbones. Her face was swollen, red, and blotchy. Sarah had noticed how her hands and feet had grown bigger over the past couple of days, and wondered maybe this wasn't normal swelling. Back in her old community, stories from women in different plantations would advise sending for the wise woman. The smell of the tea would filter through the little wooden huts as the songs from the homeland danced around the birthing hut, and the birdsong mingled with the women's cries. Miss Fisher would know what to do.

The front door slammed, breaking her free from the ghosts.

"Straight up the stairs Dr Hutton, second door on your left."

An older, stout of a man barged through the door, followed by Joshua. He peered over the doctor's shoulder and then weaved passed him.

"How is the patient doing?" The doctor stared dispassionately at the three women in the room. One in the corner, confused by the proceeding. Another, anxiously pacing, startled by the sudden noise. His gaze hovered over the black woman, who was kneeling beside his patient, holding a cloth to her head. He let out a low grunt and then shuffled towards them, bag in hand.

"That won't do any good. Step back so I can attend to my patient," he grumbled.

Sarah kept her head down and, without muttering a word, stood up and placed the rag back in the water.

"What do you think could be wrong, doctor?" asked Joshua in a hoarse voice as he knelt beside the chair.

"She seems to be asleep now, her face is puffy, but that is normal for the time she has left; two or three weeks?" Joshua nodded. The doctor placed two fingers on the inside of Bea's wrist and studied his pocket watch. "Her heart rate is rapid, but that could be because she had some sort of fright. Everything seems normal to me. She probably has experienced nothing more than a bad dream."

"A bad dream?" Beth exclaimed incredulously.

"Young woman, please, do not allow yourself these hysterics. You will wake the lady."

"It was more than a bad dream doctor. If you had only seen her when she was awake, she was in a lot of pain," offered Beth, lowering her voice.

"Women have described having vivid dreams when they are with child, and so to her it probably seemed real, pain and all. Has she been under much stress recently?"

"I- well... some stress, yes, with the move, and preparing for the birth. She was... sickly for a few months, before we were married."

"Well, there you have it. That will be it, and all she needs, therefore, is plenty of rest. Yes, bed-rest, with none of this unnecessary fussing, is what I advise. You may call upon me when it is time for her delivery."

"But... you will not check the child?"

"The lady is my patient, not the child – there is certainly nothing more I can do in that case until she goes into labour."

Bea let out another moan and shuffled on the chair. Her eyes shot open suddenly as she let out a low scream. Joshua held out his hands in front of her, not knowing where to place them in fear of hurting her further.

"Joshua – Joshua?"

"I am here, my love." He stroked her forehead and her damp, dark hair.

"Something..." she let out another moan, "something is

wrong…"

"Won't you help her doctor?" Beth shouted desperately, staring at her sister and then back at the doctor, who had frozen instantly to the spot.

Joshua, stroking Bea's hair with one hand, grasped her right hand with his other, and felt a fraction of her pain, as a sense of dread washing over him. He couldn't lose her, not like this. Hanley's baby was killing her, finally getting what he had wanted all along. After everything they had endured, making a life here, for it all to just end like this? No, he wouldn't let it happen. Joshua pulled his gaze away from Bea and glared at the confused doctor. A bitter anger began building inside of him, and he opened his mouth, ready for harsh words.

At that moment, they all heard a small knock at the bedroom door. For half a second, no one stirred, too embedded in the moment. Then Sarah let go of the small rag in her hand, dropping it into the bowl of water, and made her way to the door. Behind which the small errand-boy was standing.

"Tell me you found her?" she whispered.

"Yeah, she's downstairs, in the kitchen."

Sarah nodded her head and followed him out of the bedroom.

Highlighted by the low burning embers in the hearth, and the afternoon light straining through the basement windows, a larger black woman hovered in the corner. She clasped a small carpet bag close to her body, not yet trusting the owners of such a house.

"Miss Fisher? Good to see you again, thank you for comin."

"Why am I here? Why am I in this house?"

"My mistress needs you. I heard about yo' skills through others at meetin' house, Mma."

"Them white folk who live here, they do not want my skills; they will not want me here." She shook her head and made her way towards the back door.

"Sir, the - Mr Mason-" she still could not use the word '*Master*', having vowed to herself once she was free never to use that word again, "he asked me to send for you."

"Me?"

"Yes, Mma – they have need of a wise woman, a midwife."

"Is the baby coming?"

"I don't know, I think so, but somethin' is wrong with the Mistress."

"I will come, but for a price."

"He will pay you whatever you ask him Mma, he is good for it. I give you my word." She held a hand to her heart. In the distance, Bea's cries filtered down to the kitchen as Miss Fisher made her way up the staircase.

Chapter 8

"Sir – sir?" Sarah tapped Joshua on his shoulder as he gently stroked his wife's hand. The room was fixed in the same tableau as when she had left. "Miss Fisher is here." Joshua looked up at her, slight confusion on his face. "You asked me to fetch her, sir?"

"Where is she? Bring her in, please." Sarah nodded and made her way back towards the door.

Miss Fisher observed the stillness of the room, with the doctor standing awkwardly in the centre. Sarah made her way to Bea, gesturing to Miss Fisher to follow as she clutched onto her carpetbag, filled with herbs and tonics. Bea let out another low moan. Miss Fisher stepped back and studied her movements, how her body shook and contracted, and the swell of her skin. The baby was coming soon, but something was indeed wrong.

Sarah stood aside to give Miss Fisher space as she knelt beside the sick woman. Joshua said nothing. He hovered a foot away and watched, praying silently that she could help. Miss Fisher started at the head, feeling her forehead, the heat and sweat flowing out of her. Her hands moved over Bea's chest, and she lent closer, and tilted her head nearer Bea's mouth, listening to her breath. She heard a tightness in her chest; the baby pressing on her lungs. Next, Miss Fisher brought out a tarnished pocket watch. One side was dented, and the clock face had a slight crack across the glass. She mirrored the previous doctor's motions, placing her two fingers onto Bea's wrist. She counted the beats as she watched the tiny second-hand tick. The breathing was too shallow, and the heart too fast. She carefully placed the watch back into her dress pocket and moved her hands towards the bump. Her fingers pressed into the overstretched skin and felt for the baby. The legs were under her ribs and the bottom high. Her hands skimmed over the baby's back and towards the head. The baby was engaged. As her hand moved lower, Bea let out another low moan.

"Stop – stop, she is in pain!" Joshua called out, stepping closer to Bea.

"Sir, she – your wife - she is in labour. I need her to move to the bed."

"The baby is coming?" He said in shock. He wasn't ready, they weren't ready.

"We will help you." Beth stepped forward, looking at Sarah.

The movement in the room brought life back to Doctor Hutton, who looked startled and disgruntled at these latest developments. "What do you think you are doing? What is this - woman – doing here?"

"She is helping us," replied Joshua plainly.

The Doctor stepped closer to Joshua and muttered under his breath: "Trust me, you do not want her kind touching your wife. She needs to leave."

Joshua took a step back and shot a hard glance at the Doctor. "I asked for her to come, and she will stay."

"What can she do? How will she help? I am the only qualified medical practitioner here."

"My wife is in labour and you failed to notice, when she did not - I think that is enough of a reason for me." Joshua gave the doctor a challenging stare.

"If she stays, I will not," threatened the other.

"She stays." Joshua turned his back and made his way to the bed.

"Then I will not take the blame when she causes harm to your wife and child with her dark voodoo. I've seen this evil craft before, women with their smoke and herbs. They know nothing of the genuine science of this world, and-"

"Blood," said Miss Fisher abruptly, cutting off the Doctor's righteous flow.

"She is bleeding?" The worry was clear in Beth's voice.

"I need to examine her, properly – it might hurt."

"Joshua?" Bea's voice was faint.

"I am here – we are going to look after you, I will not leave you." He grabbed her hand, taking the pain as her fingers squeezed his until they turned white. Joshua turned his head back to the Doctor. "Leave us; send me your bill, I will pay you for your time."

Beth stood behind Miss Fisher and saw the first blooms of crimson liquid soak into the sheets.

"Joshua..." moaned Bea.

"The baby is comin', but your wife is bleedin' too soon. Her body, it is in distress, and if she gives birth, we might lose both, mother and child."

"What are you saying?" The unbearable thought refused to filter into his brain.

"We need to take the baby out." Miss Fisher said plainly.

"Cut the mother open, are you insane?" cried the Doctor, looking at Joshua, incredulous.

"Tis the only way now, sir," Miss Fisher insisted, ignoring the older man.

"You will kill her!" Interjected the Doctor again.

Joshua hesitated. The image forming in his mind was surely too terrible to give grounds to, but the alternative was to watch Bea die slowly, with the baby, in her own world of pain.

"This way I might save at least one of them." Miss Fisher turned and faced Sarah.

"Do it." Bea's strained voice filtered across the room. She moved her gaze from Miss Fisher to Joshua, the tears pooling in the corner of her eyes. "Save my baby."

"You could die... I cannot let her cut you." He pleaded.

"Please Joshua, save *our* baby." Joshua felt his heartbreak, her face straining in pain, her hands damp with sweat, and the choice she had made.

Joshua leaned in, careful not to put any pressure on her body, and kissed her lightly on the lips. "I love you," he whispered.

"I love you too." The words etched in sadness at the possibility they could be her last words to him, yet again.

"You have my blessing, Miss Fisher - what do you need?"

"This is insane, I will not be a part of this." The Doctor turned, pick up his leather bag and made his way out the door.

Joshua jumped to his feet. "How many? How many of these procedures have you performed?"

"I have seen eight, done three myself – five lived, mother and child - two under my hands."

"I have helped two others," added Sarah.

"What do you need?" Added Beth.

"I need towels, boiling water, and she needs to drink a tea before we start. It will bring down the fever. We need to be fast, everybody. Then brandy, towels, something to bite down on – for the pain."

Sarah nodded.

Beth stopped Sarah before she ran out the room. "Where are the towels? You fetch the boiling water and whatever else she needs." Sarah pointed down the hallway as they left the room together.

Miss Fisher examined Bea once more, making sure she wasn't fully dilated. Once the baby was in a decent position, they could no longer help her.

Bea let out another low moan. She reached her hand out to Miss Fisher. "Thank you for helping me and my baby." Miss Fisher took hold of her hand and nodded. After saying a little silent prayer, she let go.

Beth came back into the room carrying a stack of towels and laid them out on to the bed. As Miss Fisher lifted Bea's night dress, Beth placed two towels on top of each other, draping them over Bea's hips, allowing for modesty and to absorb some blood. Sarah came back into the room, carrying a tray. On it was a jug of boiling water, a mortar and pestle, a fine china teapot, and a small cup. Miss Fisher gave Sarah a small nod of thanks and opened her carpetbag. A smell of herbs wafted out. To Sarah it was a smell of home. Miss Fisher produced a bunch of mint leaves, moringa, and small nob of fresh ginger.

"Moringa." Sarah said, smiling.

"Nebebaye – neverdie," Miss Fisher corrected her, using the African name.

She took out a slim kitchen knife and peeled back the skin from the ginger root and shaved a small amount into the mortar and pestle. She picked the tiny buds at the top of the stems from each herb and dropped them into the grey stone, grinding everything together, scraping stone against the stone until a pulp formed. Using the knife, she scooped it into the teapot and brought out a round jar of honey from her bag, adding a teaspoon. She filled the pot with boiling water and allowed it to settle whilst she laid out the rest of her items.

"Do you have any brandy - whiskey?" Miss Fisher asked Sarah.

"Yes, a bottle for guests."

"Fetch it, my child, she will need a glass, and - he will too," gesturing to Joshua, who was turning white as he watched the newcomer take a brown calico roll from her carpetbag and spread it open to reveal a set of shining silver knives. Sarah nodded and left the room. Joshua ran his hands distractedly through his hair, repeatedly.

Bea let out another low scream, following by a pulsing groan. Miss Fisher rushed to her side and examined her. She was almost fully dilated, and the midwife could feel the tiny hairs on top of the baby's head. "We must act now, are we all ready?"

Sarah came back into the room, placed the tray on the sideboard, and poured a large measure of whiskey into two glasses. She placed one into Joshua's hand without a word and he drank it in three gulps, making his way almost instantly towards the tray for another. Sarah sat on the edge of the bed and smiled gently at Bea.

"I need you to drink, it will help with the pain." Bea attempted to lift her head, but couldn't find the strength. Sarah leaned over, gently slid her hand under Bea's sodden hair, and lifted her head a little, angling the glass to her lips. Her face recoiled at the taste, but she kept drinking until the last drop was gone. Then she poured out the tea and repeated the same motion. Sarah lowered Bea's head back and placed the teacup on the side table. She then took a deep breath and produced a wooden peg from her apron pocket. Gesturing to Joshua to come around to his wife's other side, opposite her, she took hold of her arm.

"You must bite down on this." Bea's eyes widened as she repeated the line to herself again in her head: *You are my child; you are not his – you are innocent – you are loved – you are mine.* She opened her eyes. His face was sullen with the realisation of the moment. "Joshua?"

"Yes, my love?" He forced a fake smile and a brighter tone.

"If I don't..." Her tone mirrored the same tone she had used all those months back in that dark cell.

"You are going to be just fine; I promise you."

"If I don't make it-" she stopped him before he could interrupt again, pleading with her eyes, "I need you to promise me, you will love our baby, that you will protect her and care for her?"

"I swear it - but you have to promise me, you will fight."

"I am tired of fighting." Exhaustion clear in her voice. The tears were pooling around her eyes.

"I need you to try, one last time – I cannot move forward in this unknown world without you."

She tried her hardest to nod, "I promise – I love you."

"I love you, my brave Bea." He leaned in and kissed her, like he used to do, removing the last nine months.

"I will need you to hold her down," Miss Fisher ordered. Joshua broke away at the order and placed his hands on her shoulders.

"Please – no - don't hold me down!" The fear was manifest in Bea's voice.

"I cannot have you movin'." Miss Fisher shook her head in

refusal.

"No, please get off me -NO!" Flashes of Hanley holding her down came flooding back. "No - No, *get off me* – not like this..." Her voice boomed from a hidden depth within her. She could smell his sweat once more, the sound of his voice as he laughed and grunted, the sensation of being exposed forever, unclean and violated. She had lived through the nightmares, but now it was real. She was there once again, in that moment, as she brought his child into the room. She had wanted something, just one part of her mind he couldn't touch, and yet even now he had a hold on her. She was falling into the darkness once more. "Get off me – please... No, no, no!" she screamed.

"We cannot stop now; we have no choice," Miss Fisher told the room.

Joshua stared at Bea; something had changed in her face as he held her arms down. She was no longer present. The realisation dawned on him that, as he held her down, she wasn't talking to him anymore. He looked away from the horror she was reliving.

Sarah heard the sorrow in her voice and remembered it well, from the nights where the white men would visit, and the cries she would hear, the plea in the women's voices, the plea in her own. She watched the man opposite her look away from his wife as his fingers whitened around her forearm. It was not his child they were bringing into the world.

Miss Fisher fetched the thinnest of her knives from the bowl of boiling water and held it out in front of her. She glanced down at the draping edge of the towels, was already soaking up the bright red blood from between Bea's legs. She knew she had to act. She had done this thrice before, two alive, one dead; she could find her way towards life again. She sent out a prayer to bless the room, for the mother, for the child and for herself.

"Ready?" She looked at Sarah, calm and ready. The woman's sister was holding down her other side, the bit between shining teeth, fear sketched across her taught, grey face.

The first cut was fast and clean, directly under the bump from one side of Bea's hips to the other. A heart-chilling, drawn-out scream through clenched jaws accompanied the movement.

The blood poured out, blocking Miss Fisher's view of the wound. She reached out for a towel but found another hand ready at her side. Sarah swiped away the thick, red liquid quickly and calmly. The midwife carefully sliced along the centre of the cut once more, this time going a little deeper. She felt the muscle give way, exposing the womb underneath. She took a deep breath and slit the stretched mauve material. A small gush of water flooded over the bloody towels. She could see a tiny arm and the curve of a back. Using both hands, she reached in and, with a deep groan from Bea, who was on the verge of passing out, clamped her hand around the baby and started encouraging the body out, one limb at a time. The legs came out first, followed by the back, and then with a last tug, the head, the umbilical cord wrapped around its neck. Beth stared at the rope and then looked at her sister. Miss Fisher placed the unmoving baby between Bea's legs and picked up the knife, and with tiny movements, cut into the cord. She had seen midwives before, cutting too deep, slicing the baby's neck. The cord gave way as the room let out a deep breath. Sarah grabbed hold of a clean towel and began to vigorously rub the baby. *Come on, little one, breathe for me.* She sucked the child's nose clear of fluid and continued rubbing the upper back. The seconds felt like hours until a tiny cry erupted out of her little lungs.

"You have a girl." Sarah exclaimed. She saw a faint smile on Bea's white face, and a small nod of thanks from Joshua as he comforted his wife.

Sarah pulled the baby close and moved to one side so that Miss Fisher had room to sew the wounds closed before Bea bled out. Sarah knelt on the floor and placed the baby and her towel on the seat of the soft velvet chair. She gave God a small prayer of thanks as she tied off the cord with a piece of string before rising to her feet to grab the bowl of water and a clean cloth. Clearing her throat, the baby sent out a little burst of cries.

"Oh, hush now, little one. You are safe in this world." Sarah wiped the blood from her head, moving down her body, checking for bruises or disfigurements. The little girl was perfect. She had forgotten what it was like to hold a newborn, and a silent, lonely tear trickled down her cheek for her dead son. Once the best part of the blood was cleaned off, she wrapped the baby in a fresh cloth and blanket and carried her back to her mother.

Miss Fisher had sewed the womb back together, and Beth was holding the skin and muscle of the lower abdomen together for her to clean and close. Bea was a ghost, already still in the bed.

"The baby needs to feed," Sarah told Joshua. "She needs to latch on to get the first milk and bond with her mother."

"Not now... Can't you see my wife is fighting for her life, the baby will have to wait." Joshua struggled even to look at the child, seeing nothing but the pain Bea was in, and the still-open chasm into which, at any moment he knew he could still lose her.

"She is a newborn; she cannot wait."

Beth spoke out before Joshua could block Sarah again. "How can I help, what do we need to do?"

"We need to place her at the breast; baby will do the rest."

Beth looked at her new niece and saw a likeness of Bea straight away, the curve of her lips and the shape of her nose. This is what Bea would want. "Of course." She gave Joshua an incontestable look, still holding the folds of her sister's stomach together. His shaking hand reached out and opened Bea's nightdress to expose her swollen breasts.

Sarah laid the baby down near the left nipple and watched how the baby wriggled at the smell of milk. Opening her tiny mouth wide, after two or three attempts, she latched on. Sarah lifted Bea's nearest hand and placed it on the baby's back. She watched as tears slid from the corners of Bea's eyes into each ear, and another smile spread across her lips.

Miss Fisher cut the thread and cleaned off the wound. She placed a paste of moss and cloves across the red line to help it heal and numb a fraction of the pain.

"The rest is in Gods' hands. I have done my part. Now she needs a good rest, and a reason to fight. May I use yo' kitchen to clean myself up and rest? If you will allow it, I will remain close on by?"

"Of course - rest, eat. Thank you for all you have done." Joshua reached out and took her blood-stained hands into his. "We are forever grateful to you."

"She's not out o' the woods yet, child - if she makes it through the night, she still have a long road ahead of her."

"I understand, I do, but... she is the strongest woman I know."

Chapter 9

June 1832, Beacon Hill, Boston

For the first two days, Bea fought. Miss Fisher and Sarah took care of her night and day whilst Beth looked after the baby, taking her to Bea to feed every two hours, giving her a reason to keep fighting, reminding her she needed to live. Joshua divided his time between shorter days at work, and remaining by her side, stoking the fire and trying to be helpful to both able women, all the while feeling completely lost. He read to her in their few quiet moments from her favourite books. Jane Austen had become a comfort to her in recent months. Miss Fisher continued preparing herbal tea to keep the infection away and redressed the wound every few hours with fresh moss and cloth. On the third day, Bea's colour began slowly to return, and she could acknowledge the baby when she came for her feeds. She felt the weight of the small body on her chest and the awkward little stretches she would perform as she suckled. Her hair was dark with little flecks of red that caught the candlelight. But if Bea tried to move an inch, a sharp pain seared across her hips. So she stayed still, her body aching and exhausted. Sarah gently and respectfully helped her to the toilet with a bedpan and an endless supply of clean towels, all the while humming her work-songs under her breath to put the new mother at ease.

By day five, Bea was more lucid. She was aware of everyone around her and how grateful she was to have them there. Her milk had now come in fully and the baby drank for longer, her own body responding to the smaller one at her breast.

As Beth brought the baby in for her mid-morning feed, Bea

could hear her making funny little noises as she reached up for her Aunt's hand.

"Good morning. You are looking better today. More colour in your cheeks." Beth rejoiced.

"Good morning," Bea whispered back.

"Here's Mama, little one." Beth lowered the baby onto Bea's chest.

"Thank you."

Beth smiled with a gleam in her eyes and gave Bea a brief nod, in the same way her Da used to do, one that said everything, knowing there was no reason for words.

"Hello Grace." Bea stroked the tiny mop of dark hair and held her close as she latched on.

"Grace? Is that her name?"

"What do you think? It came to me last night. It feels right."

"I love it, it suits her! She is Grace, I have never known a more contented baby."

"She is my grace, and my light." Bea said softly as she gently stroked the bare back.

"Grace Mason."

"What's this? Good morning, my love. You are looking better today." Joshua sounded happy as he peered around the door from his dressing room, still trying to tie his cravat.

"I have named the baby Grace. What do you think?"

"Grace Mason," Beth repeated with a smile.

"Yes, it's... very good." Joshua glanced at the baby for a moment before studying Bea's appearance. "How are you feeling today?"

"Better, stronger, still the pain when I move. Have you said good morning to our daughter?"

"... Yes."

"I would like you to hold her a little while today."

"You need your rest, my darling, and I need to work," Joshua interjected, dismissing the idea as if she wanted to walk barefoot in the snow.

"When you're ready, Bea." Beth shuffled out of the room before things became too personal.

"Have you held her yet, Joshua?"

"I didn't want to disturb her; all she seems to do is sleep and feed. And I have been busy at the docks and looking after you."

"I know you have, and I am truly grateful to you; you will never know how much. I felt you every second, hearing your voice helped me in the darkness." Joshua gripped tight her free hand, placing a kiss on her forehead. "But you also need to bond with your baby – she is our child."

"I need to go to work." Joshua pulled his hand out of her grip and moved towards the door.

"You can spare five minutes, surely?"

"I am needed to put out a fire. Something has gone wrong with a large shipment, and they need me on the ground."

"Please, Joshua?" she was pleading, the hurt clear in her voice.

"When I return this evening, I will – I promise – but now I really must go."

Grace gave a brief murmur, a sign she was full, and began wiggling on Bea's chest. Bea gently shuffled her upwards so that the lolling, milky head was supported just above her shoulder. Gently, she patted the baby's back. After a minute Grace let out a loud burp, and Bea chuckled.

"It suits you – being a mother." Joshua stood there for a moment and watched how she smiled, a small light returning inside of her. A quick pang of jealously entered his head, but he dismissed it as quickly as it arrived. "I'll see you tonight."

Bea nodded, absorbed once more in Grace. "I love you."

"I love you too." Joshua said as he walked out the door.

Bea felt Grace relax into her chest once more and drifted back to sleep, soothed by the familiar sound of her steady heartbeat, the pain dulled by its dainty rhythm. Bea tucked the blanket around them both and embraced the reassuring ball of weight, grasping tight to this moment of happiness. "You are my child; not his – you are innocent – you are loved – you are mine."

Chapter 10

After a fortnight, Bea was strong enough to shuffle around the room for a few minutes at a time, cradling the baby in her arms. Once she was out of danger, Miss Fisher had left to return to her own home, with twenty pounds in her pocket at the Mason's insistence: "You saved our lives; it is the least we can do. We are forever in your debt." Miss Fisher, who had never seen such a sum of money, took it with an abiding sense of disbelief, but returned every couple of days to check Bea's wound for any sign of infection. Sarah barely left Bea's side. They gave her the second bedroom to use as her own, and she insisted on staying close, making sure they fed Bea with rich, simple broths, and drinking her herbal teas.

One morning, seated in her velvet chair after ten laps of the room with Grace sound asleep in her arms. She whispered to her daughter, delighting in her profoundly tranquil face.

"I promise you, my darling, I will protect you with my life. No one will hurt you or take you from us. It is you and I against the world. You will have a life full of love, happiness and opportunities..."

There was a knock on the door. "Come in." Bea called out in a loud whisper.

Beth popped her head around the door. "Sorry, I wanted to check if you needed anything?"

"Thank you, but I think we are fine, aren't we, my darling?" Bea gazed down at the sleeping Grace in her arms, with rosy cheeks and her little wrinkly fingers interlocking around the knitted blanket. Beth nodded and edged back round the door. "Wait... come and sit with me for a moment, will you?"

"Of course." Beth dragged over a chair that was beside the dressing table. Bea watched how she moved, how she held herself. Her little sister was no longer a young lady. Without Bea realising it, she had transformed into a woman. Her face had more defined angles, higher cheek bones showed off her brown eyes and full lips. Her waist, which was once straight, had a curve to it now, emphasising her hips. Where had the time gone? It was only yesterday, when they used to curl up on the hay mattress, keeping away as their parents had yet another fight after dinner. Practising hairstyles and fashionable braids they had seen on Lady Dawn Richmond at Church two Sundays past. She was the same age as Bea, but couldn't be more different. Now look at them. How strange life was sometimes. Bea readied herself for a conversation she had been meaning to have for the past few weeks, but now it was time.

"I wanted to talk to you... now that I am recovered, and I want you to be honest with me." She waited until Beth nodded her head in agreement. "Tell me how it really is in Ulverston when you left? Da writes to me, telling me that everything is alright, but I know he is protecting me... from the truth. For example, I have only received one letter from Alice and yet, I have sent at least a dozen in return. I know things are wrong but no one will tell me... Please, don't get me wrong, I am thrilled and grateful that you are here and yet, this wasn't the plan. The fact Joshua and Da thought it best and you must have agreed?" Bea lifted her hand off Graces rhythmically rising chest and laid it on top of Beth's outstretched hand.

"We knew you were struggling, not just through Joshua but by your letters. There was no spirit in the writing. Your voice was gone. That was one reason, to be here to help you, when I should of before..." Bea was about to protest until Beth raised her finger to allow her to finish. A gesture similar to her Da's. "In honesty, I have not been allowed to talk to Alice. I saw her in town one day and she passed me a note whilst remarking on some form of nonsense before carrying on with her business. I think it must have laid in her cotton shopping bag for a while with the corners bent and smudged. And yet, all it said was sorry. For the sake of their shop we could no longer be friends and in time she hopes things are different. That was it, a life time of friendship dismissed in a few words. But I also understand, which brings me onto my other reason..." Beth had contemplated how this conversation would go, knowing the guilt Bea would instantly feel. "Life back home is harder. The family gave me notice, after working for them since I was twelve. Da's orders have slowed down. Mr Mason blacklisting the family didn't help, but the shipyards know Da and the reputation the Lightfoot rope, so they keep orders coming. Thankfully, business keeps thriving in Ulverston and they need rope, otherwise..." she didn't need to finish the last part. Lowering her eyes and the slump in her shoulders told Bea everything she needed to know. "But none of that is because of you. All you did was fall in love and no one saw what Captain Hanley was capable of. Society is quick to judge and hold you down." Beth added in a soft voice with a hint of their Da. Bea felt the tears building in the corners of the eyes. "No one in our family blames you... I don't blame you." Gently placing her other hand on top of Bea's slightly shuddering one, she gave it a brief squeeze, seeing for the first time the amount of painful guilt Bea was holding on to. "What you had to endure was enough punishment to last a thousand lifetimes, and you did nothing wrong. - I see it now, the way he looks at you, protected you when this little one was coming into the world – you belong to each other."

There was a moment of silence as Beth's words sank in and she believed her. There was no blame. "Thank you, for your honesty... I am so glad you are here." A few tears broke through and streamed down Bea's face. Beth let go of her hand and grabbed a clean handkerchief from the top clothes draw, handing it to her. "Thank you," she repeated.

"It is strange, living in a big town – city compared to Outcast – Ulverston, but I am enjoying it. There is excitement here and endless possibilities." Beth continued the conversation, smiling back at her sister.

"You have a chance to start afresh, to discover what you want to do." Both of the women giggled as Beth distorted herself so that it resembled that of Lady Dawn, with her nose held tight and grinning whilst looking rather fearful of the poor children standing close by. An appearance they had often seen at church. The laughter stirred Grace out of her deep sleep.

Sarah entered the room carrying a pot of tea on a small silver tray. "Thank you, Sarah, you read my mind."

"I am going to pass on the tea. I have some errand to do before the shops close." Said Beth, refusing the empty cup. "Sarah, I'll be back in an hour to help make dinner."

"Thank you," Bea repeated, as she felt a part of the burden lift from her shoulders.

Without a word, Beth smiled and waved bye as she closed the door behind her.

"Shall I put Grace in her cradle?"

"Yes, thank you."

Sarah lent down and scooped Grace into her arms, planting a small kiss on her forehead before laying her down. Bea saw daily how fond Sarah had become of Grace, and she didn't know what she would have done without the young woman; she had become a friend, an auxiliary mother, and a protector.

"Sarah, may I have a word?" Today was the day for honesty. No more secrets.

"Yes, Mistress... Bea."

"I have been meaning to speak to you - to explain – about... what I said during the night my baby was born."

"There is no need." Sarah shook her head, dismissing the notion.

"There are moments from my past that haunt me still, and some of that came back during the labour. You have shown me such kindness over the past few weeks, months, even, I do not know what I would have done without you."

"You would have done just fine, Mis... Bea."

"Few people would have been as patient and kind as you. I

like to think we have become friends?"

Sarah nodded, poured out a small cup of tea, and placed a thin slice of lemon and a spoon of honey into the cup, stirring pensively. She understood Bea needed to talk now. She handed the cup to her in silence. Bea took a small sip, followed by a deep breath. She told Sarah about Hanley without using his name, merely calling him 'the man' or 'the monster'. She lightly touched upon the night he had taken everything from her, without going into detail. But she didn't know if she should dare say more, whether Joshua would want her to. What if Sarah told another, even in innocence, and then they told another; before they knew it, it would taint their fresh start.

"There... there is more, but I have not spoken of it aloud to anyone but Joshua, and... I do not know if I am ready." Without thinking, her free hand drifted towards her neck and stroked her scar. Sarah had seen that mark many times before, but always on the dead bodies of men and women, never on a living soul. Bea's story intrigued her, and wanted to know more, but felt instinctively that it wasn't her place to press. The moment she had met Bea, she had seen pain in her every movement and thought. And on the night Grace had come into the world, she had witnessed it become a reality. When Bea was ready, she would be there to listen.

She took Bea's hand in hers; one woman to another, both survivors of terror, now working out how to live entirely new lives. Sarah gave Bea's hand a little squeeze and smiled.

"I'll let you rest now, Bea." She took the half-finished tea, placed it on the tray, and carried it quietly out the door.

Chapter 11

July 1832, Ulverston, England

"I feel sorry for them, I do – to think how that girl behaved, and how it has affected her family – oh I'll have a half a pound of butter too – the Lightfoots have been here for generations, and in a matter of months they've lost everything." Mrs Richardson placed her wicker basket onto the polished wooden counter.

"*Such* a shame; I know Bob well – now is there anything else I can get for you?"

"A dozen eggs, please. Yes, my Frank knows Bob Lightfoot, they used to drink together in the Bay Horse, but now I hear he won't go near the place, and I don't blame him. The questions people asked.... That wife of his rarely comes into town herself now." She tutted her head from side to side. "The airs that woman had, I personally couldn't stand her, but I wouldn't wish such a fate on any mother. Mrs Dent does her shopping for her now."

Mrs Hodgson moved closer, stretching her neck out. "Really?"

Mrs Richardson, mirroring her action, leaned forward. "It's just shameful, that's what it is."

"The nerve of that Beatrice."

"Hmmmm, indeed. Well, is there anything else I can get for you, Mrs Richardson?" The shopkeeper continued, straightening herself back up and smoothing out the creases in her apron.

"Could I have three candles, beeswax, if you don't mind. I know it's an indulgence, but I prefer the smell."

"Right you are."

"I hear they have shipped the other daughter out to join her across the sea, little Beth. She lost her job working at the big house, and no one else will have her, of course – and can you blame them?" She made the sign of the cross over her chest.

Mrs Hodgson placed the candles beside the basket. "Bob still vouches for her innocence."

"Of course, he would. Who would want to believe their child could do that?"

"He says it was that other man… to be honest I can't believe it myself; she seemed so nice when she used to come in for the shopping. Just the eggs, was it Mrs Richardson?"

"A sack of flour, if you please. What I can't believe is the Mason boy stuck by her, even when his family disowned him, and cast him out. What spell did she have over him, that poor Joshua, for him to leave his family for her?" She repeated the sign of the cross, shaking her head.

The bell above the shop door rang in the background as someone entered.

"I'll be right with you," Mrs Hodgson called out, her back to the counter as she reached out for the flour on the third shelf.

"I overheard Mrs Dent say that she has given birth a month since. But unless my memory is two months ahead of itself, or the baby came altogether too early, that baby was conceived out of wedlock?"

"Maybe that is why he stuck by her?"

"I had heard rumours of them meeting alone, in secret. Whoever the father of the child might be, Beatrice Mason wasn't the girl you thought she was."

"Well, Bob told me about the man who attacked her - it all came out in court, every single detail – he took her maidenhood, poor thing - maybe it is his?" Mrs Hodgson placed the heavy sack on the counter with a thud.

"Attacked, you say?"

A loud cough behind reminded them they weren't alone. Mrs Hodgson looked up and gave Mrs Richardson a warning look. She blushed as she turned around.

"Forgive us, we like to catch up on the local news..." She didn't recognise the gentleman standing in front of her with golden tan and clean, fine clothes, compared to his more dishevelled appearance stepping off the ship. But Mrs Hodgson knew who it was straight away.

"What can I get for you Captain Hanley?" Throwing Mrs Richardson, a quick glance, she brushed a few specks of flour from the counter as her customer let out a sharp intake of breath, and the penny dropped.

"A ball of twine and a quart of oil, please Mrs Hodgson?"

"Of course. No trouble at all," Mrs Hodgson replied briskly, searching for the items under the counter.

"Did I hear correctly that - Mrs Mason, is it - has had a baby?" Hanley looked directly into Mrs Richardson's crimson face.

"Why yes, Captain," Mrs Hodgson confirmed, reaching for the oil on the middle shelf.

"A boy or a girl?"

"A girl, I" Mrs Richardson turned around, lowering her eyes as Captain Hanley stepped forward.

"I must congratulate them that *is* good news– how much do I owe you?"

"Two shillings and sixpence."

Captain Hanley leaned past Mrs Richardson and placed three shillings on the counter and took the bottle of oil and twine with an elegant flourish. "Keep the change, ma'am." He gave Mrs Richardson a broad smile. "This has all been quite informative."

"Thank you, sir, good day..."

"Good day, ladies." Captain Hanley tipped his hat and strutted towards the door.

Once they had heard the bell and were assured that he was gone, Mrs Richardson let out a deep sigh. "So that's him then?"

"Yes."

"*Now* I see."

Chapter 12

August 1832, Beacon Hill, Boston.

J oshua stared down at the sleeping baby in her crib. She was three months old now, and he had only held her twice, both times at Bea's insistence. She was showing character now, little chuckles and smiles when Bea was playing with her. He noticed how protective his wife was over the baby, not letting her out of her sight, monitoring every tiny sound and each recent development. But he couldn't deny that being a mother suited Bea, and the baby brought back a side of her he had missed. There was a light in her eyes, and a genuine joy in her world once more. The tiny little girl was looking more like Bea every day, and for that he was unspeakably grateful.

He shuffled around the room on his tiptoes as he collected his shoes and jacket, cursing the creaking floorboards as the baby moaned and twisted in her blanket. Bea had only fallen asleep an hour ago, and he knew it would disappoint her if he couldn't leave without waking the baby. As the moans got louder, Joshua dropped his shoes and jacket on the ever-faithful velvet chair and quickly made his way over to the crib.

"Shush now, baby." He never spoke her name; calling her baby gave him the distance he needed to persevere with their new life as a family. He placed a hand lightly on top of her chest, reassuring her with a move he had watched Bea make repeatedly, to soothe and quieten her in moments of unrest. Her little hands reached out and clung on to his thumb, her eyes wide and wondering, gazing up at his face in complete seriousness. He wondered at her tiny fingers, and how enormous his hand looked against her body. She let out a gummy greeting. He smiled back. She let out a little cry, a sign to be picked up, and a demand for comfort. Bea stirred in bed, ready to jump at her baby's command. Without thinking, Joshua quickly scooped Grace up. Supporting the head, he held her tightly against his chest, feeling the little heart thump against his, and the warmth of her body. He felt her nestle in against his shirt as her morning drool created a damp patch, but he didn't mind. She smelt like Bea. He lowered his head down further and took a deep breath into her wisps of hair. There was also a sweet, lavender smell, and within a few moments he could hear her own breathing become deeper. He relaxed with her; doing it on his own terms wasn't so bad after all. For months before she was born, he had feared he would hate her, especially if she had been a boy, a consistent reminder of Hanley. To his relief, she was a girl, and he didn't hate her, but he also found that no matter how many days passed, and how much happier Bea grew, he couldn't love her either. The only thing that mattered to him in the first couple of days, weeks, and months was Bea, and the fear of her leaving him alone in this world and he would have to bring up Hanley's child alone. But Bea had survived. More than that, she now thrived as a mother, knowing that this little person was her entire world, one that she could contain and celebrate always. And for Joshua, that was enough. To gain glimpses of an old version of his love was enough for now, and he was occasionally even hopeful that in time, she would return to him completely.

He lost all track of time, watching her little hands and feet clutch at his under-shirt as she dreamed, her lips forming a pout, desiring milk again. He would have stayed there until she woke if Sarah hadn't come through the door and reminded him he had work.

She gave him a surprised smile, filled with warmth, at finding him holding the baby whilst Bea slept.

"She stirred, and I - I didn't want Bea to wake," he whispered, feeling awkward at being discovered.

"Sir, your breakfast is waitin' for you downstair', I'll take her until Mistress wakes."

"Very good, thank you Sarah."

She lent in and scooped Grace out of his arms in one swooping motion, swaying on the spot to settle her once more. As Joshua left the room and made his way down, his arms seemed naked, missing the weight from her body and the smell of her head. He tried to shrug it off, make out it was all nonsense. But as he helped himself to coffee, he knew deep down that she had done it; she had broken through his barrier. He now saw what Bea was trying to tell him, that Grace was innocent of everything that had happened before.

Joshua devoured his breakfast and almost jogged to the stables. He was running late, and he was never late. Mr Goldstein was an old-fashioned individual with traditional values, and believed a man should only interact with his child on a Sunday afternoon for a few hours, or sent to boarding school once they had turned five, never to be seen again until they were eighteen. As for wives, his attitude was remarkably similar: "Women? Hmmm, they are strange creatures, I leave them to it; don't get yourself mixed up with all their drama, my boy."

Joshua left his mare with the groom to be stabled and cleaned himself up.

"Ah - Mason, my boy, is it all done and sorted, then?" Mr Goldstein's voice barked out the moment Joshua stepped over the threshold.

Joshua could make him out in one of the side offices. His broad frame always looked unusual against his small stature, but his rich, sonorous voice made him seem like a giant. Joshua paused for a moment. "*Sir...!*" Before he could begin, he heard scurrying footsteps on the floorboards above, followed by thundering footsteps coming down the stairs as George appeared, looking panicked. He had clearly covered for Joshua and was trying to save the situation before his line manager put his foot in his mouth. George held up a piece of paper on which Joshua glimpsed details of the 'Lioness' shipment, quickly dropping it when Mr Goldstein spun round, glaring at the interruption.

"Ah – Yes, sir, the... *Lioness*, is all sorted now."

"Glad to hear it - it was a good thing you got here early, Mason, to sort it all out. Mr Carter, said customs wanted to make a search?" Trying to poke holes in his story, Joshua knew he hadn't quite believed George's explanation of his absence.

"Indeed, sir... One of their random checks. But I... I informed them of the rumours surrounding the recent Indian shipments. The fortunate result was that they postponed our checks for another day." *As soon as Mr Goldstein left, he knew he would need to inform the team on the boards to cover all bases.*

Mr Goldstein let out an alarming gruff chuckle that Joshua hadn't heard before. "Grand."

Most of the customs men were endemic racists and took any excuse to throw their weight around with the more 'exotic' traders, searching their piers and shipments at the least excuse. Whilst Mr Goldstein liked to keep certain cargo on certain shipments on a low radar. The 'Lioness' being one of them.

"Men come at night, clear out part of the cargo and declare the rest in the morning... and if you want to keep your job sir, you don't ask why... not even you." George had told him on the first day working in the office.

"Now, Mason: Mrs Goldstein is organising a Gala to raise money for some sort of charity, you and your wife must attend. It's in a month; I'll get Mrs Goldstein to send out an invitation. A chance for you to meet your fellow employees." It wasn't a question; it was an order.

"It would please Mrs Mason and I greatly to attend. Thank you for the consideration, sir." He knew Bea wouldn't be happy about making the date, but once he explained he had no choice, he was sure she would understand. After all, now with Grace here, he couldn't risk his job and reputation, not now their family was expanding.

Once Mr Goldstein had left, the office calmed down, and business continued as usual. With another strong cup of coffee in him, Joshua filled in the logbook, opened letters from ports scattered around the world informing him of any changes or difficulties they were currently facing, and replied to his local correspondents with advice or demands. The rest of the day passed with ease. He enjoyed his routine, slight break away from the desk, walking down the pier and have space to think. He loved the drive of necessity, and the satisfaction of motivation his job gave him from minute to minute. Here he felt needed, important, a boss with a voice; at home he wasn't needed - not really. Bea had developed her own routine with Grace, and both Beth and Sarah aided her with it gladly. So, he left them to it, keeping to his study, out of the way. He couldn't deny that their home life wasn't what he had imagined back in Ulverston, planning their elopement and imagining his future with Bea. But on the whole, everything was better here. Working for the Mason company, he could never really own a role; his father had made him an overseer, but for six months, that had meant little. Unwilling to relinquish his control, not even to his son, left Joshua idle. Here, he could see a clear path in front of him, to control his own future with Bea by his side every step of the way.

At five o'clock, each pier started the changeover for the evening. Day and night workers huddled together, exchanging gossip and the day's events. Envious stares from the new arrivals followed the day workers as they headed for a drink before home. A year ago, after work, like the labourers, he would have stopped by at the pub and had a couple of pints before heading home. That was one thing he missed from home, a good pub. Here they didn't seem to exist; each community had meeting houses, a familiar gathering spot, or a workers' tavern. In Ulverston, one might blur the lines between classes, as long as no one threw their weight around amongst the workers or talked too much politics. But in Boston elitism and professional snobbery were alive and well carried across the Atlantic from all over the globe, the only difference being that it was money that dictated the social strata. Beacon Hill was no exception; house by house, street by street, each community stayed in its patch: the wealthy upper classes, the self-educated middle-classes, the workers, the Irish, the free slaves, the rising black Americans, the Jewish families, the Eastern Europeans, and the tight-knit enterprising Asians. The diversity reminded Joshua of London, and the short couple of years he had spent roaming the streets and meeting people from around the world, listening to all the different languages. That was a problem with Ulverston; as a remote northern area of British Lancashire, it didn't attract a diverse community. It had seen change, and the people there weren't afraid to speak their minds, but most lived and died within a ten-mile radius of the same spot. Boston was a different world, and Joshua felt more and more that it was a better fit for his ambition and his own growth.

Joshua entered through the front door; Bea had successfully made the case that they shouldn't disturb Sarah in her tasks just so they could walk through their own front door. He had felt foolish, thinking back to all those years he had made his family butler open doors for him, as though he weren't able to do it for himself, but his father wouldn't have considered any other way. Another difference to their upbringing. He placed his bag on the side-table and hung his overcoat on the peg. For a moment, he stood and listened to the flowing noises of the house and how happy it seemed now. Downstairs, the sound of Sarah singing drifted in from the kitchen as she finished making the dinner for everyone. Upstairs, Beth was pottering about, talking to herself, a trait of Bea's, making lists and thinking out loud. Instead of the muffled sound of Bea and Grace from behind their bedroom door, there was a louder, clearer conversation which came from the sitting area. It wasn't a room that they had used much at first. Before Grace, Bea mostly stayed in her room, apart from when she was helping Sarah with jobs around the house. Beth used it occasionally when she was not sitting with Bea in their bedroom, or taking time alone in hers. When they were all at home, Joshua kept mostly to his study, his own sanctuary, and sat in front of the fire with a glass of whiskey before dinner. After dinner was done, Bea would return to the bedroom, tired, and Joshua would return to his haven and contemplate life whilst watching the flames dance and lick their way up the chimney breast. Now, however:

"What a lovely surprise." Joshua stood in the doorway, grinning at the startled Bea, on the floor with baby Grace laying on top of a blanket, wriggling around.

"I hope you don't mind; Grace was getting restless in the bedroom and I thought a change of scenery would do her good."

Joshua walked over and instead of giving her the usual kiss on the forehead, he knelt beside her. Without saying a word, he stroked her blushed cheeks and gently kissed her on the lips. He couldn't stop smiling at Bea's reaction. "Mind, why would I mind? It's good to see this room getting used."

"You're in a good mood. How was your day? I heard you were late." She gave him a playful smile, brushing her hand across his shoulders in a familiar gesture. "It was nice to hear you had a moment with Grace." Bea tickled her free hand over the baby's stomach, making her giggle.

"I didn't want her to wake you – and yes, it was... nice... holding her." Joshua nudged closer to Grace and watched her smile up at him, reaching out her chubby arms towards him, taking him by surprise.

"I think she wants another cuddle from her Da." The words finally sunk in; to Grace, he was her Da, and she was no one else's daughter. She carried nothing of the pain or jealousy he did; she only wanted to be held by him, taught by him, raised by him. They were a family; a complicated family, but one that none could break apart. He was her father. Without another thought, he reached down and picked up the giggling baby, as she kicked out her legs in a jerky, excited motion, stretching her arms out, determined to touch his face. He laughed in surprise and felt with a jolt that he was happy; they were finally happy.

Chapter 13

May 1820, Georgia.

Jessie readied herself, the same as always, once a month. She cleaned up the small wooden hut, wiping off the thin layer of muck that lay dusted over the few pieces of furniture she had gained. A discarded dresser that the main house had thrown out, no longer suitable with its broken leg, which she propped up with a stick, and a drawer missing, the gap filled with her one pair of home-made shoes. She didn't have a great deal of clothes to put in it, but she kept it because it made her hut look more presentable, and less like the grimy cotton-picker's shack, which it was. Its last inhabitant had somehow gained a chipped bedside table, certainly without the other women knowing otherwise it would have been gone before Jessie had arrived. She reshuffled the wildflowers, weeds to anyone else, in the glass beer bottle she had found in the tall grass near the woods. She placed it first on the dresser, and then on the bedside table, back and forth, unable to work out which one looked best. She decided on the dresser tonight; if she kicked her legs out, she might knock it off the table, so it would be safest there. She unwrapped the thin piece of cloth with faded flowers and splashes of greens and purples from around her head. It had once been her Mama's, a gift to remember her by on the day they sold away her daughter. She let the deep brown, frizzy, tight curls descend like a waterfall, crashing on to her shoulders. She pulled out one of the dresser drawers and carefully placed the folded piece of cloth inside.

She had been at Drayton Hall for just over a year, sold to the estate as a cotton-picker and, at twenty-four, young enough to restock with another man. But there would never be another man; no one could replace Hercules. She might be a widow, but in Jessie's heart, no one could replace him, nor her son Sebastian.

*

Hercules had been strong, like his name, working the fields, readying the ground for plantation, organising the men and protecting the weak. For years he had dreamt of running away, even before their son had arrived, and in the dead of night, when only the crickets were awake, he would talk about a path that others had used, where known people would hide and guide escapees until they reached the free states, where no man could own another. The promised land. A myth, a legend. He had said someone who told him, talked of 'station', and 'conductors' and 'the underground movement'. But those entities were merely rumours the coloured peoples clung onto for hope. Jessie herself saw it as a quick way of a slave getting themselves shot or hung, the sound of the dogs in pursuit, with the taste of a dead man in their mouths. She had experienced the cat-o'-nine-tails before, when she hadn't met the day's picking number, which was higher than the last plantation. None of it sounded appealing to her, not in exchange for a mere fantasy of escape. Men and women alike continuously dreamt of crossing the county lines and following the north star to a different life, but only a lucky few out of thousands made it. They punished the rest depending on how far they had fled, and the value of the stock. A few hours, and a simple retrieval. Then it was the cat-o'-nine-tails, followed by the hot-box for a month. If it was close on a day, and they had to use the dogs, then it would be the cat and the hanging tree, strung up by the hands for a further day, an example for all to see. But if the runaway lasted a few days out in the open, then the hunters became involved. Then the punishment varied from the 'R' brand on the face to a slow execution. Jessie could still smell it now, the acrid, sweaty tang of burning flesh. It would linger in the air for days afterwards, filling the nostrils until it embedded itself into clothes, food, skin and minds.

The last time Hercules mentioned escape was the day Jessie told him she was pregnant.

"Mine?"

"Of course."

"Not Jamieson?"

"I know to clean out after him." A rule the master introduced with any couple, to take the marriage bed first so every woman knew who they really belonged to.

Jessie had met Hercules when she was twelve and he was fifteen, sold away from her mother to the Middleton Plantation, with never a mention of her father. There was some speculation to his identity at the colour of her paler, honeyed skin, but it went no further than the slave huts. Alone and isolated in a new plantation, Hercules had showed her the way. She had shared a hut with another girl, Reed; two years older than Jessie; kind, but a slow picker. Jessie was quick, especially after the first slashes on her back. Her Mama had shown her the best ways when she had turned five and became a full-time picker. How to cover her neck from the beating sun, to keep the cloth wet, to sing out loud the workers' songs, tapping her foot to the rhythm when her hands split and cramped, to keep the girls' spirits up and to use the oil-based cream when the cracked skin leaked blood onto the cotton. At night, she heard her Mama cry out when the white man came to visit, and knew what life had in store for her. This was her life, and she had accepted that. The thought of running away was a fool's errand.

Two years passed since her farewell to her Mama and her old life. Now, at seventeen, Hercules declared his love for her, and offered his hands, his heart and his protection. They made plans to marry, sought approval from the big house and in the spring, out in the woodland church, declared their unity to the lord. Nothing would break them apart. That was the first night he had whispered words of escape, cradling Jessie in his arms after her first visit from the tall white stranger who had inducted her into the darker side of womanhood. He had found a mythical creature called a conductor who owned a station. He told her, stroking the tears from her cheeks, that if they could get to him, he might help them cross the county lines to the next station, and then onward in the same way to the nearest free state. Over the years Hercules had gathered the information gradually, gaining more and more trust from the master in order to run errands to the store, and eventually stealing a map. Tucked in between the sheets of their bed, he would talk of stories and trickle his fingers across the vast map until they reached Boston. There he said they could start afresh, as free people who could choose where they worked, how they lived, and be the masters of their own home. Jessie would listen, allowing him to dream, but knowing nothing would come of it as his fingers pointed lovingly at the different states. They were now in North Carolina, which meant crossing into Virginia, on to the Capital, and then into Philadelphia and on through another four states until they reached Boston, all without getting caught and sent back.

But stories stopped the moment he heard she had a babe in her belly. He couldn't risk the cat or worse, on her when his child was growing inside her. When their son finally arrived into the world, they both realised they couldn't run with a child. It was slow to begin with, but after time, Jessie saw the fire going out of him. He had lost hope of freedom, but gained a son.

Sebastian was strong, like his papa. There was no question of that when he was born. The mirror image of Hercules lay staring back at them, with the rich dark colour of his skin, his soulful eyes and full lips. He was clever and fast to learn, watching his mother picking the cotton as she strapped him to her front just days after giving birth. Jessie never let him out of her sight. He spent the days strapped tightly to her until he could walk, and at night tucked up next to her in bed. They were a team, with an unbreakable bond, and no one, not even Hercules, could come between them. With his untutored eyes, he saw everything. Before he could walk, he already knew the truth of his future. Jessie tried to protect him, to keep a form of childhood for him like her mother had for her. Jessie would watch him dance as the old General played the spoons and Hank drummed an old pot to the 'Miss Julie' song. He loved to sing and dance when the sun went down, shaking his hips and tapping his toes. He had the spirit of his father, a warm flame inside, burning bright - until a fever hit the plantation. One by one, the older, weaker slaves died, while the rest drank herbal teas and prayed for salvation. The main house was no exception. The white servant, Miss Teal, was the first to fall ill and die, and the Mistress was bedridden for weeks. They watched as the doctor came and went from the main house. She heard him remark, "They have a robust constitution, an African constitution, the strongest will fight off this disease." Other visitors blamed it on "the wrath of God, cleansing out the sinners: no doctor could heal that, why waste your money?"

The fever passed through every living thing, but it wasn't until they buried the first child that the fear took over. Jessie wept with her friend over the tiny grave as she clung on tight to her little boy, threatening the lord with wrath of her own if he dared take her son. And yet, he did not listen.

She saw the first beads of sweat forming on his brow as she forced the herbal tea down his throat, ignoring his cries. Two more children had died since that day, but they had been young, too small to fight off the sickness. But Sebastian had turned five last winter. He was big for his age, and strong like his father.

All night long Jessie lay by his side, placing cold damp cloths to his head, watching him fight against the fever dreams. For a while it worked, thinking they had broken the fever until the second wave hit.

She laid her head on his chest, her arms wrapped around his body, and sang lullabies from her faraway country as his last breath escaped from his lungs. Hercules fell to his knees, his fist breaking the thin floorboards as Jessie let out a heart-shattering cry. A cry that was heard across the community for days, weeks, even that night, hers blended in again with that of another. Their tears washed the small body clean as the cry gave way to a silent shudder. It broke them. It tore away the bond and left behind a gaping hole nothing could fill. Hercules lent in beside her, wrapping his arms around her shaking body. But she wanted no comfort, only her son back. For him to wake and wrap his tiny arms around her neck and tell her it was all a bad dream. But there was no life left in him. His soul had moved on and left her behind, knowing less of how to live in this godforsaken world than ever.

The day Jessie and Hercules buried their son was the day all light and hope left their unity. She fell into a pit of despair, unable to eat, or even wash herself. Whilst he turned dark, wild, and reckless, talking back to the masters and relishing in the destruction. She had never seen this side of him before, and it scared her. The thought of losing him and her son together was too much to bear.

Months after the burial, she dressed a new set of scars and deep lashes across his back.

"Let us escape... we still have our plan... The conductor-man will see us through to the next station," he growled through gritted teeth as Jessie pressed herbs into an opened wound.

"You talked to him again?"

"I did. You know we can't stay here, nothin' is left for us." He sat up, wincing at the pain.

"Our son is here."

"His body is in the ground. Our son is here!" He slammed his fist to his chest.

"Who will visit his grave? Who will remember him in his home?"

"That will keep us trapped here. Bent over his grave... he would not want that."

"We will never know what he wants again."

"We can start again, in another place, earn money for a proper doctor, not enter the earth before our time, powerless against the white man."

"You are ready to move on? To leave him behind already?"

Hercules lent forward and held her face in his hands. "We will die here if we do not move on, or they will sell us both to different plantations. This is our last chance."

"When?"

"Tomorrow night."

"Tomorrow, so soon?"

"That is when the conductor can take us. If not, we will have to wait another six months: this is our chance."

She saw a glimmer of the light returning to his eyes, something she had not seen for six years. What else did she have left to lose? "Tomorrow?"

"Tomorrow we leave, and head north."

Chapter 14

August 1832 Beacon Hill.

"Sarah?" Bea leaned over the bannister and called down through the house, forgetting the bell system. "Sarah?" On the lower floor, a commotion echoed through the hallway, followed by the sound of footsteps coming halfway up the stairs. "Yes, – Bea?" Sarah replied, smiling at the floating head.

"Would you mind coming up for a second?"

"Coming."

Bea picked up the demanding Grace off the blanket. "Aw, are you hungry, Gracie? I just need two minutes and then I'm all yours." Sarah came into the bedroom and closed the door behind her. "Sarah, I have a favour to ask, and you can say no, but - Beth has gone out for a walk, and I need to nip to the shops. I'm not comfortable going so far by myself with the baby alone; not yet. But I know you don't enjoy going out with me." She read the look forming on Sarah's face immediately. "It's just I – Joshua - they invited us to an event, a gala-thing, and I need to look like one of *them*." Bea had been dropping fragments of information about her past in recent weeks, informing Sarah that she was in fact a working-class girl without a society-driven bone in her body. Sarah liked her all the more for it. "So, I need a dress that would suit a formal gathering, and since this little one," Bea's hands tickled the restless baby in her arms, "my body has changed somewhat, and I could do with a few more day dresses too. Would you mind coming with us and being there if I need you?"

"Today?"

"This morning... Are you free? The gala is on tomorrow; Joshua only told me this morning. I think he forgot, perhaps lost track of time. Or maybe he feared I would say no if he gave me more notice... That doesn't matter now though, as long as you can come?"

Sarah hated going out with the white women of whichever house she worked, over the past thirteen years of living in Boston. She had worked for five women, four out of which had insisted she accompany them when they went shopping, a mark of their status, but for Sarah it was a reminder of the past, another white person owning her space, and her actions. Even though she was free, she was still in the bottom third of society and therefore had to walk two steps behind the Mistress. Walking side by side would signal a friendship, and that would not do, even in liberal Boston. But she saw the desperation in Bea's her face and knew that this wasn't the same as before; it was a need, a necessity, that someone had to go with her, just in case she fell or struggled. She would have chosen Sarah over anyone else in the city, and that meant something different.

"I will come."

Relief flashed across Bea's face. "Thank you, Sarah."

"When would you like to leave?" There was still a hint of reluctance in Sarah's voice she couldn't hide.

"I will feed and change Grace, and then shall we go? Get it over with?" Bea tried giving Sarah a reassuring smile and adding a lightness to her voice.

"Very well."

Sarah maneuvered the grand pushchair from around the back of the house to the front as Bea gripped Grace in one arm and locked the door with the other. She hadn't stepped out in public since Grace was born; months had passed, and she hadn't felt the need. She thought it strange how her demeanour had changed since coming to Boston, and the trial. In Ulverston she longed to get out of the house each morning, to walk beside the old harbour, the woods and the meadows. Maybe it was the fact that Boston had none of those things, not in the same way as Ulverston. She had a park, but there was no genuine beauty in it, nothing wild or wide or powerful. There was a harbour, but it was too vast and busy for a single girl, and there were no woods to forage. Joshua had promised her that when the time was right and work had calmed down, all five of them would take a trip to the countryside, *upstate*, as she heard a native Bostonian say, and take lodgings in an inn, or rent a house. She hoped it would be during autumn; she had heard the leaves turned a stunning red and gold that flooded the banks of the lakes and reached taller into the sky than any of the trees in England.

Bea placed Grace into the pram and pushed it down the hill toward the principal shopping street. Sarah walked two steps behind her. Bea hated this. Sarah was her friend, not just her employee. Society should not be able to tell her how or where her friend should walk. She glanced across the street and saw herself mirrored there, with a pram and a black servant walking behind. She noticed the other black woman looking at Sarah and giving her a nod. That was her world, her community, not her own, and it was so much harder to acknowledge. She struggled to keep a hold on the pram as it gathered momentum down the hill. Her stomach muscles were not used to this sort of strain, and she cried out in pain.

The noise pulled Sarah's gaze from an acquaintance across the road. She instantly stepped forward and grabbed hold of the handle. Her black hands interlocked with Bea's white ones as she pulled back the pram to a standstill.

"Thank you, Sarah," Bea breathed through panicked breaths. "I am so glad you are here; I don't think my body is quite ready for this."

"I should push the pram from here, Bea."

"Only if I can walk beside you?"

"That's not the way here, it ain't right." Sarah gave a look and then gestured to the women across the street.

"To hell with that. - I'm not having you push Grace behind me while I strut forward like some sort of Queen. That is just not happening!" Bea enacted a mocking display of royal gesturing.

Sarah couldn't help but laugh as Bea joined in. "We can take the looks - and if Joshua says something, then I'll put him in *his* place." Bea gave Sarah such a determined smile she had not seen before. There was no point in arguing.

As they walked on to Charles Street, they certainly got the looks, but Bea simply smiled at each stare and nodded her head at the more gentile ladies. None of them were going to tell her where she was going to walk. She realised after twenty minutes that she was actually enjoying the situation, and was proud to smile at their arrogance, but when she looked across at Sarah beside her, she saw otherwise. She saw her head held low and avoid any form of eye contact with her smile replaced with a straight line. At that moment, Bea realised none of this was about her, it was about Sarah, and her personal defiance was causing her friend pain.

"There are three shops I would like to visit; two dress shops and the haberdashery shop. Is there anywhere that you need to go?" Sarah shook her head. "This way first then."

Bea turned left and headed down the street towards a small dress shop, '*Jane's Emporium*' catering for daytime dresses. Bea held the door open whilst Sarah pushed the pram over the threshold. The lady behind the counter gave Bea a welcoming smile until she saw Sarah push the pram in and glanced nervously at the other two customers at the far side of the shop. Bea, unaware of her discomfort, gazed at the various displays of colourful fabrics and tailors' dummies styled to show off the upcoming fashions. Soon it would be autumn, but the thought of wearing a thicker dress with longer sleeves in the current heat was unbearable. She had told Joshua she would get two new day dresses and one formal dress. She decided on a lighter dress that would transition with some for now and an autumn dress for the change of seasons. Since having Grace, her shape had changed, her breasts were larger and fuller, and her hips had become wider. Joshua had told her he loved her changing body, and her new curves just the other night: "You have a woman's body now." She stared at herself in the long ornate mirror, positioned beside the examples of lace and haberdashery, designed to add fare to the simpler designs. She had a sudden recollection of Mrs Johnson's back in Ulverston. The thought of entering her shop to order two dresses had been an infrequent daydream-fantasy. What she would have given back then, to own such fabric... and the path she found herself on because of those desires. And yet, where would she be now if she hadn't accepted that so-called gift? She wouldn't have Grace or Joshua. She would probably still be feeling lost and alone in that cottage, looking for another route to escape. Either way, she was here now. She had faced hardship, but that had brought her own unique family, and nothing would make her ungrateful for that. Bea gazed at Sarah, and saw that same look of wanting on her face as her fingers skimmed across a cornflour blue muslin, dreaming of the dress it might become. Bea glanced back at the shop woman, glaring at Sarah, wondering if she really felt she would need to burn the fabric after her friend had touched it, as her expression seemed to suggest. It was the same look Mrs Johnson had given Bea if she had dared touch her own wares. What she would give to walk into that shop now, with money in her hands and a smile on her face, and order ten dresses in front of everyone who had ever looked down on her. But that would never happen. She could never set foot in Ulverston again, but she could do this. She could buy Sarah the blue fabric, a dress for her Sunday best, and remove that hateful look from the shop-woman's eyes.

Once Bea had chosen her two fabrics and designs, she approached the lady standing guard over the till.

"Good morning." Bea tilted her head, copying the other more gentile ladies.

"Good morning," the lady repeated with a slight nod to her head.

"I would like to order three dresses please."

"Very good ma'am! Can you tell me the fabrics and the designs you would like? And then we will take your measurements."

Bea pointed to a pale pink muslin fabric with tiny red roses scattered across it, the fabric she had dreamt of as a lass. "I would like this fabric made up in a summer gown - this design please." Pointing to the design in the pattern pages, she smiled excitedly over at Sarah.

"Of course ma'am; and the second dress please?"

Bea pointed to a plum-coloured fabric with shades of red flowing through it, in a heavier, thicker sateen, but one that would match perfectly with her hair colour.

"I would like this fabric, in a 'fall' design please," she said carefully, remembering the difference in vernacular. "In *this* design please," pointing to another design in the pattern pages, with long sleeves, a higher neckline and a fuller skirt.

"And your third dress?"

Bea took a deep breath and braced herself for what she was about to do. "I would like to take the cornflour blue fabric." She pointed to where Sarah was still standing with Grace, her fingers skimming the top of the fabric, unwilling to let it go.

"For yourself?" The shop woman remarked in a desperate, directorial squawk.

"No, for Sarah." On hearing her voice, Sarah spun round.

"We... I... we do not sell *those* kinds of clothes here. Maybe she would be better to visit the coloured shops?"

"No, I would like to order that fabric. Sarah, have you thought about the design you would like it in?" An old trigger uncovered a side of Bea that she thought had disappeared. A strength grew in her tone and countenance. "Would that be a problem? Do we need to take our business elsewhere?" She stared straight at the opinionated woman, remembering who she was now, the wife of a gentleman, and in a position too. "It would be a shame if we did, given that... Mrs Goldstein recommended this shop. I wouldn't like to tell her you refused to sell to me." Holding her nerve, Bea stood proudly as Sarah stood next to her, head held low, embarrassed by the sudden fuss.

"Oh! No need for that, I'm sure - we can certainly make an exception, this once. Which design would you like...?" The shop keeper grumbled. Sarah pointed to a simple design with full sleeves, a slimmer skirt and a high neck. "Lovely... I will get those ordered up for you straight away, ma'am. Now if you step this way, we can have you both measured."

Bea felt the tension in Sarah and being measured after what had just transpired would be a step too far. "Thank you, but I will send you over our measurements this afternoon." Bea bowed her head, and in a single move, turned her back on the woman and took hold of the pram. "Good day."

Sarah waited until they were far enough away not to be heard before she paused.

"Why did you do that? Make such a fool of me. What am I to do with a dress like that? Nor can never repay you." Sarah muttered in a low voice, with a hint of disappointment.

Bea looked at Sarah and realised what she had done. "Forgive me, Sarah, I did not think." Her pride had got the better of her and the unspoken rules of this new land were confusing. "I didn't mean for you to look foolish, I meant... it's just... a year ago, in early spring, I received the same look you had from that shameful proprietor, not because the colour of my skin, but the class I was in." Bea stepped closer. "To *that* woman I was nothing but a dirty wretch who should know her place, who could never afford fabric like that, no matter how many pieces of lace I produced for her, or how perfect they were... I am sorry, I saw the way you were looking at the fabric. I knew that feeling so well, and now I can stop that happening to someone else. You have given me so much kindness and strength, it is I who can never repay you." Bea coughed away, the emotions building inside of her as the pedestrians veered around them on the street. "I wanted to do this for you, and, to be honest, I wanted to remove the look on that woman's face for both of us If someone had gifted me a dress like that with no terms attached... well, maybe I wouldn't be standing here, but that's different life, and not having Grace, well –." Bea leaned in and gave a sleeping Grace a light kiss, speaking the last part more for herself than anyone else. "Maybe you can wear the dress to a dance? To church, at Christmas? I am sorry to have done this to you. I promise you I simply wasn't thinking... an old ghost came back to haunt me for a moment."

Sarah stared at Bea, and quickly her confusion and anger drifted away. She knew this unusual, mysterious young woman meant no ill towards her. She was so used to defending herself against pale-skinned women it was difficult to accept one of them might actually be on her side.

"Shall we move on to the next shop?" Sarah suggested, ending the conversation with a forgiving smile.

"Yes."

Sarah cut in front, taking the pram from Bea and guiding their way back up Charles Street. Bea watched the passers-by, how they ignored Sarah but gave her a curt nod of approval. How much she still had to learn and understand about this expanded alternative world, yet she had already concluded, in under twelve months, there were parts she would never like. The further they walked up the road, the busier and louder the traffic became as carriages rushed by and men trotted on horseback to various destinations, not focusing on anything but their next meeting. She could have sworn for a moment she had seen Joshua. Yes, it was him. Her eyes followed him down the street, and a part of her wanted to shout out to him, to show the world that this man was hers. To show him she was trying, at least attempting, to fit in and make things work. Instead, she just watched him, elegant, strong, and handsome as he rode down the street. This world was where he belonged, a gentleman, a man of standing- and how close she had almost been to losing all this for him. But recently he seemed happier, they both had. He was holding, touching, kissing her again, and it felt right.

"Mistress?"

Bea watched Joshua disappear out of sight, unaware of his audience.

"Mistress Mason?" The voice was Sarah's, but the name seemed strange to her.

"Sorry... I saw Joshua riding down the street." Bea blushed as people awkwardly slipped past her statue form.

"Mistress, the next shop is this way." Sarah gestured to a few shops down.

"Yes – yes, lead the way." Bea smiled and shook her head, placing herself back in the present moment.

They stopped outside '*Miss Julie's Dress Shop*' watching the other gentile women inside laughing and admiring one another's gloves.

"If you don't mind, Mistress, may I take Grace with me whilst I fetch a few things in one of my own shops?" A few streets away was the coloured district, where the shops were owned by black people for the black community. Boston was a liberal town, but the people, black, white or otherwise, still knew their place. There were a rare few that could cross that line, born free and gain a position, but unfortunately Sarah wasn't one of them. There was also a part of her wondered if Sarah was worried that she might order her another dress, if she stayed.

"Yes, of course. Shall we meet back here in thirty minutes?"

"That should be fine, Mistress."

Sarah veered off down one of the side streets as Bea hovered in front of the shop a little longer, reminding herself once more that she belonged in such establishments now, and that her old ghosts had no place here.

The high bell rang out a sharp tinkle, making the four women turn round and examine Bea as she stepped over the threshold. This shop was much like the last, except that the fabrics draped seductively in a line, each one peeking out a little below the others and were more luxurious than before. Willing the customer to reach out and fall in love with the soft touch of silk, the hard-crisp feel of chiffon or the incandescent shimmer of the bright, high-quality Satin, Bea didn't know where to look or which fabric to choose. She knew that the elite of Beacon Hill was going to be at this gala. They would handsomely dress the men in their finest suits, whilst women would look like queens in their fashion-forward designs and tailored fabrics. Where would she fit in all this? She couldn't let Joshua down; this was his moment. She wanted to support him, just as he had supported her. And yet, this was his world, it wasn't hers. She would need to impress people, talk to strangers, make conversation, amuse her peers. What did these people talk about, anyway?

Bea must have been standing staring at the peacock-blue fabric with a worried look on her face, because the shop assistant made her excuses to the other three ladies and glided over to Bea.

"Madam, may I be of help?" the woman drawled, empathising each word. Bea turned her head and looked at the perfectly presented woman in front of her. In a topaz chiffon, the women glowed and rustled as she moved. "Madam, are you considering this fabric? Can I ask what occasion it is for?"

"... Possibly, I'm not sure... I am attending Mr Goldstein's harbour-gala tomorrow with my husband and I am looking for something new to wear." A surprised look came into on the shop-woman's eyes, at the news that this young creature, so overwhelmed by the fabrics and the surrounding atmosphere, was going to be attending an honorary gala.

"Very good, Mrs -?"

"Mrs Mason, my husband Mr Joshua Mason is Mr Goldstein's second-hand man at the harbour office."

"Mrs Mason?" A voice came from behind her amongst the three women crowded together.

"Yes." Bea turned her head toward the unfamiliar voice. A tall, elegant woman, perhaps twenty years her senior, dressed in mint green silk gown with bold embroidery outlining the bodice and the hem stepped forward.

"I am Mrs Goldstein. It is a pleasure to finally meet you. My husband sings high praises of Mr Mason, and the outstanding work he is doing for our company." Bea blushed… "Did I hear correctly that you were picking something out for our gala?"

"I am sorry, but it's not enough time, to make a dress for tomorrow, Madam," the assistant butted in. "We usually take a week, at the very minimum."

Ignoring her, Mrs Goldstein continued the conversation with a bright smile. "I hear congratulations is in order. My husband tells me you were blessed with a baby, just a few months back?"

"Yes, a girl - we named her Grace."

"How wonderful, a girl. I have two of my own, and a little boy. How sweet they can be at that age. I remember the first few months, how time can slip past us mothers…" Bea wasn't sure how sincere Mrs Goldstein was being, There was a tone to her voice that Bea had often heard from the more gentile class, which undercut the words. But today, she ignored it and smile, this woman was her better. "So", she continued, "I am sure *Miss Julie's* can make an exception, this once, on my behalf?"

"If we have the fabric ready cut, and the design is nothing too complicated, then we might have it ready for tomorrow night. Madam will have to send someone over at six, before we close, to collect it."

"Thank you very much." Bea nodded to both women.

"I will get you samples of the fabric that I already have in." The assistant turned her back to her customers and strutted off through to a curtained off area.

"I will leave you to it, then, Mrs Mason. There is still a lot to be done before the gala."

"Thank you for your help, Mrs Goldstein."

"I was happy to step in; it was a pleasure to meet you, my

dear, and I look forward to finally meeting your husband too, tomorrow at eight."

Bea gave her a small bow as she gestured for the other women to follow her out into the street.

Bea waited patiently for Miss Julie to return as she scanned the fabrics, making her way to the pattern pages on a dark wooden desk. America, especially Boston, seemed to be ahead of England in the fashion stakes. The skirts here were bigger, fuller, with an unexpected hoop underneath. The more formal the dress, the more daring they became, with their lower necklines, exposing the first curve of the wearer's breasts. The sleeves looked like they had magical puffs of air trapped inside, to carry Bea into the sky, with their balloon-like appearance, all in the cause of showing off more of the slim curve of the waist. Bea skimmed over the designs, each one slightly different from the last. They all seemed to be adorned with some sort of bows, fabric flowers, or a structured cascade of fabric draping out to the side. At least the size of the skirt would hide her now wider hips, she thought. Finally, she settled on a design that caught her eye immediately. It was simple and yet elegant; something that Joshua would be proud of but not so extravagant that Bea would feel like a peacock, strutting around for all the company to see. There were no bows or layers. It was a simple smooth skirt, allowing the fabric to flow naturally. Miss Julie returned with swatches of material in her hand, and a flustered look. She laid them on the desk, side by side, from light to dark like the tones of a rainbow. Bea looked at the creams and pearly-white samples. One shimmered under the light and seemed more sumptuous even than her wedding dress had. Cream was her fail-safe; it was simple and didn't draw too much attention. She glanced over the other colours, and the gold also caught her eye, with flashes of the last and only ball she had attended replaying in her head.

No gold had drawn her into trouble. She wouldn't be wearing gold again. The reds looked nice, but reminded her of Christmas holly berries. Maybe she could come back in November and buy herself a Christmas dress here. She forced her attention back to the task at hand. What colour would shine with the simple design she had selected, allowing her to stand out just enough for Joshua to be pleased? Then she saw it, the colour of trees, of nature, of the woods in summer that she had left so far behind. The emerald green shining cloth called out to her, willing her to touch it.

"A splendid choice; it would suit your hair too. Have you chosen a design?"

Without saying a word, Bea pointed to the simple design she had bookmarked, and saw the relief on the attendant's face.

"It will be ready for tomorrow evening?"

"Yes, it will be ready by then. If you come this way, I will take your measurements."

Bea did as she commanded, clutching tightly to the silk square in her hand.

Bea exited the shop to find Sarah and Grace waiting patiently outside. "Hello little one." She popped her head into the pram and found a curious facing staring back with her arms stretched out, wanting her Mama. Instead, Bea gifted Grace with the piece of fabric, and watched how the mid-day sun shone through it, casting her in a green shade. "All fine?"

"No trouble at all. How did you get on? Is that the colour?"

"What do you think?"

"Beautiful, Bea."

"I thought so too... Sarah. I think I need a cup of tea and a sit down. Is there anywhere we can go that isn't too far from here – but far enough from the judgemental glares?"

"We can just head back if you're tired?"

"No, not yet - I'm enjoying being out, and I think Grace is

too!" Bea glanced down at the wide-eyed baby in her pram, flapping her newfound treasure.

"Well, I know of a place; it is a bit of a step out from here, but I do think you'll like it - and I wanted to drop by there and pick somethin' up anyhow."

"Lead the way."

Sarah gestured to take the pram, but Bea kept a tight grip onto the handle. She had missed not seeing Grace, but if she was honest with herself, it was more for the fact that she needed something to lean on as they strode back up the hill. Her wound was aching now, crying out for rest, but the thought of being cooped up back in the house didn't seem appealing.

Sarah marched back up the hill as Bea followed, struggling to keep pace as they passed the summit, and kept on for another twenty paces. Bea took a moment to catch her breath and stared down at the scene below them, glimpsing sparks of blue sea between the buildings. She came up with a plan for Sunday at that moment: they would all hire a carriage and go up the coast for a day trip to the sea. She felt the water calling out to her, reaching its powerful, familiar arms out, and longing to hold her in its embrace.

Sarah looked back and saw Bea was failing to keep up. "Not long now, it's only a few streets away."

Bea nodded her head, unable to speak for want of a breath. Now she really needed that cup of tea. As they neared their destination, Bea watched the street-fronts change from the grand town houses to less ornate buildings designed for function. Some were even wooden, tucked between the brick walls, as if they were holding it up, with its brown slats cascading down towards the pavement. As they drew further into this new community, she noticed the people were mostly black, Indian, or dressed in styles hailing from other far-off countries. She was in Sarah's territory now and suddenly felt awkward being the only white woman walking down their street. She realised, for the first time, a fraction of what it must be like for Sarah inhabiting her small space in their lives.

Sarah came to a stop in front of a large red-brick building and waited for Bea to catch up.

"We will receive a welcome here."

"And a cup of tea I hope?" Bea blurted out between breaths. Sarah chuckled at the hopeful look on Bea's face.

She noticed a sign waving back and forth in the light breeze: '*The African Meeting House.*' She smoothed down her dress and shuffled the bonnet on her head, then registered the stairs leading up to the door.

"We can leave the pram out here; it will be perfectly safe."

Without uttering a word, Bea parked the pram at the side of the building and slowly lifted the sleeping Grace to her chest.

She heard the bell chime out as Sarah held the door open for her. An apprehensive sensation grew inside in her stomach. What would she find on the other side of the door? She glanced back at Sarah, who was smiling and gesturing for her to venture further in. She trusted Sarah, knowing she would never bring them somewhere she would be mocked or made to feel uncomfortable. As she stepped forward, the light of the room washed over her. It was more like a church than a hall. She heard a voice speaking out from the back of the room, very much like that of a preacher, and saw a man standing on a podium positioned in the centre of the hall. A few of people turned round and examine her with questionable faces until they saw Sarah coming in behind.

"Sarah – welcome. And your guest - please join us." Bea felt herself being gently forced forward and directed towards a nearby pew.

Once they were seated, the speaker continued, and all turned towards him once more.

"Is this a church?" Bea whispered to her guide.

"No, it is a meeting house."

"A meeting house for what?" Sarah gestured her head for Bea to listen, so she did.

"Before we finish this meeting, I would like to read from a

letter, sent to me by a conductor in the south; a reminder of why we are here, and a push for what we need to do next. He paused for a moment, unfolding a sheet of paper.

"I was hoping to write this letter to you, informing you of a new passenger travelling north, but I have not had many ask for my aid over the past few months. There seems to be a self-imposed lock down, spreading across the plantations, instigated by our own children. After one brave rioted against his owner at the head of his fellows, killing the man and his family, managers have used his uprising as an excuse to use brutality for the slightest reason, the punishment never living up to the crime. It has therefore been quieter in this area, until two weeks ago, when a certain man came into my store, holding a list from his master. We started talking. He couldn't read English, but he told me tales of the land they took him from, and the family he had left behind. Once I knew I could trust him, I informed him of the railroad path, and the tracks that could take him northward. We arranged passage for Monday last, but when the time arrived, he was nowhere to be seen. Maybe he hadn't the chance to get away, maybe he had changed his mind. The next day I waited for the usual Tuesday order from his master, but another young man greeted me at my shop door. I politely asked after the other, who had first delivered the list and was informed that the manager had found him out in the woods two miles from the plantation. "The dogs had got to him first. He fought the leader with a branch, killed it with one blow, but the other got a hold of his groin and wouldn't let go, dragging its catch back to their owner." my face showed him sadness, grief, the losing a friend, and in that moment, he seemed to age in front of me, exposing his own sadness and despair to my own, before leaving the crumpled piece of paper on the counter. I realise these facts may dishearten; still I thought it best you discover what we are up against down here, and the em-bedded fear now strangling the hearts of all who live in shackles. I will write again soon to update you further on the situation; pray for us."

The room was still. No one shuffled or made a single sound; not even Grace dared a murmur, as if sensing the grief. Bea stared at Sarah with too many questions for her to answer. The words blurred themselves into her mind, connecting all the dots to form a picture she hadn't known how to see.

"Shall we end the meeting with a prayer for all those in our thoughts: for the imprisoned, and for those who risk it all for freedom."

The congregation bowed their heads as one and poured out their thoughts in silence.

"Lord we ask you..."

"Hear our prayers...".

Everyone moved soberly out of their pews, greeting a fellow friend, and made their way to the back room. Bea held Grace close to her and waited until the nearby folk had joined the others.

"Shall we join them for a cup of tea?"

"Why have you brought me here?"

"To have a rest and a cup of tea."

"But, why here?" Bea gave Sarah a quizzical look whilst smiling awkwardly at the new acquaintances.

"You asked me to take you somewhere that *we* could go to rest; there is no other place *we* can do that but here. My quarter would look at you with suspicion, and in the white area of town they will not permit us sitting down together, unless I'm.... But if you wish for us to leave, we can?"

"No, of course not. It is just... not expected, that's all." Looking around the room, she could imagine her Da here, standing in the corner having a debate with a fellow member. A tiny ember ignited deep down. Maybe this is what she needed. "I was wondering, the letter, what that man said – I had heard stories like that before but – did you, have you – ever *seen* something like that?" Bea kept her gaze on Grace who was drifting off as she lent her head against her mother's heart. She had perhaps stepped too far.

And yet Sarah had brought Bea here.

"Yes." A single word that said so much. "Shall we go through?"

Bea allowed Sarah to show the way as she nested Grace close to her, a protective barrier against the eventual onslaught of questions.

The slim door opened up to a square room filled with twenty extraordinary people: black, white, men and women, chatting in small groups. A rectangular table stood against the far side, set with cups and saucers. Two large teapots sat next to a plate filled with homemade biscuits. Bea hovered in the doorway, not knowing how to behave, unsure on what to say. She still wasn't sure what members did. Last year, she had spent a few evenings outside the pub, eavesdropping in on the reformers' talks, hoping for a chance to be a part of it all. And now that she was here, what would be the impact of choosing such a journey as this? Then Sarah was at her arm again.

"For you," Bea welcomed the perfectly made cup of tea with a single biscuit balancing on the saucer. "I can take her whilst you have your tea?" Without waiting for an answer, Sarah sat the tea down and carefully transitioned Grace from one set of arms to another without a single stir.

Sarah showed her around the assortment of people with as much pride as if she had been her own child. Bea watched each member place their hands out and rest them upon Grace's sleeping head, blessing her into the group. Bea guessed Sarah must have told them about Grace, by the way she introduced the child, and the acknowledgements she received. Bea kept her back against the wall, pretending to be the flower in the wallpaper, content merely to observe and marvel at the group of friends before her. There was not a single drop of judgement, and all stood equal to one another. This is what the world should be like, she thought to herself. Not to see the colours of skin, or the shape of gender, but simply look face to face each at a human being and the actions they might account for. She was grateful to Sarah for sharing this rare moment, and such a precious heaven on earth. Bea reflected on what she had heard earlier and saw Sarah's pain in a whole alternative way. Bea gazed at the other black men and women standing before her and wondered if they were born free, or if they had escaped the cruelty of the south.

"You must be Mrs Beatrice Mason."

An older Bostonian stood in front of her, his hand stretched out in a greeting. He had a full head of white hair that bled into long side-whiskers, clashing at his temples like two waves in a surging sea. His suit looked slightly faded against others in the company.

"I am."

"Allow me to introduce myself." He placed a hand to his chest and bowed his head slightly, showing off a perfect circle of a bald patch. "Mr Robert Taylor. I'm glad to see Sarah finally brought you to meet us. We have heard many a tale of her life with you."

"Indeed?" Bea panicked for a moment, but then felt herself blush, sensing it was a compliment, by his broad smile.

"All good, all good, I promise. She holds you in great esteem."

"She has become a dear friend to me. I honestly don't know where I would be without her."

"I am pleased to hear that." He smiled, and she had passed the test.

"Can I ask? Forgive me, that was you, standing at the front, reading out the letter?" he nodded to confirm it, "but - what is this gathering? This place?"

"Did Sarah not tell you?"

"I was only told it was somewhere we could sit down together and have a cup of tea." She lifted her empty cup and smiled.

"No wonder you think it strange, then. We are an abolitionist group." Realisation dawned in a flash. "We have been helping former slaves for years, to find a home, to gain honest work, to gather support. In the past eight months we have created a newspaper to spread the word of what we are doing here, in the hope of change."

"That letter spoke of a conductor and a railroad."

"I'm afraid that is a story for another time, perhaps, if you come back again?" Across the room, a small group in the corner was gesturing Robert to join them.

"I hope I can."

"Then I look forward to speaking to you on that occasion, Mrs Mason." With a single bow of his head, he disappeared into the crowd.

Bea took a deep breath; she was more intimidated, though less fearful. '*Abolitionist*', even in a free state such as Boston, it wasn't a word that was used lightly.

"There she is." Sarah broke through the circle of people in front of her with a wide-awake Grace struggling in her arms, her tiny bottom lip trembling. "Someone was looking for her Mama."

"Hello my darling." On hearing her voice, Grace's head spun round, and her smile soon returned.

"So, this is one of your many secrets? You're an abolitionist?"

"These people helped to bring me back to life when I arrived here. I am a free woman now, and I wouldn't be standin' here without them."

"They seem such strong, good people. I just never thought..."

"Are you shocked?"

"Maybe a little, but mostly I'm fascinated. This is what the world should be like – all persons together, equal, and in good faith. I would like to come back?" Bea looked at Sarah for approval. This was her group, her family, and the last thing she wanted to do was to interfere where she was not wanted.

"It is why I brought you here, to introduce you to other like-minded citizens. I hoped you would understand what we are tryin' to do". Sarah placed a hand on Bea's shoulder. "There is another formal meeting a week from now." Something stirred in Bea that she had not felt in a while as she followed Sarah to the door and down the steps: a desire for justice that she shared with her Da, and the fight to believe in change.

Chapter 15

T he following day, Beth collected the new emerald dress from Miss Julie's, as Sarah helped Bea prepare for the gala. There were so many questions she still had after her experience of the meeting house, but now was not the time. Instead, Bea was more concerned with convincing a group of social-climbers that she was as much one of them as it was possible to be.

"May I come in?" Beth peered around the door.

"Of course, come and sit next to me, and help calm my nerves." Bea reached out a hand for Beth to take. "I wish we could have secured a place for you to come too. I do not know what I am going to say to these people…"

"You'll have Joshua there; I am sure he will look after you."

"We saw it before at the May Day dance, men go off in one corner to talk about work and politics, whilst the women gossip in another."

She feigned a moustache with one of her curls and pretended to take a puff of a cigar. The three women burst out laughing.

On the other side of the room, Grace stirred from her sleep at the sudden commotion in the room. Instinctively Bea rose from her seat but felt the pressure from Sarah's hands on her head.

"I'll get her. You stay and make ready." Sarah turned her head towards Beth. "Do you mind finishing?"

"It would be my pleasure, like the old days."

Beth waited for Sarah to exit the room with a now-grumpy Grace in her hands. "I am sure you'll be fine - you have had time to accustom yourself to things here now, and you are in a better place... in your head. You have a stunning gown which I'm sure Joshua will approve of. Besides: it is just one night, if you find yourself in a huddle of gossipy wives, well - allow them to talk, and simply nod your head like so..." Beth lifted her nose up high and pulled a familiar face, causing Bea to burst out laughing, followed by Beth.

"I have missed that, laughing. It has been like living in a fog, clouding every thought or action. But recently it seems to have been dissipating, finding I can smile once more. Enjoy the small things; laughing and playing with Grace."

"There, done! I haven't done your hair since the last dance we had in Ulverston, the night you made Joshua fall in love with you." Beth gave Bea a wink in the mirror.

"I think we both knew there was something there. But so much has happened since. I wonder sometimes if I am the same woman as I was then."

"A year ago you were still a girl in many ways. Now you are a woman and have lived through so much more. It would make sense you have changed, how could you not? Now you are stronger; you are a wife, a mother and living in a new world."

Bea shook her hands, as if ridding herself of a wave of emotions. "You are right, I am just being silly."

"Bea, are you ready?" Joshua shouted from downstairs.

"Am I?"

Beth finished pinning the last braid into the sweeping bun and loose curls. "Yes, all done." She declared, sealing the hair with a kiss.

Bea stood up, smoothed down her dress and looked at herself in the free-standing mirror. She failed to recognise the woman staring back at her, in a glowing green dress that shone in the candlelight, setting off her warm skin and auburn hair. It gave a curve to her body and an elegance to her frame. "I look like one of them."

"You look as beautiful as you always do - now go down to your husband." Beth pushed Bea towards the open door.

Bea could see him standing handsomely at the bottom of the stairs, gazing upwards. He seemed not to have changed since the last dance. How elated she had felt seeing him again there, the daring touch of his hand upon hers - and now they were going together to a gala halfway across the world as husband and wife. Standing at the top of the stairs, she saw his expression change to a delighted smile at the sight of her. One hand on the skirt and the other on the banister, she glided down the stairs towards him. In one move, he grabbed hold of her and pressed her against his body.

"You look radiant. I am a lucky man to be presenting you as my wife this evening," he whispered into her ear. Something changed in him. Suddenly, they were how they used to be. His mouth met hers as though it were their first kiss all over again, pulling her tight against him, and they both felt a sense of yearning stirring between them that hadn't been there for a very long while.

Bea skimmed her lips against his. "Do you remember the ball in Ulverston?"

"The night I fell in love with you? How could I forget?" He stole another quick kiss.

"It felt like an unreachable dream - that one day you would be my husband, standing here, holding me. I hope you know how much I love you." He leaned in and kissed her again. She felt his fingers press into her back, urging their bodies into one. His hands travelled over her. One slid downwards while the other went north. Her skin became hot and flushed under the dress as a new yearning surged inside of her. Reluctantly, he paused.

"I love you too, more that you'll ever know – and now I almost don't want to go to the gala."

Bea felt her cheeks become hotter at his implication. She pulled herself away from his grip.

"We had better say goodnight to Grace." She lead the way into the sitting room, and with a disappointed sigh, he followed behind her.

They had positioned themselves on a chair, Grace leaning in

as Sarah hummed one of her tunes, rocking her back and forth.

Bea quietly crept up and crouched down beside them. "Sweet dreams my darling, I will see you soon." Grace, on hearing her mama's voice, turned and smiled at Bea, but her eyes widened in awe at the sight of the magnificent green dress.

"She will be fine. You go and enjoy yourselves. I will keep her in with me tonight."

"If she needs a feed, bring her in." Sarah smiled, seeing Bea's anxiety at leaving her child for the first time.

"Of course."

"Sarah and Beth will take good care of her." Joshua leaned in a little closer, placed a kiss on his hand, and gently laid it upon Grace's head. "Good night, my sweetheart."

Behind her, Bea could hear moaning as she walked towards Beth, holding out Bea's cloak.

"If we need you, I will send word to you." Beth replied, reading Bea's face, and the question written all over it.

"Thank you."

"Now - you go and dance the night away."

Joshua smiled at Beth as he grabbed hold of Bea's hand, drawing her towards the carriage waiting outside.

The house was lavish, a real spectacle of Mr Goldstein's wealth and power within the community, sitting proudly on the northern side of Beacon Hill. Carriages waited their turn to deposit strings of guests in front of the two front pillars, made up of the crème de la crème of the city moneymakers, amongst them all, a former Ropemaker's daughter. But tonight, Bea was not just her Da's daughter; she was the wife of a successful business manager; she reminded herself. She noticed Joshua tilting his head at certain men as they passed by in the hallway. He strolled into the principal room as though he had always belonged there, tall and proud, comfortable in his own birth-class once more.

"Don't look so nervous," he whispered into her ear, "you belong here too."

Bea nodded. Her throat had become dry and her hands were sweaty as she noticed some women staring at the new arrival in their midst.

Joshua felt her body tense against his and guided her towards the refreshment table. "This should help." He handed her a glass of champagne and took one for himself.

The bubbles popped in her mouth and caused a fizzy sensation on her tongue. She couldn't help but giggle. "That's better." He lent forward and gave her a kiss on the cheek.

She smiled. As the champagne disappeared, so did the fear.

"Shall we dance, Mrs Mason?"

"I think we shall, Mr Mason."

Joshua guided her onto the dance floor as the music began. It was a quadrille. Joshua beamed at her, seeing how much of her old self had returned. Then they both remembered: they still didn't know the steps confidently to a quadrille! A laugh slipped out from Bea, and she tried to cover it with a dainty cough. They watched the other couples do their steps first, and with their turn, in the middle, Joshua took her hand and leaned in close so that no one else could hear: "I love you."

A passionate happiness surged through her body, and for the first time since their courting days, she wished they were alone. Instead, she waited for their next turn and whispered the same sentiment. She stared at him with wonder. How did she deserve such a man?

"Are you alright?" Joshua whispered, observing a wave of emotions flashing across Bea's expressions.

"More than, this is wonderful." She smiled up at him as he placed his arm around her waist, pulling her closer.

"Come with me." He took her hand in his and weaved them away through the crowd, issuing small nods to anyone he knew.

"Where are we going?" He replied with only a mischievous

glance. One of the side doors to the now-empty hall stood ajar, and he pulled her through quickly.

"What- I don't think they'll allow us to be in here." Her eyes darting around the room, making sure they were alone.

It had a musky smell, with a fire crackling in the stuffy air, and worn leather books lining the walls. He let go of her hand and closed the door behind them. Then, in a single movement, he pressed her back against the door and kissed her. It was deep and passionate, reawakening the earlier sensation in her body at the foot of the stairs. She wanted to give in to the moment, to allow all the past inhibitions and trauma behind.

"I'm perfectly happy." She stroked the side of his face, staring into his sea-blue eyes.

There was a moment of relief and joy reflected in his expression. "I know."

Still blushing, Joshua retrieved another glass of champagne for them both. Then: "Joshua Mason, so good of you to make it!"

"Mr Goldstein, Sir," Joshua gave the broad-chested, sharp-eyed figure approaching them a courtly bow. "May I introduce my wife, Mrs Beatrice Mason."

"Good evening, my dear." They both bowed together as he inspected the woman standing before him. "I have heard a lot about you," he added in a serious tone.

"Good evening Sir, you have a magnificent home." Bea gestured, feeling an awkward tension between them.

"Yes, yes, thank you, most kind. Mason, may I pull you away from your wife for a moment, there is a gentleman I wish to introduce you to." Joshua gave Bea a quick look. He didn't want to leave her alone. "Mrs Mason, I am sure you will be more comfortable with the other wives, over by the fire-place." He lifted his hand and within seconds a grand lady was standing beside the small group. "May I introduce my wife, Mrs Goldstein - this is Mr Joshua Mason and Mrs Beatrice Mason."

"Mrs Mason and I have already met at *Miss Julie's,* my love – the dressmaker's."

"Very pleased to meet you again, Mrs Goldstein, and thank you again for your help." Joshua gave Bea a quizzical glance before turning himself to Mrs Goldstein.

"Good evening, Mrs Goldstein, what a splendid gala you have created."

"Thank you, Mr Mason - I have heard much about you. It is a pleasure to place the face to the name. So glad you both could attend." Bea and Joshua bowed their heads in acknowledgement. She graciously inclined her own, ever so slightly. "Now, Mrs Mason, would you be so kind to join me, we are discussing a certain matter dear to our hearts and would be grateful to hear your opinion."

They herded Joshua in one direction whilst they beckoned Bea in another. He gave her one last look of thanks and reassurance before they became lost in the crowd.

"Mrs Mason - may I call you Beatrice?"

"Yes, of course."

"How lovely; I am, Mary. I truly *have* heard great things about your husband, you know; my dear Mr Goldstein tells me he has become essential in the running of the company."

"Oh I – that is so good to know, thank you, I am very proud of him."

"Glad to hear it – ah! Here we are. May I introduce Mrs Louise Sears, Mrs Mary-Ann Appleton, Mrs Elizabeth Coffin, Mrs Hannah Lowell, Mrs Jane Amos and Mrs Sarah Perkin. Ladies, this is Mrs Beatrice Mason, the wife of my husband's new manager, Mr Joshua Mason."

"I am so pleased to meet you all." Bea didn't know what else to say.

The seven women huddled around her, inspecting her accent and her clothes, determining whether she was worthy to join their own elite group. All the women were older than Bea by some few years, some were old enough to be her gran. Bea smiled at an image of her beloved gran, working the land around the cottage, catching animals but would have snorted at wearing such fineries. The surrounding women dressed in a way that best showed off their influence and wealth, with fine jewels draped around their necks, and expensive but demure silk gowns. But it was also the way they held themselves which exhibited their power, an intimidating stance which cast each lady in a worthy, unquestionable light. If this had all been back in Ulverston, they wouldn't have allowed her to serve them coffee, never mind permit her to stand toe to toe in their presence. But she was no longer in Ulverston, and here in Beacon Hill she could rewrite her own history as Mrs Mason, wife to an up-and-coming gentleman, firmly established in their society. She sighed inwardly, but reminded herself of everything Joshua had sacrificed for her, and told herself sharply to stop dwelling on her past.

"What do you think, Mrs Mason?" said Mrs Elizabeth Coffin.

Bea hesitated; lost in her thoughts, she had not been listening.

"I- Pardon? I beg your forgiveness, but I-"

"You seem a little overwhelmed dear, are you quite, all right?" asked Mary Goldstein.

"Yes, I am fine, thank you – I apologise. I felt a little dizzy for a moment. The champagne... I've had nothing so... since..."

"I quite see my dear -this the first time you have been back in society since you had your child, is it not?"

"Yes, yes, it is."

"Is it your first?" asked Hannah Lowell.

"Isn't it just grand to leave them behind with the help, to venture out back out into the world again?" giggled Mary-Ann Appleton.

"I cannot remember mine when they were small at all, I must confess; it has been a long while – and now they have had children of their own!" laughed Sarah Perkins, distracted by her brooch.

"How old is yours?" asked Mrs Amos.

"Four months."

"Lord, they take so much of your time, when they are small." Jane Amos smiled fondly; she seemed the closest in age to Bea.

"Heavens, an hour a day was enough for me. They do not notice when they are that small, a nursemaid and a nanny are all that they need. We have far more important things to be doing than suckling, and singing nursery rhymes," remarked the haughty Elizabeth Coffin. This all took Bea by surprise, and she only held her tongue in response, reminding herself that these women were not like her. They hailed from a different breed.

"Either way, it must be nice to have some time in a pretty dress, with your young husband?" Jane read Bea's expression.

"Yes, indeed - it has been nice to have some time with my husband, and to choose a new dress for the first time in... er..."

"And how lovely it is." Mary Goldstein smiled, but there was an empty tone to her voice. She was not in earnest. "But girls -did you hear the rumours surrounding Mrs Garret and her music tutor?"

Bea took a step back whilst the other ladies moved forward to hear the latest gossip.

"Yes, isn't it a shame." Elizabeth replied.

"What happened?"

"Well, I heard..."

Bea disengaged from the conversation and turned away to observe the room. There were small groups of people like her own set gathering around the edges, whilst the centre was buzzing with excitement as the dancers whirled in and out of the throng. On the far side of the room were the high-standing husbands of the ladies standing next to her. These were the men on whose wealth Beacon Hill had been founded; they dictated its society and wielded its power. She watched Joshua, at ease, talking to them, a glass of champagne in one hand, and a lit cigarette in the other. She wondered how much it would take for a woman to be standing beside the men, their equal in every sense, as they had at the abolitionists' meeting house? She didn't think such a phenomenon would happen in her time, but possibly in Grace's. Bea was determined to teach her to be powerful in her own ways: reading and writing, like her Da had for her; to know her own mind, to have the acquaintance of a wide variety of people, from all classes and backgrounds, and to be afraid of nothing under the sun. She watched the black servants standing in corners or filtering through the crowd, serving drinks with keen discomfort. There was so much that still needed to be changed in Boston, in society. She was looking forward to returning to the meeting house in a weeks' time, reigniting her determination, and trying to bring about a change in her own way.

Bea turned her attention to the ladies standing next to her once more, still engrossed in society gossip.

"Please excuse me for a moment, I need some air."

They all nodded, as if they had forgotten she was still there.

On top of the hill, the air was clean and crisp compared to the lower streets, which were filled with soot from the mills, sickness from the cramped alleyways, and dust from the streets. The gardens here were grand and lavish, one advantage of belonging to the first Beacon houses, built when there was still plenty of land to be had. Bea strolled around the side of the house, taking in the speckle and shimmer of the distant sea, as the moonbeams bounced off the distant waves. She closed her eyes, and instantly found herself back at the old harbour, waiting for Joshua to join her.

"Excuse me, Madam?"

"Hello?" A figure stepped into the low light issuing from the oil lamps. The man wore a finely tailored suit matching those of the other gentleman, but his skin blended in with the night sky.

"I have intruded on your solitude. Forgive me. Allow me to introduce myself, Mr Abe Winston." He held out his hand for Bea to shake.

"Oh – a pleasure to meet you, Mr Winston - Mrs Mason," taking his hand.

"Forgive me, do I know you? Your face seems familiar."

"Possibly... I... I don't really step out into society, I have an infant at home, not yet a year old. I rely on my companion Sarah to run most of my errands."

"Sarah Bateman?"

"Yes... I?"

"You were at the meeting yesterday afternoon... What were your thoughts?"

"Yes, – we both were. It was astonishing, shocking... but somehow... inspiring. It gave me hope. Sarah is taking me back next week."

"I'm glad to hear it, Mrs Mason. Sarah told me once that you have shown great kindness to her."

"I owe so much to her. She has become a great friend, and a part of our family. I don't think of my actions as a kindness."

"It is lucky she has found such a place in your hearts. I meet not many with open arms in Boston."

"How long have you known Sarah?"

"I helped arrange her arrival, and over time we have become close friends."

"Then, can I ask - how do you know Mr Goldstein?"

"I am a merchant in some ways." He paused before continuing. "I have done business with most of the men here." It intrigued her. She could see he was hiding something.

"There you are, Bea!" The familiar voice from behind them caused her to jump and glance backwards.

She reached a hand out for him to take, their fingers interlocking. "I needed some air, and ran into Mr Winston - Sir, this is my husband Mr Joshua Mason."

"A pleasure to meet you, Mr Mason." Mr Winston stepped further into the light and held his hand out to Joshua, which he accepted.

"And you too – I hope my wife hasn't been distracting you from your business?"

"No, no, not at all - but I should return now to my companions. A delight, Mrs Mason."

"Likewise." Mr Winston tilted his head to Joshua as he walked past and made his way through the side door.

Bea continued to look out at the view, and Joshua placed his arm around her waist, standing behind her.

"Look at this view – it was making me think of our spot on the harbour." She turned around and saw a loving look on his face. She couldn't resist leaning in for a kiss, which he welcomed.

"Will you do me the honour of another dance, Mrs Mason?"

"Of course, Mr Mason."

Before letting go, Joshua took a moment to glance around him, then pulled Bea in even closer. Their second kiss was passionate, and as his tongue flirted with hers, she could feel his desire stirring.

"I have missed you." His lips hovered above hers.

"I know. I'm back now." He kissed her again.

The couple lasted another hour at the gala before Joshua made their excuses to leave. They crept through the front door hand in hand and made their way to the bedroom. Bea scanned the room for a sight of Grace, but she was nowhere to be seen, guessing she must be with either Sarah or Beth. For the first time in a while, they were alone. Joshua grabbed hold of Bea and pulled her against him, kissing her with speed and hunger. Running her hands through his hair, she slipped them down his neck and pushed his jacket off his shoulders and on to the floor. His hands mirrored her actions as they made their way down the front of her dress, undoing each fastening. The dress gave way, revealing her rounded breasts and figure-hugging corset. His lips moved from her mouth and down her neck, causing her back to arch. He spun her round and unlaced the corset. Soon they were standing in front of each other completely naked, seeing one another properly for the first time. Bea had thought she would feel frightened in this moment, and exposed – instead, there was a desire and love for the man holding his body next to hers. The warmth of his skin and the feather-light touch of his hands as they stroked over her curves generated an unfamiliar ache that surged through her, of wanting him; needing him. This was how their wedding night should have been, she thought briefly. She let out a gasp, and then a moan as his fingers stroked over her curves. Together as one, they made their way to the bed. His kisses skipping down her body, she could see his desire clearly as he crawled deliciously over her on the bed, pressing against her.

"Are you sure?" He paused for a moment, his breathing harsh, his eyes dark. Bea nodded. "If you need me to stop, just say." She wanted it, and they both needed it; the making of a true husband and wife. They became one, unable to tell where Joshua stopped and Bea began. A spike of hard pleasure erupted inside her, and the warm aftershocks rippled through every inch of her body.

Chapter 16

September Beacon Hill 1832

Since the gala, Joshua had inwardly celebrated his reconnection with Bea. He had waited for over a year to lie with her intimately, and although they took it slowly at first, getting used to each other's bodies, gauging Bea's responses carefully, he felt an excited fulfilment in her company that brightened his days as much as his nights. Life was good, and he was happy. His wife was coming back to him, Grace was growing and felt like his own child, and the house had developed its own daily rhythm that suited every occupant.

Joshua rolled out of bed and gazed at his sleeping wife, feeling his body stirring again as images of last night flashed through his head. Grace had slept with Beth again, allowing them to have more time alone, leaving Bea to sneak out and giving Grace a feed in the night. He leaned in and gave Bea a light kiss on her forehead.

"Morning my love." Bea opened her eyes and smiled. "I must get ready for work." Joshua was about to back away to find his shirt when Bea grabbed his hand.

"Do you have to; it's still early... Come back to bed?" She pulled him closer and gave him a playful kiss. His body coursed with excitement, giving him no other choice but to stay a little longer.

J oshua glided up to the stables with a grin on his face, smiling at each person who passed him. Six months ago, he wouldn't have believed that he could be this content. Beacon Hill was providing the fresh start he had dreamt of, and Bea was his once more.

"Morning George." Joshua tapped the desk of his clerk jauntily and made his way into his office.

"Morning sir, you seem rather happy today!"

"I am George, I am - can you bring through today's list?"

"Yes, sir." George quickly shuffled back to his desk and placed the desired paperwork directly into Joshua's outstretched hand.

"Thank you." Joshua glanced down at the day's appointments. "George, wait a moment. What is this? I have an appointment with Mr Lowell?"

"Yes, sir. I received a letter from Mr Lowell yesterday requesting a meeting and you had an opening in your diary today, so I sent word back."

"Without speaking to me first?"

"Forgive me, sir. I know he is an important figure. My father has told me there are certain men you cannot leave waiting."

"Your father is probably right, George, but that doesn't furnish me with any time to assemble that last quarter's figures – or enlighten me as to what the meeting is about?"

".... No, sir...",

"Fine, fine. I am sure I can answer his most likely questions. Can you fetch me some coffee, please?"

"Yes, sir." George almost ran out of the office, eager to soothe his agitated superior.

Mr Goldstein had introduced Joshua to Mr Lowell at the gala. He was an independent shareholder and business-owner in the Northlink Railroad Company. But what did that have to do with him? He knew little about the railroad, only that it was used to transport goods from mine and quarries to canals, and the potential it would likely prove to show in the coming years, in terms of trade expansion.

George came back in, carefully carrying a cup of coffee. "Anything else I can help with, sir?"

"No, that's all George - thank you."

As hours passed by, the early morning events evaporated from Joshua's mind, so much so that when a sharp knock on the office door came at lunchtime, the sound made him jump, and a small knot of tension tightened in his stomach for a moment, before he remembered his surprise engagement, and stood up hastily. He pulled his golden pocket watch out and stared at the time; he was five minutes early. "Yes?"

"Sir, Mr Lowell has arrived." George popped his head around the door, bearing an encouraging smile.

"Very good, send him up, please."

Joshua heard George shuffle off back down the corridor, followed swiftly by the firm tread of a second set of footsteps approaching his office. Joshua strode around the desk to greet his guest, one hand extended, the other clasping the documents in which he had been absorbed in moments before.

"Mr Mason, - Mr Lowell." George gestured back and forth between the men.

"Good afternoon Mr Lowell; thank you George." Joshua gave him a wink, showing they should not be disturbed, and the clerk closed the door behind him with a nod.

"Thank you for making the time, Mr Mason."

Joshua made his way back behind the desk and took a seat, gesturing Mr Lowell to do the same. "Of course, Sir - what can I help you with today?"

His finely tailored suit emphasised his narrow frame and sharp facial features amongst his sleek white hair. His overall appearance suggested wealth and around Beacon Hill, that meant power. He peered over his spectacles, gazing around the sparse room. He held a blank expression at the simple wooden chair in front of the desk. Upon sitting down, he hiked up his trousers a little; something Joshua's father used to do. Joshua smiled slightly, then the smile fell into a slight frown. "Well indeed, it is more of a question of how I can help you."

"I'm sorry, I don't follow."

Mr Lowell leaned back, then crossed his right leg over his left. "Mr Goldstein has been telling me for a while about your hard work and talent for management. After meeting you at the gala, I thought you might be the right man for a job."

"Forgive me, Mr Lowell, but I already have a job with Mr Goldstein..." Joshua felt uncomfortable at openly discussing other prospects at the expense of his current employer, no matter how intrigued he was by the offer.

Mr Lowell gave Joshua a half smile. "Your loyalty does you credit, Mr Mason, but I do not think you fully understand me. I have already put my ideas across to Mr Goldstein and he agrees. We would have you join with our responsibilities."

".... I see... and what would you be asking of me?"

"We have, as you know, developed a railway system to transport goods to and from the canal, but I believe there is much more we can achieve." His hands skimmed through the air as if telling the story. "I see the railroad spreading across Massachusetts, linking towns, cities, and states, instead of mere water ways. We want to create a new division called the East-coast Railroad Company." Once finished, he folded his hands onto his lap once more.

"It would change the very bones of the way our people travel – and revolutionise the concept of distance! Goods could travel right across the country from north to south."

"Precisely. The goods on Mr Goldstein's ships would not stop in Boston. They would travel across the states as far as Washington DC, and South Carolina. The stock would arrive there far more easily than it does via the coast by ship." Joshua rose from his seat and paced up and down behind the desk, only half-aware of his actions.

"That would be years away... but it would change how we conducted business... it would change everything... As for the cost... well... prohibitive at first, it would require extensive investment, but-" Mr Lowell cut in.

"I knew you would be the right man for the job! And you are right; we are years away from achieving that goal, but we have already started work in Massachusetts. We are determined to make this American dream a reality – and a prosperous one at that."

"Forgive me, sir, but... you have communicated no details of what this proposed job would entail." Joshua paused.

"Come round to the offices next week, and we can talk prospects; both of work and salary."

"I will, sir, and - I thank you. I am more than eager to hear you expand on these innovative particulars." Joshua grinned like an excited schoolboy.

"Capital, capital. Well, Mason, I'll be off."

"Thank you again, Mr Lowell." They shook hands once more, and almost without prompting, the office door opened. "Good day, sir."

Mr Lowell nodded his head with approval before he exited the room. "Good day, Mr Mason."

Joshua lowered himself back into his chair once George had shut the door behind the unexpected new sponsor. He was surprised and giddy at the concept of a new adventure. Certainly, he had heard wondrous things about the railroad, and had tried to talk to his father into investing in it years ago, but his idea was quickly dismissed, and just as quickly discouraged. And now, the manager of an established Boston railroad company wanted him to take part in the very beginnings of a grand new venture. But... to do what? He decided not to tell Bea of his good fortune until they settled more details and outlined the final demands on his time and person. But the idea of earning more money, to rent or possibly buy a bigger property, and gain a part of the life he had lost after their departure from England was tantalising. He was sure Bea too would appreciate the chances it would give Grace and their future children. He spent the rest of his afternoon dreaming of the security, excitement, and opportunities Mr Lowell's nascent railroad might afford them.

Chapter 17

May 1819, North Carolina.

‣

T hat night they took what they could, packed a few pieces of clothes and stored food. They told no one, knowing better what might happen to any informed persons when the managers came looking. Hercules had made a piece of cloth into a bag, and taking one last look through the door of their hut, he slung it over his shoulder and grabbed hold of Jessie's hand. The stepping was hard at first as they made their way through the nearby woods, with only the crescent moon lighting the way. Yet years of skimming his fingers across the forbidden map gave Hercules a sense of direction, stopping them both once in a while to stare at the stars, and then moving on. Even when her aching feet turned into a mass of blisters, rubbing raw on her oversized shoes, Jessie kept on moving.

But as the sun rose, they knew, despite everything, they were running out of time. With a full day's travel ahead before they reached the first so-called station, they needed to keep out of sight. The heat was already beating down. Sweat glistened across her forehead and trickled down her back. Mud stuck to her skin as they shuffled through the undergrowth beside the main road, pausing their steps, holding their breath when there was any sound from above. It didn't matter whether it was a catcher or a traveller, either would have handed them in. She saw Hercules close his eyes for a moment, and then he raised his head.

"This way." He took hold of Jessie's hand and darted across the road to a clearing on the other side. "We must go down to the river, to cross."

"To swim?"

"It hasn't rained in days; the river will be low enough to wade through."

There was no other choice. Time was running out.

At first, the sounds were faint, but as they came closer, a deep low growl precluded the high-pitched yelps and they knew the dogs had caught their scent. Hercules dropped the cloth bag, and they ran as fast as their broken bodies would allow.

Through the trees, the river appeared in a blinding, frothing roar. It was faster and fuller than expected, but now there was no other option: risk drowning in the river or caught by the dogs.

Hercules held Jessie's hand as he lowered her into the raging current. The icy water shocked her voice out of her as she gasped involuntarily. The power of the water was strong against her tired legs, but she pushed forward, full of fury. She expected to hear another splash behind her as Hercules' body hit the surface. Instead, she heard excited growls, followed by thrashing water.

"*He got one – good boy, Lucifer!*"

Jessie turned round and saw Hercules up to his waist in the water, with a dog hanging on his arm, refusing to let go. Four men on horseback, the omen for the end, called out in celebration, watching the show. Another dog jumped up and caught Hercules's other arm as he tried to punch the first dog, causing him to lose his balance and fall sideways onto the riverbank.

"GO!"

But she could not move. The horror of watching her only remaining loved one pinned to the ground, fighting for his life, caused her to freeze. Does she stay and fight or run and leave him behind?

"She's in the river…" one man called out.

"Jessie… Run…" Hercules bellowed.

Jessie turned back downstream, shutting her mind away, and forcing the dark pain searing through her heart down into her legs. Drowning alone would be better than the dogs. Without a last kiss, a farewell, or the chance to mourn, Jessie forced her feet to move. She scrambled up the muddy bank on the far side and tried to ignore her husband's screams. She ran.

Across the fields and forward, not knowing the way without him. Least of all, where the station was, or the identity of the conductor. To trust a white man seemed impossible. What would this benevolent creature look like?

She heard heavy footsteps running behind her all too soon, mixed in with heavy breathing. She needed to hide, wait him out until he lost her tracks, and then at night use the north star as her guide. Before she knew it, though, the footsteps were directly behind her, and with one swift move she was on the ground. And the man who had visited her in the night was now hitting her across the face in rage. Jamison's lip curled up at the side where the red scar touched his cheekbone as he sneered in delight. Again and again her face was slammed into the hard, dry earth, and she tasted the hot metallic liquid at the back of her mouth before the sky turned black.

H er face swollen, bloody, and purple. She stood there naked for all to see. Standing in a line of people, all ages and sizes, were exhibited before the crowd to be bought and sold like cattle. Numb, lost, and broken, they stared ahead with wide eyes. In her heart, Jessie knew he was dead, and now she was, too.

S he had been at her new plantation, Drayton Hall, Georgia, for a year. But it was like all the other plantations and masters in this godforsaken land. The hut was her prison once again, alone and void of thought or feeling. And yet, when the knock came, her stomach lurched.

"Jessie."

"Gabby?" She opened the door to find a woman not two years younger than herself hovering in the doorway. Her filthy clothes hung off her skinny body, with a fabric belt tied around the middle to keep her skirt up. The only item of clothing she kept clean was the head wrap that was her mama's, filled with reds, oranges, and yellows. The colours of a Malinke sunset, her mama told her as she whispered bedtime stories of their homeland when she was little.

"May I come in?"

"He's on his way - he can't find you here." Jessie peered behind her into the clearing for a sight of him.

"I'll be quick." Gabby shut the door behind herself and stood in the dark hut. "Where's your candles?"

"Better without."

Gabby gave her a knowing nod. "Jessie... have you heard of a... a railroad?"

"Railroad?" She rolled her eyes at whatever this new nonsense was.

Gabby lowered her head and voice, just in case the hut had ears. "A secret railroad."

"Gabby - please... I don't have time for this..." Jessie moved past her and was about to open the door.

"A man asked... he asked if I might want to travel along it. To find a new life." Gabby didn't have what people called smarts. She was kind enough, but simple.

"Well, that ain't making sense. Find me after and don't you go talking to any sort o' a man." Jessie tried to push her back towards the door but she was wasn't moving.

"Wait..." Gabby nudged Jessies hand away and gave her one of her serious looks. "He called himself a conductor... what's one of those?"

Hercules's words flashed back into her head, and all their past terrors with it.

"It's a lost cause – forget about this man, and them words he said to you."

"But... Jessie... life here is hard and what if there is a way out?"

"It's not living, it's surviving, and it's better than what happens if they catch you thinkin' thoughts like that. Now go." Jessie opened the door for her and saw a figure approaching in the dusk. "He's coming, go – now!" Jessie shoved Gabby out the door, causing her to stumble backwards. "I'll find you, after."

The walls inside her mind fractured. Tiny segments spilled out, filling her heart and her belly with all she had lost. She couldn't let Gabby go through that; they would catch her for certain.

"Survival ain't enough Jessie; we deserve to live. To be without fear, without pain, to be seen, walking down the road as a man, instead of cattle at market. To fall in love with a woman without knowin' that another has the right to come knockin' once a month. To earn a wage, to make a home, not squat like an animal in its hut. If that life, why live at all? If we are to live, we need freedom - we must live free, or die trying."

Hercules's words rang out as clear as if he was standing next to her once more, holding her hand, pleading with her not to let go. But she had let go, and she had stopped living. She had become trapped in a bitter, angry shell of survival, and she knew how disappointed he would be in her for it. What was the point of running now? What was there to live for, if not for her man and their child?

Sunlight streamed into the hut at the arrival of her new monthly visitor. As he walked past her, she paused for a few seconds, allowing the heat of the sun to sink into her dark, honey skin, and relight a little of the fire inside herself.

"I don't have long today. Bend over."

As she lifted her skirts and closed off her mind, she saw herself running free from him, and taking the hands of her beloved husband and child spirits, all three of them walking through golden fields together into the promised land.

Chapter 18

October 1832 Beacon Hill.

Life in Beacon Hill felt like home now. Bea was falling in love with Joshua more each day, spending her nights wrapped in his arms with Grace asleep in her cot. They were the family she had dreamt of. During the day he was busier at work, rushing out the house in the early morning and not arriving back until late, but he had a spring in his step she had never seen before. In the past month, Bea herself had attended a further two abolitionist meetings, listening to the stories of free slaves and the fight in front of them. It felt like she had finally discovered the part of her that was missing. For once, she was whole. There had been a fragment of this sensation sitting outside the Bay Horse last year, waiting for her father. She understood why he took the risk he did for the Reformers; it was the same fire, a spirit which flowed through from her Da, and she felt a connection to him once more. And yet, she hadn't told Joshua about the African Meeting house. Something inside her was preventing the confidence; a secret desire for this venture to remain between her and Sarah for now, for fear he might not understand.

"I'm heading out." Beth poked her head around the sitting-room door.

"Attending the girls' school?" Bea called out as the head disappeared.

"Yes - I shouldn't be long. I am meeting Rose there." She came back through into the sitting room with her new autumn cloak and bonnet Bea had bought her, almost matching the colour of the fallen Boston leaves. "They need help for a few hours this afternoon. I can't read and write like you can, but I can help teach sewing and prepare some for service. It can be a good life, if you have the mind for it."

"They are lucky to have found you." Bea lifted her gaze from the fine silk threads and bobbins in her hands.

"I feel useful, and I enjoy teaching the girls, they remind me of when we were young." Beth wrapped the woollen cloak over her shoulders and tied the ribbon.

"That seems like a lifetime ago." Bea let out a small chuckle.

"Shall I keep a plate for you?" asked Sarah, seated next to Grace on the rug.

"Thank you, Sarah, but I should be back well before supper. I won't be long, will I, my sweetheart?" Beth scooped Grace into her arms and swung her around, lighting up her face as they both descended into a fit of giggles. "We have so much now, and those girls have nothing, only the charity to supply teachers and funds. They deserve a chance in life, to know that women aren't as powerless as we're told."

"Here, here!" Sarah and Bea called out together, lifting their arms up and smiling mischievously.

"You are right - and I'm proud of you," remarked Bea sincerely.

Beth blushed at the compliment and handed Grace back to Sarah. "I had better be off."

Once she had closed the front door behind her, Bea turned to Sarah and removed the lace stool from between her legs. "We better be off too; the meeting starts in thirty minutes. I'll finish getting Grace ready, if you bring the pram round?"

"I will see you out front."

Bea could hear Sarah descend the kitchen stairs. She patted Grace's towel nappy -no need to change - and grabbed their woollen coats and hats and the knitted blanket.

Outside, the seasons were changing. The trees were awash in colour, the like of which she had never seen before, and though the air was getting cold, in the sun's rays there still lingered a hint of warmth. Back in Ulverston, the seasons didn't change like this, not with such clarity and brilliance. By now the English rain would set in before they would even see a chance of snow. Memories of stepping out into that familiar light drizzle that soaked into everything, and hung like a darkness over the day, and seeped into your bones. Last year she hadn't noticed the changing of the seasons. She had spent the days watching her body transform and the confirmation of what that meant, and all *that man* had done to her. The difference a year can make, she thought with a sigh. Bea kicked the dry red leaves like a gleeful child as Sarah pushed the pram up the hill.

∞∞∞∞

Outside, they could hear the minutes being called out as Bea grabbed hold of Grace and her favourite teething toy. They nodded their head to Mr Winston, who was chairing, as they snook into one of the back pews. Bea saw how Mr Winston smiled at Sarah, but also noted that she held her eyes on the floor.

"... and sales of 'The Liberator' has increased in the city, and further afield. Our voice is being heard and welcomed," Mr Winston continued.

Bea reached out for Sarah's hand and gave it a light squeeze. "Thank you – for letting me come again."

"You belong here - as do I." Sarah gave Bea's hand a light pat before letting her go to clap at the close of Mr Winston's address.

"now - stand with me, all, as we sing *Go Down Moses*."

The song started low and slow, "*When Israel was in Egypt's land...,*" but it took Bea by surprise when the congregation erupted in sound as they sang out:

"Let my people go!"

"*Oppressed so hard they could not stand,*
Let my people go.
Go down, Moses,

Way down in Egypt's land,
Tell old pharaoh to let my people go."

Bea felt the pain in the people's voices at the words. She gazed round towards Sarah; her eyes were closed, but her cheeks were wet. *"Let my people go."* She pleaded.

"Oh, let us all from bondage flee.
Let my people go.
And let us all in Christ be free,
Let my people go!"

Bea allowed the pain, the fear and the sorrow all around her to sink in. Grace was no longer shifting in her arms in her attempts to dance, but lent her head against Bea's chest, her mouth sucking intently on her teething toy. Bea wanted to place her arm around Sarah's shoulders and tell her how sorry she was. In this alternative world, slavery should not exist. She knew, however, that Sarah would not accept such a gesture; she was intensely private, and though she could give comfort, but found it harder to receive it.

Once the song finished, everyone took their seats. Grace reached out to Sarah and without a second thought, Sarah took hold of Grace and held her close to her chest. Bea watched Grace comfort her friend, her chubby white fingers resting against Sarah's dark honey tone skin; black, white, it did not matter. Only love mattered.

Then everyone settled themselves for the day's talk. Each meeting that passed, Bea learnt of fresh horrors surrounding the slave trade, sometimes from letters, sometimes from a travelling speaker or a brave member of their group. She didn't know yet how she could help fight against this injustice. First, she must learn who the enemy was.

"Today, we are joined by Mr Farlow, a Quaker, a businessowner, and orator, who discusses the particular horrors of the slave route, the Guinea trade, and how change is slowly but surely coming to our nation." Mr Winston ended his introduction with a short round of applause, and gestured for an older man to join him at the podium. He was tall, thin, and remarkably pale-skinned, with a long white beard, and attired in a simple dark grey suit and a white tie. What stood out to Bea was his black broad-rimmed hat, unlike any she had seen before.

"Thank you, Mr Winston. Good afternoon, ladies and gentlemen, it is a pleasure to be here with you again. I would like to speak a little of the lesser known details of the Guinea trade routes, and elaborate on the progress to which my friend just alluded – to encourage you, to take faith because history is happening, right now, in our own time."

Bea frowned a little, thinking she had heard of the '*Guinea trade*' before; but where? First came his face, and then his hated name.

"..., and in fact, the British tried to claim the line as their own, from the Portuguese, thirty years ago. A few vessels dominated the stretch, led by notorious Captain Flint, Southerton, Hanley and Anderson."

There it was, his name, that name. She recalled the morning at the harbour, almost two years since, when Joshua had told her a little of Hanley's past, and of his violent upbringing on his father's ship. She felt all the warmth drain out of her as she listened to Mr Farlow's story. She looked over at the innocent Grace, who was sound asleep in Sarah's arms. These stories were part of her heritage, a heritage that she would never know. She stared at the tiny details of Grace's facial features, wondering if there was any part of Hanley in them at all. The roundness of her eyes, the arch of her chubby cheek bones, the curve of her lips. Thankfully, all she saw was herself, sound asleep. There was nothing of him, there couldn't be any of him in her. The only father she would know was the man who loved her and cared for her every single day.

"Are you feeling alright?" Sarah muttered.

All Bea could do was nod and gesture towards the man without speaking, laying her hand reassuringly on Sarah's arm.

"Portuguese government captured Upper Guinea hundreds of years ago and traded men, women and children to northern Brazil. The seaman I mention became infamous when the British captured the island of Bolama, off the East coast of Guinea. The castle there, was like so many others, fortified against other tribes that came intent on stealing their stock. The black people were contained in the dungeons, dark holes where there entered no light, with barely any food to eat, and visited only by those conquistadors selecting a woman to violate – all of which is still happening right this second, if only elsewhere." He paused for a moment, and all Bea could think about was her own cell, the dungeon she had inhabited while awaiting trial at Lancaster, and the horror she felt both mind and body between its damp and senseless walls - how many others' entire lives have comprised the same? Sarah or her parents? Mr Winston? Other black men and women sitting in this room, who she had passed by in the street on her way to buy candles or collect an order of silk? How many across this city, across the continent? She knew the feelings of worthlessness, and she knew pain, and though her experiences, she saw, were far removed from any soul born or bought into the ownership of another human being, she knew too of the difficulty in living without fear, even after finding freedom.

"The king of Guinea Bissau gained power, riches and land under the Portuguese trading in iron, steel, gold and gems for people - criminals or captured soldiers, or those who simply could not defend their communities from slavers' raids. The Europeans took advantage of a market in human subjects that already existed in Africa, Ghana and now Guinea Bissau, but the white men were the ones who turned it into the monster it is today. From the ensuing battles came prisoners, and this meant even more slaves ripe for the taking. The brutality only increased under British rule. Traffickers even supplied guns to the indigenous tribes, but not enough to ever turn them against the slave ships.

These Captains traded on their names and their supply.

In 1807, when the British finally abolished the slave trade, their power over the ports fluctuated, as other countries laid claim to their former markets, with skirmishes springing up all along the slave coast. Without a single organisation taking responsibility for the disorder, the private slave ships became unmanageable. Southerton and Hanley's vessels were the first to break away from the mainstream trading route, and sold their services to the highest bidder. Some of you here today have had first-hand knowledge of that industry, and my simple words cannot do justice to your sorrows.

Yet, still I am here to talk about the power of the British slave traders because, after twenty-five years of turning a blind eye to these privateer ships, the government is making definitive, terminal moves to abolish slavery in their empire.

What has changed? Namely this: that six months ago, the British government passed the reform bill, giving certain working men the right to vote. This in turn has meant more men in parliament, and more voices being heard. The British government is now putting a bill together to finally make the use of slaves illegal across the entire empire."

Bea leaned into Grace and whispered into her ear, "your grand-papa made that happen." Sarah overheard Bea's words and gave her a questioning look. Bea replied with just a smile. The old gentleman continued.

"This is only the first step on a longer journey; a lot still needs to be addressed.

I would like, therefore, to end this brief address by reaffirming to you: it is our joint responsibility to speak up - to use our voices, our influences and our God-given humanist reason, to condemn this treatment, and these practices, and speak out, of equality and freedom for all peoples – the times are changing, and we will be heard. Thank you." As Mr Farlow bowed to the congregation, they all stood up and clapped. Grace cried out unintelligibly, excited at the commotion. Mr Wilson stepped forward again.

"Thank you, Mr Farlow, for your much-needed words. I would like to take this moment and reach out to anyone who wishes to tell their story. The Liberator needs fresh voices, and articles to help the fight against ignorance. Mr Farlow himself has agreed to write an article – if you too will lend us your experience, please see me after the meeting."

He stepped down from the podium, assisting Mr Farlow, who bobbed his wide black hat to his companion, and bid farewell to those who could not stay as the rest made their way into the small side room for the usual refreshments.

"A pleasure to see you again, Mrs Mason - and you too, little one." Mr Winston gave a smile to Grace and then turned to Sarah, his dark eyes lighting up. "Sarah, it is good to see you."

Sarah handed Bea a cup of tea. "Mr Winston - would you like a cup of tea?" She held out her own cup to him. "I can fetch another?"

"No, thank you. I have had enough tea and coffee today; I would not deprive you of yours."

There was a gentle awkwardness between them, and Bea saw how Mr Winston looked at Sarah with admiration and attraction. And yet Sarah kept her gaze down always, blocking his advances.

"Good afternoon, Mrs Mason... Sarah."

"Afternoon, Mr Winston," offered Bea, while Sarah distracted herself with the tea, and tried to hide the flush of colour to her cheeks.

Chapter 19

Beacon Hill, Boston.

Christmas 1832.

The smell of spices filled the bottom kitchen. Three different forms of Christmas were to take place under one roof. Though Bea and Beth knew only of a simple kind; handmade gifts wrapped in scraps of fabric, and handed out after church, the family feast made of whatever they could get cheaply from the shops, or in abundance from their own snares. Joshua's Christmases had been filled with parties and celebrations, the grand house full of visiting guests, and always swimming in the rich tang of drink and the scent of fir and chocolate. As for Sarah, she talked little about her own experiences of Christmas time; only knowing that they attended church for a special service and eaten a special spiced dish of meat and fruit that her mama had once taught her to make. Since living in Boston, fellow members of the meeting house had invited her to join their respective Christmas gatherings, but every year she had said no, not wanting to intrude. This year, however, was different. Grace had brought her into the home, and into a new family, and Sarah was a part of a new tradition of Christmas celebration.

Bea sprinkled the cinnamon into the cake mixture, and ground the fresh ginger Sarah had found at the market in the mortar and pestle. She had smelt nothing like it before. She closed her eyes and imagined she was in an exotic land. When she opened them, Beth and Sarah were giggling at her.

"What?" Bea laughed back.

They shook their heads and continued with their tasks. Bea gazed down at the ancient recipe book she had found in a bookshop on the main street. She had never owned one before; a family tradition was to pass all the knowledge down through the generations. She gazed at the list of ingredients: sugar, molasses, citron fruit, spices, eggs, suet and a whole pound of butter. She had heard of the plum pudding before, but it was a rich man's dish.

"Do you think Joshua is going to like it, I've made nothing like this before?"

"This is one of his Christmas traditions, is it not?" asked Beth, and Bea nodded. "And since you are making it for him, no matter how it turns out, he will love it - just like we always say, it is the thought that counts."

"Your gesture will mean a lot to him," added Sarah.

"I hope so."

She tipped in the rest of the fresh and dried fruit, then added the molasses. The smell alone would be worth the work. Grace, making sure everyone was still aware of her presence, tapped her rattle against her wooden chair and shouted enthusiastically at her mother.

"Would you like to smell it, my sweet?" Bea lowered the bowl next to her small face and allowed Grace to breathe in the spices and rich, sugared scent. She marvelled over the contrast of her daughter's upbringing against her own. The privileges Grace would know that Bea had not. When she was older, Bea wanted to teach her the simplicity of life; how to catch and prepare dinner, to live off the land, to create beautiful things, and not just buy them. But living in the town meant she couldn't show her the joys of the countryside. That would be her greatest wish one day; to move out of the town and into the countryside, where Grace could walk freely through the woods and the fields, like she had done. Perhaps even have her own secret spot by the sea.

Bea lined a muslin cloth against the sides of a fresh bowl, and carefully poured in the glossy, thick mixture. The clock on the mantle chimed in the background.

"You had better get ready, the both of you. Guests will be here in an hour," noted Sarah.

"I supposed I must, though I was hoping for a quiet Christmas Eve," smiled Bea wryly.

"It won't be too bad. Everyone is only coming to have a few drinks, and I'm sure they won't stay late. The snow looks like coming down pretty heavy tonight."

Another of Joshua's wishes had been a Christmas Eve party, a reminder of home, and a light-hearted networking opportunity. Bea had spent the last few days making sure the house was presentable for the Goldstein's. Back in England, she would forage in the nearby woods for foliage, to decorate the house in evergreen and holly. But Joshua put a stop to her, walking through the park and snapping off branches to trail back home. So instead, she ordered as much fir and as many seasonal flowers as she could get her hands on to decorate the house.

She tied off the cloth into a double knot and placed the bowl on the side counter. "Sorry to leave you with this mess, Sarah."

"You just make yourselves presentable now, and Grace and I will sort everythin' down here, won't we, child? And then, we might just have a night of pure mischiefin' around the two of us, and a Christmas Eve bath, mayn't we, we my little sugar?" Sarah lent down and tickled Grace from her chin down to her tummy. Grace cried out in delight and kicked her legs ferociously.

It had been hard to approach the subject, but a week ago, she had tried to explain as respectfully as possible that she didn't want Sarah serving at the party; she didn't want it to be in any way akin to the Goldstein's gala. "I will help them get drinks with Beth, or they can help themselves. I don't want people viewing you like... like that, not here, and not at Christmas. Would you stay with Grace instead?" She wished she could invite Sarah as her own guest to commune with everyone, but in her heart she knew that neither party would be comfortable with that situation.

"It sounds like you will have lots of fun. I wish I could join in."

Both Beth and Sarah heard the anxiety in Bea's voice. Attending a gala, pretending she was one of those people for one night alone was one thing, but inviting those people into the sanctity of her home was another. And yet, for Joshua, she would brave it all.

Beth and Bea made their way upstairs whilst Sarah finished the canapés, and laid out each of the tiny iced cakes prettily before taking them up. Bea and Beth had each ordered a special gown from Miss Julie's for the night's events. Laid out on the marital bed was a deep crimson dress. The silk fabric shimmered under the candlelight. Before Joshua made his way upstairs to get ready, Bea collected her handmade gifts from her hiding spot and placed them on the vanity unit next to their vacant velvet pouches. She had spent the winter evenings creating each one. For Sarah, a delicate piece of lace, as a collar for a dress, composed of tiny rosebuds and leaves. For Beth, another piece of lace filled with her favourite wildflowers. For Grace, a new Christmas dress made from a smoky red velvet, and for Joshua, she had found a silversmith and ordered a pair of cufflinks engraved with his initials. She wrapped each one carefully and wrote a brief message on each of their cards. As she slipped out of her simple blue dress and climbed into the pool of crimson silk, the door open as she was trying to fasten the back of the dress.

"Would you mind?"

She could smell his scent, that of smoke and musk, as he

stood behind her, his fingers stroking down her neck and between her shoulder blades.

"We have an hour before people arrive... I could think of something else to do first?" He moved her hair out of the way and kissed her neck, wrapping his arms around her, stroking her body. She felt herself awaken between her legs at his touch, her pulsing breath willing her to give in to his request. He spun her round and kissed her passionately, sending a shiver across her body. Reluctantly, she broke away.

"After the party, I am all yours, but right now there is too much to do." Her lips hovered over his as she saw the disappointment on his face.

"The party won't last long in that case." He grinned at her and gave her a quick kiss before letting go.

"Would you mind?" Bea gestured to the back of her now crumpled dress.

Joshua chuckled as he hooked the seams together and sealed it with a kiss on her shoulders.

"Thank you." She turned round, placed her hands on his cheeks, and kissed him. It was slow and deep, but before he could pull his body against hers again, she let go.

"Not fair! And this poor dress, how am I..." She laughed at his over acting of frustration, before letting out a chuckle himself.

There was a knock on the door. "Come in," Bea called out between giggles.

"Someone wanted to say goodnight before her bath." Sarah came in with Grace, her arms outstretched for Joshua.

He strode over to Sarah, smiled, and took Grace from her arms.

"Sweet dreams, my darling." He cradled her as she reached out her little hand for his face.

"Bea, you look the equal if not better than any lady here tonight."

"Thank you, Sarah."

"You do look beautiful, wife," Joshua added with a twinkle in his eye.

Bea grinned at Joshua before focusing her attention on Grace. "Goodnight, my sweetheart. Tomorrow will be your first Christmas." Bea stroked Grace's head and placed a kiss on her forehead, pausing a moment, breathing in her scent.

She stepped back as Joshua handed his daughter back to Sarah whilst Bea made her way over to the dresser and pulled out a large velvet pouch.

He waited until he heard the bedroom door close. "Now, where were we?" murmured Joshua, standing close behind her, about to put his arms around her waist.

"I meant what I said, *after* the party." She gave him a quick kiss and slid out of his grasp, making her way to the door as a disappointed moan issued behind her.

∞∞∞

"Can I come in?" Bea called out behind Beth's door. "Yes, I'm decent."

She peered around the door and saw Beth standing there in her new floral dress of dark blues, reds, and fern greens. "You look beautiful." Her sister had put hair up in a simple, elegant bun with a plait around the edge, leaving her long neck bare.

"Would you like me to do your hair?"

"If you have time, that would be lovely, but that is not why I am here. I would like to give you one of your Christmas presents early."

She held out the large velvet pouch in her hand, offering it to Beth. "Merry Christmas, my lovely."

Beth placed it on her vanity unit and pulled at the blue ribbon, revealing a delicate silver rope chain, and a pendant of swirling strands of silver, mimicking sea-waves, with a few pearls, and a single sand-diamond placed at the bottom. She picked up the necklace and held it up against the candlelight. "Bea... I don't know what to say."

"Do you like it?"

"I... I love it, but you didn't need to. I have seen nothing like it."

"May I?" Bea gestured to put the necklace on. Beth nodded. The pendant hung perfectly above the neckline of the dress. "A reminder of home."

Beth gazed in the mirror and watched how it sparkled and glimmered in the candlelight. "It is too much."

"I did, I could, and I wanted to."

Beth pulled Bea in for a hug. "Thank you." The emotions in her voice said it all. "Now, let's see what we can do with that hair." She blushed, fighting against the happy tears.

The dining table had a fresh machine-made lace table-cloth, a large floral centre piece, and arrangements of large and small plates piled high with Sarah's handcrafted delights. They had all covered the two rooms in deep reds, purples, evergreen, and honey-scented candles.

"You have outdone yourself my darling; thank you for all this." Joshua stood beside her in a new suit. His cream and gold waist coat stood out smartly against the light grey jacket and trousers. He was handsome and ready to greet his guests. "I would kiss you, but I fear I wouldn't be able to stop - and then where would we be?" He gave her the same knowing grin as before, wrapping his arm around her shoulder, his thumb skimming over her bare skin.

Then the doorbell rang out, and Joshua removed his arm and made his way to the door. Bea took a deep breath and readied her nerves.

"George?"

"I came early, sir, to see if you needed any help – what a lovely home you have."

Joshua gestured to take his coat, placed it on a hanger and

paused. "Thank you George. Actually, you can – would you help greet the guests and hang up their coats? But first, let me get you a drink, and introduce you to my wife."

"Lovely to meet you, Mrs Mason, you have a splendid home here."

"It's good to finally meet you too, George. I have heard a lot about you."

"Really?" A mixture of pride followed by worry spread across his face at the thought of Joshua talking about him in a personal context.

"Get that down you." Joshua offered him a small glass of whiskey and proffered a glass of red wine to Bea.

"Thank you. The snow is coming down heavily now. I could certainly do with the warmth." George took a sip, and the doorbell rang out again. He glanced at Joshua and nodded, placing down the glass and making his way down the hall.

"Good evening, sir and madam, may I take your coats?"

The room was filled with no more than twenty people; a comfortable number, and there were only a handful of cards wishing them kind regards and regrets. The Goldstein's arrived late and left early, making a cursory appearance so as not to snub Joshua. He and Mr Goldstein spent his time huddled in a corner, talking about business, whilst George ran around bringing drinks, occasionally assisted by Beth. Mrs Goldstein made pleasant conversation with Bea, remarking on the beauty of the rooms and giving an eloquent Christmas greeting before joining her usual circle. Bea hovered around the room making small talk, noting happily that Beth seemed to be far more at ease with the ladies than she. Filtering from one group to another, she set everyone at ease, taking a moment now and then to check on Bea. Once the Goldstein's left, the company relaxed a little more but as the clock chimed ten; the couples left. It was at that point that Bea noticed Beth and George speaking quietly together in a corner. Her sister was smiling brightly, whilst George was blushing, and unable to meet her eyes.

"I think that's everyone gone. It was a good night!" remarked Joshua heartily, tapping his cigarette into the dying fire.

"Look - what do you think?" Bea pointed over to Beth and George.

"George is an excellent fellow, I suppose... though I had thought she might... well... yes, yes. Why not?"

"Not everyone can be as lucky as me, Joshua." She turned round and gave him a quick kiss.

"The party is over, so, according to your previous statement, you're all mine now?" She gently stroked his hand down her cheek to her shoulders.

"You two head off. I'll tidy up," Beth interjected from across the room.

"I'll help, if you don't mind?" George blurted out, glancing at Beth.

Bea smiled at Beth. "Thank you, the two of you."

"Very good of you, George - and you have a merry Christmas." Joshua held out his hand for George to shake.

"You too Sir. And Mrs Mason, it has been a lovely evening."

"Merry Christmas George," smiled Bea, as she linked arms with Joshua's as he led her towards the stairs.

The following day was just as Bea had imagined. Sarah made everyone a luxurious breakfast before they went off to their two different churches, after which they gathered around the fire and exchanged gifts. Joshua presented Bea with a simple pearl necklace as she handed him the silver cufflinks.

"Oh, how wonderful Bea, thank you."

Bea then handed out her two gifts to Sarah and Beth; Grace was already wearing hers.

"You made this for me?" Sarah held the delicate lace against the cornflower blue dress Bea had bought her back before the gala. "Thank you."

"She has a gift, our Bea. Thank you, sister." Beth held out her hands to Bea and Sarah, and all three women linked their hands together.

Grace banged her rattle happily on the ground as Joshua smiled before handing out more of his own gifts. Grace got a set of wooden blocks and a wooden duck on wheels. Beth gave Sarah an enamel brooch, and in return Sarah handed each of the others knitted mittens, scarfs and a dress for Grace.

Joshua pulled Bea into his arms.

"I can't believe how happy I am right now. This is what we had dreamt of." She whispered, gazing into his blue eyes.

He paused, brushing a hair from her face. "I love you more than I thought I ever could."

"I love you too. Merry Christmas."

Chapter 20

January 1833 Beacon Hill.

One year passed smoothly and gladly into another without additional ceremony. Joshua had thought it would be a good idea to have Grace's christening on the first Sunday in January; a sign of change and looking forward. So, on the Saturday, they filled the church with white flowers, and prepared Grace's ivory gown with its four layers of machine and handmade lace. The invitations had gone out in late December; if the occasion had taken place in Ulverston, the church would have been packed, but here it would be ten close acquaintances at the most. She had finally convinced Sarah to attend the ceremony, to sit with the family at the front. Joshua didn't argue. He knew how it might look to other people. And yet, she felt like she was becoming a member of the family and how invaluable she had been in bringing Grace into the world safely. They also invited George, with a seat in the second row. He had made a few more appearances at the house over Christmas and the New Year, and Bea suspected it wasn't merely to run errands for Joshua.

The snow was at least a foot-deep outside, and in constant fall; she had seen nothing like it before. With the sea mist and the salty air, Ulverston had experienced some snow, but not like this. Bea made the final preparation while Beth and Sarah prepared the sitting room, in case anyone came back for a cup of tea and cake after the ceremony. Bea wore her dark green wool dress, and wrapped Grace up in as many blankets as she could find, with Sarah's knitted hat on top. There was a chill in the air that buried deep inside your bones and a cold sensation Bea couldn't shake no matter how many blankets placed around her in the carriage.

They made the brief journey to the church and stood in line with all the others filing in. The pews were filled with familiar faces, all gazing at Bea cradling their newest member. A few expressions changed at the sight of Sarah standing directly behind Bea. There were a handful of well-to-do black families who attended the church, so Sarah's was not the only one in a sea of white faces. Even so, several individuals stared at her with suspicion. George filed in behind, taking a seat next to Joshua, and behind him strode Mr Winston. He walked into the church without fear, the equal of all those who stood under its roof. Once the church was full, the elderly vicar stood forward and sighted the first half of the service. Bea, waiting for her signal to step forward, could not focus on the sermon, and glanced around the grand building. It was newer than it looked, built for the growing population of Beacon Hill, styled on older churches back in England. She wrapped the shawl tighter around her shoulders.

"Today we welcome a new member into our flock. Will the parents and godparents of Miss Grace Mildred Mason step forward, please?"

Bea took Grace from Beth and accompanied Joshua to the baptismal font at the front of the building as she and George stood to one side, ready for their cue.

"Dearly beloved, forasmuch as all men are conceived and born in sin, and that our saviour Christ saith, none can enter into the kingdom of God, except he be regenerate and born anew of water and of the Holy Ghost.

Let us pray,

Almighty and everlasting God: by the Baptism of thy well-beloved Son Jesus Christ, in the river Jordon, thou didst sanctify water to the mystical washing away of sin. We beseech thee, in the name of thine infinite mercies, that thou wilt mercifully look upon this child, to wash her, and sanctify her with the Holy Ghost; that she, being delivered from thy wrath, may be received into the ark of Christ's church. People of God, will you welcome this child, and uphold her and her family in their new life in Christ?"

"With the help of God, we will." The church spoke as one.

"Who brings this child before God?" Announced the vicar.

All four took a step closer towards the font. Whilst at the back of the congregation, Bea heard a familiar sound. Hesitantly, she glanced round and saw the few men standing at the back step aside. Her heart stopped, and her breath caught in her chest. She had feared this moment for so long, and now it had finally come. He was here. Victor Hanley's eyes set on her, and taking another step forward, made it clear he was here to claim what was his.

"Bea." Joshua's voice struggled to break through the fog that was forming inside her head. Her ears felt as though they were filled with sand, and her chest was too tight to speak.

She looked over at the vicar, who had his arms stretched out for Grace. She couldn't let her go. Grace was hers, all hers, and Bea had to protect her. Seeing the hesitation on the mother's face, the vicar instead came round to her.

"Christ claims you as his own. Receive the sign of the cross." The vicar dipped his finger in a small bowl of holy oil and made the sign of the cross on Grace's forehead. He gestured for Bea to come closer to the font as he lifted the silver bowl toward the water.

"Almighty everliving God, whose most dearly beloved Son Jesus Christ, for the forgiveness of our sins..."

She has no sin, she is innocent – she is pure – she is loved – she is mine, not his, not his...

She felt his stare bury into her, challenging her to make a move. *Not here, not now.*

"We beseech thee, the supplications of thy congregation; sanctify this water to the mystical washing away of sin; and grant that this child, now to be baptised therein, may receive the fullness of thy grace, and ever remain in the number of thy faithful and elect children; through Jesus Christ our lord.

Amen." Grace made little moaning noises as he trickled the water over her head. "I baptise you in the name of the Father, and the Son and of the Holy Spirit. Amen."

"Amen."

Once more, she shifted her gaze slowly to the back of the church. Had it all been a false vision? But standing in broad daylight, Hanley was standing there for all to see, waiting.

Sarah had seen the colour drain entirely from Bea's face and followed her gaze back into the crowd. She tried to shift in her seat to get a better look, but the angle she was sitting at prevented her from locating what was frightening Bea, though her terror became more and more unmistakable, her cheeks the same colour as Grace's dress.

Standing next to George, Beth too noticed how distracted Bea was, continually shifting her gaze to the back of the church. Then she saw him and understood the horror. Why her sister looked like death, as though she should be lying in a coffin instead of baptising her child. Hanley looked different from the last time she had seen him. But there was no mistaking the eyes, the stance, or the darkness, and now he was back.

The vicar had continued without the three women noticing. "Let us give thanks unto almighty God for these benefits, and with one accord make our prayers unto him, that this child may lead the rest of her life according to this beginning."

The vicar made the gesture for the congregation to bow or kneel in prayer.

"What's wrong? Bea?" Joshua had turned to her with a smile, but started at the fear on her face.

"Our father, which art in heaven, hallowed be thy name, they kingdom come, thy will be done, in earth as it is in heaven. Give us this day our daily bread; and *forgive us our trespasses, as we forgive them that trespass against us*. And lead us not into temptation, but *deliver us from evil*. Amen."

"Bea?"

She didn't know what to say. The perfect heaven on earth

they had created was crumbling under their feet, and she didn't want to be the one to tell him. That her actions were about to create more pain for him, that the biological father of the child he was holding was here to claim his precious daughter.

The vicar gestured to the four of them to take their seats once more. Bea closed her eyes as Joshua turned round to face the congregation. She felt his body tighten against hers as realisation seeped in, and as she opened her eyes, she saw a smirk across Hanley's face as he nodded once at Joshua before slipping back into the crowd.

Chapter 21

Hanley made his way swiftly out the side-door and collected his horse from around the back. The snow was coming down heavy and fast now. How much he wished he could observe their party as it returned home; to listen to the conversation that would begin tearing them apart. Their bright alternative world wasn't so safe anymore. Another thought flashed into his mind, that of him holding the child, watching her smile up at him, like she had for Bea, but he dismissed the notion as quickly as it had appeared. He wasn't here merely to take charge of the infant; he wanted to break the both of them, once and for all.

The idea of returning to his suffocating room at the boarding house while he was riding out such a high did not seem appealing. He needed to celebrate; drinks, cards and a woman or two.

He made his way down the south side of the slope, in the direction of the harbour, and towards his usual boarding house. He passed the black community, a cold comparison of his actual home, and then the newly formed Irish community, who were taking a lot of the labour jobs at the harbour. Past them were to be found the brothels, the slums, and the poor of every colour, crammed together in a squalid perimeter of blocks, a square of Boston where nobody felt at home - except him. Most of the buildings were wooden, with the few brick-built structures looking even more hazardous than their timber counterparts. With one match he could bring this entire community to its knees, and not a soul alive one would miss it; quite the contrary, in fact. But he would never do such a thing; Boston needed this dark corner. He needed it, a stark reminder of the real filthiness of humanity lying beneath the shine of moral society.

He had been hiding in Boston for months, following one Mason and then the other go about their days, obsessing over the tiniest of details, and contemplating various avenues of action. They had thought they were free; they had thought their life was perfect away from Ulverston and the chaos they had left behind. But what would their new friends think if they knew the truth? He had followed Bea on her small trips to the shops, seeing that she had money to spend within their modest income. He could have given her that; all she had now, she would have had with him... what had made Joshua so much more desirable to her? He noticed how happy she looked every time she bent down over the pram. A girl; he had never seen himself fathering a girl before, only a boy, and with a boy he would have known what to do. But a daughter... He had seen her face only a few times, and though she looked almost the miniature of her mother, with barely a trace of his own features visible in her own, he knew Joshua Mason had no right to father his child. When he had sex with Bea, she had been a virgin; he had felt it, and therefore this girl, Grace, well - she had to be his, and only his.

Goldstein had told him of the Christening at one of their meetings at the club. Instantly, he knew it would be the perfect setting to make himself known to them once again. To wait until they had reached their ideal happiness, as the boy ready to claim his child in front of their pitiful community. Only for him to step forward amid their pride and security, and to witness, just for a moment, their fear.

Bea looked like one of them now, but no matter how far she ran, she would always belong to him.

He dropped off his cold horse in the nearby stables, and covered her in a warm blanket, settling her with a nosebag of fresh straw. His feet sank into a fresh pile of deep snow outside the stables before stepping into the usual grimy slush running down the main street; a mixture of household waste, mud, soot, and cold water. He strutted passed the bodies of a few frozen animals, mostly rats, with the odd dog or cat, all having been unable to find shelter before death set in. Most homes around here were themselves unable to afford wood or coal for their fires. The only surplus was the mouths waiting to be fed, and the only comfort, a few moth-eaten blankets. He passed a couple of men fighting over a discarded wooden crate, with the potential to provide one family with heat for a couple of hours, and possibly a warm meal. After a single punch, the slimmer of the two landed in the freezing sewage water at the edge of the road and stared up at the winner, clutching tight onto his meagre prize. Hanley watched the despair in both faces, as each party dragged themselves in opposite directions off down the street, thinking that although many aspects of rural life were difficult and degrading, at least out in the countryside, families might find enough kindling from fallen trees and sticks to store away for the winter, or burn peat dug out from the fells to keep themselves warm. City living for the poor turned them into the animals, scavenging for scraps whilst mothers watched their children starve. Hanley kept his head down after that and slipped down one of the side alleys. The metropolis for him was a place for visiting, not living; give him a ship or a country house was his kind of home. A dishevelled man approached him as he turned down a dark alleyway, chancing his luck. But the figure stepped back quickly, both arms raised, relinquishing his attempt, when he beheld the identity of his supposed victim. There was a dull flash in the dark as he slipped his knife back into its sheath within his jerkin.

"Afternoon Ranford," muttered Hanley.

"Ah – yes... Sorry, Captain." Ranford stood to one side, his head bowed low, allowing Hanley to pass. He still bore the scar on his left forearm from his first and only attempt to part the Captain from his purse.

Hanley could smell the smoke billowing out the various chimneys and welcomed even the thought of heat. The building stood strangely in its surrounds, the only Georgian house amongst the wooden houses built up around it, like a stark stone angel bedded in the dark, makeshift forest. With its six bedrooms and large parlour, Hanley wondered how it came to be here; whether it had once been the house of a gentleman, or if the men on the north slope had built it themselves as a place of refuge, away from their cold, unaccommodating wives. Inside, the house exhibited some of its former glory; the faded bespoke wall paper showing off exotic animals and birds, and the peeling paint around the gilded rose work on the celling, now streaked with sooty lines from the cheap candles constantly burning.

An older lady dressed in a blue silk gown glided towards him from the side room. Her dress hinted at temptation, but she wasn't for sale. She was in charge. Her painted face gave visitors a glimpse of past beauty, equal to any of her girls twenty years ago.

"Hanley, we have missed you. It disappointed me greatly to receive your note informing us you were staying elsewhere. I thought we had offended you somehow. Tell us, how can we make it up to you?" She stepped forward, close enough so that he could smell her perfume.

"Afternoon Madam. Not at all. Your establishment could never disappoint. I had business in the North slope, but I am returned now, as you see."

"Excellent! So now, what do you desire? We have a hot table in the back room. A drink in the lounge, and then a bath upstairs? Your usual room is free."

"A bath to start, then an evening of cards and pleasure. Is Mai available?"

"Of course – and I believe she is, I shall make her aware of your happy arrival." She smiled before walking down the corridor toward the back rooms as Hanley made his way upstairs.

He sat in front of the fire, his back against the base of the bed. He pulled his sodden shoes off slowly, allowing his feet to dry and the sensation to return to his toes. He watched the flames flicker like a magic lantern, and his mind wandered back once more to the morning's events. His grin returned as he pictured the babe in Bea's arms, kicking out with vitality and strength: his daughter. What would he do with her?

A small knock came at the door as two girls brought in a squat copper bath and placed it in front of the fire. He stood to attention as Mai entered behind them, her silk shift flowing delicately over her body, resting tentatively on her breasts and hips, transparent against the firelight. She muttered something to the girls before they left and closed the door quietly. Then without a word, she placed her arms around his neck and kissed him, awakening his body, and prompting an image of Bea to spring, ghost like, into his head. He wrapped his arms around her waist, the smooth, firm flesh of her buttocks warm beneath his fingers, and instantly gave in to his fantasy.

Chapter 22

"**B**eth, please could you take Grace upstairs whilst Bea and I talk?" Beth nodded her head and walked over to Bea, who was still holding tight to her sleeping child.

"Bea, dearest... may I take baby? Just for a little while, upstairs?" There was something void in Bea's eyes; she wasn't present in the room.

"I... I must protect her. He is out there. He can't have my baby." muttered Bea indistinctly.

"I promise to protect her," Beth whispered in return. "Please?" Beth reached out and eased the sleeping baby out of her sister's grasp.

Joshua was pacing the still-decorated sitting-room, and Sarah had made her way to the kitchen.

After the service, Hanley was nowhere to be seen, and Joshua had made excuses to their guests. Explaining that Bea wasn't feeling herself, and they would have to defer their celebrations to another time.

"What is the devil doing back here? *I should have killed him when I had the chance.* How on earth did he find us?" He continued to pace the length of the room, his tight fists at his sides.

Bea stood in the centre staring at the pattern rug. "I... don't know..."

"And what was he doing at the Church - that stance, that gesture? Does he... does he want Grace? My child?"

Bea backed away from Joshua's increasing temper. The world

around her was swirling, making her dizzy and disoriented. *How? Why? Had she not suffered enough?* Her legs gave way as she crumpled to the floor. She hadn't seen him since the trial, and the moment they told her she would die. It was that smile, the same one that was smeared across his face today. A smile that rejoiced in her pain.

Joshua stopped pacing and watched the life evaporate out of his wife once more.

"Bea? Please..."

She shuddered at his touch and shuffled backwards between the armchair and the wall. She said nothing.

"Bea, come back to me? Bea, *I need you*... I've only just got you back, I can't lose you again..." Her eyes were closed, battling between being back in her former cell and the person she was now.

"BEA!"

Running footsteps came from the kitchen. "Sir?" Sarah saw him standing in the middle of the room, his back arched, staring into the corner with his clench hands turning white. She took a step to the side and saw Bea hiding by the wall, and knew that image all too well. "Sir, may I?" Sarah took another step towards Joshua, who looked completely bereft.

"Bea it's Sarah. Can you talk to me? Can you tell me how I might help?"

The wave of emotions built up inside Bea until she couldn't cope. She opened her mouth and let out a sharp, piercing scream, followed by a wave of silent tears. An act she hadn't done since the days in the dark, godforsaken cell. An act no one knew about.

Joshua said nothing, but stood there in shock and cried at his wife's pain.

"Bea?" Sarah gave her no choice and threw her arms around the ball. Bea fought her at first, but as Sarah squeezed harder, she resisted less and less until she was just a sobbing, trembling mess in Sarah's arms.

They said nothing, because there was nothing to say. Sarah

knew that pain. She had witnessed it before, and she had felt it before. The room fell silent as they held each other.

"Sarah, could you – would you mind - some tea?" Joshua whispered.

"I will be back," Sarah muttered into Bea's ear.

She shuffled out as Joshua took her place and threw his arms around Bea as another set of emotions hit her at her husband's touch. They both wept together.

Sarah watched, and it reminded her of her past, the night she had lost everything, and Hercules had placed his arms around her as she had wept, and screamed up to the sky with pain. She sent out a prayer as she made her way back down the stairs, rubbing her arms as though the air was cold.

"I'm sorry, I am so sorry." Bea's voice crackled into his wet shirt.

"I love you. There is nothing to be sorry about. This - he - is not your fault." He tried to lift her head up to him. "Look at me." She peeled her eyes open. "We are in this together now."

He kissed her softly. Her body eased.

"I love you... I am so sorry!" She lent her head against his chest, her body vibrating against his as another wave of terror and grief hit her. Knowing the future pain this man can cause.

Chapter 23

Drayton Hall, 1819

Jessie had spent the last month questioning Gabby about the mysterious man of whom she had spoken to, and what exactly he had said, never allowing her far out of her sight. She found out he was in fact another conductor of the underground railroad route, based twenty miles away, but that by day, he worked as a carpenter. Once a month, in a little valley at the intersection of three small neighbouring plantations, most local slaves came together for an evening church service. It was where husbands met wives, fathers, mothers and children, and where future relationships began. The plantation staff allowed it to happen because it brought a sense of peace to their workers, a chance of normality for a few hours, and to be amongst friends and music; this all curbed any small instances of unrest. They would sing their hymns and their workers' songs together, share skills, and swap stories. Jessie watched, and waited, and made new acquaintances, and one day, her chance came along once more.

"Are you Elijah? Miss Gabby, the lil' one, from Drayton, told me of your knowin' a certain road; of your knowin' a way... to another place?" The man standing alone next to the campfire, tapping his foot to the song being played, had on the green cap Gabby had told her about. She also noticed the strange mark down one side of his face, a mark she had seen plenty of times before, and guessed the hat was there to hide a missing ear.

"She shouldn' ha' done that, so she shoul' not." He moved away from her.

"I understand. I 'ave heard of it. A few years past on another plantation. *The railroad.*" The last part came as a loud whisper.

He paused, looked at her properly for the first time, then back at the fire. "Come child, come o'er here fo' me." He reached out and took her hand, leading her away from the music to a nearby tree; far enough away so that any listening birds might not sing songs back to their master.

"I have told no one, and I shall not tell it, never." She held her hands up as though he were a drunk overseer aiming his gun around, fearful of what he might do.

He stepped closer and yanked her hands down. "What do you mean you 'ave heard it before?"

"One state over I believe, my husband was- my late husband, they approached him, we..."

"I understand. And you're still willing, missus?"

"Yes. But, why haven't you... taken the road?"

"My job is to recruit, child."

"You stay here, in this place, just to tell others? That don't make no sense!"

"I will travel that way myself, once it is time, but for now, I keep my head down; do my work, and once a month, I tell someone new, see if they have what it takes."

"It would mean death for her. She is but an innocent – trust me." Jessie raised her eyebrows and gave him a knowing look.

"She brought you to me, did she not?"

"It could cost us both dearly." She shrugged her head away from his stare.

"But you missus, you is willin' to do it again?"

A sudden image of Hercules smiling at her in encouragement made her catch her breath for a moment. "Yes."

"I wouldn' do it alone, missus, you be safer in a group."

"Better if it's just me – I'm sure, I know it," she replied in a stern, determined voice.

He held his callused hand out to her. "Meet me back here next month; I'll have what you need."

"A month? Can't you tell me now, sir?" She went to pull him back, but her hand missed his sleeve.

He stopped and leaned back towards her. "I need to speak to another, to take time over it, set up a route for you. Caution, and quiet is best, missus."

They heard the goodbye song ring out amongst the community groups and knew it was time to leave.

"Under this tree at the next meeting. Your name?"

"Jessie." He gave her a swift nod before turning back to the congregations, leaving Jessie nursing a dark hope that this time she would outrun them all.

She followed Elijah's advice and kept her head down, picked the cotton, and lay silent as the master visited her room, ignoring the smell and the damp of his broad frame pressing down on her, and his musk-scented chestnut hair covering her eyes; she had made herself disappear before she had even left. A month passed, and she walked out the door of her hut to the September church service with a firm tread. She waited under the large tree, looking out at the cotton fields, grateful for the shade. The summer heat was bearing down, with no let-up from even the night sky as the dark, sticky heat clung to her skin.

She paced on the spot, listening to one song after the other. Maybe he wasn't coming, maybe he had betrayed her, or worse; maybe he had been caught. Then she saw the green hat in the distance, accompanied by another man.

"I was thinkin' you weren't coming."

"I was late receivin' a package - this is John."

"Hello." She threw Elijah a mistrustful glance. "Have you changed your mind?"

"John is just goin' to take you part of the route, missus."

"I said I was doin' it alone."

"He can take you halfway to the blacksmith, the first station. It's ten miles, he runs errands and got clearance by the master to attend the shop. He knows this land, child, when you do not."

"But..."

"You gotta be quick as you can, girl, to get as faraway from your master before the morning count. There ain't no time to argue."

"What *now*?"

"Yes, now. Here are your papers."

Jessie took hold of the parcel. In it was a few dollars; she had never held money before, and the coins were heavier than she had imagined. She looked at the papers in disbelief. "Sarah? And the description - it don't sound like me."

"We all look alike to them; 'tis the best we could do at brief notice."

"We need to go now - Sarah." John stepped forward.

"It's Jessie." Feeling insulted somehow, she pulled her hand away from his.

He grabbed hold of her papers with force. "No, it is Sarah now. You are leaving Jessie behind. Jessie is a slave, but Sarah is free." He stared at her. There was something glorious in what he said.

She nodded; *Sarah, I am now Sarah, and she will be free.*

"Thank you, Elijah." She placed her hand on top of his for a moment before taking back her papers from John.

He nodded his head in return. "God bless you on your journey, child; live well for us."

John put his arm around Sarah as though they were going off as a couple to be alone. Once they rounded the corner of the perimeter fields, they ran.

∞∞∞

John picked up a cloth bag left hidden in the scrub beside a small tree, and opened it to show her a loaf of bread, a parcel of cheese and some nuts. They ran north through the trees and the swamp fields as they followed the river, stopping at any sound that wasn't from an animal. It was all too familiar to Sarah. Every time they stopped, she kept an ear out for the dogs, waiting in her heart for them to come close up behind with their angry jaws and capture her once more. John ran without thinking; his feet knew where to go and hoped that Sarah could keep up. After a couple of hours, they stopped for ten minutes to gulp down some bread and water in the shadow of a large bush. Sarah, remembering how her feet had become broken and bloody after her last attempt, tore off the hem of her dress and wrapped the cloth around her toes, up to her ankles. The shoes she wore had always been too big for her, passed down from a former hub woman when she first arrived. Now that her feet moved less and didn't rub, she could run.

They kept moving through the night, keeping close to the river at all times, the moonlight that bounced off the still water making it easier to see. She wondered how many times John had done this before, but she didn't ask questions. Silence was their friend.

Just as the sun rose, they made it to a small shack on the outskirts of a sleepy village which looked to Sarah more like a trading post than a shop.

"Stay here." He left her in the undergrowth as he made his way inside. As she leant against the tree, the heat of the sun already breaking through, she closed her eyes for a moment, feeling herself drifting. Suddenly she jumped at a noise nearby, cursing herself for letting her guard down. She stared around her, trying to hear further sounds, but nothing came, only the pounding in her chest echoing in her ears. A tap on her shoulder caused her to shriek a little.

"Come," said John.

Sarah did as he commanded, following in his footsteps to the back of the store. He pushed an overgrown bush to one side and slid a wooden panel upwards. The gap was small. She lay on her stomach in the dry dirt and pushed herself through, now trapped in the hot, stuffy space. It was worse than the hot box they had forced her into when she was ten. Punishment for stealing an extra portion at dinner. John handed her the cloth bag with a few remaining pieces of cheese and nuts, and sealed her in without a word. The space was dark. She reached out her hands in front of her; the tips of her fingers could stroke the roof, which gave her about two feet in front of her face, and she could stretch out on either side without contact. She guessed it ran at least halfway across the foundation of the building, enough for three or more slaves to hide in. Footsteps moved about above her, accompanied by a low, muttering voice. A tinkling bell rang out and then came a blinding light. She covered her eyes with her hands.

"I'm Franklin. You're safe here, girl."

Sarah peered through her fingers and saw an old man, with skin tanned red by the sun, and a white beard peering down at her through an open rectangular hole. Maybe their version of God was correct, she thought dazedly.

"I'm..."

"Sarah, yes, my dear. John told me you were coming. You are to rest here today, and I'll move you part of the way to the next station."

Sarah moved her hands from her face. "You ain't a black-smith. I was told I was going to a blacksmith."

"He's another six miles downriver, but your master will be out looking for you by now, so we thought it best to wait things out until nightfall, and then I can take you the rest of the way by wagon."

"Thank you, master." White men only had one name.

"Franklin, child; I am no one's master, especially not yours - you are free now! I have some water, bread and cooked meat here – there you go." He handed down another cloth parcel into the hole. "Rest and sleep; you have still a long road ahead of you."

"Thank you, Franklin."

He placed the floorboard back over above her, leaving her in darkness once more.

∞∞∞

Sarah guessed she must have slept for a couple of hours until a sudden noise woke her. The space was thick with heat, her skin dripped with sweat and soaked into her filthy head wrap. Disorientated, the voices broke through the wooden flooring as though they were whispering in the cramped slot with her.

"You seen a nigger-woman this mornin'? A runaway, wantin' food?"

Sarah held a hand over her own mouth, scared she would make a single sound and seal both their fates.

"No sir, I have not. The only black slaves I have seen for the past week are the two black men who come in regular with lists for goods. I checked their papers myself."

"You sure?" She didn't recognise this other voice.

"I'm sorry, sir, but I have seen none around here, specially not a woman. I will keep a lookout. What plantation is it she escaped from?" Franklin's voice sounded calm.

"Drayton Hall; Master Hanley wants her back, and he will pay for any information you can give, so you mind that."

"I know of it; I will keep a lookout and send word if I see her."

"Good day then, sir."

The men, animals themselves, made a low growl, followed by the sound of the shop bell. It was the greatest blessing Sarah could have prayed for, the fact they hadn't brought their dogs. On the other side of her pen, she could make out the sound of horses kicking up dirt, and then a yell. Silence descended over the wooden hut.

∞∞∞

As nightfall descended, the wooden panel to her side shifted open, and a hand slipped in.

"We need to get going." Sarah slid out carefully and found Franklin standing over her, holding out some fabric. "Here, put this on. It will help you blend in better than those rags. I'll hitch up the wagon, meet me round front." Sarah simply nodded.

The cotton dress was a little big for her slight frame, but it was clean and presentable to look at. She grabbed her parcel out of the hole, relived herself; who knew when she would get another chance and made her way round to front of the shop. A single horse and covered wagon stood waiting, with Franklin already seated, reins in hand, ready to move.

"Climb into the back and cover yourself with the blanket. We have little time."

She did as instructed. The blanket was more akin to a hessian sack and scratched at her face. But she now realised after last night's journey, it was still incomparably better than braving this journey on her own. The horse followed the narrow path beside the river, veering away from the north star.

"Are we not going north?"

"We are too far south to go northward yet; besides, that's what they'll expect you to do - to head through the Blue Ridge Mountains, which would only slow us down."

"Where are we going then?"

"The blacksmith, he will explain further. Now cover yourself back up and try to rest."

Sarah lowered her head down and placed the sack back across her face, wondering if she would ever see daylight again.

Chapter 24

February 1833, Beacon Hill.

I t had been a few short weeks since Captain Hanley had made his reappearance, and it left a shadow hanging over the house. Bea spent her days inside, refusing to leave. As if creating a fortress inside her mind, she locked the doors and windows and stayed in the central part of the home, away from the impending threat of Hanley. He could generate hell. He had done it before without succeeding, and it wasn't in his nature to lose. Beth and Sarah stayed around her whilst Joshua went to work, constantly keeping Grace by her side. They watched her as she stood on the edge, risking slipping back into her former, disordered self and twisting the tangled piece of lace around her wrist. Whilst Joshua struggled to decide the next step with no father for advice and no friend for comfort. They couldn't run again, not now.

Standing by their bed, he peered down at Bea, sleeping with a constructed nest for Grace next to her. His baby girl was getting bigger. Her sweet, round cheeks and wisps of auburn hair made his heart ache. This was his daughter sleeping there, and the love he felt for her was all-consuming. He would, he must, be the only father she would know and yet... he knew Hanley could take that treasured future away from him?

Joshua trudged through the freshly laid snow, the cold soaking into his boots. It was still dark; he missed the sun during the long winter months. The street-lights bounced off the white ground, and he pounded his hands together inside his mittens. For days afterwards, he and Bea argued about the threat of Hanley and leaving the house. He refused to be controlled by that man. Every day he resisted the urge to react, to yell as the anger boiled up inside him once more. Work was important. At the office, he could command each occurrence, and the power to divert things as he wished. He collected his horse from the stables and resisted the desire to gallop, missing once again the fields and fells around his former family home. He loved Bea with all his heart, especially since he had loved her physically in the months leading up to Christmas. It had been the life he had wished for and dreamt of during dark times. Was that all it had been, a dream, and now he was awake to the icy reality before him? A broken wife; a child that wasn't his by blood; a man obsessed to the point of madness.

He slammed his numb hands together once more as the horse lead the way. The harbour streets were full of freezing workers and labours, taking turns around the small fires in metal cages spread across the walk like warning beacons.

He handed his horse to a waiting stable boy and stepped into work, instantly switching off the dread surrounding his domestic life.

"Morning George.".

"Morning... Joshua, sir," responded George, striding after him with coffee pot in hand, still unsure what to call his superior now that a friendship seemed to form between them.

The fire was already lit. Joshua poked an iron rod into the flames, sparking it to life. He slumped into the wooden chair as George poured their coffees.

"George, we've gone over this: Joshua is fine, except in front of Mr Goldstein. Mr Mason reminds me too much of my father." He picked up the cup and took a sip. "Thank you." He took out his silver case and tapped a cigarette on the top in his time-honoured way.

"Talk me through today's agenda."

∞∞∞

T he day passed by like all the others, with two shipments to organise and some logistical compromise to be arranged between ports.

"Joshua." George peered his head around the corner of his office door.

"Yes, what is it?" he sighed.

"Mr Goldstein would like a word with you down at the harbour."

"When?"

"Now, if you're free."

He grabbed his pocket watch out from his vest pocket and flipped the lid open. The lamp light glistened off the engraving left by his father. There was enough time. Joshua collected his overcoat from the hook by the door and made his way down the stairs. Mr Goldstein was standing at the furthest point along the pier, beside a ship he didn't recognise. "Good afternoon, sir. What seems to be the problem?" Joshua tried to keep a lightness to his tone.

Another man, some yards behind Mr Goldstein, raised his head from the letter he had been perusing, turned, and stepped forward, smiling at Joshua. "Oh, no problem, Mason, I simply wanted to introduce you to someone - Captain Victor Hanley. Hanley, this is Mr Joshua Mason; he's been invaluable to us this past year."

"A pleasure to meet you, Mr Mason." Hanley held out his hand to shake.

Joshua stared at the hand before him. If he didn't play along, it would seem rude and strange to his employer, and more importantly, if he told Mr Goldstein how he knew Hanley, the past would become unearthed. Joshua shook the proffered hand. The other smiled again and gave his hand a tight squeeze. Joshua smiled back and returned the same gesture a little tighter. *If that's the way of things...*

Mr Goldstein continued, paying no attention to the interaction between the two men. "I have been doing business with the Hanley family for years. We have formed a formidable partnership, eh Victor."

The realisation of the statement sank in like a damp fog; Joshua knew what business the Hanley family primarily dealt in, and that meant that Mr Goldstein must know the extent of their dealings, too. It made him suddenly suspicious of other ships that docked at their pier.

"I did not know that Sir; I haven't seen the name in the books."

"Oh, something has somewhat preoccupied me over the past year – woman trouble!" Hanley looked at Mr Goldstein, and they both laughed. Joshua called upon all the restraint he could muster and remained rigid. "Anyhow, I am back now, and will continue my regular visits; you won't be able to miss me. I will be here that often. I almost feel as though Boston harbour is my second home." Hanley stared at Joshua, telling him everything he needed to know.

"Indeed," Joshua muttered through gritted teeth. Mr Goldstein patted each man on the shoulder.

"Well, I better be off gentlemen; I have another engagement. Victor, I'll see you at the club later?"

"Of course, Richard."

The gentlemen doffed their hats to one another before Mr Goldstein left. Joshua waited until he was out of earshot.

"Why are you here?" His voice was controlled, but the anger was palpable.

"I should be I asking you that, shouldn't I, Mason? My family has been working with Mr Goldstein for over twenty years, and then suddenly, you too have found a place in the company. How did that come about, I wonder?"

"If I had known of the connection, I would never have accepted the job. I have no interest in your history or how you earn your money. Only in that you stay far away from my wife and child."

"The distance I keep from your wife is between her, myself and... our child."

"Grace is not your child." Joshua was willing himself to remain calm; Hanley had baited him all too often in the past and resulted in two fights.

"I can assure you sir, your wife was a virgin when I fucked her." Hanley whispered into Joshua's ear.

Joshua pushed him away and took a step back. "You are less than human, Hanley. Do you know that? Walk away now, before I do something I regret." Joshua's knuckles turning to the colour of the snow.

"You're right, of course. Who would protect Beatrice and Grace if you're in prison? It is certainly something for us both to think about." Hanley sniggered, turned his back, and began walking off down the wooden boulevard.

"Stay away from us, and from my daughter!" Joshua yelled, but there was no response.

J oshua picked up the crystallised snow and formed them into some sort of ball before lobbing them into the dark sea. He repeated the motion until his hands became numb. Manic thoughts chased through his head one after the other, creating a cloud of dust in his vision, blocking his sight ahead. He needed a distraction to ease the pain, if only for a while.

Joshua stormed into the office and startled the nearby staff. "George!"

"Yes, sir?" George ran down the stairs, taking two at a time.

"There aren't any more shipments or urgent matters to attend to today, are there?" Joshua snapped.

"No s- Joshua."

He saw the fear on George's face and took a deep breath. "Then grab your coat; where does a man go for a drink around here?"

"Is... everything alright?" George looked concerned, hesitating at the foot of the stair.

"Yes, yes, I... I just need a drink, that's all." The junior clerk studied Joshua's face for a moment, then said cautiously. "Between you and me, I've never liked that Captain Hanley fellow. Always put me on edge."

Joshua smiled. George was a simple man, but undeniably kind-hearted, honest, and easy to talk to. Exactly the friend he needed.

"Where to, George?" Joshua let out a little chuckle at his confused friend as he grabbed his coat off the stand.

"Not far. There's a little place called the Boardroom. Cheap food, but decent ale."

Joshua smiled at a cowering clerk hiding in a nearby doorway. "Lead the way." He flung his arm out for George to go first and felt lighter already.

The small tavern took up the basement of a tenement building, with only one window that lead out to the arched walk way above, and which barely let in any light. Ancient wine bottles acted as the candlesticks, dotted across the room in tiny nooks and on the assortment of battered tables. The stale smell of unwashed men and women, along with tobacco, vinegar and hops, was embedded into every inch of the interior. Joshua followed George into the back rooms, who pointed to a small square table in the corner, and two chairs, which looked like they might crumble into their individual components at a single touch. Joshua sat down carefully and smiled at George; he had never imagined the young man would bring him to a place like this.

Joshua leaned on the table, his sleeve sticking to the remains of what looked like a supper left behind by the previous customer. He wiped his sleeve on the edge of the table and leaned back again, trying hard to hide his disgust.

"How... did you find this place?"

George laughed a little. "I can take you to more gentile quarters if you wish?"

"No, no, this is fine; a perfect place to forget my troubles. Do you, er, come here often?"

"I live a few streets over, so I come in now and again, on the way home from work."

"Hello Georgie. You're early tonight, d'you want your usual? Who's your friend?" The serving-woman who had appeared from nowhere gazed down at Joshua and winked at him. Her face was pretty but tired, with dark circles under her eyes. Her dress more grey than blue under all the filth, with a few top buttons conveniently undone to give the customers a suggestion of temptation, encourage them to leave better tips. She pulled out a stained rag from her leather belt, bent over the table and gave it a quick wipe, her cloth sticking at the same point as had Joshua's sleeve. She smiled over at George and then back at Joshua.

"Yes, thanks Claire. This is Mr Joshua Mason, he's a manager down at the docks, and he'll have the same as me."

"Nice to meet you, Joshua. I'm Claire - and I'll be right back."

"Thank you, Miss." Joshua tipped his head to her and returned the smile. She walked back through the adjoining room and slapped another serving woman, younger than her, on the shoulder for getting too familiar with a labourer.

Joshua raised his eyebrows. "She seems nice."

"Claire? Oh yes, she is – she practically runs this place and monitors the newbie staff. She has a sound mind, and we often talk."

"Does Beth know?"

"Oh... No. Not... that's not the way of it. We are friends. Claire doesn't go in for anything more than a flirtation with the customers; there really is nothing to tell Beth." Even in the dim candlelight, Joshua could tell George was blushing.

"Do you have true intentions for her? Beth, I mean?"

"Yes... I suppose there's no use hiding it from you. I think she's an angel. She's kind, beautiful, and I can talk to her – about anything. She is so unlike the women I was brought up with..."

Joshua laughed. "Yes, the Lightfoot women do have that effect!"

"If you don't mind me asking, then... how did you meet Mrs Mason?"

"Fate really. It was a chance meeting, on the old harbour road back in England... She appeared like some sort of sprite creature, always when I least expected it... You know their background - Bea and Beth - what their father does?"

"Yes, Beth has told me, with pride, may I add. He sounds like a strong character."

At that moment Claire entered through the low open doorway with two plates filled with grey-ish looking boiled meat and potatoes, and a pair of two-pronged forks. She placed them on the table and left, smiling without saying a word. Joshua stared at the plate before him, suddenly not hungry. George read his thoughts.

"Simple food actually doesn't taste that bad - it soaks up the ale, at any rate."

Joshua watched George take a bite and followed his lead, trying hard not to judge. He was right; it didn't really taste that bad. "Sorry, you were saying...?"

Claire entered again with two tankards of ale and placed them in front of the men. "Enjoy!"

"Thank you," Joshua toasted her, taking a gulp of the ale. It had been a while since he had proper ale. The sweet, malted tang of the hops trickled down his throat. It took him straight back to his usual spot outside Ulverston, filled with workers just like these. He had forgotten that part of himself. "Bea and I met early one morning at the harbour, nothing like here. It's crumbled into the channel now." Joshua paused for a moment, thinking how to phase the next part. "You know about the English class structure?"

George nodded. "We have our own form of it here."

"Well, back in Ulverston, the Mason family, my family, are gentile, having money and property, though they have been business-owners for over a few generations, as well as seated landowners, whereas the Lightfoots... they are a family of working class... if not lower. And yet... I hold Robert Lightfoot, their father, in the highest regard. Higher than that of my father, by far." Joshua took another gulp of ale and pushed away his plate. "George... can I confide in you? Under the strictest of confidences?"

"Of course. We are friends now, are we not?"

Joshua took a moment, gazing down into his tankard, and then it all came spilling out, like a sinner at the confession box. He told George about Bea, and about Hanley. How he himself had fallen in love with Bea, but against his better judgement walked away from her, putting his family first, and had thus left her to the bitter mercies of a drunken Captain Hanley and one terrible night, now almost two years ago. He took another couple of gulps, and described his duel with Hanley, after she had confessed to him about the rape, and how he had left him for dead in a clearing not long before the trial, and their escape to America.

"He killed a man...? In front of her? And after you fought... how is he still standing?"

"He framed Bea for the murder," Joshua continued in a hushed tone. "They tried her at Lancaster Castle and found her guilty. He had people vouching for him, and of course, Bea's word held little sway with the jury."

"Then how is she...?"

"Because Bob Lightfoot is a clever man. He sabotaged the hangman's rope, though even he didn't know if it would work."

"The rope? That is a stroke of brilliance!"

"They deemed the rope failing an act of God, and we slipped Bea away to safety after they released her, under cover of the reformers' protest, also orchestrated partly by Bob." Joshua smiled wearily.

"So, you fled here for a new start, and... now he has found you." Joshua nodded as he finished the second tankard and tapped out a cigarette.

"Yes - he showed himself at the Christening."

"That makes sense now, why Bea – God bless her soul – suddenly turned into a ghost. What hell she must go through."

Joshua saw the sympathy pain on George's face for Bea and himself. "She is... a shell again."

"I- does that mean, Grace..."

"Is his, yes from the attack." Joshua lowered his eyes and stared at the bubbles at the bottom of the tankard.

"You are a good man, Joshua, to take on so much. You love her dearly, though. I have seen that. I have always thought you were a better man than I; now I know it."

His eyes darted back up and leaned across the stable. "Hardly. I have shot him, I have stabbed him, and I failed to finish the job at either event. Worst of all, I left Bea vulnerable to his attentions when I should have been the first to protect her. I believed I was a good man until all this, now I'm... not so sure." He leaned back against the chair and wished there was another gulp of ale.

George lowered his voice, and it was his time to lean across the table. "Surely you must see, if you had killed him, you might have been caught and hung beside Bea, and then who would have saved you? Every choice you have made sets store by your character and speaks of your courage and conviction. You have both wife and daughter now, while Hanley has nothing - and they need you."

"She is a part of me. I love her completely, but sometimes..."

"It can be too much?"

"I sometimes wonder what my life would have been if I had never met her."

"You wouldn't be sitting in front of me now, that is for sure." George let out a small chuckle.

"No... they would most likely have had me married to Lady Dawn Richmond, and both of us living at my family home, with my father running the family businesses, and our children riding ponies about the lawn."

"But would you have been happy in that life? Were you happy before Bea, truly happy?"

Claire came back through with two more tankards, and Joshua finally reached the hazed, numbing sensation he had been searching for.

He waited for her to leave again. "No. I don't think I was, not that I knew it myself. And I know I wouldn't have been happy with Dawn."

"I have seen how happy you can be here. You need to keep on fighting for your family and Grace is more your child than she could ever be his, without a doubt. I have seen you both together. She loves being in your arms."

"You are right, George, but how do I keep fighting?"

"Patience, unfortunately, wait and see what circumstances demands of you."

"Thank you, George; for your counsel, and for not judging us. You are a good friend."

"I am no one to judge." George shifted his gaze away from Joshua and picked at a crumb wedged between a slit in the table. "In fact, I admire you and Bea, to stay true to one another after all you have overcome together."

"It... does not taint Beth for you? I know how much you like her."

"I love her, if it's possible even more than before, to have gone through so much, and still be so kind-hearted. I prize her, and I respect her integrity - and that of Mrs Mason, too. And yet..."

"What?"

"You know fine well that I cannot provide for her at the level you can at present,- not on my wage. My father, well... I want to prove I can accomplish something on my own."

"I thought you wanted to return to your father's business after gaining experience with Goldstein?"

George refused to look at Joshua. "Right now I am enjoying my current work with you."

"Then I had better see what I can do to help, when the time comes." Joshua took another gulp and finished his ale. "I had better make my way home before Bea worries." He pulled out his gold pocket watch and the word honour caught his attention. The hour was already late.

"I will see you home."

"Thank you, my friend," Joshua laughed as he stumbled freely from the chair. "I should have eaten that supper after all."

Chapter 25

"Bea, will you not come with me? Run some errands, get some fresh air? Please, dearest, you haven't left the house for a month – I'm worried about you. It will do Grace so much good to get out." Beth bounced the infant in her arms and stared over at Bea doubled over her lace tool, fixed on a knot.

"Not today, maybe tomorrow." She muttered.

"I understand you might be scared, but..."

She dropped the bobbins and suddenly spun on the spot. "He is out there, Beth. The man who gave me this," and pointed to her neck, yanking the lace down and followed the line of the rope. "I was a fool to think I could escape him; he is here to finish what he started." She glared, her hand falling to her knees.

"He can't touch you, not here. You've done nothing wrong, Bea."

"But I have. This is all my fault, all of it, if I hadn't..." her voice trailed off.

"What about Joshua? We are worried about you."

"I'm the one who lived it," Bea muttered, turning back round and picking up the bobbins.

"What was that? Bea?"

"Please, leave me alone for a while, I need to focus." All she wanted to do was close her mind off to the trance of the rhythmic motion.

"Can I at least take Grace with me?"

"No!" Bea jumped up off the floor, knocking the tool over.

"No, she cannot leave my side, she is mine." Panic sketched across her face.

Hearing the raised voices, Sarah made her way up the stairs and entered the room.

"I'll take her, Beth; you leave them with me; you take yourself off now, for peace and air." She whispered, as Bea making sure her daughter wasn't leaving the house, picked her tool up and continued knotting together the delicate threads.

Beth nodded and handed over a worried-looking Grace gratefully. She gathered up her purse and bonnet, and with a last look of anxiety and betrayal toward Bea, she left.

Sarah crouched down onto the rug, cradling Grace, and gazed down at the hands weaving in and out, followed by a calculated knot. Bea looked exhausted and had barely touched her food.

"What are you makin' there?" Sarah tilted forward, gazing over Bea's shoulder whilst Grace reached her hand out for a grab at the dangling wooden bobbins.

"I need a replacement." Bea replied in a blank tone, gesturing towards the piece of lace wrapped around her wrist, hiding the scratches along the scar. It had become frazzled at the edges with all the pulling and twisting.

"I see." Sarah moved back and placed her hand on Bea's shoulder, tapping her fingers. "Well, me and this little one are going to make us all somethin' delicious for dinner - roastin' chicken, I know how much you like it. – Come down when you're ready."

"Thank you." Bea breathed, not taking her focus off the blossoming rose.

∞∞∞∞

That night, she was back in the cell, but her jailer was not the man she knew; instead, she saw Hanley's face leering down at her in the dark, ridiculing her with scraps of food, teasing her, pulling her hair, threatening he could do more. But this time, there was no visit from her Da, no word from Joshua - and then it was time to face the noose once more. The harsh daylight blinded her as the gulls screamed overhead as she let out a heart-shattering scream, and fought the air, clawing for freedom.

"Bea! Bea, it is Joshua! You are safe, you are home - in your own bed - it was just a dream."

Bea could feel hands and arms around her, and the sound of crying. She peeled her eyes open, but her tears were silent; instead, it was Grace screaming in distress in the cot, frightened by what she had just witnessed.

"It was just a dream," Joshua repeated softly.

"N-no! It - it was real, it was not a dream." Hearing the pain in Bea's voice, Joshua pulled her in close until she relaxed. "Grace," Bea whispered in a broken tone.

Joshua let her go and picked Grace up from out the cot and placed her on the bed. She was still crying, but more softly now, comforted by the nearness of her mama.

"I am sorry my darling; I am so very sorry." Tears dripped on to Grace's wispy hair.

"What can I do?" asked Joshua quietly.

"I don't know what anyone can do, I don't know how to stop feeling so scared, and powerless."

"You're not powerless, my love. He cannot touch you again. You are safe here. He won't lay hands on you again, not now. This is our home, our family."

"I know, you are right, thank you." Grace had fallen asleep between them. "I'll put her back in the cot." Bea scooped her up and whispered. "Forgive me, my darling," and kissed her on the forehead before laying her down.

Joshua reached out and pulled Bea back into his fold. She listened to his steady heartbeat as it lulled her back into a deep sleep, anchoring to his body.

∞∞∞

"Morning Sarah," Joshua strolled into the kitchen and poured himself a coffee into the waiting cup.

"Did I hear Bea again last night?" She slid the eggs out of the pan and onto the plate next to the slice of gammon.

"Yes, third night in a row." He took a mouthful of eggs and couldn't help but smile.

"And all day, she was working on that piece of lace. Have you seen her wrist? I'm goin' to make up some balm for her, that might help."

"Thank you, Sarah, I know she'll be in excellent hands, with you both." Joshua glanced back at Beth as she ambled into the kitchen half asleep. "I better be off, busy day." He rushed down one last mouthful of gammon, followed by a mouthful of coffee. Then darted up the kitchen stairs.

"I worry about him," said Beth. "He is carrying a lot on his shoulders. They both are... blaming themselves, when there is only one person to blame here." She poured herself some coffee and sat at the table. Sarah nodded. Finished plating up the breakfast and slid one in front of Beth, who had her eyes closed, inhaling the caffeinated steam.

Bea was sitting up in bed, playing with Grace as Sarah strode into the room.

"I thought you might like some breakfast," she noticed Bea unconsciously scrunch her face at the idea of food. "And Grace can pick at the eggs as usual," Sarah added. She placed the plate down on the wooden tray, balancing on the bedcovers. Straightaway, Grace's little hand grabbed a handful of scrambled egg and spilling half of them before they reached her mouth. "I heard you again last night. How you feeling this mornin'?"

Bea sighed. "I keep reliving it again, now that he's back... He didn't just attack me." Bea pointed to the scar across her neck, which was barely visible now. "I haven't told you everything."

"And you don't have to." Sarah gazed at her whilst lightly rubbing her shoulder.

"But I want to. Beth knows most of it, and it might help me talk about things, finally to someone who really knows me."

"If you think it will help." Sarah sat beside them both, Grace still distracted by eggs.

Bea paused for a moment, trying to decide where to start. "Were you... I mean, did you see the man at church, at the christening, the one who..."

"No, not from where I was sittin'. I couldn't get a clear sight o' him - and then he must 'ave left."

"His name is Captain Victor Hanley, he who caused my entire world, mine and my family's, to come crashing down."

Sarah tried hard to keep her face blank, but she felt a wave of cold shock hit through her chest, realising for the first time that the man Bea was describing was the same monster she herself knew, one of the many faces that reappeared time and time again in her nightmares.

Bea started at the beginning this time, leaving nothing out. There was no point in hiding it anymore.

Sarah listened in silence. A rope-maker's daughter...? Pieces of her companion's puzzle finally slotted into place.

"What I didn't tell you, when Hanley attacked me, was that there was someone else with him." Sarah silently placed her hand on top of Bea's as she held Grace. Bea lent down her neck and kissed the sleeping baby, her face wet with tears. "It wasn't enough for him to beat me, and rape me, for the other man then tried to... do the same. I tried to fight him off. I got a couple of blows in. But he kept telling me how he was going to kill me afterwards when suddenly... Hanley stabbed him – twice - in the chest." Sarah looked at her with pained eyes.

"There was so much blood, it soaked into my clothes, and he just fell on top of me. I couldn't move, I couldn't breathe with his dead weight pressing down on me, and I was in too much shock to fight it. Hanley stood there, smiling at me, and told me he couldn't let me get away with what I had done to him." Bea explained how she had been found with the dead body hours later; about the planting of her father's knife; the inquest; crossing the sands and the sickening weeks of mindless dark in the county prison, waiting for the end.

"He had every detail planned; the men of the jury only saw one thing, a guilty woman, and they sentenced me to hang."

"How? How then are you here now?"

"I don't know how they did it, but whilst I was in that cell counting down the hours until that fateful day, Joshua and my Da came up with a plan. There is a law in England, it still holds today, that a person cannot be hung twice; that if the rope shall break, or they survive the execution, then that is deemed an act of God, and they may be set free." Bea continued on, explaining the reformers' involvement through her Da, and Sarah suddenly remembered the comment Bea had made in the meeting house to Grace about her granda helping to bring the abolition laws into force. Rebellion was in her blood; she was a fighter, just like Sarah.

"Joshua told me he had stabbed Hanley in a duel, that we might be free of him for good, and I believed him. We left for Boston not long after our marriage, and then onboard ship I found out I was carrying Grace. It has taken so much strength to build myself up after giving birth to this little one... I don't know if I can do it again. What does he want from me, Sarah? He believes he owns me... I'm scared."

"You'll never stop runnin' – but you are stronger than you think, and the runnin' will turn to walkin', walkin' forward someday. You ha' gone through so much, and sometimes you need to feel the bad, down in your belly, so you can get up, and fight for the good times again - for this little one - she needs you, she needs her Mama."

Bea took a deep breath and let it out in a sigh. "Thank you... for your kind words and listening. You are right, and yet... it's hard. How shameful all this must seem to you..."

"We all have history, none of us are clean from sin or from shame. I am here whenever you need to talk – the ghosts from our past have a habit of hauntin' our dreams and enterin' back into our lives - but we must cast them out. They hold no power over us unless we let them." Bea nodded slowly and gazed down at Grace, now sound asleep. "In the meantime, my sister, you need to build up your strength - startin' with a bath, and some good home cookin'."

"Thank you." Bea looked like she was about to cry again. "You have been a good friend; I hope, one day, I can do as much for you as you do for me..." She smiled.

"You have, more than you know. Now, I'll bring the boiling water up for the bath and get it ready for you."

"I'll help." Bea gave Sarah a reassuringly stern look before she could argue and slid her arms out carefully from under Grace.

Sarah was right. A bath was exactly what she had needed. The steaming water, infused with a few drops of lavender oil, had eased her muscles and her mind. She dressed herself in a light chemise and her dressing gown, and joined the now wide-awake Grace, along with Sarah and Beth, downstairs in the kitchen. The hot food smelt good; she had made another roast chicken with garlic and herbs, and a side of crushed potatoes and carrots. They all sat around the table, and for a moment it reminded her of her parents' home. Grace sat proudly in a tall wooden highchair and picked at her dissected morsels, exploring her newly found taste-buds whilst Beth sliced some meat for Bea.

"You look much better Bea, I'm glad to see you," said Beth gently, as she placed the chicken on her sister's plate.

"Thank you. I am sorry, about... about before." Bea slid her hand across the table for Beth's and received a light squeeze. "And I am building my strength up, bit by bit." She smiled first at Sarah, then at Beth.

"There is no need to apologise - it will take time, but I'm glad to see you have taken the first steps."

She glanced again at the clock on the mantelpiece; it was later than she thought, and Joshua was still not home. Lying in the bathtub, she relished in the love and support he had given her, night after night. And yet, she had forgotten to acknowledge his own pain. If they were going to fight against any plan, their monster might enact, then they would only be stronger together.

Chapter 26

June 1819, the South.

"You need to move now." Franklin grabbed at the hessian sack and pulled it off a sleeping Sarah. "They are coming and this time with dogs." The words startled her awake, for fear that they were already here. "You need to wade into the river. It would take too long to go via the bridge and the dogs can't track you in water." He saw the horror in her face as she stared at the river once more. It was happening all over again.

"I will distract them, and it ain't too deep. We haven't had rain for a month. – if you stick with me, they will find us and kill us both. - two miles east you'll find the blacksmith on the outskirts of a town. If you keep east, they won't think to look there, hopefully they will head north. – Go - now."

Sarah climbed off the wagon, clinging on tight to her cloth bag. "Thank you, Franklin, for your kindness."

"God bless you on your journey." He turned and made his way back toward the wagon.

Sarah gazed at the river. *Freedom or die trying.* She held her bag above her head and climbed down to the bank. The current was strong. She clamped her lips shut, sealing in the involuntary sound of shock as the cold water splashed against her legs. The wind carried the sound of the horses and dogs getting closer. She ain't going back there, and if they found her, they would lynch her for all to see. A second time runner that failed again hanging from the tree would be a good inducement against anyone else trying the same act. No, there was nothing else to it. She needed to keep running. Her feet touched the bottom of the riverbed as the waves lapped around her chest. It was hard to keep her feet planted to the bottom as it tried to carry her downstream. As she approached the centre, the dirty water surged into her mouth, making her cough. Her legs kicked out against the rocks below, creating enough momentum to propel her forward and gain footing again. She scrambled up the far riverbank; the water causing the dry mud to become sticky and cling to her shoes and hands. Bent over, the last of the river water spurted out of her lungs as the night air shocked her chest, causing her to cough continuously. Her sodden clothes clung to her shivering body. She needed to keep moving. She looked back across the river. But Franklin had already gone, disappeared into the night. The sounds of dogs barking had got louder. Quickly, she held her cloth bag against her chest and ran into the hedgerow, pushing through until she reached the fields of wheat. Branches, thorns, stinging weeds scratched and scraped against her skin. She crouched down low and listened. She waited until the sound of horses, men shouting, and dogs barking came and went. She kept low, shuffling through the tall stems. For the first time in her life, she was glad God had made her small. She reached the nearby woods and paused for a moment, grabbing a handful of nuts. The North star stayed by her left shoulder as she headed east.

Sarah came to a small clearing in the woods with a single large tree in the centre with low swinging branches, but as she got closer, not all of them were branches. Black men and women swung in the light breeze, highlighted by the moonlight. The bodies hung like strange fruit on a tree. A stark reminder of what she was running from. They had been there for days, some weeks. As she got closer, the smell was overwhelming and the sight unbearable. Animals and birds had clearly been picking at the fruit. Her brothers and sisters from a distance family punished for nothing more than the colour of their skin.

Freedom. Once she was past the tree, she sent out a silent prayer and kept moving.

Franklin had said it was only a few miles until the Blacksmith, but it felt longer. She gazed up at the stars, but a scattering of cloud made it difficult to see. She kept walking straight through fields and woodlands. Her mind second guessing if she was going the right way. Sarah's exhausted body ached and her feet felt raw against the worn leather. She investigated her cloth bag; a piece of cheese was all that was left. After two bites, she placed it back in the bag, just in case, and kept moving. Large fencing sprang up, which signalled another plantation. She followed it around the edges, keeping in the tree line, ready to hide at the first sight of anyone, white or black. The clouds were getting thicker, blocking out the moonlight, making each step more difficult than the last to see. Tripping over the overgrown tree roots. Her failing body longed for sleep once more, but she couldn't risk it. She had to make it to the blacksmith by dawn. The trees gave way to fields laden with cotton and guessed she was on the outskirts of the plantation now. In the distance, men's voices got louder. They sounded like they were discussing, arguing about something, but they didn't sound like they were on a hunt. Sarah kept low, scurrying through the rows. The cotton was shorter than the wheat had been and made it harder to hide. Maybe that's why the masters liked it so much. The cotton soon gave way to a grass meadow. With the last fragments of strength, she ran until her legs collapsed. She veered right a little, aiming for another patch of woodlands. The scent in the air changed to an herbal flower smell. The heat was rising, which meant dawn was coming. She cursed herself for not knowing where she was going, for wandering in the dark with no clear path in front of her. How foolish she had been, thinking that she could run and be free. All she knew, she could have been walking in circles this whole time. There was nothing to it but to keep moving forward and hope fate was on her side.

Light on the horizon broke through the trees and highlighted a cluster of large wooden and brick buildings, with smoke billowing out of one of them. She approached with caution, keeping in the tree line. The place was quiet, except for a few men moving in and out of the buildings. Was this the place she had been looking for, if she were wrong, it would seal her fate. She jumped from one tree to another, attempting to get a better angle. A sharp banging noise came from the brick building that produced the smoke. At her first plantation, there had been a makeshift blacksmith run by a slave. It was cheaper to get them to repair the horseshoes and fences than to ask a white man and his price. This building seemed similar to that one, enough to take a chance, and if she didn't act fast, the sun would take away her ability to hide.

She took a quick glance around her. When there was no sign of anybody about, she ran to the building. She tried to stay as flat as possible against the wall, hugging it as she shuffled around the edges to the opening. A smell of burning wood and coal became stronger as the banging noise grew louder. *This had to be the spot.* The other wooden buildings were barns or stables, housing a few horses or carts to fix. The front of the brick building had two wooden stable doors facing into a makeshift courtyard. She peered into the space; nobody was about the courtyard. She shuffled along the front and stared through the open gap between the panelled doors. A man had his back towards the door, poking a bar of metal into the large pit of fire before pulling it out and whacking it with a mental hammer. She steadied herself for a moment and before she could change her mind, took a step into the building. The noise masked her footsteps. The man unaware of his new audience. She took another step forward and waited until he finished monitoring the door at all times.

"Excuse me sir, my name…"

He jumped at the sound of her voice and swung round with the metal bar and hammer still in his hands. "Child, you gave me a fright." He starred at her, the whole of her. She couldn't tell if he was white or black. It covered him in that much dirt and soot. "Sarah, is it? I expected you hours ago – where is Franklin?"

"Yes, it is sir, - Mr Franklin had to leave me by the river. I made the rest of the way by myself."

"That must have been hard, but you're here now."

"Yes, sir."

"No more sir, my name is Jeb – follow me – I'll hide you until dark and then take you to the next station. I don't get many doing this journey alone, family?"

"Only me, the rest are gone." He gave her a look as if he understood.

Jeb took her into one of the nearby barns. "It ain't much, but it comfortable." It looked like he was taking her to a dead end, at the back of the barn, until he pulled two hay bales away from the back wall and revealed a small door cut into the wooden panels. He pushed it open and climbed through first, Sarah followed in behind.

It was about six-foot-wide and spread the width of the barn. It could house ten or more slaves. But today she was alone. There was hay and a few scattered blankets on the ground with another cloth parcel.

"I have put some bread, meat, and fruit in there for you and a jug of water. Rest, eat, and I will collect you once it is time. No one else knows you are here except me. Do not make a sound. If you need the toilet, there is a clean bucket in the corner."

"Thank you – Jeb."

"Push the door shut behind me and lock it with the clasp, I'll place the bales back on my side."

Sarah nodded. There was no escape.

For the rest of the day she kept quiet, listening to the daily activities of the forge whilst nibbling at the food left behind. She wasn't hungry, but then again, when would she have the chance to eat once she left here. Only God knew the next step in her journey. Sarah laid down on a blanket. It had a musty, sooty smell. Weirdly, it reminded her of Hercules standing next to the fire pits. She used that one like a pillow and grabbed another as a blanket. Taking a deep breath, she breathed him in, imagining his arms wrapped around her whilst she held their child. For the first time in a while, they were with her, travelling alongside of her to freedom. She closed her eyes, every inch of her becoming heavy with exhaustion, filling her dreams with fragments of her old life.

A light tapping at the door woke her.

"Sarah – its Jeb, we need to go."

She grabbed the last of the food and placed it into her cloth bag, brushed the straw from her dress, and undid the clasp at the door. A dragging sound on the other side meant she could push the door open on her side. What if it was all a trick? She had to trust him. What else could she do.

Dusk was descending, ridding them of the last of the light and casting them in twilight. Jeb stood there, watching Sarah climb out of the hole. She noticed he was a little cleaner than this morning, dressed in more respectable clothes, and yet his skin was dark. Not as dark as hers, but not white either.

"I have a cart outside, follow me."

Sarah nodded and did as he commanded.

There were two horses attached to an open-air wooden cart, full of pieces of metal; how was she meant to hide amongst all that without a blanket in sight? Jeb strode up to the side of the cart and let down a side panel. There were two bottoms to the cart, one holding the metal in place and another smaller, cramped space designed for her to climb in between. There was barely enough space for her tiny body. What if she had been a big man, how was he meant to fit in there?

"It will be tight, but it's safe – hurray, climb in."

Again, she said nothing, but moved forward. She handed him her cloth bag filled with her only processions and awkwardly slid her body into the gap. The pitch-black space was hot, and she barely had enough room in front of her face. He handed back the cloth bag, laying it beside her before closing the side panel.

"Wait, where are you taking me?"

His hands held on to the side. "To the coast, there are too many checkpoints north now."

"A boat, I can't get into a boat."

He lifted the panel once more. "We don't have time now, we need to go." he paused, leaving a gap. "If you want freedom, this is the path in front of you. – you have come this far alone; you are stronger than you think."

Darkness.

Chapter 27

Beacon Hill, March 1833

B ea glided the knife across the skin of the carrot, peeling off the dirt and the first layer. Sarah, next to her, mirrored her actions with the potatoes before dicing them into large chunks.

"It is such a dismal day out there; some of my Gran's stew is just what we need. I still can't believe you could get decent beef at the butchers." Bea threw in the diced carrots into the pot bubbling away on the stove.

"You can get it if you have the money to pay for it." Sarah gave Bea a knowing look before scoping her potatoes off the chopping block into the pot.

"Even when we had money, sometimes the butchers in Ulverston still didn't have it. Or maybe it was me? Do you think they would have rabbit? Then, it would be my Gran's stew."

"Rabbit?"

Bea chuckled at the look Sarah gave her. A knock on the back door interrupted, "My Da...".

Sarah opened the door to the small runner boy she uses occasionally.

"Miss Sarah, I have a note for you." Sarah stared at the handwriting on the paper. "That smells good." The boy commented as he walked closer to the stove.

"If you come back in a couple of hours, Sam, you can have a bowl if you like?" Bea could hear the crack of wax and the unfolding of paper as she reached for a plate on the kitchen table.

"In the meantime, would you like a biscuit?"

"Cheers, Mrs Mason." Sam took one for his hand and two for his pocket.

"Sam, tell him I'm on my way." Sarah placed a dime in his hand, "go quick." He nodded his head as if reading her mind and bolted out the back door.

Sarah took her apron off and walked over to the stairs.

"What's wrong?" Bea called out.

"Nothing, Mr Winston needs help with a matter."

"Sarah, I know when you're withholding from me. Let me help if I can be of use." Sarah paused on the first step. "Please, Sarah."

"Bea, you haven't been out of the house in months, and it is too risky. I thank you for the offer, but please stay here with Beth and Grace." Sarah turned back around and headed up the stairs with Bea following her.

"Why is it risky? What's wrong?"

"It is an urgent matter for the meeting house Mr Winston needs help with. Bea, I don't have..." Sarah placed on her cloak.

"I'm coming with you. I want to help."

"Bea..."

"Why take me to the meetings if not to help?" She grabbed her cloak from the hook as Sarah opened the hallway cupboard and took out a large bag. "Let me tell Beth we are leaving."

Sarah nodded her head, knowing she would not win this battle. In a matter of seconds, Bea was back downstairs and followed Sarah out the front door to a waiting carriage.

Bea remained silent on the ride, watching them pass the unfamiliar houses as the carriage headed down the south slope. The children played in the narrow streets, running alongside certain carriages. They were all skin and bone, with their dirty rags hanging off their slim frames. It brought her back to the scene she had witnessed in Ulverston, when Joshua came to her aid as she helped poor David to his feet. It had only been a few years. But how readily she had forgotten. That even across a vast ocean, people, living conditions, hunger, never changes. Even in Boston, on Beacon Hill, they force families to work night and day with little to show in their pockets and no food on the table. A surge of guilt hit her that she was now in this comfortable position, able to afford fine pieces of meat from the butchers when there were others starving. What would her Da say or do?

The streets gave way to the harbour. A scene she had not seen since she first arrived. She glanced around for a sighting of Joshua. What would he say if he saw them now? Without realising it, she leant back, away from the carriage window. The harbour was loud from men shouting to one another as they removed crates from the ships. Horse's hooves clicking against the cobles as carts slipped past, and the overwhelming smell of manure mixed in with salt and burning wood filtered in through the window.

"Bea, when we get out – what you will see might shock you at first, stay close and I will tell you what needs doing."

Bea spun the lace around her wrist and nodded. "Don't worry about me. Just tell me how I can help."

The carriage stopped in front of a warehouse. The door opened and Mr Winston greeted them.

"Sarah, thank you for coming – Mrs Mason?"

"She wanted to help."

He gave Sarah a disapproval look before continuing. "Martha is inside waiting for you."

"Is it bad?"

"They lost one on the journey." Mr Winston said in a disappointed tone. He opened the door to a vast, dark room filled with large wooden shipping crates as he held a lantern out in front of him, lighting the path. Bea felt her heart beating fast in her throat as past images flashed into her mind. She felt her hand being grabbed as Sarah glanced back at her. Slowing her breathing down once more. Mr Winston placed the lantern on a crate as he moved it to one side, revealing a hidden door. He picked the lantern back up and signalled for them to follow him. Bea's eyes adjusted to the warm light which filled the secret room and couldn't believe what she saw.

In front of her were five metal framed beds. Men, women and a single child occupied three of them. One man looked injured, whilst they lay the other man on a table with a woman bent over him.

"Martha, Sarah has arrived." Mr Winston announced.

"Sarah, did you bring your bag? Good, I need more cloth." The woman glanced back as Sarah instantly made her way over to the bent over woman.

"Miss Fisher?" Bea remarked, struggling to comprehend.

"Mrs Mason?" Said Martha, mirroring the same tone.

"She came to help." Added Sarah.

"Then come here, I need you to hold this." The command shook Bea out of her daze. She took off her cloak and stood next to Miss Fisher and placed her hand on top of the blood-soaked cloth and pressed down on the man's thigh. "Firmly and when I tell you, I want you to lift off the cloth whilst I replace it with another." Bea nodded. It was a strange sensation as the warm, red liquid pooled over her fingers and stained her hands. She gazed at the unconscious man. His black skin had a tinge of grey and yellow to it and looked like he had already crossed the veil. Without warning, a flash of Mr Gregson's face and his eyes, void of life, crashed into her head as the smell of blood filled her senses. "Now." Martha's stern voice brought her back to the present. Bea lifted the heavy rags off the gaping hole and dropped them to the floor. "Press down again." Bea watched as the blood seeped into the cream rags, creating shapes before it consumed it completely. "Keep your hands there. I need the bleeding to slow down before I can sow the wound shut."

"Yes." She couldn't think of anything else to say. She watched

Miss Fisher make her way to the other wounded man. Standing side by side of Sarah as they worked together on the man's shoulder. What happened to these people? She noticed the Mother and child clinging on to one another, staring at Bea with a fearful, suspicious look. Then she realised she was the only white person in the room. For them, she represented what they had escaped from, who did this to these people. Bea shifted her gaze on to Mr Winston, who was talking to another man on the far side of the room. He had his back towards her, and the other man held his head low. She couldn't see his face, but could tell they were deep in conversation. He planned all this; he was the one who helped these former slaves to freedom; but how?

Without noticing, Miss Fisher was standing next to her once more, lifting her hand. "Good, the bleeding is slowing down. Pass me a needle and thread."

Bea took her hand off Miss Fishers and made her way to a small table where everything was laid out. There was a bobbin of blue cotton thread, a knife, and a small, dented metal tin with a few scattered needles in it alongside a stack of torn pieces of fabric. As Bea reached out for the thread, she noticed her hands covered in blood. Her heart raced as the same images flashed into her mind, but before they could take hold, she shook them free. Not now. She searched for a cloth to wipe them clean. "Now Mrs Mason." Without thinking, Bea wiped her hands across her dress and then grabbed hold of the thread, cut a yard off with the knife and picked up a needle.

"Good. Now I need you to stand at his head. He might stir or wake whilst I do this. You need to hold him down and try to calm his nerves. Can you do that?"

"Yes." Bea said firmly. She gently placed each hand on his shoulders and felt the muscles underneath contract at Miss Fisher's actions. Her face was calm, as if it were a sock she was mending. Bring together all the threads to create a single line. But the more she sowed, the more the man stirred.

Without warning, the man's eyes shot open with a look of

horror in them as he stared straight at Bea. "No." He yelled out and tried to move from her hold. A coat of sweat covered his skin as he cried out in pain.

"Please, you need to stay still. Miss Fisher is healing your leg." Bea whispered.

"Find something to bite on to, I'll take over." Mr Winston slid his hands over Bea's as she pulled hers out. "Calm, you are free, and we are fixing you."

Bea raced over to Sarah's bag and searched for a wooden peg, something.

"Here." Sarah put her hand in her pocket and pulled out a wooden peg before turning her attention to her man.

"Thank you." Bea grabbed the peg and raced back to man crying out in pain. "Bite down on this."

"Bite down." Mr Winston repeated. The man shifted his gaze and did as he commanded.

After they did all they could, Sarah and Miss Fisher packed the wounds with moss and herbs, as they had done on Bea, and then wrapped them with a clean cloth.

"The cart is outside waiting. It is dark enough to transport them to the boarding house."

"I will come with you. They need some tea for the swelling, and I'll stay to watch them through the night." Ordered Miss Fisher.

"Thank you, Sarah – and Mrs Mason, for your help this evening." Mr Winston hovered, reaching out his hand to shake. Sarah took it and removed her hand just as fast. Glancing up at his face and blushing at his smile.

"I'll come by in the morning and help, but we had better be going." Sarah turned and gathered her supplies back into her bag.

Mr Winston enclosed his hand around Bea's. "Thank you for

coming." Bea was void of words and replied with a smile. She carried Sarah's bag as she helped the wounded man back through the warehouse and on to the cart. The harbour was quiet now, with only a few men gathered around the fire pits darted along the wharf, waiting for their next shipment.

"You and Mrs Mason take the carriage back. I will ride with the cart."

"Thank you, Abe. I will be round at eight." He nodded his head and turned towards Bea.

"You're made of stronger stuff than I had imagined." And he smiled at her filthy, bloodstained dress.

"If I can help, please let me know." He replied with a tilt of his head.

In the shadows, Hanley watched as they loaded the black slaves into the cart, followed by Bea and then someone he hadn't expected to see. It had been fourteen years since Jessie had escaped. And even though she had aged, he knew it was her. But what was she doing standing next to Bea?

Chapter 28

The night before, Sarah hid their dresses in the wash house as they came up with excuses for their late outing. The meal had been served and finished. Beth and Grace were settled in their beds, whilst Joshua was in his study. The house was still and quiet. Bea tried to process what she had seen and her newfound regard towards the members of the meeting house. Was it the link she was looking for regarding the underground railroad?

Joshua had bought the explanation of her joining a new charity, helping the poor, which she fully intended to do today. Beth knew a charity connected to the school she volunteered at and gave her the address before she left for the day.

"Would you like me to come with you?" Said Sarah as she stacked the wooden blocks in a tower alongside Grace.

"No, but thank you. I think its best if I go alone." Bea smiled as she watched them play. "Yesterday, when we were in the carriage, for a moment I had forgotten what it was to be poor and what I had seen in Ulverston could be mirrored in any town. When I saw those children and the living conditions on the Southside – I realised I need to do more to give back, and I'm now in a position I can do that."

"Don't be so harsh on yourself and you are giving back what you did for those people last night and – being a mother. You needed time to heal. But it is good that you want to reach out. I think…" Sarah paused for a moment. "You need to tell Joshua the truth and that you are part of the meeting house. He will find out one day and it's best if it came from you. What are you worried about?"

Sarah was right, she needed to tell him. She felt awful lying to him this morning, but she also knew that he might put a stop to it and that couldn't happen.

A knock at the door cause them both to jump. "Are you expecting anyone?" Asked Sarah.

"No." Bea held her hand out to stop Sarah from rising. "I'll get it." She smoothed down her dress, double checked her pieces of lace covering up the scars, and saw her unruly auburn hair flying out of her bun in the mirror before opening the door. But she wasn't ready for what she saw. "Captain Hanley?"

He stood there in a gentleman suit, the same one she had seen at the christening. His skin still held a honey tone to it, although it had seen a winter in Boston. He was clean and respectable to anyone seeing him at the door, but his scent remained. Bea took a deep breath as images flashed into her mind. *Not now.*

"I thought it was about time we had a brief chat and for me to finally meet my daughter." He placed his worn leather boot across the doorway. There was no closing it now.

Bea instinctively backed away from the door and stood in front of Grace as he closed the door behind him.

"She's not your daughter, Captain Hanley. She is Joshua's child."

"We both know that not to be true." He gave her a suggested grin that brought an old pain to shoot through her body and catch in her throat. "I give him credit for taking on another man's child, but I am her father." Hanley pulled out his pipe and filled it from a pouch in his pocket. Behind Bea, Sarah picked Grace off the floor and held her tight. "You can't hide behind Beatrice, Jessie."

"Jessie? Her name is Sarah, and she is part of this family." Bea watched him as he walked into the sitting room, towards the fireplace.

"Would you mind?" He picked up a splinter of wood by the fire and lit it without waiting for a reply. A billow of smoke engulfed his face. "I think someone hasn't been telling the truth. Jessie here is my slave, my property, who ran off some fourteen years past, but she is still mine. Just like you are and so is the child." His tone was smooth, like silk. He exhaled another cloud before taking a seat in the armchair by the fire.

"She is not your child – she is mine; she is loved, she is innocent." Bea could feel herself getting pulled back into the dark pit. Using all her strength, she yanked herself back to the present. "None of us, belong to you. I think you had better leave." Bea reproached, stepping between them once more.

"That's the fire I love." He jumped to his feet like an excited child and stepped in front of her. "At the trial it had gone out, I would have thought you'd have fought harder, but you gave up." He reached out to touch her face. Bea battered it away and took a step back.

"What you did, broke me. Why? Why did you do it?" Her voice cracked. She reached her arms around her back, protecting them.

"Look what came of it, my sweet daughter." There was a laughter to his voice that brought a chill to the stuffy room.

"What do you want?"

"I want what is mine. You think what you have here is real, but it's all a delusion. The boy trying to rebuild what he lost because of you. Forcing you to play a role which isn't you. This society, his society. I have been watching and I know you're not happy, unless you're sneaking around behind his back. What would he say if he knew?"

"You can't tear us apart. You've already tried that, and it didn't work. Is that your plan?"

"I gave him this," gesturing to the house and placed his pipe on the mantlepiece. "And I can take it all away, unless…"

"Unless what?" The anger was exploding out of her as she

stared up at him, causing him to grin. Grace behind her began crying as Sarah gently bounced the little one in her arms. "I'm not yours. I never was. Neither is Sarah nor Grace. I think you are the delusional one here, Victor."

He leaned in further, his face floating above hers. She could see the lines under his eyes and whispered, "we shall see about that." Bea took a step back and glanced at Sarah, holding Grace with a fearful look on her face. "I will make you come to me. All of you." He said a little louder, pointing at each one.

"Leave!" Bea bellowed.

Hanley strode around Bea and tried to stroke Grace's cheek as Sarah pulled her away. "It's good to see you again, Jessie. What luck." He laughed as he pulled his hand back.

Bea moved towards the door and held it open for him. "Leave." She repeated with a more of a controlled voice.

He stopped in front of her, leaned in, and said. "You loved me first, you'll love me last."

"Goodbye, Captain Hanley."

"See you again soon, Mrs Mason." As soon as Hanley stepped over the threshold, Bea slammed the door shut.

Sarah turned pale and placed Grace back onto the rug. "How? Why?"

A nauseous sensation surged in her gut and knew she had brought this man back into her life.

"You know, Hanley? Was he..." Sarah quickly raced into the hallway and grabbed her cloak.

"Not now – I need to find Winston." Sarah turned back around and faced Bea. "Once Grace is down tonight, I will tell you all of it, my journey and the part that man played in it, but for now, I must find Winston." She turned, checked to see if Hanley had left, and dashed out the door.

Chapter 29

Joshua spent the morning going over his papers as George flitted in and out of the office, either bringing fresh cups of coffee or more papers for Joshua to go over. He tried to remove Hanley from his thoughts. Convincing himself that he couldn't do anything. None of them had done anything wrong and exposing their past would only expose Hanley to his? Today Joshua worked through lunch to clock off early to spend more time with the family.

"Mason, can I have a word?" Mr Goldstein barged through the office door, followed by George.

"Sorry, sir," George muffled, before Mr Goldstein slammed the door in his face.

Joshua jumped to his feet behind the desk, almost knocking his chair over. "What can I do for you today, Mr Goldstein, everything is running in order."

"I have no doubt, Mason; it is not your work capability that is in question here."

"Forgive me, sir, is something a miss?"

Mr Goldstein dismissed the notion to sit and remain fixed on the spot, glaring at Joshua. "I hate to be so blunt, but are you aware of what your wife is up to when you are at work?"

Joshua let out an involuntary laugh at the surprised question. "Caring for our child, I presume." he removed the smile off his face at the snarl on Mr Goldstein's. "Forgive me sir, but why do you ask what my wife, Mrs Mason, gets up to?"

"I have it on very good authority that Mrs Mason has been attending a meeting at the Negro house."

"At our servant's house?"

Anger gave way to disappointment. "No man, at the abolitionists meeting house – now it is not my place to concern myself with your wife's affair's but if she is in with that troublesome crowd then it needs to stop. What they are about could destroy a lot of livelihoods... including your own."

"I am not aware of her attending any meeting, sir, and do not know how she would learn of them. Who has been saying this?"

"A man that I trust, believes it to be so. – is her father not a reformer? I've heard about those English troublemakers and what they are trying to do. I hate to say, but bad blood will out."

There were only two men in Boston who knew about Mr Lightfoot, and he knew George wouldn't betray him. This is how Hanley was going to cause trouble. But it was a lie, it had to be. "Sir, that is my wife you are talking about."

"You are a good man, Mason, but I think you need to get your home in order. I cannot have a man working for me when he has a wife causing no end of trouble for my company. It makes me question where his loyalties lie."

Joshua held his hands up in front and lowered his voice. "It must be a mistake, sir; I am loyal to this business and what you are trying to build for the future of this company and this country." All this could cause the railroad position to disappear. "I will speak to my wife tonight and get this matter resolved."

"Make sure you do, Mason, for all our sakes. – this might be a free state for some, but we all know where the Negros belong in all this." The last part confirmed Joshua's fears and suspicions. He kept his head down and nodded, unable to agree with the last part. "Good, we will say no more about it for now." Mr Goldstein declared as he slammed his hand on the back of the wooden chair.

The owner briskly left the office and slammed the door behind him as Joshua slumped into his chair. After a couple of minutes, George peered his head around the corner of the door.

"I thought you might need this." he held out a glass holding a large measure of whiskey. "I have a small bottle hidden for occasions such as this."

Joshua tapped a cigarette out on his silver case and lit it. After taking a deep inhale, took the glass and swallowed the drink in one. It was American whiskey, not as smooth as the Scottish variety he was used to, but it did the job.

"I need to get home and speak to Bea." Joshua stood from his chair and finished the cigarette in his hand.

"Do you think there is any truth to it?"

"Knowing Bea, yes, she has her father's spirit and looks for a cause to fight – but I don't think she realises at what cost."

"Who would have known and told Mr Goldstein?"

"Hanley – he is making his move. He must have found out somehow and told Mr Goldstein – he means to cause trouble and divide within; I won't let that happen – but how could she." Joshua could feel the anger rise inside.

"Is there anything I can do?"

"I will find you at your lodgings if I need you – thank you, George."

Joshua picked up a few things off his desk and made his way out of the office, flicking his pocket watch out before shoving it back in his vest. Leaving George hovering on the spot.

On the ride home, Joshua kept reeling over certain parts. He had overlooked Bob's involvement with the reformers, as in the end they had served a purpose. He remembered once that Bea had mentioned hiding outside the pub to hear the meetings and wanted to be a part of it but this. Not telling him she was now a part of the abolitionist movement and how it would look like to his employers. She probably guessed he would be against it and decided not to tell him, and yet that made it more disappointing that she lied. – Is that what his marriage it based on, secrets and lies. After everything else she had put him through, he now had to contend with this.

By the time he had reached the door, his blood was surging through his body, and he could no longer hide his anger.

"Bea." He yelled out, slamming the front door shut. He rode into the sitting room and noticed a strange, distinctive smell lingering in the air. He could hear her feet running up the kitchen steps. "Bea, is it true?"

She followed his voice and ran into the sitting room in a panic. "Is what true? What are you talking about?" She came to a stop when she saw his face.

He took another step towards her; she could feel the anger emitting out of him. "Have you learnt nothing – on top of everything else I hear you're involved in the movement?" He saw the frightened look on her face. She had never seen this hidden side of him before. Few people had.

"What are you talking about Joshua – and please calm down you are scaring me."

His restless feet paced on the spot, causing Bea to take a step backwards. "We have – *I,*" pointing hard at his chest. "Have worked hard to establish us here, in this community, and all the while you have been going behind my back and attending meetings."

"At the meeting house, yes, why is that a problem?"

"You are an abolitionist?" He snapped.

"Why should that surprise you, what is wrong with that – I mean, Sarah?" She gestured down the stairs.

"That is different." He brushed away the air with his hands.

"How? Boston, Massachusetts is a free state, why shouldn't we stand up for what is right, slavery is evil or are you saying differently?" She crossed her arms and raised her eyebrows at him, daring him.

"Of course, slavery is an evil act, we should treat no one like that." She took a step toward him; she wasn't backing down.

"In the south they do, and it needs to stop. People need to be aware of what they are doing. It is a just cause to fight for."

"You sound like your father."

Her tone rose as she took another step closer. "What is wrong with that, I am proud of my Da. He helped to bring about change and fought for something he believed in and I am doing the same. It is in my blood – I have finally found my voice." There was a different fire inside of her, a passion he hadn't seen before and was proud of her, but it still needed to stop. Then a realisation hit him.

He took a step closer and stared her straight in the eye. "Be honest with me, is that where you were last night, helping them and not a poor charity?"

Her arms unravelled as they fell to her sides, as she cast her eyes downward. "Yes. They needed help. You should have seen the state they were in coming off the ship, bullet wounds and god knows what injuries across their bodies." She lifted her gaze upward, pleading with him.

"You helped ex-slaves cross into the state?" Barely an inch between their faces, with anger and passion seeping from one into the other. He could have kissed her, but resisted.

"I helped Sarah and Miss Fisher to save them. They would have died otherwise."

"And you don't care what others think or how it will affect this family – This might be a free state but helping them cross the border is against the law... Never mind, abolitionists are still a taboo, many business owners are against what they are trying to bring about – and if you thought it so innocent, then why hide it from me – why did you not tell me? How long has it been going on?" Past pain broke through the anger as he took a step back from her.

"For nine months and I did not tell you – because I thought you would not understand – I wanted something that was mine - you are not a fighter like me." She regretted the words the moment they exited her mouth.

"*How dare you!*" He boomed. "I fight every day for this family. I fought for your life, for our love, to bring us here and then fight for a position so that we can have a roof over our heads and food in our stomachs. You will never know how much I fight for this family." Is this what she thinks of me after all that I have done? *Does any of it matter?*

In the corner of his eye, he saw her trying to reach out to him, but he couldn't have her touch him. He would only crumble. "I know, I am sorry, I did not mean - there is a connection we share, Sarah and I, she understands my pain, she knows it."

The words felt like they had pierced his heart. "Do we not, Beth and I?" He took a splinter from the fire and lit a cigarette and moved over to the whiskey.

"You both try to, but you do not know it, have felt it and though it is different circumstances, she has felt it and once I heard the stories of what other people go through, what the slaves go through, I couldn't stand by idle. They are equal to us, the same as us, and yet how they are treated horrifies me." He watched the tears pour down her face. What she was saying was true. But to him, this had become more than slavery. This was about them. About her lies.

"How much I wished I could have swapped places with you, that night and all the days after, to see the shell of the woman I love tore at me, made me feel helpless. – I tried to be there, to fight for us when you could not. I even accepted and love our child – is that not enough? But all the while you have been keeping a secret from me that could bring all this, all what I have been fighting for to its knees." He put the empty glass on the mantlepiece and saw the burnt-out pipe sitting there. He picked it up and stared at it. That was what he had smelt, and there was only one person he knew smoked that tobacco. "What is this doing here?" He held the pipe in front of her and watched as her face changed. "Tell me he hasn't been in my home... that you didn't let him in while you were alone?"

"I didn't have a choice, he pushed his way in and Sarah was here holding Grace, while I asked him to leave."

Joshua threw the pipe in the fire, resulting in a cracking noise and a puff of smoke to billow out the grate, filling the room with his smell. "What did he want? Did he hurt you?"

"To cause trouble, to divide us but I told him that can't happen." The dense scent of Hanley's tobacco caused her to wretch in her throat as she fought back images flashing in her mind.

"I think you're right, I believe he is the one who told Mr Goldstein, that you are part of the movement."

"He said he has been watching me." He heard fear in her voice and wanted to comfort her. His arms yearned for her, but he couldn't move.

"If that is the case, then you need to stop. No more meetings, helping people."

"What, I should stay inside and hide, let him control my life again and become a shell of my former self? For the past three months I have been doing that and as a result, I watched you all worry about me and hear comments whispered in the corners. Which one is it? Snap out of it or hide?" She pulled at the lace around her wrist. Twisting it back and forth as it rubbed against recent scratch marks.

"No, I'm not saying that, but if he is watching you? Do you not see that your safety is at risk and the cost attached to this – I could lose my position..."

"Why – because your wife is an abolitionist?" She said in a dismissive tone.

"*Yes* - Mr Goldstein..." he paused, realising his own secrets. "Has connections I did not realise before and I don't think – no, I know he wants to see an end to it and as for Mr Lowell..." He forgot he had not told her about the railroad.

"What has he got to do with it?"

"I was going to tell you once the deal is close to final – he has offered me a job to manage part of a railroad he wants to build – all with Mr Goldstein approval of course," he tried to grab hold of her hand and clench it tight within his but she had turned her back. "– but do you not see what this job could do, more money means we could buy our own house with more land and garden."

She spun round. "We don't need that. Why? To replace what you have lost due to me?"

She was seeing it from the wrong angle again. "Yes and no – it's not like that, but money brings security..."

Her hand dropped from her wrist and waved it back and forth in the air. "At a price, as long as you do as they command and me with it. – I told you, that day in the woods, when you choose to walk away, that money did not matter to me like it does to you."

She still held that against him. "Why would you bring that up now? - But I chose you, no matter the consequence – now we can - I can have both – my parents didn't bring me up in your world – money matters."

"So, do lives, people matter more than money – that was the world I was brought up in – that if you find an injustice, you fight it."

"Think of Grace, what your choices might cost her, - we could afford a governess, social standing, a suitable position..."

"I am thinking of Grace. None of that means anything if all we are teaching her, is that money means more than lives do. I'm not a society lady." She pointed to herself, how false the grand dress looked compared to the old cotton blue dress she used to wear.

She still held the pure spirit that made him love her, and wished he could agree with the notion. "That is an ideal Bea. And if we are disgraced, then what? How will we place any roof over our heads if I can't get a job, have you thought about that? Your actions have consequences. Last night, you broke the law by helping slaves to cross the border."

"I know about consequences," she blurted out. "I live with them every day, they are burnt into my mind and can't get rid of them." A sudden burst of anger emitted from her.

"Bea, I did not mean.... I don't want to see you back there again. Back in a cell." He reached his arms out to her, but she fought his gesture as she tried to hide back the tears.

"I won't stop going." She said, like a child refusing a parent. She twisted the lace around her wrist.

He grabbed her arms and pulled her close. The sorrow clear on her face defused the bomb inside of him. "What about what I want, does that matter?"

"You knew the person I was when you chose me."

"I thought I did." His hand fell from her arms. "It is the same conversation all over again – maybe we are too different – Hanley doesn't need to break us apart; we do that all on our own. You want me to change for you, but you cannot change for me – where does that leave us?" He stepped away. He needed a drink and to work out the next step before he said something he would eventually regret.

"What are you saying, Joshua? I love you. That is the only thing that matters." Bea tried to reach out to him, but he stepped back further.

"Sometimes love is not enough... I can't keep doing this," he muttered under his breath and made his way back towards the door.

"Joshua - where are you going?" He said nothing, but opened the door. "Please come back in and talk." He ignored the tears building in her voice and calling out to him one last time before banging the door shut. Had the first time he walked away been the right choice all along?

Chapter 30

Hanley stepped back and watched as his plan unfolded. A simple mention of watching Beatrice enter the meeting house to Goldstein was sufficient for him to react. He knew what impact the abolitionist would have on Goldstein trade and bottom line if they got their way. Fear was a powerful motive. No matter how much they tried to hide it, the two of them had barely changed. He had watched Joshua saunter around Beacon Hill like he owned it. Money and power held sway over him. As for Beatrice, she was still naïve to how the world really worked, believing she could make a difference and keeping lies to do so. He knew one word to Goldstein would force him to confront Joshua, which would then force him to confront Beatrice. It had worked perfectly.

Hanley stood in the shadows outside the house and listened to the argument. She had left him for that boy, and now she was seeing him for who he truly was. Hanley hadn't imagined that after everything Beatrice had put Joshua through, that he would still stand by her, but he had. The boy had even claimed Hanley's child as his own, - but that could never stand. Hanley listened to the cracks form in their relationships. All their emotions they had buried came spilling out. Neither one listening to the other. He watched Joshua leave the house whilst Beatrice called out after him. He gave Joshua a head start, guessing where he would head to and listened to Beatrice break down over the fear of losing him. There was a slither of sorrow for her, but it was all her own doing. If only she had chosen him. None of this would have happened. Hanley climbed into the waiting carriage and followed Joshua to the tavern. Grinning with anticipation of the entertainment about to ensue.

∞∞∞∞

He slithered in and sat at a nearby table, close enough to overhear the boy and his puppet talk.

"She didn't want to listen. None of what I wanted made any difference." Said Joshua.

"Did she explain why?" Asked George.

"She wants to fight the cause, make everyone equal and expose the injustice of the south – which I understand and in different circumstances, I would support. And yet, we can't risk all that I have built. We need to keep our past a secret – something I wouldn't have to do if she..." Hanley grinned at Joshua's words. It had been easier than he thought to tear them apart.

"So, what are you going to do?" Asked George.

"Drink." Joshua said bluntly.

"And after that?" There was a chuckle in George's voice.

"I don't know – I have forgiven a lot of her past deeds but this - it is not the fact she attended the meeting that has me so angry, it is the fact she has been lying to me, keeping it a secret because she wouldn't like my response. How can I trust her?"

"From what you have told me, none of the past deeds where her fault *and* she has paid heavily for it..."

"I know; I see the scar it has left behind every day."

"And now you are what? Willing to walk away, leave her and your family behind? All because Mr Goldstein says so. And the fact she kept it a secret, you yourself have been keeping your own from her. Maybe you don't trust her?" Said George, the question lingering in the air. Hanley rejoiced at the thought.

A young serving woman dropped off another tankard at Hanley's table.

"Would you do me a favour," Hanley held up a dollar coin in front of the woman. "Tempt that man over there, provide drink and encouragement, and in return I'll give you ten more of these."

"I'm not a whore," exclaimed the woman.

"I'm not saying you are. However, I have watched how you behave in here. I am merely doing it to protect a friend. I don't trust him and believe him to be untrustworthy. You only need him to think he has." She nodded her head and took the coins. How easily people can be manipulated into doing your deeds if you use the right words.

"Excuse me, miss." Joshua's call carried over the increased voices as she stopped what she was doing and strode over, rolling her hips, which Joshua watched openly.

She leaned in a little closer and dropped her eyes, and shifted her dress around her breasts. "Yes, handsome?" She said. Her long eyelashes fluttered for a moment before gawping at him.

"I was wondering, do you serve any whiskey or something stronger than ale?" He smiled at her blatant flirting.

She stroked down the side of Joshua's face, carving her dirty fingernails through his evening stubble. "For you, I'll have a look." Her face was so close he could have kissed her.

Hanley watched as Joshua fell for the bait, the way he looked at her – the need to escape. He knew that look all too well. Beatrice didn't see Joshua for who he truly was, and Hanley was the one to show her – prove to her. He will make her come to him.

"Thank you." Said Joshua suggestively.

"I know how you can thank me." She whispered.

"Is Claire working tonight?" Said George, spinning in his seat to see if he could spot her. "This is not acceptable, and he is not the usual man in here. It's Lisa isn't it?"

Both pretended George wasn't there, as Joshua laughed and gave her a wink.

George waited for the woman to leave. "What has got into

you? You're playing with fire and she is the kind of woman that will burn you. Think about Bea."

"All I do is think about Bea, that's what got me into all this mess. I walked away from my family, my position, my reputation because of her. Then all the mess with Hanley, saving her from the noose, almost killing a man which I now regret since he is back, planning God knows what. I should have killed him when I had the chance. Raising a child that is not mine, building a life here in Boston which I thought would be safe, but now, that could come crumbling down for what? - What could Bea do for that cause anyhow, how is she helping them? She is jeopardising everything to hear a few stories and break the law. I realise my feelings don't matter to her. She's not interested in what's important to me?"

"And what is important to you? I'm afraid to say but she is right, lives matter more than money."

"You sound just like her." He pulled a silver flask from his pocket and took the last mouthful to George's surprise.

"What has got into you? This is not like you."

Hanley watched the serving lady bringing back two glasses filled with a clear liquid. He had seen, drank moonshine before, and you remember little of the night before. It was perfect.

"Joshua, I think it's best if I took you home now, get you back to your wife." George said the last part more towards Lisa, who had taken a step towards Joshua and was ignoring George.

"And what do we have here?" Joshua picked up a glass and gave it a sniff, scrunching up his face at the harsh, bitter smell.

"Oh, just a little Moonshine we make out back. It hits a hard punch. Only the genuine men drink this." She gave him a challenging look before smiling, showing some of her darker yellow teeth. He raised his eyebrows, lifted the glass up to cheers and in one gulp, drank the clear liquid. Followed by a cough as the liquid burnt his throat.

There was a pang of anger stirring in Hanley as he watched Joshua flirt. He had taken the bait. The boy who was meant to be better than him now had another woman, a whore, draping her arms across his shoulders and Joshua wasn't doing anything about it. This was the boy she left Hanley for? Grace and Beatrice should be with him, not this boy who had tantrums when he doesn't get his own way.

Joshua took the second glass, stumbling on his feet. "I'll see myself home," and gulped it down and slammed it on the table. Ensued by a barking cough.

"Do you want to get me some more?" Joshua mumbled, his words sticking in his mouth as he tried to speak.

Hanley pulled down his hat over his face as George stormed past, cursing the foolishness of his friend.

Hanley's work was done for the evening. He contemplated heading over to Miss Julie's establishment one last time. Instead, he made his way back to the confiding boarding house; he had a busy day tomorrow he must prepare and pack for his journey south.

Chapter 31

"Would you like another glass?" smiled Sarah, already taking the empty vessel out of Bea's hand.

"A small one please, it's medicine for my thoughts." Bea let out a small chuckle. "Oh, Sarah, what am I going to do? We can't be at odds with each other, not when Hanley is out there. Only God knows what he is planning, and we are doing all his hard work for him... I just want my husband back."

"He will come round tonight; he'll have gone a-lookin' for young George, and a drink."

"I hope you are right. What a day. But, how are you feeling now, after this morning?"

"Do you mind?" Sarah pointed to the dark red decanter for herself.

"No... I think we all deserve one!"

They both sat in silence, sipping for a moment, and then Sarah spoke.

"My name isn't Sarah. He's right, it's Jessie. Well, that was my slave name."

She started at the beginning, speaking of her life in the plantation, of her husband Hercules, and then, slowly, of her beloved son. She spoke of their first attempt at freedom and starting her journey on what they called the underground railroad. Being sold to Hanley before escaping once more. Both women cried silently together, Sarah reliving the pain of the past, and Bea weeping for her friend.

"The smell of the sea was strange, salt lingered in the air as gushes of wind surged around the darkness. There was a low glow of an oil lamp casting a figure in shadow standing beside what I guessed was a boat. Jeb raced toward the figure. I had no other option but to follow. The man waiting for me was as black as the night itself and introduced himself to me as Winston. Before I could thank Jeb properly, he headed back to the cart and kept heading down the road. Winston held out his hand and guided me towards a small rowing boat. He rowed us out to a ship waitin' a mile from the shore. My Mama had told me of the ships her parents came on; the chains, and the smell of death she carried with her until her last breath. But when Mr Winston lead me into that great wooden belly, they had filled the room with blacks of all shades, dressed in fine clothes. I stood there like a statue, frozen in surprise at the sight before my eyes.

It took a week, I think, to travel up the coast to Boston, and still the reality of freedom hadn't set in. For days we had nothin' to do - first time in our lives. We docked one sticky night, away from the larger tradin' ships. Even at night, Boston was so loud, and movin', all the time. Three carriages were waitin' to take us to a nearby boarding house, where I spent my first year. They taught me my letters and numbers, to get myself into havin' a job. I'll never forget the feelin' of holding my first wage there in my hand! After a while, Mr Winston introduced me to the meetin' house and there I found a new family. The thing is, you are never really free. It seems like it; sometime it feels like it, but your heart is always knowin' fear. I saw it in you too, when we first met, and I understood." Sarah took a deep breath. "And so, I told Winston today that Mr Hanley had found me, and he's put a plan together to hide me once more."

"You're leaving? He can't take you; we won't let that happen. You live in a free state."

"If he wants me back, he will do it. Once I am back across the border, he has the papers to say where my belongin' truly is. We both know it."

"What you have been through... I could never imagine – I am

so sorry." Bea placed her hand on top of Sarah's.

"What we have both been through."

Bea shook her head. "My pain is nothing compared to yours."

"Do not belittle what you have experienced because it is different, sister. It is your own, and few women could 'ave survived it in the manner you have, never mind find a kind of compassion inside themselves to help others."

"You have, and so have others; in the meeting house, and all across this town."

"That is true, we all have our own stories."

"And I understand why you did not tell me yours before now."

The two women embraced, wrapping their arms around one another protectively. "Shall we go downstairs and see what has happened to Beth and Grace?" said Bea finally, smiling through her tears.

Chapter 32

Bea had stayed up all night waiting for Joshua to return home, Sarah's story and her own, mingling in her mind. Dawn crept through the curtains, highlighting, in a rosy glow, the space on the bed where her husband should be. She threw a woollen shawl over her shoulders and made her way down to the kitchen.

"Mornin'."

"Morning Sarah, you are up early – I thought I would take some coffee."

"You were up all night, Bea? What time did he come home?"

"He... he hasn't."

"Here." Sarah grabbed a cup from the side and placed it on the table beside the coffeepot. It smelt welcoming to Bea's fatigued brain.

"I kept thinking about what I would say to him: how sorry I am, and how important the meeting house has been for me. Try to get him to see it from my side. But now I'm just worried about where he might be. Why hasn't he come home?" Bea watched the black liquid blend lovingly into the creamy milk as she placed the pot back down on the table.

"He's probably with George."

"I thought that, at first. But what if he has run into Hanley, and is lying on the ground somewhere, with a bullet in his back?"

"I doubt Mr Hanley would be that bold. Not in the city. Have somethin' to eat now. Do you want eggs and bread, or gammon? You ate little of your dinner last night."

"Thank you, but I will stick with the coffee for now."

"Look who is awake." Beth made her way into the kitchen, holding a noisy, squirming Grace in her arms. "I think she wants her Mama, and her milk"

"Thank you, Beth. Good morning, little one." Bea took hold of Grace, who instantly calmed down in her mother's arms.

"Still no sign of him?" Beth's eyes scanned the kitchen as if she were hoping to find him there.

"No," said Bea flatly.

"He is probably sleepin' off a bit of liquor with your George," Sarah quickly suggested.

"I hope not too much liquor. George is picking me up in an hour; he wants to show me a couple more sights of Boston, or something of the sort, and then he mentioned tea somewhere – Joshua will surely return with him."

"That will be nice," said Sarah. "You two have got quite close?"

"I like him... We can talk; he listens, he makes me laugh - and I think he is fond of me – there are no secrets, no pretence. I like that."

"I think he is more than fond of you." Bea smiled.

Blushing, Beth took a cup from the dresser and poured herself a coffee.

"There is no rush – he wants to prove to his father that he can make it on his own as a business person before..."

"You are right, there is no rush – you must take your time to know each other first." There was a hint of regret in Bea's voice that Beth picked up on instantly.

"You and Joshua know each other inside out; better than any couple I've known, even Da and Ma! You will get through this. Lord knows you are stronger together, and you love one another, and Grace, regardless."

"Yes, you are right. Well, on that note, I had better feed this little one before anything else, hadn't I?" They watched Bea as she made her way back up the stairs, rocking Grace gently.

"I'll bring some more coffee up." Sarah called up after her. There was a slight nod from Bea before she disappeared round the banisters.

"Do you think she will be alright?" asked Beth warily.

"Only time will tell, honey, but I'll monitor her today when you're out. I'm sure he'll be back soon."

∞∞∞

A n hour later, George had arrived and left without sign or sound of Joshua. Back in the kitchen, Bea kneaded the bread violently for dinner, hitting it, slamming it on the table, and then hitting it some more. Sarah raised her eyebrows.

"I think that will do for the bread, hmm?"

"Sorry, Sarah... but he refused to look me in the eye!"

"Who?"

"George. He wouldn't look at me; he knows where Joshua is and he can't look at me for fear I'd guess the truth."

"You don't know that, now. There are many reasons he might a' been kept away, and it ain't the one in your head."

"But what if it is? What if he has left me?"

"He loves you, you are his woman."

"So, where *is* he?" Grace cried at her mama's raised voice, and Sarah scooped her up from her chair and cradled her tenderly. "I'm sorry – both of you." Bea stroked the top of Grace's head and gave her a light kiss.

"Why don't I take Grace out for some fresh air, give you some space to let it all out." She smiled "We won't be long, will we sugar? Twice round the park. Joshua might be home soon; it will give you a minute to talk."

"We'll see. Take layers, the air is chilly and her bag, if she needs anything and keep a lookout." She gave her a warning look.

"I'll be gone an hour, Bea, maximum. There is no need for the bag."

"Oh, please... For me?"

"Alright, alright!" Sarah chuckled, shaking her head fondly.

"I love you, little one." Bea gave Grace another kiss on the head, and she smiled up at her mama, showing her wooden rattle excitedly. "See you both soon." She watched them leave through the back door and out of the yard.

The house maintained an eerie silence after that. Everyone was gone. Tears dripped from her cheek and splashed on to the dough, making it sticky. She sprinkled more flour over the mound and kept hitting it. This was all her fault again; she had caused yet another rift, and she didn't know how to mend it. Was there something wrong with her? Why didn't she fall in line like all the other women she knew, why did she keep making trouble for herself and her family? Then she heard the front door open and shut with an empty bang. She ran into the hallway, with flour across her face and apron.

He stood in front of her, pale and clammy, and he too couldn't look her in the eye.

"Where have you been? I have been worried sick that something had happened!"

"I was with George; I drank too much last night and slept at his lodgings."

"Is that the truth?" demanded Bea, bluntly.

"Of course, it is. What kind of question is that..." he replied dismissively, trying to slip past her toward the stairs.

"George came by about an hour ago, and there was no mention of your sleeping at his. Why would he come alone if you were with him?"

He kept his back to her and set a foot on the first step. "I was far more the worse for wear than he... I asked him to tell you I would be back soon. I don't know why he didn't pass on the message."

"Look me in the eye, Joshua," she scolded.

"Don't be foolish, I am in no mood." Still, he stared down and to the left, at the edge of the stair carpet.

"Stop Joshua – we can't keep lying to each other, you need to tell me the truth, if we are to have a future."

He spun around at her words. "What do you mean, *if* we are to have a future? What are you saying?"

"You left me last night, after our argument, saying maybe love wasn't enough - you walked out that door telling me that. All night I waited for you, to tell you how sorry I was, and how much I love you. But you never turned up, until now, in the middle of the afternoon, and now you're just telling me lies. What am I meant to think? You can't even look at me!"

He jumped off three steps and landed slightly unsteadily in front of her. "There." He grabbed tight of her, holding both arms down by her side. He smelt of alcohol and something else. He stared straight at her. "What do you want me to say? That your words last night didn't hurt me? That I went drinking with my friend, didn't know when to call it a night, and woke up in a storage room somewhere, with no money left in my pockets and no idea how I got there?" He saw the fear in her face and let go of her arms as his own eyes returned to the ground.

"What? George just... left you somewhere? Drunk? That's not like him."

"No... When he left me... I had only just started drinking heavily. I promised him I'd have one more and take the long way home to clear my head. I don't think you even realise how much pain you caused me last night. How much I have struggled and sacrificed for the past two years just to see a smile on your face?"

"So you wanted to punish me, is that it, by not returning at all, making me believe the worst?"

"You think I would sleep with another woman, after everything we have gone through? I love you; can you not see that?"

She wanted to give into him; ignore the feeling in her gut that he was hiding something. But she couldn't, not now. "I mentioned nothing about a woman. I meant... Hanley! He is still out there, isn't he? The thought of you two crossing paths down a dark alley is my worst nightmare, especially drunk."

"He wouldn't be that foolish, Bea. His plan is to destroy us without the need to show his face and we are making it far too easy for him."

She reached her hand up to his face. The rough stubble compared to his usual clean-shaven face reminded her of the early morning at the harbour. "I love you, Joshua. I couldn't imagine my life without you..." She held his stare and glided her thumb against the grime smeared across his cheek.

"And what - you think I could?" He leaned in and leant his forehead against hers. *If only she could read his mind.* Engulfing her in a strange scent, she couldn't quite work out what.

"Since last night... I don't know any more... it would be easier for you without me, I know that." She whispered. "I sometimes think you would have been better off if you had abandoned all ideas of us as your father wanted – all that you are trying to regain now is because of me, what I have cost you."

"You make me happier than I ever thought possible – most of the time." He was trying to make her smile, and it was almost working. He pulled back a little so she could see the sincerity in his eyes. "I picked you because I love you, and I couldn't live without you. Maybe I am trying to replace a little of what I have lost, but I have also gained more with you beside me than I could have done a thousand times over, had I married for my parents." He placed his hand under her chin as she blushed at the sentiment.

"You mean that?"

"Of course, I do; why would you doubt it?"

"Yesterday you asked me to change who I was. As though it surprised you to find me involved in the movement – as though you didn't know me at all."

"Let's not speak about that just now. After I've had a bath, and some food, we will talk, and get it all sorted - tonight."

"Alright, you are a bit..." He leaned in and this time kissed her on the lips, and she could finally work out what that smell was, mixed in with that of sweat and alcohol: perfume, the cheap kind. She caught her breath.

He smiled. "Can you get Sarah to draw me a bath upstairs?"

Bea took a step backwards, distancing herself from what that smell might imply. "She is out with Grace, getting some air – but... they should have been back by now." She glanced over at the grandfather clock chiming away in the sitting room.

"I'm sure they will be back soon."

"Yes... well, I'll start drawing you a bath in the meantime."

"If you boil the water, I'll take it upstairs." He gave her a quick kiss on the cheek before making his way up to the small dressing room, one hand grasping the banister.

∞∞∞

S he heard the front door slam shut as she ran upstairs to meet them, but her face fell when she saw only George and Beth gazing back at her.

"Did you see Sarah and Grace on your way back? They left hours ago and haven't returned."

"No, we didn't see them on the street, did we, George? Do you think she might have gone to the meetinghouse?" Beth offered.

"I don't think there was a meeting planned today, but I'll check, anyway. I won't be long."

"Bea, they will be back soon, I promise. You don't need to go out," said Beth kindly, placing a hand on her shoulder.

"I... it's just... something doesn't feel right, Beth; I can't explain – I'll be back soon, alright?"

"I'll come too."

"No, I shouldn't be long. Dinner is ready. You eat, and I will be back in ten minutes, to check the park and the meeting house."

"Are you sure?"

"I will come too, don't worry – I need to head off now anyhow." George glanced up the stairs and then back towards

Beth. "Thank you for a lovely afternoon."

"Thank you, George. Tell Joshua I'll be back soon, won't you Beth?" Her sister nodded.

Bea grabbed her cloak from the hook and made her way towards the door, George following behind, bidding a last silent farewell.

"If we check the park first, that's where she said they were going - and then the meeting house. Thank you again, George, for coming."

"My pleasure, it's the least I can do."

There was an awkwardness between them as they walked in silence up the street and turned right at the junction.

"Can I ask – what happened last night?" George kept his eyes down and stared at the cobbles in front of him. "He said you left him at the tavern?"

"Yes - well, I didn't fancy a late night myself, knowing I was meeting Beth today and he... wanted to keep on drinking."

Bea paused in her step and stared at him, but he still couldn't hold her gaze. "Why didn't you say anything of it this morning? Or why would you leave him to get drunk and not try to get him home? There is something you are not telling me, George... Please."

"I think that is a conversation you need to have with Joshua."

"Why can't you tell me? What oath would you break by telling me now? What are you hiding?" She caught him up and overtook him, blocking his path.

"I'm not hiding anything! I didn't tell you this morning..." He veered round her and kept walking toward the park.

".... Because you didn't know where he was? He told me he woke in a strange place."

George stopped and gazed at her, wondering if this was some sort of test. "Is that what he said? Last night he merely told me he wanted to drink, to a destructive degree, and I told him I did not. He wouldn't listen to reason, so... I left."

"And when you left, he was by himself?" She took a step closer.

George kept his eyes glued to the ground "Of course! I can't comment on what happened when I wasn't there – I'm sorry Bea but I can't say any more than that." He turned and kept walking.

Her eyes scanned the manicured park. Dusk was descending, casting low shadows in the corners shrouded in trees, waiting for the lamp lighters to arrive and dispel the worst of the dark. There was an intrepid nanny with a pram, but they could see at a glance that it wasn't Sarah. Otherwise, only an older gentleman sitting on a bench, and occasionally glancing at his watch. No Sarah, and no Grace.

"They're not here. Shall we try the meetinghouse?" There was an edge of panic in her voice that she couldn't hide.

"Let's; I'm sure they'll show up there, caught up in a conversation with someone."

The building was quiet, as she thought it would be, but the door was open. The warmth inside was a welcoming relief from the frosty chill setting into the evening air. A few lamps were lit, and the stove in the corner was burning low, but no one was about.

"I'll check the back room; would you wait here, please?"

George automatically picked up a newspaper from the sidetable, stacked neatly for the next meeting, and sat down incongruously in a pew.

There was a seam of light breaking through the gap between the door and door frame. She hovered for a moment, not knowing if she should knock, or merely enter. She raised her hand up to tap on the left panel, but the door suddenly opened.

"Oh! Good evening?" Mr Winston stood there with the door a jar with a shook expression.

"Good evening, Mr Winston, I- I'm sorry, could I please speak with you, quickly?"

"It is delightful to see you, Mrs Mason, but unfortunately I'm in the middle of a meeting." He looked carefully at her face. "Is it urgent?"

"Yes... I- yes it is. Sarah and Grace, are they here? I can't find them, they have not returned home after a visit to the park and yet, I expected them hours ago... I wondered if they were here." It was all Bea could do not to sob.

His face became serious. "Do you mean they are missing?"

"Well, yes, I am sure of it. She left four hours ago to take Grace for some air whilst I finished preparing dinner, and they haven't returned. She would never... I am sure she would not lose track of time like that, not with Grace. I've come out looking for them, but I'm so worried. I don't know where else they would be!"

"Leave it with me. I'll have a word with the community and see if they know anything. I know where you live, I will let you know what I find as soon as I have word of any clues."

"Tonight?"

"It will be late."

"I won't sleep; I won't be able to, not without them *both* back, without knowing they're safe. – Do you think it could be Hanley?"

Winston nodded his head. "I pray that it's not. Let me reach out and I will speak to you soon, tonight."

"Thank you." She held her hands up to him, almost in prayer, and then pulled them back. He nodded his head again, this time much preoccupied, and closed the door, leaving her in the semi-darkness once more. She made her way back to George. "They're not here." Her fingers twitched at the lace.

George stood up, holding the newspaper in one hand. "What are you wanting to do next?"

"Winston is going to enquire amongst his community and send word – would you come with me and do another circle around the street? Otherwise, I can't think of anything but wait, and... and hope that... After, will you come back with me, and have some food? You must be hungry." There was a desperation in her voice.

"Thank you, I don't want to intrude..."

"You are family now, and that's what we need... anything else, well, it's just not important. Please?"

Chapter 33

They all sat in the living room, fractured bursts of conversation passing between them, and then a thin, tense silence. Bea sat transfixed by the dancing flames leaping off the coals in the fire. Finally, Joshua stood and made his way to the ornamental table in the corner, and poured himself a whisky.

"Can I please have one of those?" Bea asked, her voice void of emotion.

"Are you sure? You might not like the taste."

"Please." She pulled her gaze from the fire for a moment, the glow glistening on the tear rolling down her cheek. She needed something to numb the pain, just like him, and the feeling of helplessness.

Joshua said nothing, pouring out three measures, topping up George's along with their own, then knelt beside Bea on the floor. He placed their two glasses on the rug and wrapped his arms around her as her silent tears dripped off her jaw and onto his chest.

"They will be back soon, you'll see." He whispered into her ear, leaving a quick kiss behind.

He was right. She didn't like the taste, nor the harsh burning sensation it left at the back of her throat. But she took another sip, willing it to do its work. "Where are they? They wouldn't disappear, she wouldn't be gone for this amount of time and not send word. What if... he has got them?"

Joshua pulled back from her at the mention of Hanley. "Why on earth would he do that? How, why?"

"To take back what he thinks is his."

"Kidnap? He wouldn't be that foolish, surely? And why take Sarah?"

"He wouldn't take them in the open like that, and Sarah wouldn't go willingly, would she?" added Beth encouragingly, leaning down to her from the armchair.

"But she would go willingly if it meant protecting Grace," George muttered, putting down the newspaper that hadn't left his side since the meeting house.

"Sarah told me last night that Hanley was her former owner. She escaped slavery thirteen years ago and made her way to Boston. That is why she took me to the meeting house in the first place; to help me understand."

"Sarah? Hanley?" stuttered Joshua, with a blank look.

"Yes."

"But I thought..." said Beth, but Joshua cut her off.

"She belonged to Hanley? Why didn't you say anything earlier?"

"I only found out while you were still sleeping off the drink in that storeroom, wherever that was... I had guessed she hadn't always been free, but I did not know that the same man caused both our sorrows."

A loud knocking at the door halted the conversation as Bea rose to her feet, but Joshua ran to the door before she could rise. For a moment, there was silence apart from the hiss and crackle from the glowing coals.

"Good evening, Mr Mason, forgive me for the late visit. I'm Mr Winston."

"I remember - from the gala. Come in."

"Thank you for coming, Mr Winston. Do you have any news?" Bea twisted her hands together until her nails dug into the skin.

Mr Winston stood in the shadowed doorway in his large overcoat, unwilling to come any further. "No one... no one is certain. She has visited none of her usual places, and she's not home."

Bea stepped a little closer. "Uncertain?"

"A person saw someone matching her description in the park earlier, walking a pram, and talking to a tall white man with dark hair in a smart coat." He glanced over at Joshua and George, and then back at Bea. "Apparently, all three left the park together, but my friend didn't see where they went."

"So, do you think it is him, then? – Hanley?" said Bea, her voice trembling.

"Possibly. That would be bold of him. - I have never met him but I have enough stories to suggest it's in his character." Replied Mr Winston quickly, and yet there was no little doubt in his voice.

"*He* could do anything!" Bea couldn't stop herself; her body shook. "I am going out to get them back. Where could he be? Hiding in the city, or would he have taken them out by now?" She directed at Mr Winston.

"Bea, stop. Think first." Beth tried to grab her hand and saw the damage to her wrist.

"No." Bea yanked her hand free. "I don't have time. My daughter, my friend, is with that man. That godforsaken man and I don't know where they are! So, don't tell me to stop and think, all I can do is think, that is all I have ever done for the past year." She yelled and fought against Joshua's hold. "I have to do something." She pleaded.

He held her face in his hands. "We are doing something but you can't spend the night walking the streets."

"I will enquire further, and let you know if I obtain any more news," Mr Winston murmured, taking a step back.

Joshua let go of Bea and dashed to let Mr Winston out. "Thank you, Mr Winston. Is there anything I can do to assist you?" Joshua held out a hand for him to shake.

"You know people down at the harbour; if you trust any of them enough, then ask around for word of Captain Hanley, and I will do the same."

"I will, thank you."

"I will drop round again tomorrow." He looked at the grandfather clock, and seeing it was already the following day, added, "in the morning sometime."

"Thank you." George added, standing beside Beth, holding her hand.

Joshua paused for a moment and looked at Bea. "Mr Winston knows about Hanley?"

"He was one of the people that helped Sarah to freedom; her passage, and her employment. He knows everything."

"He is part of the movement?" The anger had returned to Joshua's voice.

"Yes." George answered for her, glancing down at the newspaper again.

Joshua poured himself another drink and lit another cigarette. "How many more secrets are you hiding? How deeply involved in this movement are you, exactly?"

The sudden change in his tone surprised Bea. "What?"

George held out the newspaper in front of him, willing Joshua to take it. "Maybe you should understand it better before judging them, Joshua."

"Joshua, this is not the time," Beth pleaded.

Bea absorbed some of Joshua's anger and threw it back at him. "*I'm* keeping secrets? I found all this out last night when you were God knows where."

"I'm heading to bed; we all need some sleep." Fearful of where this conversation was heading, Joshua turned his back to her and made his way out of the room.

"How can you sleep when our daughter and Sarah are out there, with him?" Joshua returned to the doorway and placed a hand on each side of the frame.

"We don't know where they are. What good would it do if we spent the night walking the streets, as you suggested? – If Hanley has got them, then he has planned it out to the finest detail, just like before and we are yet again racing to catch up."

"So, we should go to bed and wait? For what? I *need* them back now! – I promised my daughter I would protect her, and I have failed." She no longer fought the tears streaming down her face.

"Bea." Beth added tenderly.

"What should I do, tell me? Race after them? To risk all that we have. We don't know where they are."

"How could you say that? I would risk everything to get them back." Bea stormed forward as Beth tried to hold her back. "*How dare you!*" George quickly stepped in between the couple and began pushing Joshua towards the stairs. "She loves you; as a protector, as a father. Are you telling me you'd rather let Hanley act like her father? I am telling you he has them and I will find them and bring them back, with or without you. What is all this for, if not for our family? You think you can build a life for us here, and now you're not willing to fight for it?"

Regretting his words instantly, Joshua turned and faced Bea, seeing the pain his words had caused on top of everything else she was already dealing with. "No... I didn't mean..."

"*LEAVE!*" Bea's voice filled the entire room, taking everyone by surprise.

"Let's all get some sleep and put the whisky down. Fresh heads for tomorrow," George spoke calmly, but was still pushing Joshua with some force towards the stairs.

"Bea, I didn't mean... you know I love her..." Joshua tried to move round George to get to his wife, but she had turned her back on him and made her way back to the fire. She spoke icily, and quietly, but loud enough for all to hear:

"Go to bed Joshua, and why not see if you can sleep. Whilst I will come up with a plan to get them back and do all I can to ensure they are both safe."

"I will stay with Bea - you two get some rest." Beth stared at George, both of them forming a plan together without needing any words.

The thick air hung around them, and nobody spoke, almost in anticipation of another explosion. Then Joshua turned and made his way up the stairs, George following cautiously behind. Bea heard the door slam and poured herself another whisky. She was either getting used to the taste, or needed it too much to care.

"You know he didn't mean that?"

She rubbed her fingers deeply across her forehead. "My head is full of things I know and don't know. Last night my husband asks me to change who I am so that he can continue climbing the ladder at work, when we already have a house and a lifestyle that serve our needs, then he tells me he doesn't know if our love is enough for him, before leaving me for an entire night. Returning late the next day with the smell of cheap perfume all over his clothes. Now my daughter and my friend are missing, probably held against their will somewhere by Victor Hanley, all for the sake of his plan and disturbed mind..."

"You think Joshua... last night – there was perfume?" She glanced up the stairs and lowered her voice. "He wouldn't be that foolish, would he? Surely it was just an unfortunate encounter with someone soliciting on the way home, or... the wife of an acquaintance...?"

"I don't know! Beth, why is all this happening? I don't know how much more I can take." Bea finished the glass in one gulp and made her way for another one.

"I don't think that will help."

"It seems to help him." Bea gestured through the ceiling and towards the bedroom.

There was nothing Beth could say to that, and so she watched Bea's shaky hand pour another two glasses, passing one to her.

"No, I- I don't think I'll like that."

But Bea wasn't listening. She crouched down by the fire once more and stared at the flames. Beth knew she had to stop her sister from thinking the worst over and over in her head.

"So, what's the next step in the plan? I know you're forming one, you don't have to pretend you're helpless in front of me." There was the smallest hint of a smile in Beth's voice, and Bea appreciated it.

"My gut is telling me that Hanley has taken them – I don't know why or how, but his words yesterday morning keep sounding in my head: "I'll make you come to me." So, that's the next bit, really: where would he take them – are they still in the city, or does he have other plans?"

"Wait, when did this happen?"

"Hanley came to the house yesterday." Beth tilted her head to the side and raised her eyebrows. "He told me he wasn't ready to give us up – including Sarah. Except he didn't call her Sarah, he called her Jessie. I think he wanted me to... to admit he was right about everything, somehow, and go to him. - Later that night, after Joshua stormed out, Sarah told me everything – what she went through to become free, only to come face to face with that man again, who had done her so much wrong. And now, he has two out of the three of us, just as he said. He's probably waiting for me to come stumbling through his door too, in search of them, just so he can show me how foolish I was to think I could ever have a life on any terms but his."

"But if you're right – and that's exactly what he wants, then he must keep them somewhere he can control, somewhere you would find yourself at a disadvantage. What is your gut telling you?"

"I don't know." Bea stabbed the fire. "– I don't know, I can't think straight right now. He knows this entire country better than I do – he could be anywhere! Oh god, what chance do we have at finding them?"

Beth grabbed Bea by the shoulders and stared her straight in the eyes. "We can't think like that; we will find them. It is up to us to bring back our family." For the first time, Bea saw a bright, familiar fire in her sister's eyes: the Lightfoot fire.

"Yes!" They chinked the glasses together, grimaced, and downed the rest of the whisky.

T he fire was still burning when they awoke, but someone had still placed a blanket around them. But in the morning, nothing had changed. The house was strangely still. There was no Grace waking her up, calling out for her Mama, no noises or singing coming from the kitchen as Sarah made breakfast, or warm smells filtering up the stairs. It was as if the rooms were still asleep. Unable to wake. Bea's engorged breasts ached sharply, another reminder that Grace was missing, and Bea was lost without her. At least Sarah was there; she would protect her as though she were her own. Bea glanced at the clock; it was already past nine and then back at Beth. There was a thick fog clouding her thoughts and blurring her vision, calling out for coffee. The result of too much whisky, and too much emotion. Downstairs, there was a used pan on the side covered in fat, and a lukewarm pot with a thick scum of coffee lining the bottom. The men must be gone for the day without having said a word to anyone. Maybe that was for the best. She added a couple more logs and sticks to the stove before filling up the coffeepot again and placing it back on the ring. As it rumbled, she made her way up to her bedroom.

Scattered in a pile on the floor were Joshua's clothes from the night before. She lent down and picked up the shirt. The nauseous, feminine smell was still there; she had not imagined it. She threw it back on the ground and made her way to the wardrobe to pick out a clean dress for the day. There was already water in the bowl on the washing stand. She scooped up a handful and splashed it into her face. As she blinked rapidly, recovering from the cold, and the vigorous rubbing she had applied with the small hand towel hanging from the washstand, she made out, on her velvet chair, a neatly folded piece of paper.

My love,

I am deeply sorry for the last two nights, and what was spoken.

Forgive me.

I am heading to the harbour with George to gather information on Hanley's latest movements.

We will find them, my dearest, and make our family whole again. I will see you tonight.

All my love, Joshua.

The paper fell from her hand, landing back on the seat upside down. Her heart was numb; she saw the words, but couldn't wholly take them in.

She dressed and pinned her hair back up. Taking one last look at the tainted shirt on the floor, she closed the bedroom door behind her. Downstairs in the sitting room, the coffee pot sat steaming on the side, next to a pair of cups, and a wide-eyed Beth.

"I thought I would let you sleep."

"The smell of the coffee woke me."

"Joshua left a note in the bedroom. The men have gone down to the harbour." There was still a bitterness to her voice. Beth nodded and sipped her coffee.

"Did you want any food? I couldn't stomach it, but if you want something, I'll-"

"No, no, I'm fine for now – those two glasses of whisky would not agree with any breakfast." Beth pulled a face, and Bea couldn't help but chuckle.

They drank the rest of the coffee in silence.

"I'm going to get changed too." Beth placed her cup on the side just as a large knock came from the front door.

Bea shot to her feet and ran to open it.

"Mr Winston, please come in." Bea stood to one side and allowed him to pass. "Can I get you a tea, or a coffee?"

"Thank you, but no." Again, he hovered in the doorway to the sitting room, refusing to enter and take a seat. "I have some news. I wanted to tell you straight away. A member of the community spoke to an informer at the docks who spotted Hanley leaving on his ship yesterday... with an infant, and a black woman."

"Oh god, I knew it! Do they know where he went?"

"No – but I have my suspicions. I believe he has taken them to his plantation."

"Where Sarah escaped from?"

"How are we going to get them back?" Beth stepped closer to her sister.

"By the laws of the South, he still owns Sarah; she is his property, and, forgive me for saying this, but Sarah told me something of your situation: your child is also his?" He raised his eyebrows at her, but there was no judgement in his tone.

"Sarah told you?"

"We hold no secrets." Bea could see the love and the pain in his face all at once and what he must be going through too.

"Then, what can we do – we must be able to do something?"

"I have sent a letter to a conductor." He instinctively lowered his voice as if the walls themselves had ears. "I will then be able to get news of them as soon as they arrive back at Drayton Hall."

"No." Mr Winston and Beth looked at Bea, both concerned at her tone. Beth put a hand on her arm, as though about to speak. Bea continued. "She is my child, my family. I have to do something, I cannot stand by and wait for letters or news."

"But what do you propose to do – go down there yourself?" He said in disbelief.

"Don't you see, that's what he wants... That's all he wants! He said to us, all of us, '*You will come to me, the three of you.*' The only way I will get my baby back is to do it myself; to make him think he has won. If anyone else tries to act in my place, he will only twist the knife in harder. I will travel to the south, and bring them back, somehow. I am a white woman of some class now; nobody will look twice at me."

"By yourself? It is not safe – you don't know..."

"I will go with her." Beth interrupted, placing a hand on Bea's shoulder. Her sister nodded.

"We can say we are visiting family."

The activist shook his head vehemently. "You may well be able to travel through to the Southern states, but getting your child and Sarah free is another matter."

"I have faced Hanley before. I'm not afraid of him anymore; not now. I will do anything for my family, to get them back home again. With or without your help."

Mr Winston saw the determination on her face. It might just work. Two white women, dressed well, travelling together to visit family wouldn't attract too much attention, if they could rely on some kind of support network. "What about your husband?"

Bea swallowed. "It will only be the two of us." Beth squeezed her hand. Their companion sighed, then bowed his head slightly. Looking up at them with a small smile, he held out both hands to the sisters.

"Meet me at the harbour in an hour."

Chapter 34

"What are you going to tell Joshua?" asked Beth bluntly.

Bea shrugged her shoulders, as if suggesting there was only one option open to them. "I'll write him a letter – if I told him now, I know he would try to stop us, say there is another way and I can't have that. I truly believe this is the only way to get them both back."

"He might want to come and help us. Having a man at our back could be useful." Beth saw the stubborn side of her Da in Bea.

"He can't leave work for that amount of time; he wouldn't have a job to go back to, and he wouldn't risk that." Bea took another sip of her coffee as she tried to come up with what she was going to say to her husband.

"Surely that won't matter compared to the chance of getting his daughter back?"

"You heard him last night. He doesn't want to risk losing this. – I know he fought hard for me once, but I don't know how far he would go for Grace and Sarah." The pain of betrayal was still biting in her chest. "I will go as far as I need to. Can you honestly tell me he would let me?"

"Now Bea, you know that was said through a haze of drink, pain and anger."

"I know him well enough – he meant it."

"He loves that little girl, adores her, even."

Bea placed down her cup back on the side table.

"Grace grew inside of me, right here. I fought so hard to bring her into this world. A mother's love is different, its hard to explain but I would sacrifice myself for her... And if Hanley wasn't coming after me, he wouldn't have found Sarah and now... she has become family, another sister, I can't let her live that life once more." Bea paused, images of Sarah's story flashing in her mind. "I promised, and it is my job to protect Grace from life's evils, including her natural father... never mind him bringing her up in that world. It is time for him to be stopped."

Beth grabbed hold of Bea's hand and looked her straight in the eyes. "I am with you every step of the way – I just wanted to check that you had thought it through."

"I have."

"Then I will pack us a small trunk, and we will take our finest clothes; it will look more realistic if we have luggage for a family visit. You write your letter to Joshua, before the carriage gets here."

Bea sat and stared at the blank piece of paper whilst Beth charged up and down the stairs carrying random items of clothing and small trinkets. What could she say to Joshua that would make him truly understand, without leaving him angry and feeling betrayed once again, severing their love for good? At least this way he could still keep his job, and his reputation; still have all this... what really mattered to him. She wrote.

Beth answered the knock at the door as Bea placed the letter carefully on the mantelpiece.

"Yes, we are, thank you... could you take this trunk please?"

"Very good miss." The coachman nodded his head and lifted the heavy trunk with ease down to the carriage.

"Are you ready?" asked Beth, placing a travelling cloak round her shoulders.

"Yes." Bea gazed around her home one last time, as if saying goodbye. "Oh – did you pack some things for Grace and Sarah?"

"Yes."

Bea gently placed a hand on Beth's shoulders. She was so grateful to have her sister with her this time. "Thank you for doing this, for coming with me." Beth smiled at her warmly.

"I promised myself a long time ago that I would not let you go through anything alone again."

"I love you." Bea pulled her in her tightly.

"I love you too."

∞∞∞

The harbour was busy, loud, with men heaving cargo into the warehouses lining the banks. The carriage weaved in and out of traffic until it came to a stop in front of the same narrow pier that they had brought her to several nights before. Three ships stood in front of her, two as large as the fells she left behind in Ulverston, and a smaller vessel to their left. Mr Winston appeared at the top of the hazardous gangway connecting this lesser ship to the pier and walked down it quickly towards them.

"Mrs Mason, Miss Lightfoot."

"Good morning, sir." There was a determination to Bea's voice that needed no further expansion.

"Please load the trunks on board, my good man," Mr Winston instructed the ruddy-faced coachman. Then he turned back to Bea.

"You have a shared quarter on board; this is my ship, and the men are mine as well. I trust them, and know you will come to no harm during your journey, under their watch. A man called Jeb will meet you once you reach the docks in Georgia. - Once I left you, I sent word on a smaller, faster vessel that I use occasionally. But, the ship will leave you, and will return in two weeks. This is all the time I could give you; after that it will be another two months before it returns to the Carolinas. But I am warning you, if Hanley hears about a Mrs Mason or Miss Lightfoot in the area, he will learn about it. I would be surprised if he does not have eyes and ears in most of the larger towns. You must use false names. Jeb will know you from my description. He will greet you with the words: '*The sky is clearing*'; you must reply '*Yes, it looks like sunshine.*'"

"Thank you," said Bea, placing a hand on his arm. "She is still alive – he needs her to look after Grace." He nodded and shook first Bea's and then Beth's hands without a word.

For a moment, as they mounted the last feet of the gangway to the deck, Bea thought she glimpsed Joshua, six or seven docking stations up the boulevard, but she blinked hard, and told herself she was just imagining things. Grasping Beth's hand, she took one last glance back to the chimney-pots of Beacon Hill, and pulled her skirts over the foot-rope and onto the creaking wooden deck. *I'm coming, my love, I'm coming.*

A week had passed, and at last land was in sight. They packed their trunks quickly and paid their respects quietly to the captain and his crew. The small stone harbour shifted under their feet, unaccustomed to a stationary surface, and they grasped one another's arms, as though standing on ice. A member of the crew helped them with their luggage as they stood there, awkwardly, unsure whether to make the first move. No one had really told them what Jeb looked like, and there were a handful of men standing around with various carts and wagons waiting for cargo to be unloaded that might be the guide they were looking for. Then Bea noticed one man standing beside a cart full of scrap metal. He seemed to be in his late thirties or early forties, his skin slightly darker than most other local traders, and she thought he kept glancing their way, all the while monitoring the positions of his neighbours. One by one the other men approached the sailors and gave them sheets of paper, before being allowed to load goods onto their wagon. But the man Bea had spotted stayed put.

Once most of the men were satisfied, and the small harbour was almost empty, the stranger walked forward. His expression was blank, and his broad frame stood out proudly from under his clothes, which were covered with soot.

"The sky is clearing."

"It looks like sunshine."

"Come this way." He grabbed hold of their trunk with a barely perceptible smile as they followed in silence.

He placed the trunk on top of the metal, wedging it between two large rusting poles. Then he stood at the side and held out his hand to help them climb up onto the small front seat. Beth went first, followed by Bea. It was a snug fit for them on the single plank of wood. The restless horse kicked up his hooves at the dry dirt, signalling his desire to move. Once Jeb himself had climbed up, he lifted his reins and then slapped them down in a short, graceful movement. There were no words, and no other gesture as the cart jerked forward.

They were now heading deep into the South, and what was more, had less than two weeks to save Sarah and Grace and make it back to this spot alive.

Chapter 35

J oshua ran towards the pier and watched, helpless in the distance, as Bea and Beth climbed the small plank to board the ship. He wanted to reach out to her from the other end of the docks, as though she would feel his arms beckoning, and understand that she needed to wait. He wanted to run after her, climb on board, and not look back, just as she was doing, as thoughtlessly brave in his actions as she had always been with hers. But the pain and confusion of her betrayal glued his feet to the spot, and he merely watched as his wife left him behind. Seconds later the ship moved weightily out of the harbour, and he felt the blood return to his hands and feet, but he didn't know where to go, or what to do.

"Joshua?" George was trying to catch his attention. "Joshua: I just spoke to some of the St-Hélène crew. I thought they might give me a tip or two, but no one has seen Hanley these past two days, nor a black woman with a child in tow. I got some rather particular looks, though. Did you have any luck? What's wrong, man?" George stared at Joshua, following his line of sight, and then back at his friend, confused.

"She's... gone."

"We will find Grace and Sarah again, I promise you."

"No... Bea and Beth have just left, on." Joshua gestured his hand towards the open water.

"What... what do you mean?" George patted him on the back, trying to guide him away from the pier and back down the docks toward the town.

"I have just watched them leave – she has left me." There was a hollowness to Joshua's voice that made the hairs on George's arms stand on end.

"Maybe a rest and some food might do you good. Besides, we should probably get back to Bea; she and Beth will be anxious, alone at home, waiting for news."

Joshua didn't respond, but obediently tore his eyes away from the small ship, making its way into the bright horizon, and weaved through the bustling men meekly behind the optimistic George.

They locked the door. Joshua pulled out his key mechanically and stepped into the soundless house. He made his way over to the mantelpiece and saw the letter almost immediately.

"Bea – Beth?" George called out, racing down the steps towards the kitchen.

Joshua stared at Bea's handwriting, fearful of the message inside. He heard George re-enter the sitting-room, held out the piece of paper in a limp hand, and sank into a nearby chair.

My dearest,

Please forgive me for leaving this letter instead of saying goodbye. Time is not on our side.

Mr Winston has just arrived at the house, and informed us that Hanley was seen leaving on his ship with Sarah and Grace yesterday evening, believed to be making his way with them to his Georgia plantation.

Beth and I, with the help of Mr Winston and his community, will leave on a private vessel in an hour and will dock in Georgia in a week.

That is all I know. I believe that all this trouble, our losing Grace, is my fault, and so it is up to me to confront him once and for all and bring them back. I need to do all that I can to save them, however I can't ask that of you again. This way, you can explain to Mr Goldstein we have left on a journey to visit family in the South, and we need attach no scandal to your name.

Please know that I love you more every day and I hope that love is enough, but I have always known that I cannot be someone I am not. I need my daughter back; I need Sarah back.

I feared telling you before, but when Hanley was here, he told me he wants me to come to him. Therefore, I might have to do something you won't agree with and I can't let that stop me, not whilst they're in danger.

I hope you understand and I pray in a month our family will be whole again... if you will take me back. Please thank George for his help and send him Beth's fondest regards.

I love you now and always. Forever yours, Bea.

"Does it say where they are?" George's fury aroused Joshua quickly from his stupor. He couldn't find the words himself. "Is that what you saw down at the docks, staring out at sea - you saw them, didn't you? Why didn't you stop them?"

"I... I couldn't." Joshua contemplated picking up his glass from the night before from the side-table and fill it with whiskey.

"What do you mean you couldn't – you could have tried, at least? Shouted, called to them, tried to stop the ship!"

Joshua, resisting the urge, turned round and glared at George. "And what would that have done? Bea believes I would not risk it all again for her, that I would have stopped her. What I have done and said over the past couple of days has broken our marriage. I couldn't hold her prisoner."

George's voice rose further, fuelled with frustration at the thought of losing Beth. "So, instead of breaking her heart, you would have them breaking their necks?"

"George calm down."

"It is true. This is my country. The south is a different world. God, if they manage to get to them, Hanley surely won't let Bea escape twice – not from what you have told me. Then what will happen to Sarah, and Beth - and Grace your own child?"

"They have already left. What am I meant to do?"

"We go after them!"

Joshua let his head fall into his hands. "She is right though: if I leave, I will lose my job – and so will you. Then we will lose this house, and our only source of income…"

"Are you telling me, all this," George flung his arms out with force, "is worth the life of your wife and child?"

"No… of course not. But how am I meant to support us all if we do bring them back unharmed?"

"Good god man, there are other jobs, more modest houses. But none of that matters. If I make arrangements – if we leave tonight, we might just stand a chance of catching them up." George paused a moment and looked at Joshua earnestly. "I can't lose Beth. I love her." He gripped Joshua on the shoulder, and took his left hand by the ring-finger, raising it so that the gold band was directly in front of his face.

Images flashed into Joshua's mind: the moment he had first seen Bea, her hair wet with sea spray at the old harbour, laughing at the nimble waves; dancing with her in her golden gown and the instant attraction he had. Their first kiss in the frosty morning air, and the perfect, inexorable sensation of knowing that there was no going back. How it had felt, months later, seeing her caught like a frightened animal in the castle cell, and seeing, despite everything, her courage to fight returning day by day, little by little. Last of all came the guilt-ridden memory of holding Grace the first time she had smiled up at him, and a wave of anger at the idea that they could take away her from him.

"I have been a fool, George." Joshua stood up swiftly and rubbed his face vigorously. "We will leave tonight, if we can find berths to accommodate."

"Good. I know a few ships heading south on the evening tide. I will enquire about a passage. Pack lightly and join me again at the docks by six tonight."

Joshua changed his clothes, packed his bag, and closed the door behind him without looking back. He placed Bea's letter in his chest pocket, close to his heart, and made his way up the street, turning left at Candlemaker Row. There was one stop he needed to make before he joined George at the harbour. He stood outside the unobtrusive set of doors. He could hear voices inside as he entered as quietly as he could. It differed from what he had imagined. He had pictured a grimy back room or a secret cellar in some sort of boarding house. Now he felt foolish as he gazed at the church-like setting, with a podium at the front and pews down the sides. *I suppose it is God's work they are doing, after all.* The people in the pews glanced at him for a moment before turning their heads back to the podium and sat a little straighter as they continued to listen to their speaker. Joshua scanned the crowd for him, hoping he was here, and spotted him near the front. He flicked out his gold pocket watch, imagining the words his father would say declare about the new situation and studied the time. He didn't have long.

"... Now, we will hear from Mrs Woodhouse from Washington, and the encouraging progress of our efforts in the capital." It impressed Joshua at the reach these people had, but he couldn't wait. Bracing himself, he coughed loudly. He glanced back at Mr Winston, who was now looking at him. Mr Winston tilted his head to his left and rose from his pew. Joshua followed gratefully.

"She told you then?" Mr Winston spoke in a tense, hushed

voice.

They stood by the door leading into the smaller meeting room. "Do they know, what happened to Sarah? That you sent Bea after her?" Joshua tilted his head towards the congregation.

"A few do, not all. But I didn't send anyone, Mr Mason. It was your wife's idea to go after them. I suggested a very different plan, using my own connections. Bea was the one who wanted to go after them supported by her sister."

"I don't doubt that."

"Then what are you doing here?" Mr Winston asked cautiously.

"I need to know where exactly they are going. My colleague and I will follow them to do whatever we can to turn the scales in our favour – though I will certainly admit, regarding my wife, no one is more fearless."

Mr Winston gave Joshua a half smile in agreement. "The success of the railroad is that no one person holds knowledge of all the connections. I know where they are docking, and the name of the person collecting them. He is to take them to an inn for their first night; after that it is the extended community who will judge how best to get them close to Hanley – that is, Drayton Hall. If I give you the information, it is vital that no one else be privy to it. In the wrong hands it could have devastating results."

Joshua laid his hand over his heart, and unbeknownst to Mr Winston, Bea's letter. "I can easily make that promise."

"Very well, come with me." Mr Winston guided Joshua through the door and into the side room. The young man wondered how many times Bea, Sarah and Grace had stood in this room and held multiple sobering conversation with everyone, a hidden part of her that she had scared to share with him. All she had wanted to do was make the world a better place. Without him realising it, he had turned into his father.

Mr Winston headed over to a small desk in the corner, pulled out a piece of paper from the side, and scribbled down a couple of lines. He rolled the blotter over the top of the writing and then folded it in half before striding back to Joshua.

"I give you this, but you must promise to burn it once you have memorised the information. No one else must see it." Mr Winston held out the piece of paper, waited for Joshua's reply before handing it over.

"I will burn it before we leave. Thank you, Mr Winston." Joshua placed the note next to Bea's as the older man walked back to the far side of the room and opened a small, panelled door, gesturing for him to depart. "Bring Sarah back to me. If she is still alive, don't leave her in the hands of that man." For the first time Joshua realised that the man in front of him was in love. *That was why he helped Bea so readily,* he thought.

"Sarah means as much to our family as my daughter does; we will do everything we can to bring them back."

He held his hand out for Mr Winston to shake. "Thank you again." Without another word, the door behind him closed, and within moments, he was back out on the street. He slammed the door shut behind him and ran to the harbour with the leather bag in his hand.

"There you are! Good. I've bought us a passage on a ship heading south; they will make a stop for us. It was more money than I thought, however." George dropped his voice as two men walked past, heading to the harbour.

"I have some money about me, don't worry... and I found the exact dock in Georgia they plan to disembark at." Joshua resisted touching his chest pocket in public.

"Excellent." George patted Joshua on the back and lead him through the harbour crowd. "I understand the ship we are leaving on is faster than theirs, so it should enable us to gain some time. Follow me, it's this way."

Twilight was setting in as they both weaved in and out of the bustling men, heaving things into the warehouses or huddled together doing trade on the side. They continued down the entire harbour for almost twenty minutes, passing various piers until George stopped in front of one of the larger wharfs, with a tall ship standing ready to set sail.

Chapter 36

Drayton Hall, Georgia 1833

S arah kept Grace close, never leaving her sight. She had torn up part of their bedding on board ship to make a wrap, to tie Grace to her body, just as she had done with her own son so that she could work the fields when he was a baby. That way no one could steal Grace out of her arms. Hanley too had thought of everything. In the ship's cabin were extra dresses for Grace to wear, slightly too big and some rags for Sarah to wear, resembling her former slave clothes. She tore them up determinedly and used them as nappies for Grace. He had even brought a pair of goats on board to produce milk for the child. At first Grace reacted happily enough to her new surroundings, as though it were all an adventure, but as time passed she became restless, crying at the smallest mishaps, and sleeping poorly, clearly missing her Mama and her home. The men on board hated the child's wails, and when Hanley wasn't looking, threw Sarah more than a few threatening gestures. But in truth, no one would dare touch Hanley's child, not without losing their own life.

The ship came to port in Savannah, Georgia, the breeze from the sea soon giving way to the hot, muggy air of the growing city. Two carriages and two carts stood waiting for them as they disembarked; Hanley took one, whilst Sarah and Grace had another to themselves as the men, goats and other belongings were crammed onto the remaining carts. Shanty-houses along the riverbank soon gave way to larger, half-built dwellings, obviously being constructed for the rising numbers of middle-classes appearing in the city. The strange convoy made its way through the main street, then turned left, passing a large open square with a stage built in the centre. Sarah could hear a man with a deep southern accent shouting out prices and confronted with her new reality. She was a slave once more. A line of naked men and women shackled in chains, half-starved and beaten, were waiting to be sold to their new owner. There was no escape for any of them now, including herself. She leant back against the soft cotton seat and shielded Grace away from the degrading scene. But soon the city gave way to the burgeoning plantations, and she could hear the cotton pickers' song through the open window. Their voices, despite the sufferings she had known during many an afternoon singing the words, felt somehow like home, and she sang along to them quietly, rocking Grace to the verses:

"He sits on a horse just as pretty as can be

Hoe Emma Hoe, you turn around dig a hole in the ground, Hoe Emma Hoe

He can ride on and leave me be

Hoe Emma Hoe, you turn around dig a hole in the ground, Hoe Emma Hoe

Master he be a hard, hard man

Hoe Emma Hoe, Hoe Emma Hoe.

Sell my people away from me

Hoe Emma Hoe, Hoe Emma Hoe.

Lord, send my people into Egypt land

Hoe Emma Hoe, Hoe Emma Hoe.

Lord, strike down Pharaoh and set them free

Hoe Emma Hoe, Hoe Emma Hoe, Hoe Emma Hoe."

Soon the bell rang out to signal the end of the working day. and the land grew silent once more. They travelled through the night, but Sarah slept little.

The first glow of light broke through the carriage window as the birds sang out, signalling another day in the South, and a step closer to her long-delayed fate. She looked out the window and recognised the river beside them, the water that had been her road to freedom all those years ago. Which meant they were nearly there. The canopy of trees, wrapped in Spanish moss like expensive furs, framed the driveway to the grand plantation house. On the left was a blanket of cloud as far as the eyes could see, with heads popping through before disappearing. As the old foreman, his wide brim hat covering his face in shadow, strode back and forth across the field, clinging tight to his ever-faithful whip. On the opposite side was swamp land and recently ploughed fields for rice.

As the carriage came to a stop, Sarah clung to the child one last time, and bracing herself for what was about to happen next.

"Come with me." Hanley opened the carriage door and held out his hand for Sarah.

She stepped down, but refused his hand, and followed him onto the porch of the main house, with its white walls and pillars, the only colour that mattered in the south, cotton, skin and purity.

Hanley smiled down at Grace and stroked her rosy, hot cheeks. "I am putting you and Grace in a room upstairs." He casually pointed towards the stairs. His grin widened at Sarah's shocked expression.

There was no mob dragging her away from the child and placing a rope around her neck? Instead, he was issuing her a room in the main house. She shook herself and sat Grace up a little in her arms. Protecting her was all she really needed to concentrate on.

An elderly, slim-framed black man, dressed in a formal suit, his head held gracefully high, marched through the open front doors.

"Good morning sir, I hope you had a pleasant journey?"

"Good morning Albert. It is certainly good to be back. This is my daughter, Miss Grace Hanley, and Jessie - you might remember her - now my daughter's nurse. Please give her everything she needs to take care of Miss Hanley." The master ordered, making sure his butler understood.

Sarah watched the old man in front of her guardedly, staring first at her, and then at the child she was holding. His eyes flickered through one expression after another, without saying a word. But she saw it all too clearly; after all the bastards that Hanley had created, why did he care so much about this one - and a daughter at that?

"Very good, sir." Albert nodded respectfully.

"Is everything ready - regarding my instructions?"

"Yes, the child and her nurse are located next to your own room. If there is anything amiss, I am sure Jessie here will let me know." Albert gestured up the main staircase to the right slightly, throwing Sarah another look. But she was no longer paying attention to Albert. Hanley had made it clear he wanted to keep them close, in case they tried to escape. Her mind flashed back to her life fourteen years ago, when he used to visit her once a month in her tiny hut, designated for her at the foot of the slope, nearest the house. After everything she had survived, nothing had really changed.

"Albert, show Jessie and Miss Hanley to their room. I am sure they will want to settle in and observe that everything is correct, and present for their needs."

"Of course, sir." Sarah spoke for the first time since he had accosted them in that quiet side-street in Beacon Hill, surround by four other men.

"May I ask for some milk and food for the child as soon as possible?"

"Of course, Albert, see to it immediately and get Ruby to run me a bath to wash the journey off. I will be back in half an hour." Hanley leaned in and kissed Grace softly on the cheek. "Welcome home my darling." He breathed in her ear. "Soon, we will be one happy family." Sarah shuddered at the thought and resisted the urge to pull the child out of his reach, but she knew that wouldn't be wise. If she was difficult, he wouldn't let her stay, and she needed to stay, for the child's sake, for her own. Keeping her head down was the best way to survive.

"Very good, sir."

Hanley patted Grace on the head and strode back through the front doors whilst Albert made his way to the foot of the stairs.

"I'm not here to serve the likes of you." Albert hissed. "I heard all about you, the famous Jessie who fooled the great Hanley and escaped. Now look at you. Right back where you started, holding his baby in your arms. Yours?" He questioned whilst examining her up and down.

"No."

"Why he should care so much about this motherless bastard anyhow?"

"She has a mother." Albert was the sort that talked trouble when the master was away, to only get you to confess and then, when you crossed him, use it against you. She had met people like him all her life. Just because he was a slave didn't make him any less bitter and the willingness to survive at any cost.

The staircase circled round to the gallery at the top, decorated with portraits of a fictional lineage. Lies for the American's who had lived in the south for generation's, that Hanley too was a well-bred English Gentry instead of the truth. That at heart he was still an abused little boy who grew up on the slave ships.

Grace's face was awe-struck, as she marvelled at the assortment of colours of the flower petals in vases up the stair-way, all the unfamiliar painted faces looking down at her, and the glittering gold of the morning sun coming through the large, gilt-framed windows.

Albert paused for a moment in front of the bedroom door, waiting for them to catch up.

"I think you'll find everything is satisfactory. Mr Hanley wanted only the best for the little Miss," he said with a sarcastic tone to his voice.

"Thank you. I'm sure it will be fine. If you could send us up some food an' milk for her; I would be grateful, Albert." The deep channels across his forehead squeezed together as he raised his eyebrows at her request. Then, remembering his orders, bowed his head in compliance before making his way back down the stairs, muttering to himself.

Inside the room was a beautifully crafted wooden cot-bed in one corner, and in the other, a single metal-framed bed that looked like they had removed it from a hob-hut, its white paint peeling off in large patches. On Grace's side of the room were some small wooden toys laid out, tempting her to play, and a large rocking horse that smelt like a real one, with a silky pale mane and tail, meant for an older child. Sarah sat Grace down next to wooden blocks as she continued to survey the room. He had spared no expense decorating for the child and gifting her with toys. It baffled her to why he would go to such extremes. Inside a large chest of drawers lay fine silk dresses, miniatures of the ones she had gazed at with Bea in the Boston silk shops, and Miss Julie's. But there was nothing a child could roll around in and play. They were garments designed to parade out and exhibit, if not for company, then to staff – and slaves. Grace picked up a wooden block with a letter 'G' carved into the side; on the other, a creature with a long neck and patches across its body. She munched down on the corners, pressing it against her gums.

There was a quick knock on the door, followed by a house-slave holding a tray of fruits, biscuits, some form of soup, bread rolls and a glass bottle of milk.

"Thank you – I-" Sarah looked up and gave a sharp intake of breath. "Gabby?" She was no longer the young semi-innocent girl Sarah had known, but a woman in her late twenties, and the years hadn't been kind. Sarah couldn't help but stare at the deep scar across her left cheek.

"I'd heard rumours, it was you, but I had to see it for ma self. The liar... the cheat... the one that got away. But look at you now!" After all these years, the friendship had turned to anger and betrayal left by Sarah.

"Gabby, I can explain..." Sarah rose to her feet as Gabby took a step forward, clenching her fists.

Gabby narrowed her eyes, taking another step forward, as Sarah moved in front of the child as protection. "You know he went crazy after you left, questioning people until they talked." She lifted her right hand up and, using her index finger, stroked the indent cascading from underneath the eye to her jaw. "They didn't believe me for a while that you never told me, your closest friend, what your plans were."

"I wanted to tell you."

"How you do it? Did you just run, or was it that guy after all? The one who you said was lying." Sarah could tell Gabby was relaying a speech she had rehearsed countless of times over the years.

How much had she told them under torture? Whether she told them about Elijah and if, by helping her, he had hung from a tree and confessed his own secrets.

She couldn't take that chance. "At the gathering, I just ran... took my chance... headed east instead of north." Sarah said blankly, preying Gabby believed her.

Gabby dropped her hands and slumped her shoulders. "Why didn't you take..." the grief and anger still clear in her voice.

For the first time, Sarah felt the guilt of leaving her friend behind. She had only been at Drayton for a year. Told herself that Gabby wasn't strong enough for the journey but in reality, she made the choice for her alone. "I watched my husband die whilst running and I couldn't risk it if they found us."

"Was it worse than this?" Gabby jabbed a finger at her face. "Or the others you can't see?"

"I am - so sorry." Sarah wanted to reach out and comfort the child, the way she had done countless of times. But that friend was gone.

"And now your back, in the big house, looking after that.... what was the point?"

"Gabby, let me...." They heard heavy footsteps coming up the stairs, making their way towards them. Gabby held her hand up, nodded, and took her leave, passing Hanley in the hallway.

"She is hungry." Hanley stood in the doorway and gazed at

Grace, who was still chewing a corner of one of the wooden blocks.

Sarah shifted her mind from Gabby back to Hanley. "Sir, forgive us. She is teethin' and likes to chew on hardened things, like the wood..." Sarah paused, unaccustomed to actually holding a conversation with her former owner.

"I hope she finds this more agreeable." He pointed to the tray on the table beside them. "Does she need anything else?" He hovered on the spot, as though waiting for advice.

Her mother, her home. Sarah thought to herself. "No, that should be plenty, thankin' you, sir."

He took a step closer, gazing at the child. "And the room? Anything amiss?"

"Sir, I noticed she doesn't have any play clothes... The dresses are lovely, but she is growin'; and attemptin' to crawl..." Hanley replied with a baffled and annoyed expression. "She needs clothes to stretch out her limbs, and roll about in. If I had some fabric, then I could..."

Understanding finally clicked into place and flicked his hand towards the door. "Tell Albert what you need." Hanley moved to leave, satisfied that he had thought of almost everything.

Sarah, feeling unusually bold, took another step forward. "Sir? May I ask, why am I..."

He spun round. "Still here, still alive?"

"Yes."

"Grace; she needs you. She knows you, and for some God forsaken reason she loves you... that is, if an infant can love." He paused and studied Grace, dribbling on the square block. "So, for now, you have a place here, as long as you do nothing foolish." He gave her a familiar warning look.

Sarah dropped her eyes obediently. "Yes sir – master."

"I will leave you now to take refreshment, and if you need anything, I'll be *right* next door." It was a reminder. Sarah bowed her head. For now, she was safe.

Chapter 37

Georgia, April 1833

He waited until the small harbour was no longer in sight. "I'm Jeb, by the way."

"Miss Woodlands; this is my sister." The name still felt strange to say, leaving a bitter taste in her mouth.

"Nice to meet you, Miss – Miss." He nodded at each woman. "About ten miles down the road we'll be comin' to a travellers' inn, where you can spend the night, before an acquaintance of mine will meet you tomorrow, and take you further on, towards your journey's end."

"Thank you," murmured Beth.

They didn't know what else to say, or what not to say, so they remained silent as the flat land stretched out in front of them, and the road vanished behind them into a hot, hazy dusk.

"Did you get much sleep?" Asked Beth, gazing at her sister, fully dressed and staring out of the bedroom window at the early morning sun across the pasture.

"Not really, the sticky heat, and that feeling of..."

"The unknown? I know! Do you know what we are to do next?"

Bea turned round and faced Beth, sitting up in bed with the

pillows squashed comfortably behind her back. "Jeb said we are to wait here quietly until a man called Franklin comes and collects us at some point later today."

"Should we pack up and see what they might have for breakfast?" Beth ambled over to the washstand and splashed cold water across her face.

The Inn was more inclined towards serving tradespeople and travellers than two women voyaging alone. Most of the rooms had either a single bed or a double, though they had the luck of the only twin accommodation. Bea climbed back onto the bed and waited for Beth to get ready. Her hands stroked the thin sheets absent minded, which had been itchy, and scratched at their skin throughout the night. Beth continued to wash and placed on a fresh dress made from cotton this time instead of silk. She sat in front of the old speckled mirror and attempted to pin her frizzy hair back up.

In fact, it was more like a boarding house, with a single sitting room, populated by a handful of tables and chairs. There were several men within, all sitting by themselves, one at each table, and a rather more dishevelled pair in cahoots in the corner. Each smiled and nodded at the sight of the two impeccably dressed women entering the room, but to their relief, no one attempted a stab at introductions or conversation. Bea and Beth nodded and returned their smiles whilst the young server showed them to a table.

"What would you like, miss?"

"Ah... can I get a coffee, and some eggs please?" *Like Sarah always makes*, she thought with a sigh. Beth looked around at the other plates to find out what might actually be on offer, catching two of the men's eyes, to their apparent delight. She smiled nervously and pivoted back to the waiting girl, looking confused.

"She will have the same as me," offered Bea.

"Very good, miss." The young lady, now with a closer inspection, could no more be twelve or thirteen, bobbed her head.

"Thank you."

After ten minutes, the young server came back with two coffees and a note, which had been discreetly placed under one cup. Bea guessed it was from Mr Franklin, and that this boarding house was part of the community who were eligible to lend their assistances with escapees along the railroad. Bea took a sip of the welcomed coffee, which had a strong bitterness to it, and slipped the note under the table to read.

"Finish your breakfast as normal, then please meet me outside the far stables. Joshua."

She read the note three times and struggled to hide the baffled look on her face. She raised her eyes and searched the room for a sight of him. Was it some sort of cruel joke? Did Hanley know she was here, and it was another one of his tricks? It resembled Joshua's handwriting, but the words were cold and disconnected.

"Is everything alright?"

Bea paused, thinking how to tell her sister.

She lifted the note into her palm and carefully slid it across the table, dragging against the slightly murky tablecloth.

Beth skimmed the note and exclaimed. "What?" slightly louder than she had intended, and with her northern accent coming through. She lowered her head sharply and continued quietly with an apologetic look. "Do you think he is here? Should we both go?"

"What if it's a trap? I don't see him." Whispered Bea, glancing around the room.

The young girl brought out the eggs with chunks of bread and a small nob of butter on the side. "Would you like some more coffee?"

"Please," replied Beth as she took a hesitant mouthful of eggs.

"Are you both from Scotland? Looking to settle?" The Americans' often struggled to place their northern accent. It wasn't the first time someone had made that mistake, but right now, it might just benefit them.

"Er… Aye, visiting family in the area."

The girl looked overjoyed that she had made this correct detection and skipped away to fetch more coffee.

"Scottish?" Bea giggled.

"Aye!" Beth bust out into a peal of laughter, almost spitting her eggs back across the table.

They finished their breakfast casually, then rose 'for a stroll around the yard to stretch their legs'. Bea was tearing and twisting a napkin she had taken unconsciously from the dining table. Her heart was pounding, and she felt clammy and sticky in this dreadful heat. A line of stables with a carriage positioned in front, with bales of hay stacked into a haphazard pyramid on the far side, skirted the building. Beth reached out for Bea's hand, telling her they were in this together.

Then they spotted them: two men standing together, in the shadow of the stable door, looking rather down-at-heel and dishevelled.

At the sound of their feet, the men turned to face them. They had beards and their worn and tired faces were smeared in dirt. And yet, she knew those sea-blue eyes and his warm smile.

Joshua gestured for the two women to follow him, and guided them round behind the door, as though to show them a fine horse amongst the stables lot. Then he stepped forward, holding his hands out to her. But something made her stop.

"Joshua... what are you doing here, what happened? Is that you, George?" Bea stayed fixed to the spot. George gave a brief, warm smile to Bea, and moved towards Beth.

"Are you not glad to see us, my love? After I read your note, we purchased passage on a ship that very evening, and have been chasing after you without a breath ever since." Joshua took a step closer to Bea as George and Beth embraced one other.

"How glad am I that we found you, my love," George whispered in Beth's ear. But Bea was in no mood for embraces. There was a frustration building inside of her which overshadowed any joy of seeing her other half. "Why are you here? I am not going back. If that is what you want, I'm going to free Grace and Sarah, no matter what you say."

Joshua stepped closer and softened his voice. "I wouldn't ask that of you – we came to help. I understand why you left as you did, and I don't blame you..."

"Blame me? For our - or should I say *my* child - getting kidnapped, for bringing Hanley back into our lives? Or..."

"Leaving me behind?" He was standing in front of her now, and could feel her body shaking. He wiped away the tears rolling down her cheeks as she noticed lines on his breaking through the grime and the tiredness. He pulled her in and held her tight. "I'm sorry."

"So, am I." His beard tickled against her face as he kissed her like he used to. She felt her body relax and give way to him, her belly fluttering with love once more.

But she pulled away suddenly, surprising them both, and took a step back. "We can't – we're single sisters! If people see us together, they will either think we are... whores... or untrustworthy. It would jeopardise everything. We have to be smart about this."

"Then what can we do?" Entreated George, now stepping

away from Beth and glancing around the yard through the break in the stable doors.

Beth placed her hand on George's grimy vest. "There is someone meeting us from the community today and taking us on to the next stopping post. If you follow behind..."

"Then we can support you from a distance, without posing a threat?" Suggested Joshua, staring at Bea.

"Yes – and as soon as we come to know more, and arrive at Drayton – or as close to it as might be safe, then we can come up with a better plan." She said with an encouraging half-smile.

"Understood." George smiled at Bea and then back at Beth.

"Get yourselves cleaned up, and rest, and we will let you both know once the person has made contact and we understand where to go," suggested Beth happily, ushering the men away.

Once the men had disappeared, and left them stroking the noses of a pair of handsome black mares, one with white star, Beth glanced at Bea. "Are you alright?"

"Yes, but... it just complicates matters, having them here now." A torn sensation washed over her. She was happy to have Joshua here, supporting her, fighting for their family. He was doing what she had begged him to do. But she knew if push came to shove, he would also hold her back from what needed to be done. She set her jaw and continued stroking the horse's nose, calmly and rhythmically. She concluded, if it came to it, she would venture past all of them alone.

Chapter 38

Drayton Hall, April 1833.

Hanley tapped on the door before entering the nursery. "Good morning, my dear."

There was, of late, an undeniable sense of new beginnings to his life, something he had never felt before. At first he had wanted to take the child merely as a jaded form of payment, to enact his ultimate revenge upon Bea; punishment for thinking she had escaped him and believing she had the perfect life with that boy. But now he couldn't deny that he honestly enjoyed waking each morning, and hastening the few steps down the corridor, eager to see this little girl's face. He could give her a life built upon happiness, surround her only with good things; she would love him naturally, freely, and with all that she was. One day she would look back up at him as a young woman, with all her strength and beauty, and see only a loving father. And it was here, it was possible. Pushing the door open gently, he found them both on the floor, Grace attempting to crawl to Jessie across a padded quilt, stumbling now and then, but always continuing, with grunts of determination. She paused as he entered and stared at him with her huge green eyes. There was no judgement, no pain. He was just someone who made her smile. Someone she needed.

"And how are you this morning, my little one?" She clapped her chubby arms willingly to his chest as he lifted her up and touched his face curiously in an awkward pawing motion. He could almost believe she loved him.

This was his life now; spending his days here at Drayton with his daughter. That would finally make him happy.

"Did she sleep well, Jessie?"

"Yes sir, she only woke the once, an' she ate a substantial breakfast an' milk this mornin'."

"Aren't you a clever girl?" He threw her into the air and caught her quickly, making her squeal with excitement. "I'm about to do my rounds. Would you two like to join me for some fresh air?"

"I'll... fetch her cardigan." Jessie made her way to the drawers.

"Meet us downstairs."

"Yes, sir."

Hanley waited for her on the front porch with Grace balancing delightedly on his lap. There was a floral scent in the air, and the night's chill was disappearing quickly into the day. She swayed there, supported by his enormous hands, pulling at his hair and prodding affectionately at his bent nose, his brown, long-lashed eyes, and chiselled tanned jaw. He noticed that, from time to time, Grace would look about for someone almost as though she had heard a voice she recognised, its owner waiting just out of sight. He had also grudgingly realised how much she missed her Mama, calling out for Bea, the anguish in her little noises clear for all to interpret. But now she seemed far more at home, comforted richly by Sarah, and entertained meanwhile by his deep voice, strong hands and uncharacteristic patience.

"There you are." Jessie had appeared behind the odd pair, and she bent down, about to place a light cardigan around Grace's shoulders, ready to feed her arms through the tiny holes, when she was met by Hanley's hand, stopping her.

"... Would you like me to fetch the pram' round, sir?" Jessie stepped back and gave way to him.

"No, there is no need, I'll hold her." He gestured for the top, and gently placed Grace's arms through the holes himself, tugging the sleeves over her rounded wrists. "There. Snug as a bug!" She mirrored his broad smile, kicking her legs out and shouting something unintelligible, but unmistakably enthusiastic.

For the past few mornings, the three of them walked around the whole plantation. He would explain the finer details to Grace in jest, and explain carefully that all of this would be hers one day, to enjoy, and to manage. Jessie always joined them and not wanting to let the child out of her sight. He watched how the slaves, one by one, noticed the black woman at Hanley's side, and how low Jessie held her head each time they walked past the cotton-pickers, or walked through their makeshift hob-village. Muttering to one another how there wasn't even a mark on her, that she was living in the big house now with the master's child. He knew there was now nowhere she truly belonged. Outcast and bathed in suspicion, she could no longer return to them.

This morning they cut through the meadows; Grace loved to watch the butterflies flit from one wildflower to another. Hanley used his free hand to pull at the stalks, creating an instant bunch in his hand for Grace to admire.

"Have you heard from Beatrice at all, Jessie?"

Jessie paused in her step, thrown by the question. "No, sir. I ain't spoken to no-one."

"Because, I hear that two women, two *Scottish* sisters, are travelling through the south looking for their extended family – do you not think that such simple-minded subterfuge smacks of Beatrice Lightfoot?" He looked innocently over his handful of daisies to his escort and snapped the head off the largest flower.

"No, sir," repeated Jessie, unable to move. "I promise you, sir, we have not corresponded. I do not know where she is. But if it is... I mean, how would she know where we are? Her Mister, he would never let her come alone like that. My guess is that she's still in Boston."

Hanley let the rest of his bunch of stalks fall to the ground. "I told her I would make her come to me and I think she has. I will therefore invite her here, alone; show her how well our daughter is doing and suggest strongly that she should stay permanently. I want us to be a family... but if she does not agree, or tries to take my beloved Grace, then I have no choice but to-"

Jessie quickly interrupted. "If this woman is Beatrice, sir, then... she will see what you have built fo' yourself here, and how much you love your child, and... I am sure she will *not* want to take that away from you. She knows what's best."

Hanley laughed at Grace's infectious giggle as he tickled her neck with a spare daisy. "It is your job to make that clear, persuade her that this is the only option she has if she wishes to remain the mother of our child."

"Sir."

"She is to come for dinner tomorrow."

Jessie took a step forward and held out her hands, almost pleading with him. "Allow me to make up the house for her likin', sir, to show her how much she'll be wanted here. Like you said sir, it is her only option."

"Very well." Stretching his arms up, he threw Grace in the air, causing all the petals she had clutched a hold of to cascade out of her little hands, before she landed once again in his firm grip, the ground around his feet strewn with trampled flowers.

Chapter 39

Each evening, their new protector, Mr Adolphus Franklin, moved them from one town to another, booking them into modest establishments and half-built towns. In each place they stayed, there wasn't much to see, with their wooden buildings, a handful of stores and, if they were lucky, a church in the town centre. Yet, each one had a single large brick building, a statement built by a plantation owner that not only did they own their slaves, but the town and the white population inside. By the third day, they were only five miles away from Drayton Hall. Every night they would find a place to come together and try to form a plan to free Grace and Sarah. Bea had found out Sarah was now Jessie by Hanley's command. But none of their plans could work. Hanley kept them beside him night and day. How could she slip past him? And if Bea suggested anything too risky, Joshua put a stop to it. There was a hopelessness descending on the group, especially Bea. What had she been thinking? That she could simply walk into the plantation and take them back and that Hanley would do nothing? If he caught her, this time she wouldn't escape the noose, not by his hand, not in the lawless south.

They were running out of time. Mr Franklin had to leave them at this town and return to his store before they missed him, and they now had less than a week to free Sarah and Grace and make it back to the ship before it stranded them for months. They strode past shop windows displaying bonnets and dresses, without really taking anything in. Bea stopped outside one front and gazed at her reflection in the bright panes of glass. She looked tired, as tired as she had been while pregnant with Grace, and the dreams... they had resurfaced too... She caught her breath. Her hand automatically went to her stomach. No, it couldn't be. She hadn't had regular monthly bleeds since Grace had been born, but then... She counted back the days and realised that this month hadn't come. Nor had the last. But she couldn't possibly think about another baby, when her first-born was missing. *If Joshua knew she was pregnant with his child, would he stop her from saving Grace?* She hated herself for thinking it but now she couldn't stop wondering.

"I think I am going to head back to the inn and rest a little, I suddenly don't feel too well." Bea rubbed her hand against her forehead, suggesting she had a headache.

"Are you alright?" Beth studied her sister's face and saw the familiar burden weighing heavily on her shoulders.

"I haven't been sleeping, that is all." Bea patted Beth on the shoulder and attempted a smile. "I would like to rest before we meet tonight."

"Would you like me to come with you?" Beth asked gently, a hint of worry in her voice.

"No, you stay out a little while longer. The men are not far away, and I shall be just across the square. I just need... a moment."

"Of course, dearest, I understand. I'll check on you in an hour."

Bea nodded gratefully and turned back across the street to head round the square through the park. She arrived at the Inn which was in the centre of the small town, with its painted white wooden walls and shutters on the side of the windows.

There was a porch that stretched along the edges of the building, sporting a few wicker seats on either side of the front door. An elderly man sat with a folded newspaper in one hand and a steaming cup in the other. He stared at the people walking past, commenting to himself obliquely on their appearance, or where he imagined they might be going. He had been there last night when they had arrived, again first thing in the morning, and he was there now, looking Bea up and down as she walked back up the steps, alone, but she was in no mood for a conversation.

She dashed through the hallway and headed straight to their room. The space was cool and dark; Beth must have closed the shutters against the early afternoon sun. Bea pulled at her ribbons, her bonnet slipped off her head, and she placed it down on the small vanity unit. She paused for a moment, and caught sight of a card, with her make-believe name printed elegantly in the centre. She froze, the hairs on her arms standing up with fear. Even Mr Winston didn't know of their false name. On the back, a pool of solid red wax, with a crest pressed into it. She recognised it, but for the life of her, she couldn't think where from.

In an instant the seal was cracked in two and there it was, his name.

Dearest Beatrice,

It delighted me more than I can say to discover you had, so swiftly, taken up my offer to visit us in the South.

The family is well, young Grace is thriving here, smiling more and more each day, and attempting to crawl. She has her nurse, Jessie, with her at all times.

We spend the days walking the plantation and overseeing the workers, and she sleeps contentedly each night.

*It would delight us to receive **you** for a little dinner, and kind con-*

versation, this evening, should you be available? I will send a coach to pick you up at six so that you have time to greet Grace before her bedtime.

As ever, yours affectionately,

Captain Victor Hanley.

This was it. A clandestine attack wouldn't work now. She had to do it alone tonight. She knew Joshua would protest, along with Beth and George, but she had no other choice. And she didn't have long to get ready. Thankfully, Beth had packed one of her more elegant dresses, the green one she had worn to the gala. The cold water left over in the washing jug was refreshing as she splashed it across her face and down her neck. Using a fresh wash-cloth, she wiped away the remaining sweat. She wasn't fond of this muggy heat of the south, and it wasn't even summer yet. She did not know how people coped.

She sat down at the vanity unit heavily, and placed both hands on her waist, trying to slow her breathing, and took up the small set of quill pen and writing paper the inn offered each of its occupants. If Beth didn't return in time, then she needed to write it down. She had already decided not to tell Joshua of her plan, knowing he would only stop her; knowing he wouldn't understand. She wrote a letter to Beth, on one side instructing her where to meet should their escape be successful; on the other side, a loving apology. She paused before starting with her husband's letter. He was the love of her life. And yet, she realised it was all just words; that her actions sent out a very different message. That he wasn't worth more than their child, that she didn't trust him, and that she felt no compunction in leaving him behind once again.

She had just finished pinning up her hair in a simple design and putting the finishing touches to her dress when the door opened.

"What... what are you doing? I thought you were ill?" Beth walked into the room, a shocked expression on her face.

"I received a letter. From Hanley. He knows we are here and has invited me... to go... alone." Bea held up her hands and stopped her sister's protests. "We are in his world now. I have to play by his rules if I hope to get them back."

"And if it's a trap?" Beth furred her eyebrows, folded her arms whilst blocking the door.

"Then it's a trap." Bea gazed across at her face in the mirror, observing her own pale cheeks and tight lips, avoiding her sister's stare.

"Bea, you can't..." Beth pleaded.

"I have to try; we are running out of time." Bea pointed to the vanity unit. "I have written to you of what to do if I am successful – meet me there tonight, it's what we have already discussed. If I don't appear an hour after midnight, then you run - *all* of you."

"Bea.... wait!" Beth stood firm in front of the door.

"The carriage is arriving at six. I have to go." Bea grabbed hold of Beth and pulled her in tight. "I love you – be happy. I think George is the one. Above all, know that I am sorry." She released her and placed three other letters in her hand. "Keep these safe," she instructed as she made her way to the door, "and give Joshua his letter only if I don't... if I cannot meet him." Beth nodded, stepping mutely aside, and the door closed quietly, with only a swirl of skirts and the creak of the handle as the latch clicked back into its bracket.

Chapter 40

Drayton Hall.

The carriage turned down the drive to the house. Bea's stomach churned with anxiety at the role she needed to play if they wanted their plan to succeed. The house was larger than she had expected, with its pillars framing the porch, and the gilt decorations wrapping themselves discreetly around the edges of the building. Placed perfectly one storey above and between the two columns was a balcony with French windows. As if on cue, they swung open and Hanley stepped out, dressed in a grey suit. He looked like he was at home here, finally where he belonged. He watched the carriage pull up to the doors, another display of power, before languidly retreating into the house. Bea fidgeted with the frayed piece of lace wrapped round her wrist. "You are my child; you are not his – you are innocent – you are loved – you are mine."

The coachman jumped down and opened the carriage door, offering her a hand. She could hear footsteps getting closer as a spit of sick entered her mouth, suddenly noticing her hands were wet with sweat. She saw the front door open in the corner of her eye, and saw him stride forward, offering his hand as a replacement to the coachman. Her heart pounded in her chest and found it difficult to breathe, as it felt like the lace tightened against her throat.

"Beatrice. I am so glad you took me up on my offer." He sounded like the Hanley she had met over two years ago back at the house and Mrs Johnson's; secure and dripping with

279

charm. How wrong she had been. She wanted to shout at him, to scratch his eyes out for all the pain and heartache he had caused, but she politely tilted her head. "But of course." *Play the game.*

"Before we get settled, shall we head up to the nursery to see little Grace?"

She couldn't help but pause in her steps as her chest cried out in longing. "... Please." He stared down at her, seeing the pain all too clearly in her face at being apart from her child.

"Jessie has cared for her night and day. She has wanted for nothing." He encouraged her towards the stairs. "They are in the room besides mine." Bea nodded her head, unable to talk as she held her breath. The closer they got to the landing, the more she could hear them. A chuckle of pure delight resonated out the bedroom door and down the stairs, causing a blend of joy and grief to wash over her. It was a sound she had missed with every fibre of her body for the past three weeks, and yet it was now somehow a little different. She moved a little faster. "She has a wonderful laugh; it reminds me of yours." There was a sincerity in his voice there that she had never heard before. "She is a happy child."

The door opened, and the sight of Sarah and Grace greeted her, playing with a set of coloured wooden balls on a velvet rug. Sarah looked up first, and her eyes widened to saucers at the sight of Bea. Then it was Grace's turn to notice the visitor. Bea fell to her knees and stretched her arms.

"Mama." Her little voice formed the words with a kind of brave delight, and she crawled towards her mother eagerly.

Bea couldn't stop the tears from starting at the sight of her child. It had been over two weeks; how much she had changed. "My darling... My baby! How much I have missed you. Look at you crawling to Mama." Grace stumbled a few times and Bea made to move closer and pick her up, but Sarah placed her hand out to wait, showing her how strong her daughter had become. As Grace reached Bea, she scooped her up, pressing her little body against her chest, feeling how she had grown since last she had held her.

"I love you, my little one... how much Mama has missed you. But I'm back now, and will never leave you again."

Hanley crouched down beside Bea and stroked Grace's cheek, which had become wet from Bea's tears. To her surprise, at this gesture, Grace turned her head and held her hands out for him to take her. Without a word, he slipped his broad hands in between Bea and her child, and slid her into his arms, Grace beaming up at him, overexcited at the sight of her Mama after so long a separation. "We have become very fond of each other, haven't we, my sweetheart?"

Bea wanted to snatch Grace back, to shout at him, to never take her baby away from her again, but she held her tongue. She glanced at Sarah, who was giving her a warning look. How much she had missed her friend. Bea stood up and walked over to her, took the outstretched hand.

"It is good to see you again. Are you?" Bea muttered under her breath.

"No." She confirmed, shaking her head. "I have stayed with Grace the whole time."

"Jessie was about to get Grace ready for bed and give her a bath. Would you like to stay and help? We can have dinner in an hour?"

"Can I? I would be so grateful." Bea gave Hanley a broad smile, playing the dutiful lady.

"Of course, you will want to spend as much time as possible with them. I will see you in the dining room in an hour." He handed Grace back into Bea's longing arms.

"Thank you, Victor."

Bea noted his expression at her using his christian name.

Hanley was both his name and his trademark, like his father before him. He didn't say another word, gave them all a deep bow and then left, closing the door behind him.

Bea paused for a minute, waiting to hear the footsteps head down the hallway. "Thank you, Sarah, for taking care of Grace – I am so... He hasn't hurt you?"

"No, not a jot... he has kept me by Grace's side the whole time like a true nurse, thank goodness. I didn't know if..."

"Of course I came for you – so did Beth - and Joshua and George followed too, ignoring my request." Bea pulled a familiar look that reminded Sarah of Beacon Hill.

"You have a..." The nursery door opened, and two black women came through with a small copper bath for Grace. They were all dressed in the same peacock blue the uniform for Drayton house slaves.

Sarah pointed to a spot in front of the fire as Gabby came in, holding one jug of boiling water and another of cold. Bea could see they weren't exactly happy talking orders from Jessie, but no one spoke out of turn. They gave Bea a wary look as they brought in two more jugs of water, adding slosh after slosh until Sarah was happy with the temperature.

She stood up and moved closer to Gabby. "We are leaving. Come with us. I left you behind last time. You are strong enough to make this journey; you don't belong here." Bea tried to stop Sarah after her first words, but it was already too late.

"When? With them?" Gabby spun round and studied her former friend, aghast.

"Yes. I will send word to you when it is time."

Gabby stepped closer to Sarah sharply, causing Bea to rise to her feet. "Tell me now!"

"Gabby, we must trust each other. If everythin' goes to plan, I will come and find you." The sound of footsteps grew closer once more from down the corridor.

Gabby left quickly in the opposite direction and made her way down the stairs. Bea kept her eyes on the doorway for a few moments, her mind full, feeling intensely uneasy.

"Do you think... do you think that was right, to tell Gabby? What if she tells Hanley?" she whispered, as Sarah came to sit beside them once more.

"I owe her... the last time I fled, I felt that... it doesn't matter, the point is, I left her behind. From the mark on her face... he took his anger out on her when he couldn't find me. She was only fifteen."

Bea saw the guilt Sarah held. "I trust you. So if you trust her, then it's fine with me. I just hope she is as brave as you, for all our sakes."

"**S**he has grown so much - and in the space of just a few weeks." Bea held her naked baby out in front of her, inspecting her delightedly, as she wriggled around in her hands, excited for her bath. She noticed how her form had changed; how her legs and arms were slimmer somehow, no longer those of a chubby baby. She was becoming a young child now, a little girl who was growing into herself.

She placed the bouncing Grace into the bathwater, which she splashed about instantly, making little noises as her imagination came alive. Bea couldn't help but laugh along with her daughter as she played in the water. When Sarah joined in too, it felt as though no time had passed at all and they were back in Beacon Hill, almost a family once more. A thought came to her: the chase had changed for Hanley. She had seen it as he held Grace, the love he had for her – or his version of what love was... he would never give that up. There was only one way this could end with Grace, Joshua, Sarah and herself being free from him forever.

Sarah laid the thick cloth on the rug beside them. "We don't have long; you'll need to freshen up soon." Bea noticed how Sarah's voice had changed, her accent taking on a southern twang again. "I have found our way off the plantation. Each mornin' Hanley struts me and this little one, around the grounds, showing off what he says will be hers one day – well, one o' those times I saw a small path leadin' north through the swamp."

"Swamp?" Bea's expression reflected the image that flashed into her mind; the pair of them wading slowly through treacherous swamps in the darkness, clutching Grace as Hanley raced after them.

"Swamp land and mountains surround the north in Georgia, that's why it is so hard to find freedom headin' out by foot. Winston came up with the plan for us folk to head east to the sea, and secure tradin' ships. But that only helped a few, else they'd have caught on to us; the rest had to try the way north."

"He misses you. I think that's why he has been helping me." Bea gritted her teeth. "I'm sorry."

"You need to stop saying you're sorry! None of this is your fault. I knew the chances of bein' found and brought back."

"There are laws against what he did."

"It doesn't matter, law or no law, to them I'm property, an' reputation come to that. Ain't no white man in these parts goin' to turn a blind eye to a double-escape. They will always want what they own." Sarah shook her head as the old, morose thoughts spun webs in her mind.

"But we can't head north; they are waiting for us eastward, at a dock on the river."

"If we head through the swamps, the tracks will show less, and show North, but from the woodlands, past the mire-edge,

I know a way back round to the river."

"On foot?" Bea picked up Grace, swaddled tight in towels, holding her tight against her body.

"Unless you have a carriage or a cart, it's by foot - we can strap Grace to us – if we are to run, this is the only way." Bea saw the determination in Sarah's face and nodded.

"It has to be tonight, to meet the boat."

"You keep the Captain happy and I will pack what we need." Sarah rose to her feet and walked over to a small wooden chest in the corner of the room. She opened the lid and dug her hand in deep and pulling out a blanket. She laid it out in front of Bea and unwrapped it like it was Grace in her hands. The silver sparkled in the fading sunlight before she realised what she was actually looking at.

"Where on earth did you find that?" Bea said in a harsh whisper.

"The community smuggled it in."

"Sarah... we can't..."

"We might need to fight, and this will help." Sarah covered up the loot and gave Bea an uncompromising stare. "He won't think we have this. The men, the slave catchers he'll send after us, won't expect it either. I ain't coming back here ever again. I will find my freedom again, or die trying."

The new reality weighed heavy on her and the journey ahead of them. With a small smile, Bea passed the now sleepy Grace to Sarah, and gave her a light kiss on her head. "Mama loves you, darling."

She stood up, straightened down her skirt, and fixed her hair in the mirror. It was the best she could manage. She moved to the door as Sarah stepped forward, leaned in and gave Bea a hug with Grace still in her arms, who seemed to enjoy being sandwiched between the two sweetly scented bodices. Sarah slipped a small parcel from her pocket and slid it into Bea's hand. "You know what to do."

Chapter 41

Hotel, Georgia.

"What do you mean she has left – *again*?"

"Hanley invited her to the house – what could she do? He found out that she is here; I don't know about you two– we thought it was the best chance to get them out. We are running out of time... Unless you have a better plan?" Beth rounded on Joshua, her stern voice more than a match for his anger, and it remained him of Bea, always fixed in her resilience.

"We need to trust Bea; she always has a plan," interjected George, stepping between them.

"She told me where to meet her tonight, with Grace and Sarah." Beth waved the letter Bea left with instructions.

"Where?" George held his hand to see the note.

"We need to get hold of a boat and meet her at an old dock up the river." Beth turned her back and continued to pack the wooden chest.

"And what if she doesn't turn up?" Joshua couldn't stop fidgeting. Shuffling on the spot, opening and closing his fists as he fought against sinister thoughts.

"She will be there." Beth replied with an irritated tone. "So we need to be ready for when she is."

Joshua marched over to George and asked to read the letter. He slumped down at the writing desk and studied each word to form a plan. Beth continued to throw clothes at the trunk in silence. Whilst George looked like he was drawing in the air as he mumbled to himself.

"So," Joshua said, smiling ever so slightly, "Where are we going to get our hands on this boat? I have a plan."

Chapter 42

Drayton hall, Georgia.

Drayton butler stood at the foot of the stairs, waiting for Bea. "Mr Hanley kindly asks if you would join him in the drawing room before they serve dinner, Mistress."

Her body gave an involuntary shudder at the name. "Thank you."

"If you would follow me, Mistress." Bea walked behind him, her dress making a crunching, shuffling sound down the echoing corridor. A door stood ajar, the warm illumination from within flooding the end of the hallway. Her hand picked at a loose thread from her lace. She couldn't shake the nauseous feeling in her gut. *For Grace*, she told herself, *for my family*.

Hanley stood grandly against the light of the fire, a large glass of whisky in his hand. The butler strode behind Bea and picked up a silver tray from a sideboard, offering Bea a glass of wine.

"I wasn't sure of your newfound tastes in such liquors."

"Wine is... thank you..." Her hand shook a little as she reached out to take the glass.

"Please." Hanley placed his hand out to suggest one of the comfy seats beside him as he himself took one.

Bea took little slips of the delicious wine. She felt her nerves subside a little as she drank. Silence fell between them. What was there to talk about in this mirage of an occasion?

Hanley held his glass out for the butler to refill. "Thank you,

Albert. So, Beatrice: how are you finding your first visit to the South?"

Bea, taken back by such a civil question, paused before speaking. "I- ah... hot, the heat is sticky."

"Yes, nothing like Ulverston." He let out a small chuckle. "It can be quite hard to acclimatise to it at first, but I'm sure in time you'll settle in around here."

Settle in? He's expecting her to stick around, and this was now home. She hadn't realised she had finished it until she found Albert topping up her glass. The wine tasted good, and she enjoyed the relaxing sensation it brought, but she couldn't let her guard down. She cast her gaze around the room; anything to avoid casual eye contact with the man who had violated her, tried to take her life and now kidnapped her child.

The silence was deafening. She wanted to scream at him, hit him, ask him why. But that wasn't part of his game, and she had to play by his rules. Tonight, however, he wasn't his usual aggressively self-assured self; he seemed nervous somehow as he drank another glass of whiskey.

"You have a lovely home." The words stuck in her mouth as if she was chewing on a stale biscuit.

"You think so? I don't find that I can spend as much time as I would like here. I bought it just over fifteen years ago from another British family. It makes a pleasant home with a child about – you and Grace would be happy here. She is a merry girl -," he smiled as if reliving a memory of her laughing, "you have done an outstanding job of raising her." He reached his hand out and gently placed it on top of her own. He did not grip it, did not stroke it. Instead, simply pressed her hand into the arm of the chaise. His touch felt strange. As if it was his twin sitting next to her.

Bea took another sip. Her throat was dry and had an unusual taste. "Thank you... I dearly love her – I couldn't...." She stammered.

At the sound of the dinner bell chiming in the distance, Albert reappeared and politely cut her off. Hanley removed his hand and sat back in his own seat.

"Dinner is ready, sir."

"Thank you, Albert." Hanley rose to his feet and gave the empty glass back to the butler. "Shall we?" He held out his other hand in front of Bea for her to take.

"Thank you." This time she placed her hand gently on top of his, shutting off her emotions. *It was all a game.* Albert held out the silver tray to collect her own half-finished glass of wine as Hanley guided her out of the room.

The dinning room was large enough to hold a grand dinner party, with twenty chairs tucked underneath the polished mahogany table. Nearest to them, at the end of the table, two chairs remained out, with a bouquet of roses and wildflowers presented between them. They were her favourite flowers. Next to them were two sets of cutlery and an assortment of plates, each with a thin gold rim. Dotted around the room were four house-slaves, dressed as English footmen standing behind each chair. Bea glanced at the slave behind her who had his head down low, but he seemed to sense her uncertainty, drew the chair out for her to take.

"Thank you," she whispered, so that only he could hear.

The head house-slave, the housekeeper in fact, she presumed, raised her hand for two other women to enter holding plates filled with various dishes. Another, who looked ten years their junior, collected a wine decanter and made her way to the table. The eldest woman poured the red liquid in to the cut-crystal glasses in front of them. Each person waiting on them kept their heads down as they served, and Hanley did not look at them in his turn. Rather, he continued to stare at Bea, who was morosely transfixed by the silent staff before her.

"This must be strange for you."

"Pardon?"

"I know about your feeling towards slavery, here in the South; how you attend the abolitionist meetings, and the unconventional relationship you have with Jessie." Hanley spoke in a matter-of-fact tone, as though discussing a minor difference in local politics as he tucked into the fish which had arrived on their plate.

Bea kept her eyes down and picked at the fish, which she did not recognise. Her churning stomach made it difficult to eat.

"You probably know about my past, and my... prior experience of the slave ships. Yet you never asked about my version of events."

"What could you possibly have said to justify what you did to me?" Her tone was full of bitterness as she held his gaze.

A smirk crept across his face. "We will never know, will we Beatrice.... you were so ready to judge me."

"I did not judge you – not until you raped me and offered me up to be hung for murder!" She scrunched up her face at the accusation.

"You judged me as soon as your precious Mason boy told you I was no good. Nothing has passed between us of that nature when you turned me down." There was almost a chuckle in his voice. "You are not so innocent, not as righteous as you like people to believe, Beatrice."

"I never claimed to be righteous. I have my faults, like everyone else. But what you did..." She paused, remembered people were listening, and forced herself to eat a few mouthfuls of fish before one of the house slaves took the plate away. She took another gulp of wine, steadying her nerves. He was trying to bait her into saying or doing something that she might be ashamed of later, and she couldn't rise to it. Another plate filled with roast beef, potatoes and gravy. The meat crumbled into the juices in her mouth and reminded her of Ulverston, when they would have braised mutton on special occasions.

"We are more alike than you might think," he replied calmly, placing a mouthful of food in his mouth.

"We are nothing alike, you and I."

He let out another chuckle at the look of disgust on her face, followed by her unexpected reaction of pleasure at the food. "We both came from an angry household - not so much your father, I grant you – but we both have tried to free ourselves from our constraints and find our own path, to the dismay of those about us. And we have both failed."

"What you did to me..." The words spilled out of her mouth, removing the smile on his face instantly. Her voice cracked as she blinked hard, appalled by his perspective. The images flooding back.

"I... cannot excuse my actions toward you – my mind wasn't right... I drank a lot in those days." His voice was low and had lost all form of laughter.

"And now – taking my daughter?" She gripped the knife until her knuckles turned white and glared at him.

"*Our* daughter."

"Is your mind *right* now? Taking her away from me, forcing me to chase after her as though it were all some kind of game?" The tension rose between them as she allowed her anger toward him to express itself fully. "You think making me dance like a puppet is how to prove that you've changed and now, a father?"

"You must understand I needed you alone, to come here – and I knew you would not consider coming of your own free." He placed down his knife and fork and tried to grab hold of her hand.

Bea snatched it away, out of his reach. "You do not own me, nor do you own my child."

His tone became softer, with a hint of disappointment. "I do not wish for that – you shall see. Let's not spoil a lovely evening now – give me a chance to prove it to you."

"Prove what?"

"That you could be happy here, with me." He picked up his cutlery and continued to eat the rest of the dinner in silence.

Her body trembled. He was insane, and more worryingly, unwilling to listen. She needed to continue, however; she was so close to reaching the moment she needed. Taking another gulp of wine, almost finishing the glass, she continued to pick at the roast beef in front of her, finding it hard to swallow.

∞∞∞

"Shall we have dessert and coffee back in the drawing room, where we might be more comfortable?" Hanley suggested in a pleasant tone.

"Let's." The kitchen staff cleared the rest of their plates as the footmen pulled back their chairs. Hanley offered his hand, and she took it.

The fire was still warm and welcoming, but the low candlelight gave the room a sultrier feeling than it had before. But that might be the effects of three glasses of wine, she thought bitterly. Albert stood guard at the sideboard, ready to serve them more drinks.

"I note, Beatrice, that I failed to mention earlier how beautiful you look this evening. I noticed in Boston how motherhood suited you, and seeing you again now, I can observe that it has made you into a true woman." He gazed at her with unashamedly lustful eyes. Her cheeks blush but a tight pain rippled through her pelvis and into her gut. She gave no reply. He moved to sit down beside her. "Forgive me, I did not intend to make you feel uncomfortable – I forget you are unlike the other women."

"I..."

"I still love you, you know." He reached out and stroked the side of her face. She couldn't hide the shock in her expression, and she turned towards him, shaking his hand away. "I know what I did to you was... unforgivable, and words cannot express the sorrow I now feel at the remembrance of my actions. I am trying to change, to bring back what we had." He paused, remind her thoughts. "There is no excuse. I can only say that my old ghosts still haunted me back then, and I suppose I let them reign free."

"Victor..." She knew he was almost where she wanted him, and she glanced pointedly at the few faces still staring at them. "May we be alone?" Without hesitation, he lifted his hand and gestured towards the door. She waited until everyone had left before continuing. "You sent me to the gallows, I had a noose around my neck; I still feel it there some nights. Thanks to the quick-thinking of my father, and the support of my husband, I lived - but I am only alive inside because of my child, because of Grace. She brought a light into my darkness. Then you stole her away too." She didn't fight back the tears or hold back the words. This was her last chance. Maybe due to the wine, she felt more confident. Regardless, they washed down her face and dripped onto his hand, clasped over hers. "I am... so very sorry for how I treated you - and maybe you are right; I judged you harshly after Joshua told me about your past, and I didn't seek to know your side of the story. But – you raped me, beat me, and killed one of your men in front of me to frame me for murder, all because I fell in love with another man, and honestly and truly declined you."

He sat motionless for a while, "hearing it from your lips... my actions... I hope in time you find it in your heart to forgive me. If you stay with me and be a family, then I can show I can change. Give me this chance you had refused me once before," and then raised his hand slowly from her lap, and with the tips of his fingers, caressed the back of her neck and the top of her exposed shoulders, producing an unconscious shudder to course through her body. He leaned in and said softly: "But you loved me first, Beatrice, I know you did. He stole you away from me."

She spun round, catching him off guard, their faces inches apart. "I do *not* belong to you."

"I wouldn't want you to be. But, you could be happy here, I see it in your face – you, me, Jessie and Grace, all together, all where we are meant to be. Grace deserves to be brought up by her true father - someone who loves her with every part of his blood, bones and soul. I have seen Joshua with her. Granted, he took on another man's child when I could not, but that wasn't for her sake - it was for you. He looks at her and sees me; when I look at her, I see love, and happiness. I couldn't be without her now."

"What are you saying?"

"Stay here with me. Love me." He leaned in and kissed her tenderly. She closed her eyes and braced herself. *Not long now.* She blocked out flashes of that night the last time he had kissed her. *It was all a game*, she kept telling herself. *For my family.* He pulled her tighter against his body, and she felt the yearning building up inside of him. *No. not again, not again...* At the pressure of his groin against her corset it suddenly became too real, too sickening; not a game anymore, but a nightmare. Pain exploded in her mind at the touch of him, and at his smell. She pulled back, and he stopped.

"I... I need another drink – w-would you like one?" Her cheeks were flushed, and her lips were full and red.

"Of course! I'll get..."

"No, allow me." He smiled and handed her his empty glass. She returned the smile before heading to the sideboard. Carefully lifting the parcel out of her pocket, and shielding it with her body, and the crackling of the fire, she poured the fine powder from a yellow flower into his glass before adding a double measure of whiskey, giving it a brief stir. "Do you like ice - or water?"

"Neither – thank you." She poured out another glass of wine for herself and made her way back to their seat.

She handed him the glass as he made to kiss her again. "Cheers." She held her glass up, blocking him.

"What are *we* toasting to?"

"A... a new beginning."

"Do you mean that?" She nodded her head, and watched him down the whiskey in one, in a joyous, triumphant motion.

He placed his empty glass and her wine on the side-table, then wrapped his arms around her, pulling her tight against him. "Say that you love me; that we will be a family here." He transferred her smile onto his lips as he kissed her, with more passion this time. She closed her eyes and pretended it was Joshua's lips, waiting with a thudding heart for the powder to take effect, pushing the dark thoughts into the corners of her mind. He paused for a minute, his body swaying a little.

"Forgive me..."

"Perhaps we have had a little too much to drink. We should retire now for the night and resume our talk in the morning?" She adopted a soft voice, as though talking to a child at the end of a long day.

He rubbed his head with his hand. "I... think you might be right." She went to stand, but he grabbed onto her. "You know... no one has ever loved me. My father hated me, and I never knew my mother. I was told she was a house slave on an island plantation when my father was the overseer, her father was the master. So, I was a bastard, part slave, in his eyes. - My mother died a few years after I was born and when I was old enough, they made me join him on the ships. Claimed, bought, I do not know. He taught me to hate them and myself. A monster who has this black blood in me, bad blood, I was told." She sat down beside him. "No one knows. I have darker skin because of the climate and chestnut hair from my father. To be in constant battle with yourself. To see the hatred in the eyes of those who are meant to love you and believe their horrid words. – When I found you, I thought all of that would change – that someone might love me after all – that I was worthy of it." Images of her own mother flashed into her head and realised that she too was crying until he wiped away her tears. "When you picked him and treated me with fear like I was a monster – I questioned it, that maybe I am, maybe it was all true... So, then I acted like a monster to you." He held his hands up. "It doesn't condone it but maybe if you knew the truth."

She felt a form of pity. Knowing what it was like to have a bullying parent. "You are not a monster."

"Maybe I am like that Frankenstein monster, made up of parts – always seeking love and never finding it?" He saw the surprised expression wash over her face. "– I saw you read it once, so I read it too." Possibly it was the powder making him say such words, finally telling the truth, but it was all making sense. "Tell me now, you love me."

She looked at him straight in the eyes; one last lie to say goodbye. "I love you Victor."

"I love you, Beatrice. We are going to be... happy here..." His eyes closed as he spoke, the powder seeping into his bloodstream..

"We can talk more in the morning, now: let's get you to bed." She placed his arm around her shoulder and lifted him from the chaise longue.

"I should have spoken freely... long time ago... I am glad...

yes... we have had this time..."

"So am I."

Chapter 43

Bea's bedroom door opened at midnight exactly. "You did it?" Sarah stood there, Grace still sound asleep, held against her body in a wrap created by pieces of a torn sheet. Bea had changed into a simple dress, in a blend of cotton and wool, with her boots on, ready for the journey. The taste of their kiss was still clear and bitter on her lips.

"It worked."

"When the girls go to wake him in the mornin', they will think he is sick, and send out for a doctor - that will buy us even more time." Sarah smiled at her. "Here you take this." She handed her a heavy pistol, and a worn leather belt.

"I can't take this!"

"We don't have time to argue, Bea. I cannot take a gun, not while I've got the baby strapped to me, and we be needin' it! Do you know how to use it?"

"Da showed me once." Bea studied the gun in her hand and remembered the deer she had shot one autumn in the woods surrounding Ulverston quarry when food had been scarce. After that experience, she had stuck to their snares.

"Put the belt around your middle and slide the gun in, tight against you."

"And... shoot, if they come after us?" She couldn't believe

how serious Sarah was, the idea of shooting at someone. Flashes of the deer and Gregson, as the life faded from their eyes, filled her thoughts as she held the cold metal in her hands.

"They won't hesitate, and neither must you." She stepped out into the hallway, using only the balls of her feet, and gestured for Bea to follow.

∞∞∞∞

They crept down the stairs and instead of going out the front door, bolted shut by Albert, they made their way through the cook-house. The rooms were dark and cold, the last sparks of life from the burning embers in the fire grates emitting a faint, warming glow. The moon cast shadows across the hallways, making Bea believe they were being watched. The cook-house still smelt of their dinner. She noticed the pudding and coffee sitting on the tray that had never been delivered. One cake exhibited a few surreptitious bite marks.

"Gabby?" Sarah called out in a low whisper.

A movement behind them caused both women to jump. Gabby stood there quietly, the low light cast through the shutters creating slices of light across her face, following the line of her scar. But there was no bag, no belongings on her back or at her feet. Bea swallowed hard.

"We have bought ourselves some time, Gabby. Are you coming?" Sarah stepped forward; there was a stern tone in her voice. She wasn't wasting a second.

"How d'you know he won't come runnin'?"

"We slipped him some herbs; he will be sick come morning, and too dozy to realise we are missing until it's too late," Bea reassured the girl, reading the worry on her face.

There was a moment of stillness, during which Bea could have sworn none of them took even the slightest breath. Then, without saying another word, Gabby suddenly turned and ran out the room and back into the main house. Sarah gasped, then grabbed Bea's hand and hissed. "We need to go - now!"

∞∞∞

Gabby raced through the hallway and bounded up the stairs. Without knocking, she charged into Hanley's bedroom to find him hunched over, half dressed, holding his stomach.

"Sir?" Gabby crouched down and rubbed his clammy back familiarly.

"I... need... to vomit..." He made a retching noise, but nothing came out. "Get me some charcoal... from a dead fire." Gabby stared at the fire still burning in his room and knew she had cleaned the other fireplaces out. "*Now!*"

She dashed out the room and took the stairs two at a time. She made her way towards the kitchen. The traitor had gone. She sprinted out the back door to the hot-ash bucket and dug her hands deep into the powder until she felt a lump. Placing the charcoal on the counter, she smeared her filthy hands across her dress and grabbed a glass of water from the jug on the side.

On hands and knees in the centre of his bedroom, Hanley cried out in pain. "Sir, my love, I have it – eat." Gabby bounded into the room and collapsed by his side, holding out the charcoal and water as she panted for breath. He chewed on the edges of the black lump, smearing a dark stain across his face and teeth. Next, she handed him the water, quickly fetched the chamber pot, and placed it underneath him. The blend of the water, charcoal and the sour stench caused his stomach to convulse as black liquid poured from his mouth, and the whiskey burned his throat once more.

He repeated the action three times before his stomach was fully emptied. The muscles in his chest and abdomen ached as it continued to cramp. "Where are they?"

"Gone, sir."

"Call for the patrol... I am going to kill that Jessie myself...!"

"It was that harlot of yours, sir, who did this!" Hanley slapped the girl hard across the face before collapsing once more onto the rug, gasping.

"Don't you dare... she loves me, she confessed to it... She would never... it's that girl, *that girl*, causing trouble again... Grace? Where is she?" The realisation finally sank in.

"All three gone, sir... you don't need that... woman. You have me and our child." Gabby shuffled backward, fearful of another blow.

He staggered to his feet, struggling to straighten his back, fighting against cramping muscles. "You and that child mean nothing to me compared to her. Now, get me my horse, send word to the men, and to my brother, that Beatrice and my daughter are not to be harmed - they can do what they like to that Jessie... Go, now! Or you'll get more than a scar for your trouble."

Chapter 44

Outside, the air was crisp. The heat of the day had subsided for now. They had three hours to make it the first five miles if they followed Bea's plan, but if they went Sarah's way, that would add an extra three miles to their journey. With Grace strapped to Sarah's chest, there was no way they would make it.

"We need to head east; cut through the cotton and sugar fields, towards the river where they are waiting for us." Bea gestured out the path with her hands.

"They will track us faster if we go that way. Trust me, we must head north first, throwin' them off, then east through the swap lands."

"But now Gabby knows we've run, we won't make it in time!" Bea stared at Sarah. She had made this journey before. She knew this alien landscape, and Bea trusted her friend. "But... if you say that's what we need to do, then... lead the way."

They cut along the side of the cotton fields and the manicured lawn in front of the house. They kept their heads down low and crept along the fence as Sarah searched for an opening. In the distance, footsteps sounded. With their hearts in their throats, they stopped. Bea watched Sarah wrap her arms around Grace, making little sounds of comfort in her ears and bouncing her on the spot to prevent her from crying. Bea placed her own hands across her mouth as she stared at the man strutting past them. The crunch of his boots on the dry earth was deafening against their silence. He stopped for what felt like a lifetime and gazed around the landscape for any sign of disturbance. He held his lantern at arm's length out in front of him with his left hand and tightly gripped a handgun of some sort in his right. The firelight sprayed a flickering tinge of orange shadow across his face. Sarah held her hand up, indicating they should stay put until the man was out of earshot, and then they crawled along the fence once more. There was a notch carved into the top of a fence post, and with just a little push, it swayed on the spot, allowing enough room for them to slip through, one by one. She watched Sarah and Grace go first, saying a silent prayer as they dashed across the clearing and into the nearby woods. Sarah darted around one tree and then another, acquainted with the way already. The undergrowth became denser, making it hard for the moonlight to reach down and highlight their footing. Bea scrambled over branches, through bushes and fallen trees. She watched Sarah move without hesitation, her body turning like a dancer as Grace, still sound asleep, was rocked back and forth in the wrap. Then without warning she stopped, staring up at the night sky and the stars shining boldly above.

"This way."

They were finally turning east towards the boat; towards Joshua, and towards freedom. But the ground shifted under their feet. The marshy land reminded Bea of the old salt marches along the estuary back home in England: one wrong step there too, and your feet would be sucked tightly into the bog, making it difficult to move without losing a shoe. After about an hour the marsh-mud gave way to a stream, and then to a river. They must only be a few miles away. The moonlight rippled and glistened off the raging current. But just as Bea was about to smile, and allow a sliver of hope into her heart, she heard the dreaded sound of thundering hooves behind them.

"*Stop!*" Bea looked up at Sarah, not wanting to see who she knew was coming up behind, but knowing instantly what to do. Hanley was charging towards them on a sweating black stallion. Bea took a step backwards, toward him. "We must only be a mile or so away from the boat – run! Take Grace away from here – please, save my daughter."

Sarah didn't even stop to nod in her promise as she ran as fast as she was able along the river banks. Bea closed her eyes, sending all her love out to the tiny child she knew she might never see again, and held her ground. Without a second thought, she pulled out the gun and held it out steadily in front of her. "Let them go, Hanley."

Chapter 45

"Beatrice, step aside – you will not shoot me!"

Bea held the gun in front, pulled back the safety clip and squeezed the trigger hard. The kick-back almost knocked her off her feet, and there was an instant, sharp ringing sound in her ears. She had aimed high above his head as a warning.

"What the bloody hell are you doing? You could have killed us both if the horse had bolted!" Hanley climbed down and made straight for Bea. Bea clenched the gun in front of her, arms straight and direct, struggling to hear his voice against the constant ringing. "Victor..."

He stood only a foot in front of her, fury exploding out of him. "Don't you Victor me!"

"You need to let us go – let Grace go – we can't stay here in the south – this isn't the life I want for her. It's not your choice." She demanded in a stern voice, gripping onto the gun.

"What? Without her father? And don't tell me for a second that poor excuse of a boy can claim to be her father when she was born of me?" He punched his arms in the air with a hatred to his voice.

"I don't want this for her." Her anger matched his as she held her ground.

"You're a good little actress when you want to be Beatrice, but I know part of the evening was not acting – that kiss was real. I love you, and I believe you love me. We can be happy, as a family. We *will*!" He intensely leaned his body closer, taking small steps towards her, reaching out.

"I mean it, Victor, don't come an inch closer to me. You need to stop – to stop all of this! I will protect my child to the death; you know that, if you know anything about me."

He held his hands up, his voice dripping with charm, as he took another step forward. "Don't do this Beatrice – don't take her away from me. I will find you both again. You won't be able to run from me."

"We don't belong to you!"

"Are you really going to shoot me, Beatrice?"

"Yes." She said in a bitter tone.

"No, you're not. Give me the gun Beatrice, and when we get back home, I promise I won't punish Jessie for putting this idea into your head."

Anger boiled up inside of her. "This was all *my* idea! And her name is Sarah. You don't own her anymore, you don't own us – no person has that right."

In one move, Hanley jumped forward and tried to grab the gun out of her hands. Instinctively, he swerved his body to the right as she resolutely pulled the trigger. "Bloody hell... *Give me that gun!*" Blood pooled on his shirt from the bullet which had grazed his side. The commotion and the sudden gunshot caused his horse to panic and rear up. Within moments, he had bolted into the darkness. Hanley's eyes had turned to black, and she knew she couldn't let go. She had to fight once more for her freedom, and despite his size and strength, her hands remained clamped round the gun like a vice. Their bodies pressed together as he yanked at the gun, his sweat and blood, and the heat of his breath pouring down her neck and pooled over her clenched hands. "*Let us go!*" She screamed.

"Never..."

She didn't know what came first, the sound of the explosion, or the shock shooting through her like a punch to the chest. Hanley's arms tightened around her for a second. He let out a small, surprised murmur, then slumped to the ground, his hands now removed from the gun and clutching his stomach. The crimson liquid flowed over his fingers as he pressed harder into his abdomen.

With a thud, the gun fell to the earth. Bea stood motionless, looking down at him.

"Leave..."

"I... I-"

"My men, my brother... they will hear the gunfire and... come looking – you need to run... Grace, she needs you..." As he coughed, blood splattered out of his mouth. For the first time, he looked scared, a man fearful of what he might find on the other side. Then his eyes lost their light, and his chest stopped heaving.

"Goodbye Hanley," she muttered over his dead body. Was this what winning felt like? Staring down at the man she had just killed, the man who had caused her so much pain, not just to herself, but to countless others.

The ground rumbled beneath them. A drumming sound of men on horseback was getting closer. He hadn't been lying about that. Without thinking, she grabbed the gun and jumped to her feet.

Chapter 46

"**I** can hear someone coming, get the boat ready!" Joshua shouted from the shore. He stared into the darkness, his eyes adjusting to the shadows across the bank.

George and Beth stood on the ram-shackled steamboat; a makeshift design by a tradesman who had added a steam engine to a large, long fishing boat. An oil lamp attached to a hook swayed back and forth on the prow, echoing the motion of the waves. George stood at the back of the boat and held the rope in both hands, ready to pull it free, while Beth was positioned awkwardly at the engine. They had discovered that the craft moved fast enough, but it was loud, and steam clouds filled the area in an artificial sea-mist, making it difficult to steer.

In the distance, they could hear gunfire. The sound crackled through the night sky like thunder, making them all instinctively duck. Joshua could feel the ground vibrate as the sounds of human activity grew closer. Through the gloom he could make out... was it? Yes, the silhouette of a dress.

"They're here." He peered past Sarah, who was running towards him. But there was no Bea. "Sarah, thank God – where's Bea?" The bundle strapped across her body wriggled and cried out in fear. "Quickly, get on!" He held his hands out and guided her towards the ramp, constantly staring into the black. "Sarah, where is Bea?" But he realised she couldn't speak for panting, and instead kept pointing behind her.

Beth sprang forward. "Sarah, thank goodness. Here, let me help." She brought Sarah down onto the deck and guided her toward a bench at the back. George fetched a leather pouch filled with fresh water and handed it to her.

"Hello little one." Beth peered into the wrap and saw Grace staring back at her with an anxious expression on her pale face. She unwrapped the child quickly and sang gently to soothe her. After a few more mouthfuls of water, Sarah's breathing calmed.

"She's back there, Joshua – that Hanley found us, he caught up on his horse. She told me to run so she could hold him off – she has a gun..."

"I'm going after her."

George jumped off the ramp and raced over as he grabbed Joshua's arm. "That isn't a good idea."

"What if they hurt her – what if he now has the gun and has shot her?" The taller man fought with George to break free from his grasp.

"You don't know where they are, and if Hanley comes this way, then we need to leave immediately. That's what Bea would want – that's why she sent Sarah and Grace ahead."

"Get off me George, I'm not leaving her behind."

With his free hand, Joshua was about to punch his friend when another shot rang out. Grace cried out at the startling noise. Within a second, Joshua pulled himself free from George's grip. He glanced at Beth, trying to soothe Grace in her arms, but all she wanted was to be back in Sarah's. Bea had risked everything to keep those two safe, possibly her own life. But life without her seemed impossible.

"You can't stop me – I'm going to look for her." Joshua sprinted forward until he glimpsed a figure, frantically running towards the boat.

"Bea?" Joshua called out.

"*Go.*" she screamed through desperate breaths, her figure getting closer.

The group didn't hesitate. The sound of the engine bursting into life quietened even Grace, resulting in steam engulfing the boat. George lifted the ramp off the side and pulled the rope free. Joshua held his hand out and helped her to jump on to the boat.

"Bea, Bea. Are you alright?"

"It's not my blood." A thick, bright red smear mixed in the dirt covered Bea's dress. Joshua's eyes darted from her face and down her body, staring at the outfit, a stark reminder of her being locked in the cell. "We need to go now, they're not far behind!"

"Who? Hanley?" Joshua crouched down in front of his wife, who had staggered over to sit beside Sarah, glancing from Bea to the riverbank and back again. Beth placed a woollen blanket around her.

"Hanley won't be coming. He won't be coming." She stared at her red stained hands. "It's his men – the patrollers – looking for us." There was a blank expression on her face.

"Oh, Bea." Beth wrapped her arms around her.

"Tell me what happened, my love?" Joshua cradled her head in his hands and using his thumb, stroked her cheek, smearing the tears and blood away from her mouth. She could feel him tugging at her, dragging her back to the land of the living, but all she saw was Hanley's sullen face. She had killed him. Now all those lies were true.

"I... he... I didn't mean it to happen, but it did."

"What happened? Is he dead?" The look of horror she gave to Joshua frightened him.

"I am sorry, but we don't have time for this. Joshua, I need your help if we are to escape." George put a hand on his friend's shoulder and motioned for him to help feed the engine. The sound of the horses grew closer, and they could all hear men calling out to one another. He obeyed.

Bea watched Joshua, bent over, shovelling a heap of coal, with a thick golden beard and grime smeared across his face, his once-elegant white shirt now grey and ragged. How far he had fallen. This was a path he had never wanted. The unforeseen path.

The sound of hooves grew around them from both sides of the river.

"They are close." cried Beth as she stopped searching the boat and pointed at the opposite side of the bank.

An armed man with a strong southern accent broke through the tree-line, galloping behind the boat. "Beatrice Mason, you are wanted for the death of Captain Victor Hanley, for the previous theft of his property, and the kidnapping of his child... Stop the boat or we will open fire."

Time froze. Each person on the boat stopped what they were doing and stared at the figure on the bank, helpless. Then, as if on cue, the rest of his group joined him, emerging one by one out of the shadows, as a single gunshot fired out into the dark.

"*BEA!*"

Coming on 9th November 2021

The Unforeseen Path,

Book 3 in the Ropewalk Series,

Available now on pre-order.

What will happen next, will they escape the south and what happened to Bea?

Don't forget to sign up to H D Coulter newsletter to keep up to date on the Ropewalk Series, sneak peeks and giveaways.

Please keep in mind to rate

and review your copy of

Saving Grace: Deception. Obsession. Redemption

across all platforms. It helps to support the author
and recommend to other readers.

Acknowledgements

Firstly, I would like to thank you for reading and supporting the Ropewalk series and leaving a review. It means a lot to me that you are enjoying the journey of Bea Lightfoot as she orienteers through life, finding love and dealing with the challenges.

Secondly, I would like to thank Andy and Mina, for all the love and support as I write away in my little nook.

Thirdly, I would like to thank Grace Liddiard my editor and friend, for her patience and being one of the first person to believe in my writing and falling in love with the Ropewalk series. Plus my talented cover designer, Aimee Coveney for bring part of the Ropewalk world to life.

Next, I would like to thank my friend Lorna Gillies aka author Claire Gillies, she has been there through the dark times and the light. A constant sounding board, encouragement when things get hard and celebrate the wins.

Next, I would like to thank my fellow writing friends who have supported me; William J. Kite who has been great beta reader with valuable feedback and support. Anne Woodward, another great beta reader and helped me to see through the trees. Steve Gowland, who has been a great beta reader and encouragement. I would also like to thank the two Mark's who created the Bestseller Experiment podcast and face book group, it is through that I have found amazing writing support and fellow writer friends.

I would also like to thank mine and Andy's family and friends for the love and support during the launch of Ropewalk, book 1 in the Ropewalk series. Their encouragement has meant the world.

T here are so many more people who continue to support myself and my new found author career by the help of the ARC reader team and companies.

Thank you!

Books By This Author

Ropewalk: Rebellion. Love. Survival

Book 1 in the Ropewalk Series.

Saving Grace: Deception. Obsession. Redemption.

Book 2 in the Ropewalk series.

The Unforeseen Path

Book 3 in the Ropewalk series.

Printed in Great Britain
by Amazon